INTO THE Storm

HUDSON SECURITY

CHRISTINA SOL

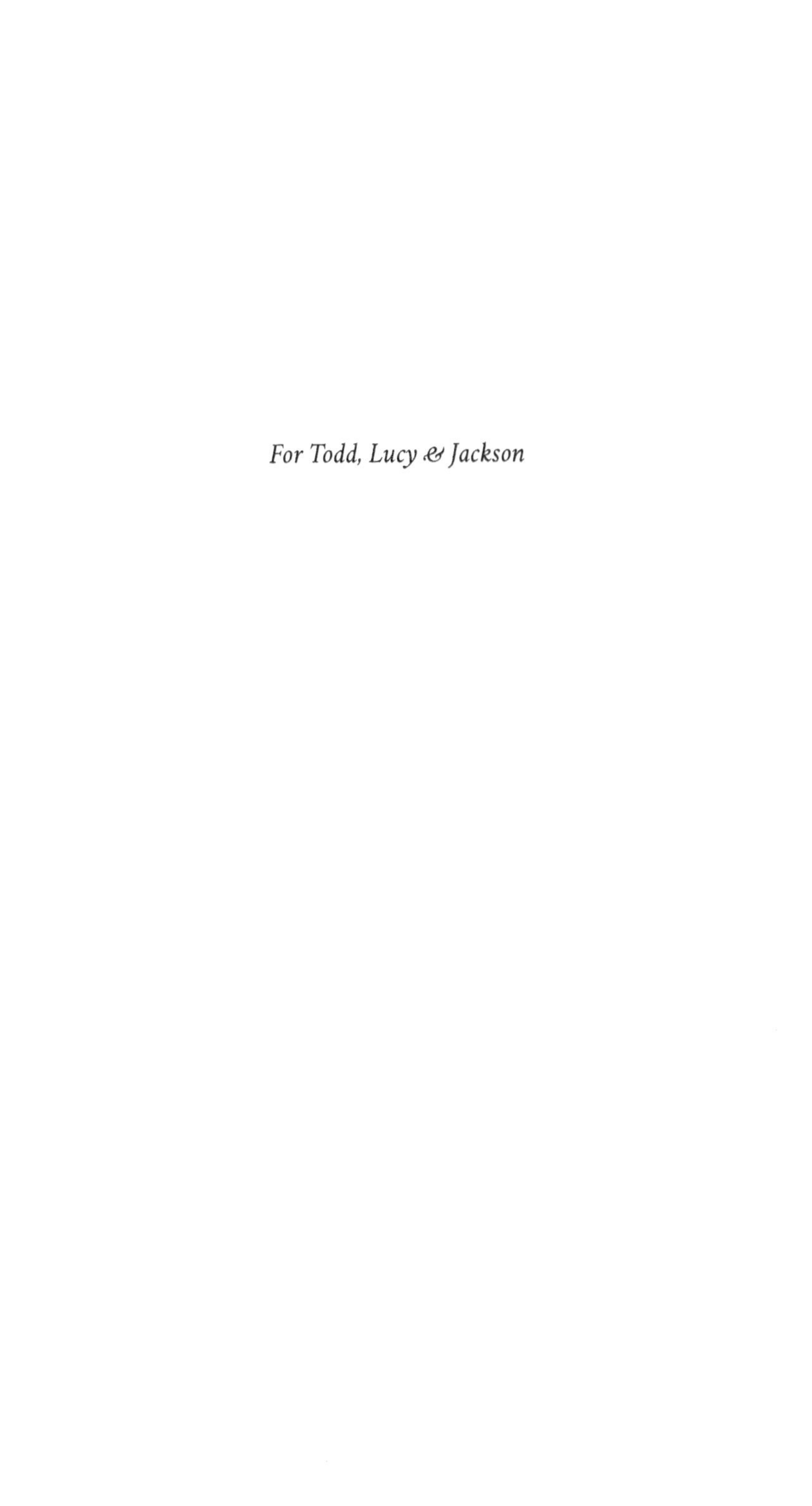

For Todd, Lucy & Jackson

AUTHOR'S NOTE

Into the Storm is the second interconnected standalone in the Hudson Security series. It contains mature and graphic content. Reader discretion is advised. A full list of content warnings can be found at www.christinasol.com.

CHAPTER ONE

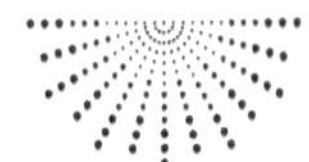

Being a hairstylist wasn't supposed to be a dangerous job.

Freya Hansen blinked as time slowed. Shock consumed her. She met her client's surprised gaze in the mirror and then shifted her attention to the angry man rushing up behind them.

Her client, Janie, gasped.

Freya's spa manager hurried toward them, chasing the red-faced man.

Before Freya could react, the man grabbed her by the shoulders and flung her to the side. She crashed into the salon chair beside hers, toppling it. Its lightly padded metal arm slammed into her ribs. Fire tore through her chest. For a split second, her breath locked in her throat, and all she could do was stare, unable to take in the pandemonium that had exploded around her.

"How dare you, bitch!" he screamed at Janie.

He tried to yank the woman out of the salon chair, and Janie cried out, clinging to the chair with one arm, covering her head with the other as he slapped her.

All the while, Claire—Janie's sister, who'd been seated at the station next to them—shouted, "Call 911!"

Claire pounced onto the man's back, trying to drag him off her sister.

Chaos. It was utter chaos.

Freya untangled herself from the overturned salon chair and surged to her feet, ignoring the pain that shot up her side. Joining Claire, who was now punching the back of the man's head, Freya grabbed the man's right arm and yanked, hoping to get him off Janie.

The man continued to slap at Janie while screaming vile curses at them, but Freya clung to his arm like a spider monkey.

Then time stopped.

Freya's eyes widened when she registered the black gun clutched in the man's right hand.

She opened her mouth to shout out a warning, but before the words left her mouth, a deafening bang sounded. The mirror in front of them shattered. Screams rent the air, and the acrid scent of gunpowder filled her nose.

Her ears rang, but she held on to his arm.

"Let go of me, you bitch!" he roared. His brown gaze locked on hers, and fear chilled her blood, but she clung tighter to his arm.

"No!" someone screamed.

He reared back and smacked his head against hers.

A loud crack reverberated through Freya's skull, and her vision wavered. Dazed, her grip on his arm weakened, and she crumpled to the ground.

The man sneered down at her, a trickle of blood dripping from his forehead. "Touch me again, bitch, and I'll blow your fucking head off," he spat before turning his back to her.

Heart racing and vision blurry, Freya scrambled backward over the broken pieces of the mirror. She ignored the sharp stings on her palms and tucked herself under her workstation. Less than ten feet away, Janie was huddled on the ground with Claire, both still wearing their salon capes. The man stood over them, arms flailing wildly as he waved his gun at the handful of women still in the salon.

"Janie, Janie . . ." He tsked. "When will you fucking learn?" With a deranged laugh, he fired again, striking another workstation's mirror. Then again into the drywall. And again into another mirror.

Hugging her knees to her chest, Freya made herself as small as possible, covering her head with her arms. More glass shattered, more screams filled the salon. Her body trembled with each heart-stopping gunshot.

"Police! Drop your weapon!"

Freya buried her face tighter against her knees and held her breath, too scared to move.

"Fuck you!" the man shouted.

Three more gunshots rang out. Freya jerked with each one.

For a moment, there was silence. Then the sounds of women crying and whimpering, muttered curses, and the crunch of glass underfoot replaced the quiet.

A deep groan, followed by a scuffle of some sort, had Freya opening her eyes.

The man was on his stomach while the sheriff cuffed him and read him his Miranda rights. A growing puddle of blood pooled beneath the man's right shoulder. Two deputies stood sentry, while Janie and Claire were huddled together a few feet away.

After a few moments, a pair of EMTs rushed in.

Freya didn't move. Not a single muscle twitched while she watched from her hiding place as the man was moved onto a stretcher and recuffed. The EMTs worked on his injuries despite the guy cursing everyone around him. He carried on about "suing you motherfuckers" the entire time.

Eventually—she'd lost all concept of time—the EMTs hauled him away. The sheriff followed closely behind, but the two deputies remained.

"Everyone can come out now," the older of the two deputies said, but she remained tucked under her workstation, her heart still beating wildly.

"Is anyone hurt?" the younger deputy asked. "More EMTs are on the way, so if you're injured, please gather over here." He gestured to the sofa in their waiting area.

"We'll also need to get everyone's statements, so please don't leave." The older deputy crouched beside Janie and Claire and lowered his voice. "Ladies, are you both okay?"

Soft murmurs overtook the room as Freya's salon and spa colleagues, along with their clients, rose from where they'd taken cover. She let out the breath she hadn't realized she'd been holding and willed her body to stop trembling.

As fast as the madness had started, it was thankfully over.

"Miss Hansen?"

Freya startled, and her attention swung to the deputy in front of her.

"I'm sorry," she murmured. With her shaking, now-bandaged hands, she raked her long dark hair away from her face and recrossed her arms over her chest. Leaning against the waiting area's sofa, she cleared her throat. "What was your question again?"

Deputy Chase, the younger of the two deputies, gave her an understanding smile. "Can you tell me what happened before the suspect arrived? What your day looked like leading up to the incident?"

She nodded and took a deep breath, hoping it would steady her nerves.

It didn't.

Surveying the destruction around her, she frowned. The salon area of the Pacific View Resort's world-renowned spa was in utter disarray. Two of the four stylist chairs were toppled over, and the mirrors at all four stations were shattered.

Deputy Chase cleared his throat, and her gaze swung back to him.

The *incident*. Right.

Exhaling another shaky breath, she willed herself to focus. "It was just like any other day, really. I arrived at eight thirty, and my first client was scheduled for nine. I had three back-to-back haircuts and styles that went until eleven thirty. I took a half-hour lunch break and had a color scheduled for noon that finished up just after two. Then I had another break until four o'clock. That was Janie's appointment . . ."

Freya's gaze caught on her stylist chair across the room. It was still lying on its side with a single bullet hole splitting the seatback's dark-brown leather.

"And once she arrived, Miss Hansen?" Deputy Chase prodded.

She tore her eyes from her workstation and looked to where Janie and Claire were speaking with the sheriff at the opposite end of the room.

"You don't need to call me Miss Hansen. Freya is fine," she murmured and brought her attention back to Deputy Chase, her mind scrambling to keep up with the conversation. Her concentration was absolute shit, and it took a moment for her to recall her prior train of thought. "Um, Janie showed up with her sister, Claire. Janie wanted to get a dramatic cut, and Claire was scheduled for a blowout with my colleague,

Hazel." She gestured to the spa's check-in desk where her friend was giving her statement to Deputy Garwood. "Basically, Claire was here as Janie's moral support."

Deputy Chase's brow furrowed. "Moral support?"

Despite the chaos and terror of the past hour, a small smile tugged at the corner of Freya's lips. "Janie had hair down to her waist, and she wanted me to give her a pixie cut. Even though it was something she really wanted, she was still nervous to have that much taken off." At the deputy's blank stare, she asked, "Do you know what a pixie cut is?"

He shook his head. "No, ma'am, I don't."

She gestured to the mid-fade textured crop of his bright-red hair. "In essence, it's a feminine version of your haircut, but a bit longer on the sides." She glanced over at Janie again. She'd only been able to cut the woman's hair chin length before her estranged husband had charged into the salon.

Deputy Chase's eyebrows rose in obvious surprise. "That's quite the change. I can understand what you mean by her being nervous."

Freya nodded as sadness swarmed over her. Knowing what she did now, knowing *why* Janie wanted the shorter cut, her stomach turned.

She opened her mouth to continue but hesitated, unsure if it was her place to say anything. But a glance at Janie's swollen cheek—hell, even the throb of her own ribs when she took a deep breath and the lingering headache six Tylenol couldn't ease—reminded her of that awful man. Of his hate and rage. Of the terror on Janie's face as he'd attacked her.

Whether it was Freya's place to say anything or not, she wanted that asshole to pay for what he'd done.

Blowing out a breath, she sent a silent plea out to the universe to forgive her if she was betraying any confidences. "Janie and Claire are at the resort for a girls' week of sorts, but not the usual mimosas-and-yoga kind." She dropped her voice. "As you probably already know, the guy who did all this"—she waved her hand at the destroyed salon area—"is Janie's estranged husband. She left him two and a half weeks ago, got a restraining order against him, split town, and hasn't had contact with him since."

"Is she a regular client of yours?" When Freya shook her head, Deputy Chase's eyebrow arched. "So you know all this because . . ."

Freya shrugged. "Because I'm a hairstylist. That chair?" She gestured in the direction of her destroyed workstation. "It's like a therapist's couch. When she got here, we chatted for a little bit about what kind of style she wanted, and why it was so important to her."

It had hurt Freya's heart to see the pain on Janie's face, to hear what she was sure was a very watered-down version of what the woman had endured. But Freya also saw Janie's strength and resolve, especially with Claire's unwavering support.

"She shared her journey with me while I cut her hair," Freya said and nodded to the woman across the room. "We only got it to chin length before . . . I'm sorry, I don't know what her estranged husband's name is. They only referred to him as POS."

The corners of Deputy Chase's lips kicked up. "It fits."

"No kidding," she muttered, blowing out a breath. "But we only got that far before he stormed in here."

They spoke for a few more minutes about how the man had thrown Freya to the ground, and how when she'd tried to assist Janie, he'd headbutted her. She explained how she'd taken cover when he'd started shooting.

"Thank you, Freya. If you think of anything else, please feel free to call me or anyone at the sheriff's department." Deputy Chase handed her his card and inclined his head toward the two remaining EMTs who were treating a couple of spa clients for what looked like scratches and cuts. "Make sure you get your head and ribs checked out before you leave."

The pain along her side had dulled to a throb that matched the one in her head. "I will, thank you."

He turned away, paused, and faced her again. He lowered his voice, concern evident on his face. "Freya, why did she want that shorter haircut?"

She could see in his eyes that he already knew the answer. But if he wanted her to say it out loud, so be it. "Because she was done getting dragged around by her hair."

His jaw clenched, and he gave her a brief nod before heading toward Freya's spa manager, Miriam. Letting out a breath, Freya crossed the room to Janie and Claire and waited as they finished up with Sheriff O'Conner.

"Are you both okay?" she asked when the sheriff stepped away.

Janie nodded, her eyes welling with tears. "Freya, I'm so sorry."

Freya was shaking her head before the woman finished speaking. "You have nothing to be sorry for. Nothing at all." She stepped closer and took the other woman's hands in hers. "Did you need to get checked out by the EMTs?"

Janie shook her head and let out a small chuckle that held no humor. "This"—she waved at the bruise forming along her jaw—"is nothing."

Emotion squeezed Freya's chest tightly. "Is it okay if I hug you?"

Janie nodded, tears spilling down her face.

Careful not to squeeze too hard, for both Janie's sake and her own, Freya wrapped her arms around the other woman. "I'm so thankful you're okay."

"I'm so sorry," Janie repeated, pulling away.

"Nope," Freya said, retaking Janie's hands. "There's *nothing* to be sorry about. You didn't do this. *He* did. It's all on him." She gave the woman a reassuring smile, hoping to inject a little bit of calm, a little bit of comfort. "I know this place is a disaster, but what do you say I grab some scissors and finish your cut?"

Janie's eyes brightened, and she swiped away a few stray tears. "Really?"

"Hell yeah."

"But what about your hands?"

Freya glanced down at her bandaged hands and stretched her fingers. "The EMTs cleaned them up, and they're fine. Really." The pain meds had eased the soreness in her hands, unlike with the low-grade headache that continued to throb. "Besides, not only is that bob horribly uneven, but I think the pixie cut you're thinking of will be a wonderful fresh start. And that fresh start begins today. You up for it?"

"Thank you," Janie said, releasing Freya's hands to wipe away more tears. "Thank you so much."

"Give me a few minutes to talk to my manager about finding a room for us to use." She met Claire's gaze. "Do you want me to check with Hazel about finishing your blowout too?"

"Only if it's no trouble," Claire replied, her eyes bright with unshed tears and her arm wrapped around her sister's shoulders.

If Freya had to pay Hazel out of her own pocket, she was making sure Claire got her blowout. Both these women had gone through so much—not only just now, but with everything leading up to today. Yet they were still standing tall. They deserved some pampering.

"It's no trouble at all," Freya said, meaning it with her entire being. "I'll be right back, ladies."

CHAPTER TWO

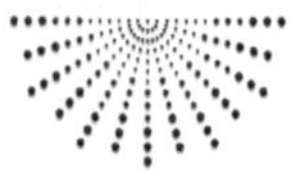

An hour and a half later, Freya settled on the stool at the end of the bar and gave a tired wave to Maya, the head bartender at the resort's Orca Moon Lounge.

"Holy shit, lady," Maya whispered, laying a coaster down in front of her and topping it with a glass of ice water. "I heard what went down at the salon. Are you okay?"

Her chest squeezed, and she fisted her hands to keep the tremble away.

Was she okay? She wasn't quite sure.

"It was crazy. I'm just relieved no one was seriously hurt." It could have gone so badly.

"I hear you. Your partner in crime showing?" Maya gestured to the empty seat next to her and shook her head, frowning. "No, that's not right. Hazel's more like the bad angel to your good angel."

Freya chuckled and took a big gulp of water. Maya wasn't wrong. "Yeah, she's on her way. She was still chatting with the boss when I snuck out."

"Speaking of your boss," Maya said, setting an empty shot glass in front of her. "Miriam said all the spa ladies get a drink on the house tonight, and that you and Hazel get two for being in the thick of it all. Mir suggested some top-shelf tequila, but I know you like the Jolly Rancher shots. Personally, I'd go with a Washington Apple. It has a little more kick. What's your poison tonight?"

Freya couldn't help but smile. After everyone's statements had been taken, and she'd finished Janie's cut, and Hazel had styled Claire's hair, Miriam had been their rock. Having already spoken to the spa's two front-desk girls, Miriam had pulled her and Hazel aside to reconfirm that they were okay and to reassure them that they'd be given the week off with pay while management got the salon area of the spa back in order. Miriam had also offered the names of a couple of counselors that the Pacific View Resort would cover the fees of should the staff need to speak with someone in the coming weeks.

Freya was still a bit numb, her emotions still a little too raw for her to really absorb everything, but the gesture—of both the paid time off and the counseling—was kind. Though it wasn't surprising since the management group was amazing. Not something Freya thought she'd ever say about what she'd once considered such a hoity-toity place.

The Pacific View Resort was a world-famous luxury wellness resort and spa. Hudson Island was shaped like a slightly tilted number seven, and the resort was located on the island's northwestern tip. It featured a Michelin three-star restaurant that was also open to the public and had a months-long waiting list. It also had multiple high-end, mindful-dining options for the resort's guests. The people who worked at the resort had every opportunity to be as stuck-up and pretentious as some of their guests, but for the most part, the staff—management and ownership included— were honest-to-God good people.

Now what exactly did "mindful dining" entail? She still

wasn't quite sure, but she supposed it was a swankier way of saying fancy, local farm-to-table, and surprisingly delicious. And the drinks they served at the Orca Moon Lounge were phenomenal. Plus, all the mixers were made in-house and were organic, so that had to be a bonus.

All Freya knew was that after the longest, most chaotic day of her adult life, she needed a drink. She wasn't the biggest drinker, but she needed something strong to combat her unsteady nerves. Yes, she still had to drive home, but if she took her time and got a carb-and-protein-heavy dinner, she'd be fine. Hopefully, food and the company of her colleagues would ease the adrenaline still coursing through her, because the idea of going home to her cozy one-bedroom apartment to stare at her not-quite-decorated walls and over-analyze everything that happened today was awful. The last thing she wanted was to be alone with her riotous thoughts.

"What's my poison?" Freya asked, leaning back on her barstool. "I learned a long time ago to never argue with the bartender. I'll leave it up to you. But please make it strong." She pressed her lips together. "But not so I can actually taste the alcohol, you know?"

"Oh, I know, Frey." Maya laughed. "You like your drinks with a kick so long as they taste like candy. Plus, bonus points if there's a cute little umbrella too. Am I right?"

She tapped the tip of her nose. "Ding, ding, ding."

Maya worked her magic behind the bar and poured a pretty, electric-blue concoction into a large shot glass. "Blue-raspberry cotton-candy shot." Maya cringed as she added a little plastic mermaid to the sugared rim. "Holy shit, that made my teeth hurt just saying it. You can shoot it, but it's a good sipper too. Do you want to order food now or wait for Hazel?"

"I'll wait." Freya took a taste of the pretty shot and

grinned. The sugary flavor lingered in her mouth. "That's delicious. It's like a blue Jolly Rancher had a love child with some cotton candy."

"There's a shit ton of vodka there, my friend." Maya grinned and then narrowed her eyes. She leaned toward Freya, dropping her voice. "Don't look now, but you have an incoming guest with his eye on you. Good luck, because he looks like a douche. Wave if you need a rescue."

Lovely. That's all she needed.

Employees, when off work, didn't generally hang out at the resort. The lone exception was the Orca Moon Lounge. The only rule was they had to meet the dress code: resort/business casual. The spa staff had a strict uniform of logoed, upscale black scrubs. However, it was different for the smaller salon staff, which included four full-time stylists and two part-time makeup artists. Their uniform was simple. All black and chic. During work hours, they simply added a logoed salon apron on top. So basically, whenever she hit the lounge after work, she easily blended in with the resort's patrons.

Freya plucked the mermaid from the rim of her glass and kicked back the rest of her shot. Her cheeks puckered at the sweet, sugary goodness, and she grinned at her friend as she replaced the mermaid onto the rim. "Can I start waving at you now?"

Maya snorted. "If you're lucky, Hazel will show and take one for the team. I mean, he's not bad looking. He's just got that slightly . . . ick thing going on." She tapped the bar top in front of Freya before turning to the approaching man. "Good evening. What can I get you to drink?"

"I'll have a Crown and Coke," he said, settling into the empty seat next to Freya. "And whatever drink this lovely lady wants."

Freya inwardly cringed. "Oh, I'm good, thank you." She took a sip of her water. "I'm actually waiting for a friend."

"That's fine. I'll just keep you company until they arrive. And please, I insist on buying you a drink."

"Oh, um, okay . . ." He held her gaze until she shot Maya a glance, worried the panic coursing through her was evident on her face. She wasn't the greatest when men flirted with her. And she was especially awkward when pushy men were the ones doing the flirting. "Lavender lemon drop?"

Maya met her gaze and gave her a reassuring smile. "Half?"

"Yes, please," she replied, grateful her friend could sense her discomfort. Half a shot of liquor would be sufficient after the candy vodka bomb she'd just downed. It would keep the edge off but let her keep her wits about her. Especially if she had to make small talk with this man. Not that she was a stranger to small talk, but it had been a *long* day.

Maya placed their drinks in front of them, and he tapped his glass to hers, giving her a giant grin. "Cheers, gorgeous."

Her face heated as she took a small sip of her cocktail. Quickly gathering her thoughts, she set her martini glass down and straightened her shoulders. Yes, this guy made her feel so damn awkward, but she could fake it with the best of them. Turning to him, she gave him her most professional smile. "So how are you enjoying your stay here at the Pacific View Resort?"

Fifteen minutes later, it took everything Freya had to not roll her eyes.

No. Forget rolling her eyes. It took everything she had to not get up, leave the lounge, and go home.

"I'm telling you, gorgeous," the man seated beside her said, eyeing her in a one-step-away-from-sleezy kind of way. "It's the next big crypto. I have a knack for this kind of thing."

She took a sip of her cocktail and deeply regretted

allowing him to buy her a drink. She also deeply regretted that Maya was busy at the other end of the bar with four new guests who looked infinitely more fun than the guy beside her.

She stole a glance at the lounge's entrance and willed Hazel to materialize. Unfortunately, the damn entrance remained stubbornly empty.

Not that Freya was surprised. Punctuality wasn't at the top of Hazel's list of priorities, but this was a bit much for her friend. It was only a five-minute walk from the spa building to the lounge—and that was if you were walking at a snail's pace.

The man droned on, and Freya gripped the stem of her martini glass. It was either that or gouge her own eyes out with said martini glass's stem.

She was a hairstylist, dammit. Which meant that along with doing hair, she was a professional small talker. Having worked at the resort for the past year, chatting with people who had more money than God—many of whom lacked humility—was not uncommon. In fact, she was well versed in it. However, this guy was wearing on her last nerve.

"Did you hear what I said?" Brandon asked.

Or was it Brennen? Bryson? Braxton? *Shit.*

Turning her attention back to the man whose name she was pretty sure started with a Br, she smiled. Though it was probably more of a pained grimace. Not that the guy noticed. She took another long drink of her cocktail and nodded. "Crypto. You're raking it in and have an early lead on the next big thing." She definitely should have asked Maya for a full shot. Hell, there wasn't enough vodka in the world that would make this man tolerable.

Oblivious to her sarcasm, he grinned and continued to prattle on. About what? She didn't really know or care.

Glancing at him, she pegged him to be somewhere in

his mid to late thirties. He was tallish and blond and handsome in a generic kind of way. However, the more he talked, the less handsome he became. From a professional standpoint, he probably used as much hair product as she did—and it took a *lot* of product to get her stick-straight hair to hold a curl. That alone shouldn't irritate her, but it did.

In a nutshell, the man appeared harmless. A bit douchey, but still harmless. But damn, did he like the sound of his own voice. She should have gotten up and left when he initially sat beside her. She should have told him the seat was taken. She should have refused the drink.

But did she do any of those things?

Of course not.

Because she didn't rock the boat. Ever.

Being a people pleaser who hated confrontation, she'd stayed glued to her seat, wishing she had the guts to tell this guy to go away.

"Now, I asked myself, Bray, are you going to let that little lady sit all alone?" He chuckled, shooting her a wink. "I just couldn't do it, gorgeous. And since you've let me talk your ear off, how about you let me buy you another drink?"

Brayden. That was his name. And of course he talked about himself in third person.

She caught Maya's gaze across the bar and widened her eyes. *Please, help me!* When her friend gave her a slight nod and held up a single finger, she thanked the female-telepathy gods.

Freya took another gulp of her drink, set her glass back on the coaster, and shook her head. "No thanks, I'm good. Like I said, I'm waiting for someone."

"So you've said, but yet you've been sitting here with me for the last ten minutes."

It was going on twenty, but who was counting?

She was going to kill Hazel when the woman arrived. If she *ever* arrived. "Because my friend isn't here yet."

He flashed her another smarmy grin. "Isn't that convenient?"

This guy needed to seriously go the hell away. "She's just running late. In fact, she should be here any moment."

He gave her a look that said he obviously didn't believe her. "How about I buy you dinner and we get to know each other better?"

Simmering irritation had heat flooded over her cheeks. "No, thank you."

"Oh, come on. How long did you say you were staying here for?"

She hadn't. In fact, aside from her name, she hadn't mentioned *anything* about herself. She'd barely spoken a word since he'd sat down, and considering the man had been talking nonstop, he'd also never asked.

"I'm pretty sure Freya's boyfriend wouldn't appreciate her having dinner with some random guy," Maya said, refilling her water glass. "Need anything else, sweetie?"

Food. But not while Brayden was still sitting here. Instead, she gave her friend a grateful smile. "I'm good for now, thanks."

"Boyfriend, eh?" He waggled his eyebrows.

Maya snorted and waved at her. "Dude, of course she has a boyfriend."

She didn't, but good God, did she love her friend.

He clapped his hands together. "Well then, challenge accepted."

Wait, what?

She frowned and held up her hand. "Uh, there's no challenge. Look, it was kind of you to buy me a drink, but I will happily pay you back for it because . . . just no."

"Loosen up, gorgeous. How about this?" Brayden leaned

closer, and she leaned away. He flashed her a smile that she was certain was supposed to be charming. It wasn't. "If your friend doesn't show up in the next five minutes, you let me buy you dinner. Your boyfriend doesn't need to know."

There was no way this guy could be serious. But one look at his slimy, lecherous smirk said otherwise. Gross. Her brain scrambled for a snappy come back and—

"Shit, dude. You're a persistent one, aren't you?" a familiar voice huffed.

Turning in her barstool, Freya let out a thankful breath.

"Sorry I'm so late," Hazel said and then glanced at Brayden. "You're in my seat."

Brayden held up his hands, gave Hazel an appreciative once-over, and smirked as he stood. "Just keeping your friend company." He turned back to her. "Freya, it was lovely meeting you. As I mentioned, I'm here for the next week. We should get together before you check out. Another drink or dinner or . . ."

She internally winced as he let the innuendo hang there. "Brayden," she said, giving him a nod. *Gah! What is wrong with you? Fuck off is the appropriate response to the creeper!*

Hazel cleared her throat as the man lingered. "Chop-chop, buddy. You're blocking my seat."

"My apologies," he said, stepping aside and holding his hand out to assist Hazel.

"I'm good," Hazel said, brushing his hand away. Once she was settled on her barstool, she turned to him and smiled sweetly. "You can go now."

Brayden chuckled and nodded to a table in the corner where two similarly dressed men sat. "If you change your mind about dinner, Freya—or about anything else—I'll be over there. And just so we're clear, I have no problems with you having a boyfriend. I can be discreet."

As he walked away, Hazel shook her head and muttered, "Holy shit. Why were you sitting with that douche?"

Freya arched an eyebrow at her friend. "You're kidding, right?"

Hazel arched an eyebrow right back. "And when did you get a boyfriend?"

"Uh, when you took your sweet-ass time getting here?" Maya thunked a glass of water down in front of Hazel. "The poor thing was like a deer in headlights with that guy. Now what can I get you?"

"Geez, I said I was sorry." Hazel held her hands up before checking out the placard with the drink specials. "Miriam said I get a couple free drinks, so can I get a shot of Patron and the spicy prickly pear margarita?"

"You got it. But you owe her, Hazel," Maya replied, pointing at Freya. "Big-time. That guy was a lot."

Hazel met Freya's gaze and cringed. "I really am sorry, but I have a good excuse for why I'm late this time. I swear."

Freya held back an eye roll. Barely. Hazel always had a good excuse. Sighing, she waved her hand in a circular get-on-with-it gesture.

"Do you remember that really hot guy I told you about?" Hazel's smile was gigantic. "The one I met at the gym a few weeks ago who works for the security company? Sandy-brown hair, tall, ripped, could be a cover model, oozes sex appeal?"

"Please." Maya scoffed, placing Hazel's drinks in front of her. "You've basically just described every single guy who works out at that gym."

Freya chuckled. Her friend wasn't wrong.

The De La Rosa Gym was an elite fight gym located on the northeast corner of Hudson Island, not too far from the resort. Some of the world's top MMA fighters, boxers, and martial artists trained there.

They were open to public membership, but Freya wasn't a member. However, since she drove by the gym on her way to and from work, she should probably join one of these days. She'd taken a few of their self-defense classes, and distractingly hot guys aside, it was a really nice, low-key gym. Get fit had a perennial spot on her running to-do list, but after being on her feet all day, working out at a gym didn't sound nearly as good as vegging on her couch.

Hazel's perfectly painted lips pursed. "True. But this guy is like *hot* hot. Frey, remember I told you how I asked him to spot me last week?"

"Oh, holy shit, of course you did," Maya grumbled, shaking her head as she made her way down the bar to the other guests.

Freya snickered. Hazel's excuses for being late always involved a hot guy. Her friend attracted the stupidly hot guys of the universe, while she unfortunately tended to attract the Braydens of the world.

Freya knew she was cute. Growing up, she'd been called her mother's mini. She'd inherited her Filipino mom's petite frame, tan skin, and long black hair. The only difference between them were Freya's ice-blue eyes that she and all her brothers had gotten from their Norwegian father. A familiar pang squeezed her heart at the thought of her parents. Shoving the uncomfortable feeling away—this was neither the time nor the place for a pity party—she focused back on her friend.

Hazel was on the opposite end of the spectrum of cute. Simply put, the woman was unfairly stunning. She was a green-eyed, taller version of Margot Robbie.

Yeah. Ridiculous.

Standing at five-two, Freya looked like a child next to her friend's statuesque five-ten. When she'd first started at Pacific View and met Hazel, she'd been intimidated as hell because of the whole Margot Robbie-doppelganger thing, but after five minutes, she'd realized Hazel was not only fiery and sassy in a way that Freya envied, but she was also really sweet.

"So this hot guy . . ." Freya prodded before taking the final sip of her lavender lemon drop.

Hazel let out a dreamy sigh. "So after I met with Miriam, I was on my way here and ran into him—Carmichael—in the hallway outside the lounge of all places. What are the odds, right?"

Freya's eyebrows rose. The guest areas of the resort were just that. Exclusively for guests. It was a rare thing to run into a local who wasn't an employee. "Yeah, that is a surprise."

"Right? Anyway, Carmichael and I got to talking, and I lost track of time. I hope you don't mind, but I kinda sorta invited him to join us. Is that okay?"

Freya couldn't help but laugh at the hopeful smile on her friend's face. "That's fine. The more the merrier, right?"

She could use all the distractions she could get this evening. Besides, the more people she met, the better. Though she'd worked at the resort for a little over a year, she'd only moved to Hudson Island a month ago and was still settling in. Aside from Hazel and Maya, she only knew a handful of other coworkers who lived on the island, so it wouldn't hurt to meet more people.

Even though her work as a hairstylist had her talking to strangers on a regular basis, she was an introvert. An introvert who did a damn good job pretending to be an extrovert. Truthfully, the only reason she knew Maya was because she'd ridden Hazel's 1000 percent extroverted coattails. Since Hazel was always running late, she'd gotten to know Maya as she sat at the bar waiting for her friend.

"Oh my God, he's here," Hazel whispered, straightening her shoulders and waving.

Freya turned and bit back a laugh. The man making his way toward them—with his focus entirely on her friend—was exactly as Hazel had described. *Hot* hot. Like he'd walked right out of a soap opera. Of course Hazel and this guy had hit it off. The two of them together made Ken and Barbie look pedestrian.

"Ladies," he said, standing behind their stools.

Hazel beamed at the man. "Carmichael, this is my friend Freya that I was telling you about."

"Hi," Freya said, holding out her hand. "It's nice to meet you."

"Likewise," he said, shaking her hand. "Do you mind if I join you two for a drink?"

Freya waved at the open seat on the other side of Hazel. "Not at all."

The moment he sat, Hazel swiveled his way, peppering him with questions. The only pause came when Maya came and took their dinner and drink orders.

Freya listened with half an ear as Hazel was all smiles, compliments, and chatter. It was like they hadn't had the craziest workday ever. Like they hadn't hid under their workstations and behind their salon chairs as a man beat up his estranged wife and shot up the salon.

A shiver tore through her. Had that really been only a few hours ago?

Freya couldn't blame her friend. People processed things differently. Apparently, Hazel's process included flirting, giggling, and tossing her hair.

Freya bit back a cringe. *Yikes. Snarky much?*

She had to give Carmichael credit, though. The man did try to involve her in some of their conversation, asking what Freya did at the resort, and how she and Hazel knew each other. But every time he tried to include her, Hazel steered the conversation back to herself. Which was fine, because as Freya listened to Hazel talk about some sort of weight machine at the gym, a wave of exhaustion washed over her.

"You good, lady?" Maya asked, refilling her water glass.

"Thanks. And yeah," she said, rolling her eyes as she tilted her head toward their friend. "I think the day is catching up to me."

"Your food should be out shortly. That will help with the adrenaline crash." Maya gave her a sympathetic smile and headed toward the opposite end of the bar.

Freya leaned back in her barstool and stifled a yawn. She was done. All she wanted to do was eat her dinner, let the steak and mashed potatoes soak up her two drinks, and head home.

She took a gulp of water and then slid from her barstool, tapping Hazel on the arm. "I'll be right back."

Hazel glanced at Freya's water glass and frowned. "Do you want me to order you another drink? On me?"

Freya shook her head. "I'm good, but thanks."

She made her way to the restroom, took care of business, and then took her time washing her hands and finger-combing her hair. She didn't want to be irritated with Hazel but could admit she was definitely on her way there. She'd hoped to talk with her friend about what they'd gone through today. While she was beyond grateful no one had been hurt, the entire ordeal had left her shaken. Still. Even after a few hours had passed.

It was obvious Hazel's focus was now on Carmichael. Which, again, was fine. But after the day she'd had, being the third wheel was the last thing she wanted.

Letting out a weary sigh, she met her gaze in the mirror. "Eat dinner and go home," she murmured. She could figure out her feelings on her own. Like always.

Squaring her shoulders, she left the restroom. At the end of the hallway, she turned the corner and came to an abrupt halt.

"Oh, sorry," she said, nearly crashing into a man.

"So we meet again, gorgeous."

Brayden. She was too tired to hold back a cringe. He loomed over her, and his eyes were a little glassier than before. He'd obviously had a couple more drinks. At least.

"Excuse me," she said, stepping to the left.

He stepped in front of her.

She tilted her head to the side. Seriously? "Can I get by?"

"How about we get that dinner?" He gave her an oily smile that turned her stomach.

Though they were still in the hallway entrance leading to the restrooms and he was blocking her, she was able to peek past him. Hazel and Carmichael were still cozied up at the end of the bar, and Maya was talking with another guest.

She shook her head. "No, sorry. I have a boyfriend, remember?"

"See, I don't think you actually do." He stepped closer, and she took a step back. "I think you're just saying that."

She stepped to the right, and he stepped in front of her.

Setting her hands on her hips, she glared at him. Anger and nerves had her heart racing and her voice rising. "I don't care what you think. Now get out of my way."

"Touchy," he muttered, holding his hands up in capitulation and stepping to the side.

She quickly moved past him and caught Maya's gaze before Brayden grabbed her wrist and turned her. She yanked her arm free, and he held up his hands again. "I'm sorry, Freya. Can we try again? I'm coming on strong because I think we'd be good together. We could have a lot of fun this week. So can I buy you dinner? Get your number?"

Douche magnet. That's what she was. "No, Brandon—"

"It's *Brayden*," he bristled.

Oh, good freaking God. "Whatever. I have a boyfriend, so no. I'm not giving you my number or having dinner with you." She was conscious of the fact that they were drawing the attention of the people around them, but she didn't care. The faster this guy got away from her, the better.

A smirk grew on Brayden's smarmy face as he crossed his arms over his chest. "Oh yeah? Well, where is this supposed boyfriend of yours?"

Heat tore over her face. "I owe you *zero* explanations." She spun and stalked toward the bar, making a beeline to the center where Maya was waving her over.

Brayden kept pace with her. "You're at a bar by yourself accepting drinks from guys who aren't your boyfriend. You're asking to get hit on. No real man would allow that. I mean, what kind of man lets his girl talk up another guy at a bar?"

Her jaw dropped as she glared at him. Of course that's what this d-bag would think.

"Those are some big words, bud," Maya said, a smirk lifting her ruby-red lips.

A smirk that had Freya frowning. What was her friend up to?

Maya crossed her arms over her chest. "You gonna call out her boyfriend's manliness to his face?"

"Absolutely." Brayden scoffed as a haughty do-you-know-who-I-am expression settled over him. "If she actually had a boyfriend, I'd definitely tell him what's what to his damn face."

"By all means then," a deep voice said. The grumbly baritone had the fine hairs on her arms standing at attention. "Feel free to tell me what's what."

Freya's gaze shot to the left—to the man she hadn't

noticed standing beside Carmichael—and was rendered mute.

Holy. Crap.

How had she not seen him? Not only was the man enormous, but he was breathtaking.

Before she could blink, he was beside her. His strong arm settled over her shoulders, and he tucked her close. She had a split second to take him in, but that was all she needed. Shoulder-length dark hair pulled half back into a bun, stunning dark-brown eyes, high cheekbones, a chiseled jaw with the sexiest five-o'clock shadow, full lips, and massive shoulders.

Her breath caught as he bent and dropped a quick kiss to her lips.

"Hey, baby." A smirk lifted the corner of his mouth. "Sorry I'm late."

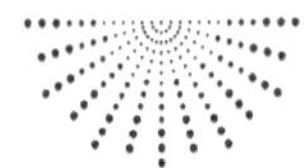

CHAPTER THREE

"We'll look around before we head out, but we'll be back tomorrow with a bigger team," Xander Bonetti said, shaking the hand of Gabriel Ortiz, the owner of Pacific View Resort.

"Thank you. I appreciate you coming right out."

"Not a problem. Also, Gavin Frazier sends his regards," Xander said, referring to his boss, friend, and the founder of Hudson Security. "He said he'll call you later this evening to touch base. He'd be here personally, but he's currently out of town."

"I understand. Believe me, I know how busy you all are, and I appreciate you fitting us in on such short notice." Gabriel let out a sigh, shaking his head. "I get what happened today was an isolated incident, but that guy should never have been able to make it to the spa. If you're not already a guest, you have to check in at the front desk to get an access card for our spa facility. We have a secure entrance to our grounds, so I'm not sure how he got past the front desk."

Xander knew that secure entrance or not, most people were lax when it came to security. Especially at a place like this. People didn't want to offend anyone by inadvertently denying a guest entry. Xander hadn't seen the man who'd stormed the spa, but Sheriff Quinn O'Conner, a personal friend he'd worked alongside with on various cases, had briefed him when they'd run into each other earlier.

The man responsible for all the destruction was Jason Edwards, the estranged husband of a guest at the Pacific View Resort. Edwards was a middle-aged white male who worked in finance. Average height, average build. Short brown hair and brown eyes. Dressed in khakis and a polo shirt. Basically, he'd blended in with the guests. Hospitality staff at a high-end resort wouldn't stop and question someone like him because of their own biases and because most people avoided confrontation. So yeah, Xander was nearly 100 percent sure how Edwards got past check-in, but he didn't want to burst Gabriel's bubble. Yet. That was for tomorrow.

"It's something we'll examine more in depth," Xander said, choosing his words with care. "My team will not only assess your current security protocols, but also how your resort is accessed by both guests and staff. We'll also talk with your current security staff and make recommendations. Do you know if the media has gotten wind of what happened?"

Gabriel shook his head. "Not that I know of, but there's extra security personnel stationed at our main entrance. If any news crews come by, security has been instructed to move them along. We sent a notification to all our staff and instructed them to forward any and all press inquiries to my office. We obviously closed the spa facility after what happened. Luckily, it was near the end of the day, so only a handful of guests were affected, but with the police presence and EMTs, I know rumors are buzzing among the guests. We sent out a text to let them know there'd been an incident and assured them that it was isolated and there were no lingering safety issues. We also informed everyone that salon services are cancelled for the week, but spa services will resume tomorrow as scheduled." '

Xander's eyebrows lifted in surprise. He'd seen the aftermath and the place had been a disaster. "Really?"

Gabriel nodded and glanced at his watch. "Sheriff O'Conner said he'd be releasing the scene in about an hour or two. I have a cleaning crew on standby. The way the facility is set up, the spa and salon areas are on opposite sides. We're going to cordon off the entire salon side, but that won't affect the spa areas or treatment rooms. Also, by opening tomorrow, I'm hoping it will keep the rumor mill down. We don't need this kind of publicity."

"Understandable. We'll leave you to it then." Xander gestured to his colleague who stood silently beside him. "Carmichael and I will look around and get a feel for how your evening security is set up, guest activity, that kind of thing."

"Of course," Gabriel said, walking them back to the main lobby. "Feel free to wander the grounds. Aside from this main building and our spa facility, there's a yoga center, gym, outdoor challenge course, a few meditation areas, three pool facilities, and of course our guest housing."

"You have what? Three hundred acres?" Carmichael asked.

"Four hundred, actually," Gabriel replied, pride gleaming in his eyes. "There's quite a bit that's still undeveloped, and we have an extensive network of hiking trails. We allow guests to explore on their own, but we also offer guided hikes. The sunrise hike is one of our most popular activities. Our grounds are extensive, but I'll set up an official tour for your group tomorrow morning. With our golf carts, it won't take up too much time."

"Appreciate that," Xander said, glancing around the lobby. The décor was classic Pacific Northwest. Exposed wood, stone, and metal. A black marble fountain featuring orcas and other marine wildlife was the focal point of the lobby and provided a soothing white noise.

"I'll see you both tomorrow. Please feel free to get some dinner or drinks after you check out the place. On me, of course. We have a few different dining options on our campus, but I suggest the Orca Moon Lounge. Not only is it our most relaxed dinner environment, but after the incident today, I imagine most of the guests will be there . . . mingling."

"You mean trying to get the scoop on what went down," Carmichael said with a smirk.

Gabriel shrugged as he walked backward to his office. "You didn't hear that from me, gentlemen."

Xander chuckled and lifted his chin. "See you tomorrow."

Once Gabriel was out of eyesight, Carmichael turned to him. "Divide and conquer?"

Xander nodded. "I'll head toward the guest cabanas and look around down there. You check out the main lodge and common areas."

"Meet up at the Orca Moon Lounge in thirty? Crawford said they have a burger there that's his favorite."

Xander grinned. Micha Crawford was a mutual friend from the gym who was also the head chef at the Pacific View's Watermark Restaurant. If Crawford said it was his favorite, the burger had to be damn near perfection. "Count me in. Meet back in thirty."

After walking the resort's guest villas and bungalows, Xander was beyond impressed with the facility. He knew the place could accommodate up to three hundred guests, but the way everything was laid out gave it a very private, intimate feel.

Stepping into the Orca Moon Lounge, he scanned the room. A full bar took up the opposite end of the room, with sets of low tables to the left along the windows, clusters of couches and overstuffed chairs in the middle, and high-top tables to the right. The place was crowded, and there was definitely a buzz to the room.

He spotted Carmichael seated on the left end of the bar with a pretty blonde and chuckled. Of course Carmichael had found a woman to chat up. While the guy was solid and an excellent teammate, he was an absolute and unapologetic man-whore. They all gave him as much shit as they could about it. Not that the ribbing fazed the guy. Not at all.

In a lot of ways, Carmichael reminded Xander of himself when he'd been younger. God knew, back when he'd been pushing thirty, he'd had a similar the-more-the-merrier atti-tude when it came to women. But as he'd gotten older, the excitement of being with a different woman every weekend had worn off. Now that he was knocking on forty, recre-ational fucking held zero appeal. Yeah, he'd dated here and there and had his fair share of friends-with-benefits arrange-ments over the last few years, but even that had become tedious. For the most part, he preferred his own company. Playing the get-to-know-you game, being on his best behav-ior, having to share stories about his past—none of that was for him. Especially since he knew it would lead nowhere.

He didn't do relationships. He wasn't built for them. As an intensely private person, women were an entanglement he wanted no part of.

Instead, Xander was happy to give his friend shit. He assumed Carmichael would become more discerning one of these days, but maybe not.

He strode to the bar and slapped his friend on the shoulder. "Can I join you guys?"

"Of course," Carmichael said, turning to him. With a shit-eating grin, he gestured to the woman beside him. "Xander, this is Hazel. Hazel, my colleague Xander Bonetti."

She extended her hand. "Nice to meet you. I've seen you around at the gym."

Shaking her hand, he nodded. Now that she'd mentioned it, she looked vaguely familiar.

As he pulled out a barstool, Carmichael and Hazel returned to their conversation, and the bartender dropped a coaster onto the bar in front of him.

"Hi there," she said. "What can I get you?"

Glancing at the bartender, he did a double take at the intensity of her stare. Tingles prickled the back of his neck. He narrowed his eyes and waited. The woman had something to say. What? He had no clue.

"So how about this?" She lowered her voice and leaned toward him. "You see that woman in the hallway? The one talking with golf douche?"

He followed her gaze and spotted the woman in question. Petite. Long dark hair. Attractive. And currently being cornered by some guy who towered over her.

Anger began to simmer in his gut. Men who preyed on women were scum. Men who used their size to intimidate women? Even bigger pieces of shit. Pieces of shit that needed to be taught a lesson. And he was happy to be the one to dole out those lessons.

"She's a friend of mine who's had a really shit day. To top it all off, she's had to deal with that asshole for way too long tonight. If you can go and pretend that you're her boyfriend, your dinner and drinks are on me."

A growl rumbled in Xander's chest as he watched the other man grab her by the wrist. He stood as she yanked her hand away and headed in their direction. "Dinner and drinks won't be necessary," he muttered to the bartender. "What's her name?"

"Freya," the woman quickly replied.

Freya. He rolled her name around in his mind as she approached with the man hot on her heels.

As they neared, the other man's words had Xander's frown deepening.

"You're at a bar by yourself accepting drinks from guys who aren't your boyfriend. You're asking to get hit on. No real man would allow that. I mean, what kind of man lets his girl talk up another guy at a bar?"

Xander clenched his fists. What a fucking piece of shit.

"Those are some big words, bud," the bartender said from behind him. "You gonna call out her boyfriend's manliness to his face?"

"Absolutely." The guy scoffed with a look of utter superiority. "If she actually had a boyfriend, I'd definitely tell him what's what to his damn face."

Xander prided himself on always keeping his temper in check. But this fucker?

Testing his goddamn limits.

"By all means then," he said, meeting the dipshit's gaze. "Feel free to tell me what's what."

Straightening to his full six-four, Xander stepped toward them and took satisfaction in watching the other man blanch.

Wrapping an arm around Freya's slim shoulders, he tucked her into his side, surprised how perfectly she fit against him. He glanced down at her, and her ice-blue gaze socked him right in the chest. Before he could second-guess himself, he bent down, and as she sucked in a startled gasp, he pressed a soft kiss to her lips.

"Hey, baby. Sorry I'm late."

She stared at him for a second but then cleared her throat and flashed him a dazzling smile. "Oh, no problem. I'm just so happy you were able to make it."

Xander glared at the other man. He had the guy by at least five inches and easily outweighed him by forty pounds. He had zero problems intimidating the fucker. "This guy giving you problems, Frey?"

"Um, well . . ." she stammered.

"It's okay, baby. Why don't you go take a seat," he said, softly squeezing her shoulders. The last thing he wanted was to make her more uncomfortable than she obviously already was. He could deal with this fucker on his own.

As she settled into the stool beside Carmichael, Xander met his friend's gaze. Carmichael lifted his chin in silent acknowledgement and then whispered to Freya.

Once her worried gaze left him, Xander stepped to the other man, who immediately held his hands up.

"I don't want any trouble, man. Your girlfriend came on to me. In fact—"

"I'd stop talking if I were you," Xander interrupted. "You know why?" When the other man opened his mouth, Xander shook his head. "That was a rhetorical question, asshole. See, I have eyes. And I saw you lay your fucking hand on my woman."

The man went ashen.

Xander crossed his arms over his chest and held the man's gaze. Two pink splotches brightened the guy's cheeks.

"If you even look in my woman's direction again, you and I are gonna have words. Am I clear?"

The other man sputtered, and Xander knew the exact words that were going to fly out of the guy's stupid mouth.

"Do you know who I—"

"I don't give a fuck who you are," Xander murmured, taking another step closer. "Am. I. Clear?"

The man opened his mouth but then snapped it shut, giving Xander a curt nod before quickly turning and hustling out of the lounge.

Part of him was disappointed the guy wasn't a complete idiot. That part wished the asshole had mouthed off just so he could put the guy in his place.

Instead, Xander slowly pulled in a deep breath through his nose and let it out. No. He wasn't that hothead anymore. The last thing Freya needed was more violence after the guy had had the audacity to grab her.

Turning back to the bar, he placed his hand on the back of Freya's barstool. "Hey. You okay?"

"Yeah." She gave him a sheepish grin. "Thank you for the rescue."

He lifted his chin toward the bartender. "Thank your friend." Freya's dark eyebrow arched, and he smiled. "Your friend—"

"Maya," the bartender said, holding out her hand.

He shook it and then brought his attention back to Freya. "Maya informed me I had a girlfriend, and that she needed me."

A pretty pink stained her cheeks. "Well, I appreciate your acting skills. That guy . . ." She shook her head.

His gaze shot to her wrist, looking for any sign of bruising. "Are you okay? Are you hurt?"

Carmichael snickered, and he shot a glare at his friend over Freya's head before turning his attention back to her. "Did that guy hurt your wrist?"

"Oh no, I'm fine." The flush over her cheeks deepened. "Just a little embarrassed, I guess."

"Nothing to be embarrassed about. That guy's a tool."

Maya scoffed. "Understatement. What can I get you to drink?"

He glanced at the row of taps behind Maya and then at

the glass in front of Carmichael. His friend had a clear, bubbly drink with a couple of lime wedges. Twenty bucks said it was soda water. Off the clock or not, they were still at the resort representing Hudson Security. "I'll have what he's having."

Moments later, Maya set his drink in front of him, and he took a sip. Yup. Soda water. "Thank you," he said before turning to Freya and holding out his hand. "I'm Xander Bonetti, by the way."

She grinned and took his hand. "Freya Hansen. It's nice to meet you, boyfriend."

"Pleasure's all mine. Who knew I could snag such a pretty girlfriend?"

"Ah, a charmer, I see," she said, a shy smile lifting her lips. "Can I buy you dinner?"

"Thanks, but that's not necessary." He gestured to Carmichael. "Our dinner is covered tonight. But maybe I can take you up on that offer some other time?"

As soon as the words left his mouth, he stilled. *Holy shit, what the fuck just came out of my mouth?*

He glanced at Carmichael, who was staring at him with wide eyes, looking like he was barely holding back his laughter.

Before Freya could respond, Maya called out, "Dinner is served, peeps." She strolled toward them, her arms loaded with dinner plates. She placed a giant salad in front of Hazel, steak and mashed potatoes in front of Freya, and plates with burgers and fries in front of him and Carmichael. The food looked amazing, but he gave Maya a questioning look since he hadn't had the chance to order.

"Your friend ordered for the both of you when he arrived."

He caught Carmichael's gaze and lifted his chin. "Thanks, man."

"So you guys are with Hudson Security, right?" Hazel asked from Carmichael's other side.

"Yup," Carmichael replied. "We're helping Mr. Ortiz with some security consulting."

"Oh, that's great!" Hazel said, bringing a forkful of salad to her lips. "Freya and I were working at the salon this afternoon when that guy came in and shot up the place."

Xander stilled, annoyed at the woman's chipper and cavalier tone. He glanced at Freya and frowned when he saw her shiver. It wasn't cold in the bar.

"You were there?" he asked, keeping his voice low. He'd seen the aftermath. For the life of him, he couldn't picture— no, didn't *want* to picture—the woman beside him amid that chaos.

She nodded, her eyes locked on the food in front of her. She reached for her water with a trembling hand. A hand that he suddenly realized was wrapped in a flesh-colored bandage. "My client was the guy's wife. Hazel was right next to us working with my client's sister. It was . . . crazy."

Freya's voice shook on her last word. The impulse to reach out to soothe her, to touch her, to offer some sort of comfort was immense, but he reined it in. That was *not* his place. At all. Momentary fake boyfriend or not, they didn't know each other. "I'm so sorry you experienced that. Are you okay? How are you holding up?"

When she turned to him, her smile was bright. Too bright. "I'm thankful no one was seriously injured."

He nodded. Her nonanswer didn't escape him. "Do you want to talk about it?"

Her blue eyes widened for a moment before she schooled her features. "It's okay. They offered us grief counselors and . . ." She cleared her throat before quickly cutting a piece of steak and shoving it in her mouth. Smiling around the bite, she asked, "So who cuts your hair?"

He chuckled. "Change the subject. Got it."

She grimaced. "Sorry."

"You're fine, sweetheart, and you have absolutely nothing to apologize for." He took a bite of his hamburger and groaned. Holy shit. The salty bacon, the savory beef, and the tart zing of the pickled whatever was on there was sheer freaking perfection.

"I know, man, right?" Carmichael said, half his burger gone. "This is fucking ridiculous."

Freya snickered. "So get the burger next time? Got it."

"I'm sure that steak's great, but yeah," Xander murmured. He held the burger out to her. "Want a bite?"

She laughed. "I'm good, thanks."

He took another minute to gobble down most of his burger and then set it down and wiped his hands on his napkin. "To answer your question, no one cuts my hair. Once it gets past my shoulders, I just grab some scissors and hack away."

Her eyes widened in horror, and he chuckled.

"It looks like shit too," Carmichael chimed in. "That's why it's always pulled back. The dude's man bun is more functional than fashionable."

He flipped off his friend before he snagged a fry, ran it through the sauce, and popped it in his mouth. "I used to just buzz my hair, but then I got lazy and let it grow out. I figure when the trimming becomes too much of a pain in the ass, I'll buzz it again."

"No!" Freya shook her head. "You have great hair. It's thick and has a natural wave. Women pay a crap ton of money to get highlights like yours. You can't just buzz it off."

"True," Maya said, refilling their waters. "If you have good hair, you gotta keep it. My boyfriend's going bald, so he says he has no choice but to keep it shaved."

"Yeah, but he can pull it off," Hazel said. "Micha's the definition of hot, tatted bald guy."

"Micha Crawford's your boyfriend?" Carmichael asked.

Maya nodded. "You know him?"

"He recommended the burger," Carmichael said around a mouthful of food.

"We work out at the gym together," Xander clarified. "Good dude."

"That he is." Maya grinned. "And seeing as my sweet, hot man Bics his head, he'd tell you to keep it while you've still got it."

"I'll happily trim your hair," Freya said. "Maybe you can even change it up a little and do a disconnected undercut while still keeping it long on top?"

"Ooh, a Viking look," Hazel said with a grin that made him uncomfortable. "That would be hot."

"Besides," Freya continued, "it's the least I can do after your perfectly timed rescue."

Even though he knew it was probably a horrible idea, he nodded and picked up his burger. "I'm not quite sure what disconnected under whatever means, but I'll take you up on a haircut. I'm due for one, and I'm sure you'll do a better job than me."

Her smile was electric, and he took a bite of his burger before more words he was sure to regret flew from his mouth. For better or worse, the woman fascinated him. She seemed sweet—probably too sweet for him—but it didn't stop him from wanting to get to know her a little better.

"Great," she said, cutting another piece of her steak. "Once they get the salon back in order, we'll figure out a time that works for you."

The conversation remained light over the next handful of minutes while they all finished their dinners.

"Thanks for everything, Maya," Freya said to the

bartender as she cleared their plates. "I think I'm going to head home." She turned to Hazel. "Do you want to walk out together?"

"No, I'm good," Hazel said. "I'm going to hang around a little longer."

Xander didn't miss how the other woman's suggestive gaze shot to Carmichael. Nor did he miss Carmichael's cringe. It was subtle and only lasted a split second, but he'd worked with the man for a number of years and could read him. Maybe the end of his friend's man-whore days was closer than he'd thought. That was surprising considering how pretty the other woman was. Granted, he thought Freya was hands down more attractive, but Hazel was exactly Carmichael's type. But who his friend did and didn't take to bed wasn't his concern.

"Sounds good," Freya said, sliding out of her seat. "I'll see you in a few days. Drive home safe, okay?"

Xander stood, retrieved Freya's purse from the hook under the bar, and handed it to her. "Can I walk you to your car? It's pretty late."

Her eyes widened, and she simply looked at him for a few seconds before she schooled her features. "Thanks, I appreciate that."

After saying goodbye to the others, he followed her through the resort's back hallways.

"The employee parking is separate from the main parking lot," she said as they exited the building into a dimly lit lot.

Xander frowned.

Roughly three dozen cars were scattered around the parking area. The cars along the back perimeter abutted a thick line of trees and were shrouded in near darkness. And of course, that's the direction Freya was walking. He'd definitely suggest adding more lighting back here in his report to

Gabriel, because having employees walk to their cars in the dark—especially the women—was unacceptable.

As they approached her car, a dark-colored Kia sedan, he noticed her stifle a yawn.

"You okay to drive home?"

She nodded, a sheepish smile tilting her lips. "Sorry about that. I'll be fine. I'm right downtown, so it's not too far. It's just been a long day."

"Speaking of, if you ever want to talk about what happened, I'm more than happy to listen. Sometimes it helps to talk it out with a stranger." He knew firsthand that it was often easier to talk through things with people who didn't know you well.

A smirk lifted her lips. "But we're not strangers. You're my boyfriend," she teased.

He couldn't help but smile. She really was a pretty little thing. "Either way, I've been informed I'm a really good listener."

"Well, I might take you up on that. Oh, and let me give you my number." Her eyes widened, and a deep flush tore over her cheeks. One he could see even with the dim lighting. "I mean, uh, so you can get in touch with me for that haircut. Not like . . ."

"I'd love your number," he said, grinning. God, she was cute. "For that haircut and maybe dinner sometime?"

He didn't think it was possible, but the flush over her cheeks deepened as she pulled out her phone.

She cleared her throat and asked, "What's your number?"

He rattled off his phone number, and a couple seconds later, his phone dinged.

"You have my number now." She turned to reach for her door and then abruptly straightened and turned back to him. "Oh! Do you need me to drive you to the front parking lot? I mean, I assume that's where your car is."

"It is, but that's okay. I think I'm going to look around, check out the security." He quickly scanned the area and shook his head. "It's pretty dark out here."

"Yeah," she said, wrinkling her nose.

He opened her door for her.

"Thanks again for stepping in tonight, Xander. You didn't have to, and I appreciate that you did."

"You're welcome." He waited as she settled herself into her seat and buckled up. "I'm sorry the circumstances were what they were, but regardless, it was really nice meeting you tonight."

"It was nice meeting you too."

"Text me when you get home so I know you made it back safely." As soon as the words left his mouth, he cringed. "Shit, sorry. That sounded super controlling and creepy, didn't it?"

She laughed. "You're fine. Besides, we know each other well enough. Not only am I your future hairstylist, but we've had dinner together, *and* you've already kissed me."

"That I have." He held her gaze for a moment, appreciating the blush staining her cheeks. "Drive safely, and I'll talk with you soon."

As she pulled away, he gave her a wave and couldn't help the smile that grew on his face.

Shaking his head, he let out a sigh. What the hell did he just get himself into?

CHAPTER FOUR

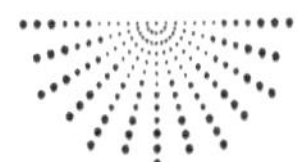

"Rumor has it that you asked a girl out," Tash said with a smirk from the passenger seat of Xander's Range Rover.

"Oh, holy shit," Xander grumbled, readjusting his grip on the steering wheel.

"What?" Tash asked, the picture of innocence. But they'd been teammates for nearly eight years, so he knew that I'm-so-innocent thing she did was a crock of shit. "I heard from a very reliable source that you swooped in and rescued her from some douche, kissed her, charmed the shit out of her, and were all googly-eyed by the end of the night."

"Moon-eyed," Abbot chimed in from the back seat. "I'm pretty sure Carmichael said Xan was all moon-eyed."

"Oh, pardon me. I stand corrected." Tash grinned from ear to ear.

It was seven thirty in the morning and way too early for this bullshit. When he'd met up with the team he'd picked to review the security at Pacific View Resort, he'd hoped for a nice, quiet morning. No such luck.

Xander was the head of the personal security division for

Hudson Security, an elite team of mostly former special forces and alphabet agency operatives. They currently had three teams of three, and he led Team One, which consisted of himself, Natasha "Tash" Silver, and Bennett Wilson, who was following them in another Hudson Security vehicle with Carmichael, who was the lead for Team Two. Samantha Abbot was the lead of Hudson Security's four-person cyber group.

He glanced at Tash. "You know, Carmichael being your *very reliable source* is nothing but trouble."

She shrugged. "You're just salty because he's not wrong. Besides, it's not like you've denied any of his intel."

"I'm sure I can pull the resort's video footage once we're there, and we can see it all firsthand," Abbot said with a little too much enthusiasm in her voice.

"It's way too freaking early for this," he muttered, scrubbing a hand over his jaw.

"Oh, suck it up, bud. How are you not used to us by now?"

How, indeed? Tash was a damn fine operative. The woman was a fierce fighter and lethal with any sort of blade. All in all, an absolute badass he was happy to have watching his six. Abbot's talents were more focused on all things digital, and she was no less impressive. He'd happily take a bullet for either woman.

However, put the two women together—a comical yin and yang of personalities—and they turned into annoying little sisters who were all about giving him shit. He didn't have any siblings, but he'd been reassured by their colleagues who did that this was normal. Standard operating procedure even. *Yay me.* All he knew was that he needed to shut this conversation down ASAP.

"Besides," Abbot said, oblivious to his growing headache, "it's your fault for being all moon-eyed in front of

Carmichael. You know the only thing he loves more than gossip is pus—"

"Eww. Nope," Tash cut in. "Do *not* finish that sentence. I swear, I don't need that image in my head this early in the damn morning."

Abbot laughed. "Sorry. You do have a point." There were three blessed seconds of silence before she piped up again. "So you want me to run a check on this girl for you?"

"Holy shit, no." He groaned, pulling into the Pacific View Resort's parking lot. He caught Abbot's gaze in the rearview mirror. "And make sure Bean and the rest of cyber don't run one either." He put the car in park, thankful they'd arrived at their destination, and got out of the SUV. Rounding the hood, he met the two women at the front. "Now, can we not talk about this? We need to focus. Be professional and shit, okay?"

Abbot snorted while Tash chuckled and gestured with her hand. "After you, oh paragon of virtue."

Rolling his eyes, he met Wilson and Carmichael in front of their vehicle.

"Thanks a lot, asshole," he grumbled to Carmichael.

His supposed friend burst into laughter. Because of course he did.

"Hey," Carmichael said with his hands raised. "Wasn't it my duty to report to the team what we observed last night?"

Xander shook his head. "I'm sure you forgot to regale them with tales of you and the blonde, though."

Abbot snickered, shouldering her laptop bag. "A blonde? Geez, could you be more predictable?"

Carmichael wrinkled his nose. "Nothing actually happened with Hazel last night."

Xander snorted, slapping him on the shoulder. "Right, dude. We're talking about the same chick, right? Tall, blond, dead ringer for Barbie, and looked like she wanted to devour you?"

"You know that no one here believes you, right?" Tash teased.

"I'm serious. Nothing happened," Carmichael protested. "Yeah, she's fucking hot, but . . ." He made a face. "I don't know. Once I found out that she was in the salon *during* the shooting, it was weird. She was really aggressive and—"

"Like you have a problem with that?" Wilson asked, his skepticism written on his face.

"I don't usually. But that place was shot to shit, and she was acting like she'd chipped a damn nail." Carmichael shrugged. "Like I said, it was weird. Rubbed me the wrong way."

"Aww," Tash drawled, bumping her shoulder into Carmichael's. "Our little guy's growing up."

Carmichael shot her a look of mock indignation. "You wound me, T."

Tash grinned and met Xander's gaze. "So getting back to this girl you like . . ."

"How about not?" he muttered.

She continued as if he hadn't spoken. Story of his life with Tash. "So do you *like her* like her, or are you gonna pull a Carmichael on her?" Tash glanced at Carmichael. "Sorry, I meant pull an old Carmichael on her."

"God, Xan." Abbot groaned. "Please tell me you've outgrown your man-whore days."

Heading back to his SUV, he grabbed a stack of tablets from the back of the vehicle. Closing the liftgate, he shook his head. Ridiculous. These people were ridiculous. "I'll admit that I had a somewhat sketchy past—"

"I heard that back in the day, you could've made me look like a damn monk," Carmichael said, taking one of the tablets from him.

Xander frowned. "Where the hell did you hear that from?" Not that it was a lie, but still.

"I don't know," Carmichael said, though he angled his head toward Wilson.

"Traitor," he grumbled, handing Wilson a tablet.

His friend simply shrugged.

"Let's just agree that both you and Carmichael are gross," Tash said as she took a tablet and powered it up. "Now the question is, if we ever see this lady who has you all moon-eyed, do you want us to talk you up or make her run for the hills?"

He sighed and scrubbed a hand over his face. "How about none of the above?"

Tash smiled, and it was all teeth. "Sorry, that's not an option."

Wilson groaned, and Xander met his gaze. "What? You have something to add?"

Wilson shook his head. "You guys gossip worse than the ladies in town. Can we actually get some work done?"

"Ugh. Always the voice of freaking reason," Abbot muttered before turning to Tash. "How do you put up with his grumpy, sour mug?"

"You get used to it." Tash shrugged and narrowed her eyes as Wilson took a step toward her. "Uh-uh. You try and put me in a headlock, I will lay you out flat, buddy. You know, just like I did this morning."

Xander chuckled as Wilson held his hands up and took a step backward. Smart man. "Alright, kids." Because swear to Christ, that's what they were all acting like. "Time to be responsible fucking adults. Billionaire resort owner at one o'clock."

Just like that, everyone straightened and donned their game faces. They crossed the parking lot in seconds, and as Xander approached Gabriel, he held out his hand.

"Gabriel, good morning." He gestured between the man and his team. "Everyone, this is Gabriel Ortiz, owner of Pacific View Resort. Gabriel, you remember Carmichael from yesterday. This is Tash Silver and Bennet Wilson. They, along with myself and Carmichael, will be looking at your grounds, operations, and processes." As everyone shook hands, he continued, "This is Sam Abbot, one of our top cybersecurity experts. She'll review your digital security and make appropriate recommendations."

"It's nice to meet you all," Gabriel said as a lean, familiar-looking man dressed in a Pacific View Resort polo approached. "I believe most of you already know Michael Kwon, our head of security."

"Long time no see," Xander joked, lifting his chin at the other man in greeting. Aside from seeing the man yesterday while on-site, most of the team had worked out with Kwon the morning of the shooting. The man was somewhere in his late forties, former Seattle PD, and one of the best Muay Thai practitioners Xander had ever seen in person.

After greeting the group, Kwon turned to Abbot and held out his hand. "I don't think we've met."

"Seeing as I'm cybersecurity and not a gym rat, that makes sense," she said, shaking his hand. "Sam Abbot. We'll be spending a lot of time together today going over the systems you have in place."

"Looking forward to it," he replied with a grin.

Sam chuckled. "You may think differently by the end of the day."

"And that's exactly why you're here," Gabriel said. "I mentioned this to Xander and Carmichael yesterday, but I'd like us to start with a tour." As he spoke, an eight-passenger golf cart pulled up to the entrance. "Our grounds are quite extensive, and we can show you them from both the guest and employee perspectives. It shouldn't take too long, then you all can do your thing."

With nods of agreement, they loaded into the golf cart. Kwon was driving, and Gabriel sat shotgun in a rear-facing seat and donned a headset. He fiddled with it for a moment before chuckling. "Apologies, it's been a while since I've done this."

Forty-five minutes later, they were back under the resort's porte cochere. As the group stepped out of the golf cart, Gabriel said, "If you'll follow me, we've set aside one of our private dining rooms for you to use as a meeting room."

There was a large round table in the center of the spacious room, with notepads, pens, and bottles of water at each seat. One wall had floor-to-ceiling windows overlooking the Salish Sea, and along the opposite wall was a banquet table with fresh and prepackaged snacks, along with water, coffee, and tea stations.

"Thank you," Xander said as his team took seats around the table. "We're going to touch base for about ten, and then I'll send Sam over to Kwon, and the rest of us will check things out."

"Sounds good," Gabriel said. "I'll leave all-access key cards for each of you up at the front desk. Sam, check in with them when you're ready, and they'll call Kwon back for you. I'll be on-site all day, so if there's anything you need from me, just let me know. You all have my cell, but if for whatever reason you can't reach me—cell service can be spotty up here—let the staff know, and they can radio me."

Once Gabriel stepped out of the room and closed the door behind him, Xander looked at his colleagues. "Thoughts?"

"The security here's a joke," Wilson said.

"I wouldn't necessarily go that far," Tash said, cracking open a bottle of water. "There were cameras and lights by the guest residences and villas. Good lighting along the main walkways."

Wilson scoffed. "Did you notice the perimeter? Their supposed 'secure entry' means jack shit when you can get on the property from countless access points."

Tash wrinkled her nose as she took a sip of water. "Yeah, that could definitely use some work, but the property is massive. Aside from fencing the entire perimeter, I'm not sure what the other options are."

Wilson shrugged. "That's exactly what we do at Hudson Security."

"True," Xander said. "We can show Ortiz how we secure our property and see if that's something he'd be interested in." He turned to Abbot. "What's your initial take on their security?"

"At first glance, it looks to be pretty high-end but basic. I'm guessing the surveillance will be standard. Hallways, main areas, walkways, guest entrances, and exits. I mean, no offense to Gabriel or Kwon, the stuff they have is good quality, but it's still your standard, bare-bones hotel security . . . just upgraded to the deluxe package, you know?"

"That's what we're here for, people. Not only to assess the physical security, but to check out their processes too." Xander placed a map of the property on the table. "Everyone's supposed to initially check in at the front desk in the main building. All other buildings are secure, and everyone is issued a customized key card that works for their guest room and allows them to access all the buildings."

"I wonder how many keys are lost during the course of a day," Carmichael pondered.

"Apparently, guests are given lanyards, but since you're talking with the front-desk staff, I'll leave that with you."

Carmichael nodded. "Will do. Plus, on our tour, I noticed two buildings had their front doors propped open, so I'll check to see what their actual policy is on that."

"Great," Xander said. "Now, the resort also offers limited day passes for the spa and salon. These folks get a key card that supposedly only gives them access to the spa building. But the guy who shot up the place yesterday bypassed the front desk and walked right over to the spa building where someone held the door open for him."

Everyone around the table winced, and Xander agreed. It was one thing to install cameras and lights, it was another thing entirely to change people's practices.

"We need to provide them some options that they can realistically implement, things that the staff will actually do. However, knowing people the way we do"—he turned to Abbot—"I'd like you to focus on really tight surveillance that also still maintains the guests' privacy. I'm sure privacy is important, but overall security holds a higher priority. I know you'll find a way to balance the two."

Abbot nodded. "Go overboard on the cybersecurity, because the worker bees won't want to confront anyone, and make sure guests' privacy is maintained. It'll be costly, but the dude's a billionaire. He can afford the upgrades."

After another few minutes of everyone sharing their thoughts, Xander doled out the assignments, and the team disbursed. Making his way to the spa, he was surprised by the high-energy atmosphere buzzing around him. Numerous guests milled about in their athleisure wear, happily chatting as they sipped on freshly made smoothies. Others hustled down the resort's paths in small groups of twos and threes, making their way to their various scheduled activities. A group of ten women laughed loudly as they followed three identically dressed staff members to the outer edge of the property for what he assumed was a guided hike.

Following the path, Xander arrived at the spa. Designed to blend into its surroundings, the building was a sprawling two-story wood, stone, and glass marvel with a cascading water feature to the left of the entrance. It was obvious Gabriel hadn't spared any expense.

Xander was glad to see a security camera discreetly monitoring the spa's entrance, but he hadn't noticed any along the pathways from the main building. Glancing around, he frowned. The spa was roughly a hundred and fifty yards from the main building. Yesterday's shooter shouldn't have been able to get so deep into the resort property without anyone noticing him or stopping him.

Fresh soothing spa scents wafted over him as he entered the building. He made his way to the check-in counter where a young woman was in conversation with two guests.

Patiently waiting his turn, he glanced around. Not that he was hoping to catch a glimpse of a certain raven-haired beauty or anything. Freya had mentioned she'd been given the week off, so the chances of running into her were slim. If he wanted to see her again, he'd have to actually reach out, which . . . wasn't something he was sure about.

It was one thing to flirt, but it was another thing entirely to follow through. Again, he wasn't sure that was something he wanted to do. She didn't seem like the casual sort. Though he was kind of over that, he also wasn't in the market for any sort of relationship. So reaching out probably wasn't the smartest idea. Yeah, Freya was beautiful, seemingly sweet, and funny, but there wasn't much he could offer her aside from a night of fun, or maybe two—

What. The. Fuck? Focus, Bonetti.

Chastising himself, he inhaled deeply, taking in the spa's eucalyptus and lemon scents and willing them to help him focus. He needed to get his head back in the game.

Looking to the left, he took in the larger spa area. Its

waiting lounge had numerous plush couches and overstuffed chairs where five women were congregated. Two women stood along the back wall perusing the bar of beverages and snacks. Past the waiting area were the locker areas, steam rooms, relaxation spaces, thermal rooms, water features, and various treatment rooms.

He glanced to the right. Instead of seeing the smaller, yet no less plush, waiting area and salon workstations, large multi-paneled room dividers blocked the entire entrance.

"Good morning," a chipper voice called out. "How can I help you?"

He turned his attention to the young woman behind the front desk and glanced at her name tag. "Good morning, Audrey. I have a meeting with Miriam Littlefield."

"You must be Mr. Bonetti. Miriam's running just a few minutes behind but is on her way." She smiled and gestured to the waiting area. "Feel free to take a seat or help yourself to some refreshments while you wait. Today, our three infused waters are cucumber, honeydew, and mint; strawberry, lemon, and basil; and blackberries, orange, and ginger."

Holy shit, he was so not fancy enough for this place. He eyed the various glass beverage dispensers across the room. "Um, is there just regular water?"

Audrey giggled. "Of course. It's the one on the far right."

"Thank you."

As he turned, the entrance door swung open. Two women walked in, and he came to a halt. His gut clenched, and he couldn't have stopped the smile on his face from spreading if he'd tried.

Freya.

She'd texted him when she'd made it home last night, reassuring him that his concern for her safety hadn't encroached into creeper territory. It had taken him an embarrassingly long time to come up with a witty reply where he'd wished her a good night but left it open-ended. To which she'd responded with a pink heart emoji.

Did he know what the hell a pink heart emoji meant? No. But still, the woman had been at the forefront of his mind ever since.

"Xander, hi," Freya exclaimed, surprise coloring her face. "What are you doing here?"

No fucking clue.

She wasn't dressed in all black this morning. She wore dark jeans and a flowy, long-sleeved, blue top with flowers. Her long black hair was wavy and cascaded around her. She looked fresh and pretty. Hell, she was downright stunning. Not that she hadn't been stunning last night. But the dark shadows that had lingered beneath her eyes were gone now.

A throat cleared, and his gaze swung to the woman standing beside Freya. Clarification: to the woman standing beside Freya who was looking at him with an amused and curious grin. "I'm Miriam Littlefield," she said, holding out her hand. "My apologies for being late, Mr. Bonetti."

Get your shit together. "Just Xander is fine. And no apologies are necessary," he said, shaking her hand. "I appreciate you making time to meet with me this morning."

"Of course." Miriam's eyes ping-ponged between him and Freya. "I take it you two know each other?"

"We met yesterday," Freya replied, a soft blush staining her cheeks. "He's the one I was telling you about. The one who helped me out with the drunk guy."

Miriam gave him an appraising once-over and then turned to Freya. "I have to grab a few things, but why don't you show him what the crew has done with the space so far."

Freya's ice-blue eyes widened. "Um, sure. Of course."

"I'll be right back, Mr. Bonetti," Miriam said.

"Take your time," Xander replied, his gaze not leaving Freya's. "Morning."

She cleared her throat. "Good morning. If you'll follow me," she said, gesturing to one end of the room divider as the pink in her cheeks deepened.

That little flush fascinated him. What would—

No. Holy shit. Hell, no.

Shaking his head, he followed her behind the screen. Didn't he just tell himself that getting together with her would be a bad idea?

Yeah, but that was before she was standing right in front of you. Like you fucking conjured her from thin air.

He internally cringed. Great. Now he was having a debate with himself. *Motherfucking shit.*

Keeping his eyes off the woman in front of him, he scanned the room, and surprise had his eyebrows lifting. Gone was the mess and destruction from the day before.

Focus, dammit. You're here to assess the place. Nothing more. Eye. On. The. Job.

CHAPTER FIVE

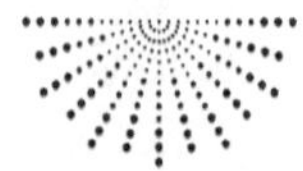

Of all the people to run into this morning, the last person Freya had expected was Xander. And damn . . . the guy was just as handsome as he'd been last night. After she'd made it home, he'd stayed in her thoughts. He'd been the bright spot in a ridiculously chaotic and surreal day. But the more she'd thought about him, the more she'd concluded that there was no way he was as larger than life as she'd recalled.

After the day she'd had, she'd been overtired. She was certain that the stress of the entire day had her painting him in some sort of heroic, better-than-reality kind of light. As she'd gotten ready this morning, she'd been certain that she'd remembered the tall, scruffy, long-haired man wrong, that she'd romanticized the entire evening.

Sneaking another glance at him, her belly fluttered.

Nope.

The man was still smoking hot. If anything, he was even better looking this morning than he'd been last night. *How is that even possible?*

Her stomach flipping surprised her. It had been a long

time since anyone had caught her attention, let alone had her feeling much of anything beyond irritation like last night's encounter with the drunk guy. Clearing her throat, she glanced around the salon and her mind scrambled for something to say.

Nothing. Her mind was mush.

"I thought you had the week off?" he asked, his voice a soothing deep rumble.

She turned to him in wonder. It shouldn't surprise her that he'd remembered her mentioning that—especially considering his line of work—but it did. In her experience, men didn't pay attention to what she had to say, let alone remember anything. Though that probably said more about the quality of guys she'd dated. Or lack thereof.

She scrunched her forehead. Not that Xander was interested in dating her or anything. In fact, if the way he was currently looking at her was any indication, the man probably thought she was a little slow—

She mentally smacked herself upside the head. *The man asked you a question. Answer him!*

Shifting on her feet, she pasted a smile on her face. "Oh, I do have the week off." She nodded to the empty area where the four salon stations had been. "But I'm meeting Janie for lunch later. Her husband was the one who . . ." She waved her hand at the room. "I figured I'd come in early and see if Miriam needed help. I'm going through everything to see what's salvageable. The faster we can get back up and running, the better."

And she needed to stay busy. The last thing she wanted was to sit at home by herself, replaying every second of what had happened.

He glanced around the salon. "It looks completely different. Whoever cleaned up got a lot done."

She nodded, following his gaze. The salon did indeed look

completely different from yesterday. Not only had all the glass, broken mirrors, and debris been swept away, but the destroyed furniture had been hauled out. The seating in the waiting room that hadn't been damaged remained neatly arranged, every inch vacuumed and wiped down. Aside from the hair-washing stations, the rest of the salon area remained empty. Meticulously clean, but empty. It was like they were simply waiting for the stations to be installed. The only indication something had happened here was the patched bullet holes in the walls, the bright-white spackle standing out against the cream-colored walls. "Miriam said once they got the okay from the sheriff's department to clean up, Mr. Ortiz had a cleaning crew come in, and they worked through the night."

"That's right," Miriam said, her heels clicking on the hardwood floors as she made her way to them with a tablet tucked under one arm and a stack of mail in her hands. "The cleaning crew left maybe an hour ago. Miracle workers, I tell you. And before I forget"—she held out the stack of mail to Freya—"these are for you. Have they not figured it out yet?"

Groaning, Freya rolled her eyes and took the mail. "Apparently not." Seeing Xander's brow knit in confusion, she explained, "I just moved here last month from Whidbey Island, but the place I'm renting downtown is new." She frowned. "Well, not *new* new, but it's a newly converted apartment, so the post office isn't recognizing it as a 'verifiable address.' I had my mail forwarded here before I got a PO box. I thought that would make things easier, but apparently, it just confused everyone even more." She held up the stack of mail and shrugged.

The corners of Xander's lips twitched, and her stomach did that flipping thing again. She glanced at her boss. "Sorry for the hassle. I'll swing by the post office again later this afternoon."

"You're fine, Freya."

Glancing down at her mail, her eyes narrowed on the large white envelope on the bottom of the stack. Quickly shuffling the mail, she caught sight of its mailing label.

Her heart stopped.

The familiar block letters bearing her old mailing address sent a chill crawling slowly down her spine like a cluster of tiny spiders racing down her back. *No. Not again.*

"Freya, are you okay?"

She startled at Xander's deep voice. Hugging the mail to her chest, she glanced up. Xander and Miriam looked at her, concern evident on both their faces. She forced a bright smile. "Sorry, yes. I'm totally fine."

Her breaths were coming too fast. She could hear how her voice had pitched an octave higher, but she couldn't do anything about it. "I'll get out of your hair," she said, her words coming out in a jumbled rush. "If you need me, I'll be in the back going over the stuff the repair crew pulled." Before they could respond, she spun on her heel and hurried to the employee breakroom.

She crossed the breakroom, dropped the mail onto the coffee table, and sat on the couch and bent at the waist. *Breathe.*

Her stomach was rolling. With her eyes slammed shut, she focused on each deep inhale and each slow exhale, willing the nausea to subside. This was nothing new, dammit. After all these years, she should be used to this. But when she hadn't received the familiar envelope on this year's anniversary, she'd thought . . . Hoped . . .

With a gasp, she opened her eyes. No, she'd never get used to this.

She slowly sat up, and her throat grew thick. Her gaze found the white envelope. Its edges were bent and creased. A familiar rock settled in her belly—sour, painful, and guilt-ridden.

With a trembling hand, she reached for the crinkled envelope. Her shoulders sank, as if a heavy weight were pushing down on her, which wasn't too far from the truth. She tore open the top flap and peeked inside. Her stomach twisted painfully.

No, she sure as hell would never get used to this. And she shouldn't. Because it's what she deserved.

Taking in a deep breath, she poured the contents onto the table and braced herself. But it was no use. Sorrow and guilt bombarded her. Her chest squeezed tightly as she stared at the four pictures on the coffee table.

All were from high school. She'd seen some variation of the photos before, but it didn't stop the grief and shame from seeping into her every pore. Nothing would.

The first two were of her and Sarah. Happy. Smiling. Laughing. She swiped away a stray tear before moving the photos aside.

The last two photos raised the fine hairs on her arms. As always, they were of her standing by herself at Sarah's gravesite. On one of the photos, her face was circled over and over again in ballpoint pen. Grooves dug deeply into the photo. A giant X crossed out her face. In the other, her eyes were blacked out and there was a message scrawled along the bottom.

The message was the same. Always the same. But like the photos, it was no less devastating. *It should have been you.*

She shot up from the couch and raced across the room, barely making it to the garbage can before her stomach emptied.

CHAPTER SIX

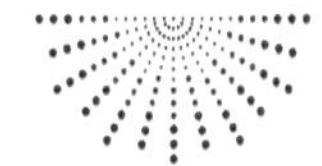

Xander leaned back in his chair and crossed his arms over his chest. He glanced around Hudson Security's conference room at his colleagues and frowned. As he listened to the woman across the table from him, his frown deepened. Esmerelda Abara was their director of logistics. She was based in the Seattle area but came to their Hudson Island office every other week or so as she handled . . . well, everything. She was former CIA, could probably kill him ten different ways, and would most definitely make sure no one ever found his body. Like all the women at Hudson Security, Esme was a badass. And she sure as hell didn't mince words.

"Of the five candidates you sent me," she said, "my recommendation is that only two of them move on to the next round of interviews."

His eyebrows rose in surprise. Only *two*?

As the lead of Hudson Security's Team One and the overall head of the personal security division, Xander had spent considerable time going through countless applications for their new Team Four. Nine candidates had passed Bean's thorough background check. Their head of cybersecurity, who was seated beside him, was one of the best hackers in the world.

It was safe to say he knew *way* more information about each candidate than he wanted. After checking their references, conducting two rounds of one-on-one video interviews, and then an off-site, in-person meeting with each candidate, he'd whittled the candidate pool down to five.

He'd thought those that remained were top-notch. Solid. That the only issue would be which three rose to the top. Each of the five had met individually with Esme over the last week, and apparently, he'd been wrong.

"In fact," Esme continued, "McNab and Stevenson are lucky I didn't lay them out flat."

His eyebrows lifted even higher as Bean chuckled beside him.

"I'm afraid to ask, Es," Gavin Frazier, the founder and head of Hudson Security, said from the video feed on the room's giant smartboard. "What did they do?"

Esme's eyes narrowed, and Xander swore he could feel her irritation from across the table.

"As you all know," Esme said, "for their interview with me, all Xander tells them is they're meeting with Hudson Security's director of logistics. He gives them the location and time. Nothing more. Nothing less. I met McNab on Wednesday night and Stevenson on Thursday." She gestured to the smartboard where Bean had added the photos of both men. "Let's just say they're both slimy motherfuckers. *Zero* respect for women. After I let them know who I was, Stevenson had the decency to act remorseful. But McNab? Nope. He doubled down on the misogyny. Suffice it to say, neither of them should advance to the next round. There's only a handful of women who work here, and there's no way I'd subject any of us to those guys."

"Fair," Gavin said, nodding. "You know we trust your judgment implicitly."

"Sorry you had to put up with that shit," Xander said. "You said only two made it through. Who else did you cut?"

"Katsaros." Esme shook her head, gesturing to the new photo on the smartboard. "The woman has all the credentials, but the chip on her shoulder is too much. She wouldn't get along with half the guys here."

"So that leaves us with Corbin and Jardine," Xander said as Bean added photos of the two remaining candidates.

"They both interviewed well," Esme said. "Professional, alert, personable, and intelligent. Jardine has a talent for languages and would be an asset for MacKay," Esme said, referring to Hudson Security's number two, Oliver MacKay, who was based in London.

"Sounds good," Frazier said. "I'll be back on the island tomorrow. Can you set up an in-office interview for next week with both of them?"

"Of course," Esme replied. "Who do you want sitting in?"

Once they determined who'd be joining the interviews, Frazier nodded. "Great. Thanks, everyone. Now, Xan, how'd the meetings at the Pacific View Resort go this morning?"

The day had gone smoothly, and his team had stayed on task. He had to admit the highlight had been running into Freya. He'd hoped to run into her again before he left, especially with how their encounter had ended. He'd been concerned with how pale she'd been when she'd rushed off. It had taken everything he had to not go after her to see what was wrong. Not only would that have been completely unprofessional, but it would have been weird. He barely knew her. Still, he'd been worried. That was the reason—the *only* reason—he'd wanted to talk with her again. Nothing else.

Right.

However, he had caught sight of her in the dining room with the woman from the shooting incident. Freya had been smiling and laughing, so he was thankful he hadn't rushed after her like an idiot.

Realizing all eyes were on him, Xander cleared his throat. *Shit. Head in the game, man.* "The meetings went well. Gabriel was surprisingly easy to work with. Abbot had a laundry list of cybersecurity recommendations that he was open to. Carmichael is going to suggest formal training for both their security and front-desk staff. He, Tash, and Wilson are working on a report with their observations and recommendations right now. They said they'll have it to us by midday tomorrow to review."

"Man," Frazier said, snickering. "I should go away more often. Looks like you've got things under control, my friend."

Xander snorted. "Uh, hell no. Get your ass back here, because as receptive as Gabriel was, schmoozing with billionaires isn't my thing."

He was more of a behind-the-scenes guy. Yes, he'd step in every now and then when Frazier was out of town, but that was a rarity. It's not like he was anti people like Wilson. He liked people just fine. In fact, he excelled at dealing with different personalities—a holdover from his chaotic childhood where reading people was a matter of survival. It was what made him a good head for their personal security group.

His colleagues were basically family, but dealing with that many alpha types and doling out assignments took a certain amount of finesse. Pairing up the personalities of clients and his colleagues, no problem. But getting the assignments and dealing with clients one-on-one? No, thank you. He was more than happy to leave that shit to Frazier.

"True." Frazier shot him a shit-eating smirk, and Xander braced for what was about to come out of his friend's mouth.

"But I heard that schmoozing and coming to the rescue of a pretty hairstylist is your new thing."

"Oh, holy Christ," Xander muttered, dropping his head back. He was going to kill Carmichael. He glared at the ceiling as chuckling sounded around him. "You would have done the same damn thing in my situation—"

"Well, I sure as hell wouldn't have kissed her," Frazier interrupted. "I value my life. Right, B?"

"Damn straight, mister," Bean said, a knowing smirk lifting her lips. "But Xan's right though, you'd totally do the knight-in-shining-armor thing—"

A brisk knock sounded on the door before it was flung open.

"Sorry to interrupt," Matt Alvarez said, stepping through the doorway, clearly agitated.

Xander narrowed his eyes. The former Seattle PD detective was their lead investigator and was always calm and collected. However, tension radiated from him now.

"Scarlet passed out at work," Alvarez said in a rush. "The ambulance is taking her to the clinic. They're monitoring her and the babies—"

"I'll drive you," Esme said standing. "Let's go."

Alvarez nodded and met Xander's gaze. "Daisy's at day care. I'm supposed to pick her up at three because they're closing early but—"

Xander stood and crossed the room, slapping a hand on his friend's shoulder. "I got her, brother. You focus on Scarlet. I'll take care of Daisy." His heart was in his throat as he squeezed Alvarez's shoulder.

Scarlet was pregnant with twins and beginning her second trimester, and Alvarez was over the moon. The guy even had the blurry sonogram picture with the two baby blobs framed on his desk, right beside a picture of his stepdaughter, Daisy.

"Alvarez," Frazier called from the smartboard. "If you need anything, man, you let us know. If Scarlet needs a medical flight, we'll get Owen in the air ASAP. Anything you guys need."

Alvarez let out a deep breath and lifted his chin, eyes blinking rapidly. "Appreciate you guys."

"We've got your back," Xander said and glanced at Esme. "Keep us posted."

She nodded, patting Alvarez's arm. "Let's go. We'll take my car. Leave your keys with Xander since your truck has Daisy's car seat."

Taking Alvarez's keys, Xander let out a breath as his friends rushed from the room. "Holy shit," he muttered, glancing back at Bean and Frazier. He sent a prayer up to the universe that Scarlet and the babies were okay. Alvarez and Scar had already been through so much.

"I'll let Owen know to be on standby," Bean murmured, her fingers flying over her keyboard. Hadley Owen was Hudson Security's pilot. She was one of only three female Night Stalkers their country had produced. If, God forbid, Scarlet needed to be airlifted, Owen would get her wherever she needed to be safely and in record time. Hopefully, it wouldn't come to that.

Xander glanced at his watch. It was nearly two thirty. "Bean, can you call Rebecca and let her know I'm on my way to pick up Daisy?"

Rebecca de la Rosa ran and owned the home-based day care Daisy attended. In the everyone-knows-everyone-in-a-small-town vein, the entire staff at Hudson Security was good friends with Rebecca's husband, Dante. In fact, Dante and his brother, Cade, co-owned De La Rosa Gym, which they were all members of. Hudson Security and De La Rosa Gym also operated a joint partnership in Hudson Tactical, a program that taught hand-to-hand combat and provided tactical training—weapons, marksmanship, and outdoor survival—to law enforcement groups, military units, and search and rescue teams.

"If she needs official authorization to release Daisy, have her call Alvarez." Xander glanced at his watch again and grimaced. "But have her call him soon before he gets to the clinic."

"On it," Bean said. "Give Daisy a hug for us."

Twenty minutes later, Xander parked Alvarez's truck in front of the two-story house just outside of Hudson Island's quaint downtown core. He checked his phone, hoping for some sort of update from Esme, but so far nothing.

Quickly getting out of the truck, he approached the front door. It opened before he could knock.

"Hey," Rebecca said. She stood with her infant strapped to her chest in some sort of wrap contraption and motioned him inside. "I talked to Bean. Any updates on Scarlet?"

"Nothing yet," he said, closing the door behind him.

"I'm so sorry we can't keep Daisy longer. It usually wouldn't be a problem, but we're heading over to Seattle in a couple hours."

"No worries." He peeked into the playroom. Daisy was seated at a miniature table with Rebecca's son, Rocco, and they were coloring. "Have you said anything to her?" he asked, dropping his voice.

"No, but I'm sure she'll be happy to see you." Rebecca gave him a reassuring smile and stepped into the playroom. "Daisy, look who's here to pick you up."

Xander smiled and waved when Daisy's bright-blue eyes landed on him. For a second, she simply stared at him, then she lit up.

"Xandy!" Daisy shot to her feet, her little mini chair nearly tipping over, and she raced toward him.

His insides warmed as he crouched low. She launched herself at him, confident that he'd catch her. And he would. Every damn time.

From the moment he'd met the sweet tiny dynamo, the little girl had him wrapped around her pinky finger. She was a quiet and shy itty-bitty thing, but for some reason, she'd immediately felt comfortable with him. Which was crazy because he knew he looked somewhat intimidating. He was six-four, solid, was more often scruffy than clean-shaven, and had wild, unruly hair. But the kid had taken one look at his man bun, declared it just like her mama's, and been his little buddy ever since. Then, as if he wouldn't already do anything for the munchkin, she'd dubbed him Xandy.

Yeah. As far as he was concerned, the kid could do no wrong.

"Hey there, peanut," Xander said, rising and settling her onto his hip. "Did you have a good day?"

"Peanut?" She giggled.

"Well, I called you popsicle last week and muffin the week before, so I figured I'd change it up again." He bopped her on the nose. "Want to go to the playground with me?"

"Yeah!"

"Great. Let's get out of here then," he said, turning toward the door.

"But, Xandy, I gots to get Mr. Slothy!" When she wiggled in his arms, he set her down. She raced toward a set of cubbies on the opposite side of the room.

"Before you get Mr. Slothy, please go potty first," Rebecca called out. "Then after you wash your hands, please get your jacket too."

Xander chuckled, shaking his head. "Bathroom and jacket. I suppose those things would be helpful. I've babysat her before, but only at their house. Never where I drove her around or anything."

Rebecca nudged him with her elbow. "You'll be fine. She's an easy kid. But you know, it wouldn't hurt to remind her about going to the bathroom every hour or so."

He frowned, his gaze going to the closed bathroom door by the cubbies. "She's good to go by herself, right?"

"She is," Rebecca said with a chuckle. "But if it's a public bathroom, I'm sure no one will have a problem with you going in with her and waiting outside the stall. Or you can take her into the men's bathroom."

Appalled, his jaw dropped. "Have you been in a men's bathroom?" He shot a glance at Rocco, still coloring, and dropped his voice to a whisper. "No way in hell am I bringing her into one. They're disgusting."

Rebecca laughed. "I'm sure you'll figure something out."

He nodded with confidence he didn't actually feel.

Daisy emerged from the bathroom, went to the miniature sink, and washed her hands. "We'll make an afternoon of it. Besides, I'm not above bribery." He shot Rebecca a grin, wagging his eyebrows. "I'm the fun uncle after all."

"I'm ready!" Daisy announced from beside him. She had her beloved stuffed Mr. Slothy in one hand and her jacket in her other, dragging on the ground.

Dropping to one knee, he plucked her jacket out of her hand and helped her into it. "Can you say goodbye to Miss Rebecca and Rocco?"

She looked toward the table where Rocco still sat and waved. "Bye, Rocco! Bye, Miss Rebecca!"

"Goodbye, sweetheart. And don't forget Miss Flora will be here the rest of the week."

Daisy nodded. "You and Rocco and baby Caleb are gonna be in Seattle to see Rocco's grandma and grandpa."

"That's right," Rebecca said, walking them to the door. "And I'm sure you'll be a wonderful angel for Miss Flora."

Again, Daisy was nodding earnestly, and Xander couldn't help but smile. The kid really was adorable.

"Thanks, Rebecca," he said, giving the woman a wave.

"Keep me posted if you can," she called out as he pressed the key fob to unlock Alvarez's truck.

After giving Rebecca a chin lift, he bent to pick up Daisy and reached for the back passenger door.

"Xandy, your truck looks just like Daddy's!"

He couldn't help but smile at how she went back and forth between calling his friend Matty and Daddy. He knew that Alvarez loved the little girl as if she were his own, and he knew his friend melted every time she called him Daddy. "That's because it *is* Matt's truck, kiddo." He opened the door and waved his hand in a ta-da gesture, which had her giggling as he'd intended. "Now hop in, and I'll buckle you in."

He set her down in the truck, and she scrambled into her seat. "Xandy?" she asked once she was settled.

He stilled at her hesitant tone. "What's on your mind, peanut?"

"Are Mama and Matty gonna be at the playground too?"

The worry for Scarlet sprouted anew in his gut. He didn't want to worry Daisy, but he didn't want to lie to her either. "No, peanut. Matt had to take your mama to the doctor. While they're doing all that, me and you get to hang out. They'll meet up with us later."

"For dinner?"

He met her gaze and did his best to reassure her. "You know, I'm not sure when they'll be done. But after the playground, if they're not done yet, we can get some ice cream."

She grinned. "For dinner?"

He shrugged. "Why not? Ice cream for dinner sounds

good, doesn't it?" He furrowed his eyebrows as he paused buckling her into her car seat. "Wait? You like ice cream, right? I mean, if you like broccoli more, we can get that for dinner instead."

She giggled again. "I love ice cream, Xandy!"

"Phew!" He mimed wiping sweat from his brow and clicked her buckle into place. "Now you hang on to Mr. Slothy, and let's hit the playground before it gets too dark."

Half an hour later, Xander's phone buzzed.

The short drive to the town's playground had been uneventful, and Daisy was running around the jungle gym with Mr. Slothy. He was thankful the place was deserted, because he didn't want to deal with other kids. Daisy was shy, and other kids, especially the older ones, often tried to steamroll her. Not acceptable in his book.

He pulled his phone from his jeans pocket and checked his messages. It was a group text with Esme and Bean.

ESME

Scarlet and the babies are okay. According to Alvarez, low blood sugar and dehydration were contributing factors. She'll be at the clinic for another couple hours. They want to monitor her blood pressure and administer more IV fluids.

Xan, you're on Daisy duty for a few more hours.

Not a problem. We're at the playground and will grab dinner after.

BEAN

Thanks for the update. How's Alvarez doing?

ESME

Trying not to freak out. Apparently, Scarlet gave him a verbal smackdown when he suggested she stop working since she's pregnant.

Xander winced. He was sure *that* didn't go over well with Scarlet.

Idiot.

ESME

Right? Pretty sure he's trying to figure out a way to get her OB to suggest bed rest without her finding out.

BEAN

Haha! Good luck with that. Unlike Alvarez, Scarlet's OB is not an idiot.

Can you ask Alvarez if they want me to bring Daisy home or to the clinic?

ESME

Sure. Hang on.

While he waited for Esme's reply, he watched as Daisy settled herself on a swing with one hand clutching both the chain and Mr. Slothy. His lips twitched as she pumped her little feet, barely setting the swing in motion.

Walking toward her, he asked, "Want a push?"

"Yes, please!"

He plucked Mr. Slothy from her hand and tucked him into his jacket pocket. "Medium, high, or super high?"

"Super high!"

Medium it was. "Hold on tight with both hands, okay, peanut?"

Setting her in motion, he grinned when her high-pitched laughter rang out.

His phone buzzed. Continuing to push her with one hand, he checked his phone.

ESME

Alvarez says that if you want, you can bring her back to their house when you're done at the playground. He's expecting they'll be home around six or seven.

Copy. We'll get dinner before we head back.

BEAN

What are you picking up for dinner?

I promised her ice cream after the playground. Then maybe some chicken nuggets and fries from Ray's Diner.

BEAN

Ugh. This is why you're her favorite.

Damn straight. Me = also not an idiot.

He grinned when both women replied with a row of laughing emojis.

BEAN

Do they need transportation back from the clinic?

ESME

Negative. I'll hang out and drive them home.

Xan, I'm staying at the cabin next to yours tonight, so I can give you a lift home from Alvarez's.

Xander lived in one of the company's cabins. After Frazier started the company nearly a decade ago, he'd bought eight acres and built five houses on it. He'd built the largest for himself, then four smaller cabin-like houses for various employees. Bean had lived in the one next to Frazier for years, but they had just recently moved in together. Xander lived in the cabin farthest away from them, and the houses in between were used as needed by various employees who were based off-island.

> Sounds good. Also, can you have Alvarez text me his house alarm code? And I'd appreciate it if you don't mention the ice-cream-before-dinner thing.

ESME

> Like they don't know you spoil that little girl every chance you get.

He scoffed. Granted, his friend wasn't wrong, but he also wasn't the only one who spoiled the kid.

> Uh, who bought Daisy a giant dollhouse for all her stuffed animals?

ESME

> It was for her birthday. She's turning five. It's a big deal.

BEAN

> Riiiiight. Her birthday's next week and you gave her the dollhouse like two months ago. You're telling us that you're going to show up to Daisy's birthday party next week empty-handed? With no new presents for her?

> Nice call, Bean.

ESME

> Whatever.

> Oh, look. Alvarez's here. I'll have him send you his alarm code. And I'll be sure to ask him what Daisy's favorite ice cream flavor is too. Just so you have the proper intel.

BEAN

Hahaha!

Brat.

He shook his head when a new text from Alvarez came in.

Dude. You have a 16-digit security code for your house? Seriously?

ALVAREZ

Call me paranoid. And it's not like you don't have an equally long code.

Mine's only 8. 16 is overkill.

Scar and the babies good?

ALVAREZ

Yes. And thanks for picking up and hanging with Daisy. Please make sure she gets some actual food for dinner as well.

Of course. Chicken nuggets, fries, and NO veggies. Not when she's hanging with me.

ALVAREZ

It's no wonder you're her favorite.

And I plan on remaining her favorite.

You doing okay?

The three dots danced at the bottom of his screen. They stopped and then danced again.

ALVAREZ

No. But I will be. I'm just thankful that Scar and the babies are okay.

Anything you need, brother. You let me know.

ALVAREZ

Thanks, man. Appreciate you.

Xander couldn't imagine what his friend was going through. Alvarez and Scarlet had already been through so much in their fairly short relationship. He wasn't quite sure how she'd tempered his grumpy-ass friend, but she had.

He knew Alvarez's world revolved around Scarlet and Daisy. As it should. His friend was a damn good man, but his family made him even better. Xander just prayed this scare with Scarlet and the twins was just a blip, that they'd be fine, and that it would be smooth sailing from here.

"Xandy?" Daisy asked, looking back at him. "Can we get ice cream now?"

He pocketed his phone and gently slowed her swing. "Sure thing, peanut."

Once the swing stopped, Daisy hopped off, and he handed her Mr. Slothy. She shoved her stuffy into her coat pocket and held up her right hand.

Smiling, he took her tiny hand in his and twirled her. Daisy's giggles filled the air as they exited the playground and turned toward the ice cream shop.

"Oh no! I dropped Mr. Slothy!" Daisy exclaimed, tugging her hand out of his and turning back to the playground.

"Here you go, honey," a woman said. The soft, melodic voice had goosebumps rising on Xander's arms.

"Thank you," Daisy murmured but didn't reach out to take her stuffed animal back from the woman holding it out.

A grin lifted his lips. "Well, hello there, Freya."

Freya's ice-blue eyes shot to his, and surprise colored her features. "Oh, Xander. Hi."

Her gaze ping-ponged between him and Daisy before she crouched down to Daisy's level. "I think your sloth friend got a little wet." She brushed off the stuffed animal and held it out to Daisy again. "But I think she's going to be okay."

Daisy took a hesitant step forward and reached for her stuffed animal. "Mr. Slothy's a boy."

"Oh," Freya said, grimacing. "I'm so sorry about that, Mr. Slothy."

Daisy hugged the stuffy to her chest. "He says it's okay." The corners of Daisy's lips kicked up in a small smile as she glanced up at Xander. "But Mr. Slothy's still kinda sad, so he prolly needs his own scoop of ice cream."

Xander chuckled. "Oh, does he now?"

She nodded sagely. "We don't want Mr. Slothy to be sad." She glanced at Freya. "Right?"

Freya grinned at the sweet little girl and then met his gaze. "Your daughter does have a good point. No sad stuffies."

Daisy giggled. "Xandy's not my daddy. Xandy's my Xandy!"

Freya glanced at him, a hint of confusion in her eyes, and he shrugged. "Honorary uncle." He placed his hand on the top of Daisy's head. "Daisy, sweet girl, this is my friend Freya. Freya, this is my best girl, Daisy."

Freya smiled at Daisy. "It's nice to meet you, Daisy."

The little girl smiled shyly at her. "Do you like ice cream?"

Freya nodded. "Even though it's cold out, ice cream is my favorite."

"We're heading to get some now." He tapped the top of Daisy's head, and she looked up at him. "Should we invite my friend to join us?"

Daisy's doe eyes widened. "She saved Mr. Slothy from drowning in the puddle. She should get ice cream for a reward."

He met Freya's gaze. "What do you say? Care to join us?"

"Sure," she said, flashing him a shy smile. A smile that did something to his insides. But he didn't want to think too hard on that.

They set off toward the ice cream shop, and Freya asked Daisy what flavors she and Mr. Slothy were getting. The walk was filled with Daisy's little voice debating whether it would be cookies and cream or chocolate.

They entered the shop, and the scent of freshly made waffle cones filled his nose. He wasn't much of a sweets guy, but for these two ladies, he'd make an exception.

"Xandy," Daisy called out, lifting her arms.

He scooped her up and set her on his hip, and they perused the ice cream flavors. He gestured for Freya to order first. She went with a scoop of strawberry cheesecake in a waffle bowl.

"What flavor do you want, peanut?" he asked.

Daisy's lips pursed in thought. "I don't know. I like chocolate *and* Oreo."

"Let's go with both." When her eyes went as wide as saucers, he bit the inside of his cheek to keep from laughing. "Do you trust me, kid?"

She nodded, a grin blooming on her cherub face.

He turned to the woman behind the counter. "A scoop of cookies and cream and a scoop of chocolate in a cup for the little lady."

"Regular scoop or kids' scoop?"

"Regular," he said, and then he quickly and silently mouthed *kid* to the woman.

She chuckled and grabbed the smaller scoop. "And for you?"

"I'll take a scoop of rocky road in a cup and a waffle cone on the side."

He caught Freya's curious look, and he shot her a wink. "Daisy and I have a thing. You'll see."

As the woman scooped the ice cream, he moved toward

the register. Noticing Freya reaching into her purse, he set Daisy on her feet. "Peanut, why don't you take Freya and pick out a table for us, okay?"

"Okay!"

"Are you sure?" Freya asked, pulling out her wallet.

"I got this. Besides, it's your reward for saving Mr. Slothy."

"Come on, Faya!"

While the two decided on a table, he paid for their ice cream and grabbed the tray with their treats. After distributing the bowls, he picked up the extra waffle cone, wrapped it in a napkin, and placed it in front of Daisy. "Go for it, kiddo."

With a giant grin, she crushed the cone, keeping it inside the napkin.

"Interesting," Freya murmured, taking a bite of her ice cream.

He forced his attention to focus on the crushed waffle cone and *not* the spoon entering Freya's mouth. "This isn't our first ice-cream rodeo together," he said, sprinkling a third of the crushed cone over Daisy's ice cream and the rest of the crumbles on his. "As much as this little lady loves her ice cream and waffle cones, she's not the fastest eater."

"It's 'cause I'm just a little kid," Daisy declared, digging into her treat.

The corners of his lips twitched. "Exactly. So we do this instead. Plus, it avoids both ice-cream-melting sadness and brain freeze."

"Thank you, Xandy," Daisy said, beaming up at him with chocolate smudged on her face.

He bopped her on the tip of her nose. "You're welcome, sweet girl."

"So, Daisy," Freya said, in between bites. "I really like your dress. Are unicorns your favorite?"

Daisy nodded. Using her spoon, she pointed to a large rainbow unicorn on her purple dress. "This one is my favorite." Pressing her lips together, her face scrunched. Then she huffed out a sigh that had his own face scrunching.

"Whoa there, peanut. What's with the big sigh?" It was like she was carrying the weight of the world on her nearly five-year-old shoulders.

She dragged her spoon through her ice cream. "Abby's brother was at drop-off, and he said my unicorn dress was ugly like my face. He's mean."

Everything inside him stilled. *What. The Fuck?* "Hold up, Daisy. He said *what?*"

After she repeated herself, her bottom lip popped out, and her big blue doe eyes turned glassy.

Anger roiled in his gut. Hell, no.

He was going to have words with this little fucker. Or at least with the little fucker's parents. Something. Reining in his anger, he made sure his voice was calm. "What's this kid's name?"

"Brock," she said with a big sniff.

Of course the fucker's name was Brock. "What's his last name?"

She looked at him blankly and blinked. Right. She wasn't even five yet. He cleared his throat. "You know what, peanut? He's stupid. And if he says something mean to you again, you tell him that."

Her little mouth dropped open. "I'm not supposa say that word."

Xander cringed. *Shit.* "Right. Well, you tell this kid to leave you alone. If he doesn't, you tell Miss Rebecca or another grown-up what he said."

She frowned. "But then I'll be a tattletale."

He shook his head. "I don't think that counts as being a tattletale. Are you allowed to hit him?" He winced when her blue eyes widened. *Fuck.* "No hitting. Got it. Well, if this kid ever talks to you like that—"

His words died in his throat as Freya squeezed his forearm. Hard.

———◆———

Freya squeezed his arm. It was either that or slap the man upside the head. Considering "no hitting" had just been mentioned, that probably wasn't the best idea.

On one hand, it was kind of cute how offended and outraged he was on Daisy's behalf, but on the other hand, the advice he was doling out wasn't going to fly. Not only was it not child-friendly, but it would most likely get him *and* Daisy into trouble.

Freya cleared her throat. "If Brock ever says anything like that to you again, you tell him—with your *words*—that it's not okay, and then you go tell your teacher." She pinned Xander with a subtle glare, and thankfully, he shut his trap. After a slight nod, she turned her attention back to Daisy. "You're right. What Brock said was mean. It was not nice at all. And you know what? He is 100 percent wrong. You are *not* ugly, and neither is your dress."

Daisy sniffed and scooped a giant bite of ice cream into her mouth. "I'm not?" she mumbled around her treat.

"No, sweetie. You're not." Goodness, this kid was adorable. Daisy looked to be around the same age as her two nieces, so Freya was somewhat familiar with the ping-ponging of five-year-old brains. And the emotions. Oh, the giant messy emotions that could turn on a dime.

A glance at Xander had her biting her lower lip to keep from laughing. She'd bet good money that Daisy was the only child this age he knew, because the poor guy was ready to throw down with this Brock kid.

"Now you said he's your friend Abby's brother," she said, trying to get more information about the situation. "Does he go to your day care too?"

Daisy shook her head, devouring another bite of ice cream. "He's a big kid, and he's always trying to boss us around."

In her peripheral vision, she saw Xander cross his arms over his massive chest. She had a feeling he was trying to keep his expression neutral.

He was failing.

"I see," she said, meeting Xander's gaze and then flickering her own to his ice cream and back. He huffed out a sigh, uncrossed his arms, and resumed eating. She turned her attention back to Daisy. "Do you know how old Brock is?"

Daisy nodded, her earlier sadness seemingly gone and replaced by righteous five-year-old annoyance. "He's six and a big meanie!"

Xander choked on his ice cream, and Freya smothered a laugh. Yup, it was just as she'd suspected. Her nieces had a neighbor Brock's age, and this sounded like one of their many arguments. But it was still admirable how Xander was 100 percent in this little girl's corner, even though he couldn't fight the six-year-old.

"How's your ice cream?" she asked Daisy, trying to redirect her attention.

"I'm almost done!" With a giant smile, the little girl showed off her nearly empty bowl. "See!"

Freya gave her an equally giant oh-wow smile. *Mission accomplished.*

Her phone, which sat face down on the table beside the crumbs of her treat, dinged with an incoming text. Then another. And then another.

"Sorry," she muttered, grabbing her phone to flip the side

button to silence it. Peeking at the message previews, she groaned.

Xander set his spoon down. "Everything okay?"

"Family group text." She shrugged, rolling her eyes. "My brothers . . ."

"You have a brother?" Daisy asked.

"I have *four* brothers," she said, wrinkling her nose. Not to be overly dramatic for Daisy's sake, but because that's how they often had her feeling.

Daisy met her gaze. "That's a lot of brothers."

She couldn't help but laugh at the little girl's serious expression. "You're telling me. *And* they're all older than me too. And super bossy."

"Yikes," Xander said. He nodded at her phone, which was now steadily buzzing. "Do you need to get that?"

Her phone went still and then started buzzing again. Sighing, she turned it over. Her oldest brother, Axel, was calling, and she quickly sent the call to voicemail. Shaking her head, she checked her notifications. He'd already called twice, and her phone showed twenty-four awaiting messages in their family group text. Lovely. Pulling up the group thread, she didn't bother reading her brothers' texts and simply typed out a response.

I'm fine. I'll call in a little bit. Busy right now.

Setting the phone down, she leaned back in her seat and met Xander's concerned gaze. "The, uh, incident yesterday at the resort made the news. Mr. Ortiz kept a very tight lid on what information was released and kept it very bare bones."

Xander nodded and his eyes narrowed. "But?"

"Hazel did an interview with one of the Seattle news stations and it aired on their noon broadcast. I assume it just re-aired." She gestured to her phone and shrugged. "When I texted them last night, I didn't exactly mention how close I was to what happened." If she had, she knew they'd want to cover her in bubble wrap and have her move home immediately.

Not. Going. To happen.

Surprise flashed over Xander's face. "Hazel did an interview with the news about the shoo—" His gaze swung to Daisy and then back to her. "About the incident yesterday?"

She frowned and nodded. "Mr. Ortiz sent out a text to all employees after it happened and another first thing this morning saying to direct all media inquiries to his assistant. Hazel met with the reporter around ten today." Her stomach churned. Unfortunately, it had nothing to do with the ice cream. To say she'd been upset at Hazel when her friend had called her earlier to gush about the interview was an understatement. "Looks like Hazel either missed the texts or . . ." Or completely ignored them. Considering the woman's phone was attached to her at all times, Freya was betting on the ignoring.

Freya wasn't surprised. Not really. While Hazel could be really sweet, the woman always looked out for herself and did whatever she wanted. Which was usually fine, usually harmless.

But this time was different.

Freya was disappointed with her friend because what happened yesterday had become personal. Not just because they had been in the thick of things with everyone involved, but because Freya had gotten to know Janie a little better today.

After the shooting, when she'd been finishing Janie's cut and Hazel had been working on Claire's hair, Janie had shared more of what she'd been through. What she'd suffered through at the hands of her husband.

That information was private. Personal. But Hazel had been more than happy to share everything and blab about it all to the press. From the man storming in, assaulting people, and shooting up the place, to the personal things Janie and Claire had revealed during what was supposed to have been their private time together.

None of that was information the general public needed to know. At all.

Freya was appalled by Hazel's actions, dumbfounded as to why she'd even do an interview in the first place.

She frowned as she recalled the giddy excitement in Hazel's voice as the woman had gone on and on about how she was going to be on television today. How she was so thankful she'd dolled herself up to go to the diner where she'd run into the reporter. How hot she thought she'd looked when the cameraman let her peek at her part of the recording.

Freya was horrified and disgusted to find this out about her friend. That Hazel could disregard other people's feelings and circumstances so easily. And for what? To be on television for a three-minute segment?

"Holy crap," Xander muttered, running a hand over his jaw. "I bet Gabriel is beyond pissed."

"I'd imagine so," she said. "Especially after he'd sent out *two* texts to all the staff."

"I take it that's not standard procedure?"

She scoffed. "Uh, no. I've been at the resort for over a year, and all communication comes from the department heads. Even the resort's GM. But *never* directly from Mr. Ortiz."

Hazel had been at the resort even longer than her. She had no clue how the other woman could so blatantly disregard the request.

Xander let out a sigh. "Damn, what a fucking shit show."

"Xandy," Daisy said, shaking her head.

He winced. "I know, sweet girl. I just said all the bad words. I'm sorry."

"It's okay," she said, spooning the final bite of ice cream into her mouth. "Matty says bad words all the time, and Mama makes him put money in a jar. Maybe Mama can make a jar for you too."

"That's a great idea," Freya said with a chuckle. "My nieces have a bad-word jar for all their uncles too." She eyed the little girl's empty cup, amazed she'd been able to eat it all.

"Do you like cupcakes, Faya?" Daisy asked, turning to her.

She blinked twice, her brain trying to keep up with the verbal whiplash. "I do. Do you?"

Daisy nodded. "My birthday party is on Saturday—"

"Next Saturday," Xander clarified.

Daisy continued as if Xander hadn't spoken. "And I'm gonna be five." She held up her hand, spreading her fingers wide. "I'm gonna have chocolate cupcakes with frosting and rainbow sprinkles, and there's gonna be unicorns on them. And I'm gonna have ice cream too. Wanna come to my party?"

Freya's heart squeezed. The little girl was adorable and made her miss her twin nieces fiercely. "Aww, thanks, Daisy. You know, I usually work on Saturdays, so I don't know if I can make it, but that's so sweet of you to invite me."

The little girl's smile grew. "If you come, it'll make me and Mr. Slothy super happy. You can come with Xandy!" She turned to the man in question. "Xandy, I'm still hungry."

His jaw opened slightly in wonder, and he laughed. "Yeah, peanut, we can get you some food." Recalling Rebecca's advice from earlier, he caught Daisy's gaze. "Why don't you go potty first, and don't forget to wash your hands really good too. I'm sure they're ice cream sticky."

She pressed her hands together and giggled when they stuck together. After hopping out of her seat, Daisy turned to her. "Faya, did you know that they have a little kid potty and little kid sink here?"

Freya glanced at the far corner of the store, and sure enough, in between the men's and women's restroom was a small, standalone kids' stall with a tiny sink beside it.

"Well, that's super helpful, isn't it?"

Daisy nodded. "The kid potty doesn't make a scary noise like the big people one."

"Alrighty, peanut, less yapping," Xander said. "Get a move on it. And don't forget to wash your hands."

As Daisy skipped toward the bathroom, Freya smiled. "She sure is a sweet girl."

He nodded, keeping his eye on Daisy until she entered the mini stall. "She is. And seriously, if you'd like to come to her party, I'd be more than happy to take you."

"Oh, that's kind of you, but I wouldn't want to impose."

Xander shook his head. "I don't think you quite understand. Believe it or not, that little girl is actually really shy. Like still-doesn't-make-eye-contact-with-adults-she's-known-for-a-long-time kind of shy. Aside from her stepdad and me, I've never seen her warm up so fast to anyone. I mean, not to pat myself on the back or anything."

She grinned. "Of course not."

"I'm serious, though," he said, rising from the table. He glanced over at Daisy, who was drying her hands. "She'd be thrilled if you came."

Freya mulled the idea over in her mind for a moment. To have the chance to hang out with the sweet little girl again would be fun. Chocolate cupcakes just so happened to be her favorite, and who didn't like rainbow sprinkles, unicorns, and ice cream? Daisy's birthday party sounded more and more appealing . . .

She rose and slipped her jacket on. "Okay. If you're sure it's not an imposition, I'll check my schedule."

Daisy raced toward them, halting in front of Xander. He crouched down and helped the little girl into her coat. Freya's stomach flipped at the sight. The tall, uber-masculine guy—man bun and all—carefully zipping up Daisy's coat and then handing over Mr. Slothy? Uh, yeah . . .

Who was she kidding? Seeing Xander again? *Sign me up.*

"Not an imposition at all, Freya," he said, standing. "Now, who wants chicken nuggets and french fries?"

Daisy's hand shot in the air. "Me!"

He chuckled, took Daisy's hand, and gave Freya a hopeful smile. "You're more than welcome to join us, if you'd like."

As much as she wanted to, she couldn't ignore her buzzing phone for much longer. "Unfortunately, I can't." Biting her lower lip, she waved her phone. She glanced at her phone's display and nearly groaned. Fifty-seven awaiting text messages. Excellent. "I should probably call my brothers back before they send out the cavalry."

"Rain check, then," he said, heading toward the door.

They called their thank-yous to the woman behind the counter and spilled out onto the street. The crisp air had her shivering. However, she wasn't quite sure if it was actually due to the temperature or the man beside her.

As they neared Ray's Diner, she said, "Well, Daisy, it was nice meeting you. Thanks for inviting me to join you guys for ice cream."

"It was fun!" Daisy said, swinging her stuffed animal in her free hand.

Xander reached for the diner's front door and then paused to crouch down and meet Daisy's gaze. "I want you to *walk* to the counter and say hi to Miss Martha. I'll be right in, okay?"

Daisy nodded. "Okay. Bye, Faya!"

"Bye!" she called out, watching the little girl hustle through the diner. The waitresses seemed to greet Daisy by name, and then she was engulfed in a hug by the older woman standing at the counter.

"Daisy's mom works here," Xander said, tracking Daisy through the diner. "I wanted to ask you if this Friday works for that rain check?"

Surprise had her stammering. "Uh, what . . ."

"Rain check. Me and you. Dinner. Like friends do." He shot her a lopsided smirk that had a flush heating her cheeks.

Good God, what was this handsome man doing to her?

His gaze swung to inside the diner and the woman behind the counter waving at him. "Ah, I've gotta go, but I'll call you." He quickly leaned down and pressed a kiss to her forehead. "Thanks for hanging out and being cool with Daisy."

Before she could blink, before she could remember to breathe, he was gone. Her heart raced in her chest, and her forehead tingled. What just happened?

Tucked in her coat pocket, her phone buzzed again. Letting out a breath, she turned down the street and began the short, two-block walk to her apartment.

First things first. She wanted to call Janie to see how she was doing after Hazel's interview. Second, she needed to check in with Miriam. Third, she'd get her brothers off her back.

Then she could fall down the overanalyzing rabbit hole. Because holy crap. She was going to go out with Xander. As friends, sure, which was absolutely fine, because she wasn't ready to hop into any sort of relationship. But that didn't mean she couldn't be giddy about going out with her smoking hot and surprisingly sweet new friend, right?

· · ·

Two hours later, Freya held her phone away from her ear and mentally cursed her life. She'd called her brother Finn, since she was closest to him. He was five years her senior—while her other brothers were even older—and she thought he'd be the most reasonable of the bunch.

She'd been wrong.

He ranted about why she hadn't been honest about how close she'd been to the shooting, and she tuned him out and thought back to the earlier conversation she'd had with Janie.

The woman had been rightfully upset, had felt betrayed that Hazel had told the reporter things she'd revealed to them in confidence. But what killed Freya was that Janie had blamed herself for confiding in virtual strangers in the first place.

Freya had tried to reassure the other woman that the blame lay solely with Hazel, but she wasn't quite sure Janie believed her. They were meeting up for breakfast tomorrow with Claire to talk some more.

"Are you even listening to me, Frey?" Finn groaned.

She jerked and put the phone back against her ear. Nope. She hadn't heard a single thing he'd said. "Sorry, you were breaking up. Reception is really spotty over here."

"Sure." His tone implied he didn't believe her.

Even though he was correct, she still bristled. Because, well, brothers. She really wondered how different her life would've been had she been an only child.

"For the *third* time, Freya, what day are you coming home for Thanksgiving?"

She frowned. The holiday was three weeks away, and that was the last thing she wanted to do. Especially now. Yes, she missed her nieces, but being the youngest of five—with brothers who were five, eight, and ten years older than her— was a lot. Their parents had passed away when she was thirteen, so her brothers were understandably protective. They'd all basically raised her. But there was hovering. And *hovering* hovering.

And then there were her brothers.

"I'm not sure. I talked to my boss right before I called you, and she said in light of what happened with the shooting, she's working on redoing the schedule for the month. She wants to meet tomorrow, so I should have a better idea after that."

"Do *not* skip out on Thanksgiving, Freya Hansen. Promise me."

She heaved a sigh. "I won't."

"Promise. Me."

She swore she could feel his glare through the phone. "I. Promise. Besides, I miss the girls. I just don't know how long I'll be able to stay. The resort is booked solid over the holiday, but both the spa and salon are closed on Thanksgiving Day."

"At least there's that. Have you called any of the others yet?"

"No. And you know what, oh favorite brother of mine?" He muttered a curse, but she continued. "I'd really appreciate it if you could call them for me. Let them know I'm fine and that I'll be home for Thanksgiving Day for sure."

"Frey . . ."

She heard the exasperation in his voice. She was so familiar with it, along with his disappointment and frustration, but she still couldn't help but wince. "I'll see them at Thanksgiving."

"You can't keep hiding from them. You know they love you, right? They just have a hard time with the whole communication thing."

"No kidding," she mumbled and then sighed. "I love them

too, but they just . . . yell." And criticize. And made her feel like an idiot who couldn't get her shit together. It didn't matter that she worked at a world-renowned resort, that people paid hundreds of dollars for her to do their hair.

Nothing was ever good enough. Especially not with Axel. He was the oldest and was truly more father than brother, and more asshole than not. His only saving grace were his twin daughters.

Her twin brothers, Oscar and Jasper, not only successfully ran their late father's construction company, but they'd expanded it over the years and now had a waitlist that was months long. Their success equated to them thinking everything she did was subpar.

Yes, she'd worked at three different salons over the last few years. It had taken her a while to find the right fit, but they didn't see it that way. Instead, they thought it was her being flakey and unable to commit.

Maybe she was being defensive. Maybe not. But Finn wasn't wrong—she and her oldest brothers had a communication problem. She and Axel especially. It was a problem that didn't look like it was going to resolve itself anytime soon.

Finn was the only one who didn't treat her like a child all the time. Only sometimes, like now . . . which was probably fair and deserved since her brothers had the ability to make her revert to a snappy, distrustful, and salty teenager.

"I get that, Frey. I do. But you need to cut them some slack."

She rolled her eyes. "Why is it always *me* having to bend to what *they* want? Why can't they meet me in the middle too? I've tried to compromise with them. You know that. But it's always their way or nothing at all."

"I know." He sighed, and she could picture him running

his hands over his face. "This is why you didn't tell us, isn't it?"

She shrugged even though her brother couldn't see it. "I knew if I told you guys that I was right in the middle of the shooting, the conversation would just devolve into them questioning my decision-making. It would be the whole you-can't-take-care-of-yourself argument we always end up having." Why subject herself to that? Especially when she'd had zero control of what had happened. "Everything was fine. The man was arrested. No one was seriously hurt. It was a freak occurrence, but you and I both know they wouldn't see it that way."

Her brother heaved another sigh. "Fine, you may have a point. I'll talk to them, okay? But promise me you'll stay through Thanksgiving weekend if you don't have to go right back to work. You can even stay with me from the get-go if that would help."

It was always expected that when she went home to Blanchard Bay, she'd stay with Axel. He was raising his twin girls in their childhood home, and of all her brothers, he had the most extra space. But without fail—adorable nieces or not—the two of them ended up bickering until she stormed off to stay with Finn. Maybe it would be better if she and Axel gave themselves some space. God knows, it wouldn't hurt. "I'll take you up on that."

"Good. I'll even run the vacuum before you show up." He chuckled. "Well, maybe."

"Wow, red-carpet treatment," she said, deadpan.

"You know it, sis. Now, aside from some asshole shooting up your salon, what else is going on? How are the new digs?"

Her gaze shot around her small apartment, and she grinned, until her eyes caught on the white envelope she'd dumped onto her coffee table with the rest of the junk mail when she'd gotten home earlier that afternoon.

Unease stirred in her stomach, but she pushed it down. Slapping a smile on her face, she hoped it would inject some levity into her voice, though she felt none. "My place is cozy and perfect. It's right downtown and above the cutest knitting shop. But have I told you about the post office drama I'm having?"

CHAPTER SEVEN

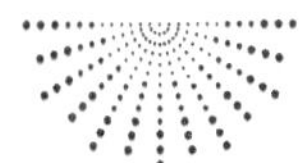

After hugging Claire, Freya turned to Janie and was engulfed in an equally fierce hug. "Keep in touch," she murmured.

"I appreciate the support, Freya, and the great haircut." Janie smiled and ran a hand over her shorter hair. "I really do feel like a new person."

Freya smiled. "I'm glad. And, really, if you're serious about finding a new place to live, you're more than welcome to come crash on my couch and check Hudson Island out. I know this place is fantastic"—she waved her hand around the lobby—"but it's not exactly reality, right?"

Janie elbowed her sister. "Unless you're Miss Moneybags over here."

Claire snorted. "Hardly."

Freya chuckled. "Like I said, if you want to check out the island, you're more than welcome to stay with me. There's also a little boutique hotel downtown and several B and Bs too."

"Sounds like a plan," Janie said as her eyes filled with tears. She pulled Freya into another hug. "Thank you again for listening and just being . . . you. I won't ever forget what you've done."

She gave Janie one last squeeze and pulled away. "I haven't done anything. Just listened."

"That, my new friend, means everything," Janie said, flashing her a smile. "I'll be in touch for sure."

"Safe travels," Freya called out as Janie and Claire waved and pulled their suitcases toward the check-out desk.

Freya's heart squeezed. She prayed everything would work out for Janie. Yes, her husband had been arrested and would most likely get a longer sentence for shooting up the salon, but the woman still had quite the journey ahead of her.

"I thought I'd find you here."

Freya turned toward the familiar voice and smiled at Miriam. "I was just on my way to meet with you."

Miriam checked her watch. "You still have twenty before our meeting." She nodded toward where the sisters were checking out. "Everything okay?"

Freya nodded. "I think she'll get there. Her sister's amazing, and I don't think Claire will give her much of a choice. Janie's looking to start fresh somewhere and is actually considering Hudson Island."

"A strong support system is everything. It's good Janie has her sister and you." A soft smile lifted Miriam's lips before she turned and began walking through the lobby toward the spa building. "It was nice of you to take an interest in Janie after what happened."

She frowned at her boss's word choice. "I wouldn't exactly call it 'taking an interest in her.'" The other woman wasn't some sort of pet project or charity case. "What happened was awful, and Janie and Claire are genuinely nice people."

Miriam held up a hand. "Sorry. That didn't come out correctly. What I meant is that it's nice of you to genuinely extend your friendship to them." She stopped as they reached the spa's main entrance and nodded to Freya. "I need to check with the front desk for a second. Go ahead into my office. I'll be right there."

"Take your time," Freya said, waving at Audrey at the front desk.

She glanced to the right where the tall room dividers still remained, blocking off the salon area. She could hear the soft buzz of activity coming from behind the partition, but considering the spa music in the lobby had been kicked up a notch, Freya was certain those who didn't work at the spa day in and day out noticed.

After making her way to Miriam's office, she sat in the guest chair next to her boss's desk. Curiosity tickled her mind. Obviously, Mir wanted to discuss something in private, but so much had happened over the last few days that it could be anything. Luckily, she didn't have to wait long. Miriam joined her after a couple minutes and closed the door behind her.

"Sorry if everything feels a little cloak and dagger," Miriam said, taking a seat behind her desk.

She shook her head. "It's fine. Though I am curious about what you want to talk about."

Miriam frowned as she clicked her mouse a few times and then turned her laptop so Freya could see the screen. It showed the salon schedule for the remainder of November.

"As you know," Miriam said, leaning back in her seat, "Hazel gave an interview to a local Seattle television reporter about what happened on Tuesday. Not only did she do so after every staff member was explicitly directed to pass all media inquiries to our front office, but she also told the reporter personal information about Janie Edwards. Is it safe for me to assume that part of your breakfast with Janie and her sister this morning was to see how they were handling Hazel's interview?"

Freya nodded. "*I* was upset by Hazel's interview." Disbelief still flowed through her and had her stomach turning. "I couldn't imagine how Janie was feeling or how angry Claire must have been."

"That's because you're a good person, Freya." Miriam sighed. "You know respecting our guests' privacy is one of the most important things here at Pacific View Resort, so Hazel has been let go."

Freya's jaw dropped. She shouldn't have been surprised, but she was. Hazel had been at Pacific View for a couple years longer than her and was extremely popular with both guests and locals.

"And that leaves this mess." Miriam waved at the calendar. "The calendar is basically booked solid this month."

Taking a closer look at the screen, Freya cringed. "Lisa's taking Thanksgiving week and the following week off. She and her family have had that cruise planned for forever."

"I know, and she'll still have those weeks off. The real issue is that Hazel was the one who predominately handled the male clients. Both Lisa and Sophie have said they aren't comfortable doing male cuts. Something about not having a lot of experience?"

"Hazel and I both completed the additional barbering program at our beauty schools. I think Lisa and Sophie just did the standard cosmetology program. I can take Hazel's male clients, and we can divvy up everyone else between the three of us."

"That's good. After the shooting, we cancelled all the appointments for yesterday and today. I held off on cancelling tomorrow and the weekend because there was a possibility we'd be able to open back up earlier than anticipated."

Her eyebrows rose in surprise. She'd seen the salon space yesterday. There was no way . . . "Seriously?"

Miriam nodded. "I was planning on reassigning your clients and Hazel's to Lisa and Sophie for the rest of this week anyway. I can't believe I'm going to say this, but we fortunately had a number of cancellations, so it shouldn't be too crazy for them."

Freya shook her head. "I don't need to take a week off, Mir. If you need me, I'm more than happy to come in."

Miriam let out a sigh that she could only describe as grateful. "I'd appreciate that."

"It's not a problem. When do you think we'll reopen?"

"Tomorrow."

Freya frowned. No way had she heard that correctly. "I'm sorry, but *tomorrow*?"

"Care to check out the place with me?" Miriam asked as she rose, a smile growing on her face.

They left Miriam's office, rounded the front check-in desk, and slipped behind the paneled wall. Freya gasped. Her jaw hung open, but disbelief had her unable to do anything about it.

Three men were busy at work. One was assembling the new workstations. One was working on the lighting, while the third was trimming out the paint. Four large stylist chairs wrapped in plastic sat in the middle of the area, along with multiple boxes which, by their sizes, looked to be the new mirrors.

Stunned, she turned to Miriam. "How did everything get here so soon? We were just talking about what kind of chairs to get *yesterday*."

The corner of Miriam's lips kicked up in a smirk. "When Gabriel makes a personal call to our suppliers"—she waved her hand at the new items—"magic happens."

"Imagine that." Shaking her head in wonder, Freya chuckled. "Maybe I should see if Mr. Ortiz can talk to the post office for me."

Miriam snickered. "The man's got influence, but I don't think that even *he* can make a difference there."

Laughing, Freya took in the space. "It's amazing how much they've accomplished."

"Like I said, we'll reopen tomorrow. If you're good, all your clients are still on the books. As you know, Sophie doesn't usually work Fridays or Saturdays, but she agreed to come in and take over Hazel's schedule. It shouldn't be too bad, because, as I said, we've had some cancellations. All Hazel's regulars."

Freya raised her eyebrows.

Miriam shrugged. "I can't confirm anything, but I'm assuming Hazel called her regular clients after I spoke with her last night."

Holy wow. Was Hazel even allowed to do that? It would be one thing if they were all renting chairs at the salon, because your clients are *your* clients. But they weren't renting space. They were employees of the resort. "Were her cancellations local regulars or resort regulars?"

"Local. So at least there's that." Miriam's face scrunched as if she'd smelled something rotten. "Speaking of resort clients, I know one of Hazel's clients tomorrow is a guy, so I'm sure Sophie would appreciate it if you took that appointment off her hands. I checked the schedule and you're open at that time."

"Of course," Freya said as she followed Miriam back to her office. The spa at Pacific View prioritized the resort's guests. However, they also offered a limited number of day passes for both spa and salon services. All the stylists had several regular clients who either lived on Hudson Island or traveled to the resort for their hair services.

Once they were seated, Miriam said, "With Hazel gone,

that leaves you as our only level-one stylist. As we discussed, you'll take over all the male clients and handle all the extension work, along with your regulars. We'll fill in colors and cuts as your schedule allows. Of course, we'll compensate you accordingly. Also, for the time being, new day-pass clients for the salon have been halted. All your regulars can still come, but the only new salon clients we'll be booking are resort guests."

Freya nodded and then frowned. "Oh, uh . . ." Her mind flashed to a certain tall, muscular, long-haired man. "Can I request one exception?" Miriam's eyebrow arched, and Freya rushed on. "You recall Xander Bonetti from Hudson Security?"

Miriam snickered. "Kind of hard to forget that one."

"When he came to my rescue the other day"—her cheeks heated, but she plowed on—"I offered to cut his hair."

Amusement danced on the woman's face. "Did you now?"

She fought to not squirm in her seat. "As a thank-you."

"That's fine. God knows, no one is going to fault you for that." Miriam chuckled. "You may want to get him on the schedule sooner rather than later. Honestly, tomorrow would probably be best." Her gaze shot to the calendar and then back to Freya. "Once we start rearranging the appointments, things are going to fill up for you. How does your Thanksgiving schedule look?"

As they discussed the schedule for the upcoming holiday, nerves fluttered in her stomach, and her mind wandered.

There'd be nothing wrong with her texting Xander, right? A thank-you haircut was no big deal. Not at all. Besides, she wasn't in the market for a relationship. It would just be a friendly, thank-you haircut that would possibly include dinner afterward.

As friends, of course.

What did it matter if she'd never had a friend that ridiculously good-looking before? It was fine. The man couldn't help how he looked. Well, she was pretty sure he worked out a lot. Like *a lot* a lot. But again, that was fine.

She was a grown woman who could control her feelings. It'd been over a year since her last relationship. A relationship that she'd thought would finally be different.

The year she and her ex had been together had been bliss. At least on her end. But as it turned out, she'd been wrong. Again. That relationship hadn't been any different from any of her previous ones. Because just like all the others before him, he'd cheated on her. And again, just like all the other times, she'd been the last one to find out.

The one difference this time was that instead of being devastated, instead of falling into a heap of tears and sadness, she'd gone numb. Over the last year, she'd received some attention from men, but aside from varying degrees of annoyance, she'd been indifferent. A hard, cold shell had surrounded her heart, protecting it from any further damage. She'd felt absolutely nothing.

Until two days ago.

Until Xander.

The moment she'd heard his voice, he'd sparked something inside her. Something she wasn't sure she wanted. Despite her uncertainty, the man was slowly thawing that brick of ice in her chest. There was just something about him . . .

It scared her. Her judgement with the opposite sex was iffy at best, and her track record was abysmal. But her body hadn't seemed to get the message, because she lit up like a barge of fireworks around the man.

Was she supposed to just go with it?

She'd always been cautious. Always planned things out. No kissing until the second date. No rounding the bases until at least seven dates. And definitely no sex until at least two months of dating. She'd stuck to those rules her entire dating life. And where had that gotten her? Cheated on by all four of her previous boyfriends.

Maybe this time around, she'd chuck all her rules out the window and just go with it. Follow Xander's lead. If he wanted to just be friends, that would be fine. If he didn't? Well, she'd be fine with that too. Right?

As much as she knew it would be best for all involved to keep things friendly, she wasn't sure she wanted to.

CHAPTER EIGHT

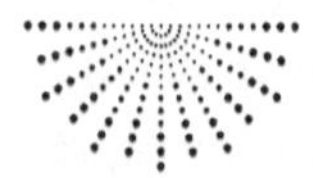

It was nearing four when Xander emailed Rizzo, Team Three's lead, asking for a few points of clarification on his team's latest mission report. Glancing around their giant work area, he saw only members of the cyber team remained at their workstations, which wasn't unusual for a Friday. Carmichael and the other two members of Team Two had taken over the security training at Pacific View Resort, and Team Three was in Seattle for the day providing extra security for a tech bigwig. Xander's teammates, Wilson and Tash, were roaming around somewhere, probably helping out at Hudson Tactical with a search and rescue group that had arrived earlier in the day.

After quickly checking his outbox, he shut down his computer and glanced at his phone beside his keyboard.

Don't do it.

He reached for his phone but yanked his hand back. He stared at his phone for a few seconds and then rolled his eyes. *Fuck it.*

He grabbed it and pulled up the text messages he'd received from Freya. Again. Did it make him a sap that he'd lost track of how many times he'd reread them since last night? Probably.

Did he care?

Maybe?

He winced. Okay, fine. Not really.

But he *should* care, because he'd spent a whole hell of a lot of time thinking about the woman when he should've been focused on work.

Glancing down at the messages, he scrolled back to the beginning and grinned.

FREYA

Hey, Xander! Good news—the salon is reopening earlier than expected. I was wondering if you were free tomorrow for that haircut?

Hi—nice to hear from you. Tomorrow should work, but probably not until late afternoon. What time were you thinking?

I can make any time after 2 work.

What's the latest appointment you can do?

The spa closes at 5:30 so usually 4:30. But if you need to do later, I'm sure my boss won't have a problem with me having you come later.

His mind had hit the gutter at her final words. Yes, he was an immature adolescent.

No, 4:30 works. I was hoping you'd join me after for dinner. Minus Daisy this time around. And not just ice cream.

At the time, her immediate reply had him grinning. Now, a day later, he was still smiling.

Count me in! Want me to make reservations somewhere here at the resort or were you thinking downtown?

Downtown. How does Monty's sound?

Love that place! And it's walking distance from my new apartment, so I'll get to indulge in some drinks.

Yikes. That sounded awful. I'm not a lush. I promise. They just make these blue-raspberry lemon drops that are absolutely divine. But I tend to end up having at least one more than I should since they go down so easy.

Yup. Mind back in the gutter.

Holy crap. Disregard all that. I really need to stop nervous texting.

You're absolutely fine. And your nervous texting is pretty damn cute.

And I mean that in the most polite, respectful non-creeper way possible.

Ha! Well, thanks. And trust me—I know creeper, and you're as far from that as possible.

I'm glad you think so.

I'll see you tomorrow at 4:30.

I'll make sure they have your info at the front desk. Just check in there when you arrive and they'll get you a pass.

But you probably already knew that
considering the whole security consulting
thing you do.

Holy crap. I'm doing it again. Erase.

And it's still cute. No worries at all. Besides, if
anyone should be nervous, it should be me.
I've never had a fancy haircut before. I did
mention that I usually cut my own hair, right?

Yes. The mere thought of that still hurts my
heart. Not that your glaringly uneven haircut
detracts from your looks at all or anything.
Because you most definitely can pull off your
lopsided do.

Holy. Crap.

I need to go put my phone down. No more
nervous texting for me tonight . . .

Haha! Well, I still stand by my earlier
statement. Your nervous texting is cute.

I'm looking forward to seeing you tomorrow.
Have a good night, Freya.

You too.

"Well, if that's not a sappy-ass grin, I don't know what is."

He startled and quickly glanced up. Tash flopped into her chair at the desk beside his and swiveled to face him. Okay, fine. *Flopped* was a bit of an exaggeration. The woman was irritatingly graceful. And so damn light on her feet. Obviously.

"What's up?" he asked, flipping his phone face down.

She rolled her eyes and then nodded to his phone. "Should I be asking you that?"

He aimed for a casual shrug. "It's nothing."

"*Right.*" She snorted. "Is it still the woman you're moon-eyed over from the resort or has another lucky lady snared your attention?"

It was times like this that he wished Tash didn't know him so well. Instead of answering her, he heaved out a sigh. "Would it do any good to say it's none of your business?"

"Nope," she replied, popping the P. The grin she shot him was 100 percent smart-ass. "Spill."

"It's the hairstylist from the Pacific View, *but*," he rushed on when Tash opened her mouth to, no doubt, give him shit, "we're just friends, and she was texting me about cutting my hair."

Tash stared at him in silence for a few moments, and it took everything he had not to squirm under her gaze. "Since I know you're actually interested in her, I'll butt out. For now."

He frowned. "*Actually* interested in her? Why do you say it like that?"

Her smart-ass grin was back in full force. "Because, my friend, if it was just gonna be a casual fuck, you'd have no issues telling me all about her."

Damn. Tash wasn't wrong, but still . . . "We're just friends. It's too early to know if she'll be, as you eloquently put it, a casual fuck."

Tash rolled her eyes. "You like her."

"Fine." No point in denying it. "You're right."

"My favorite words."

"Don't I know it," he muttered, grabbing his phone and rising. "As much as I'd love to chat, I have to get going or I'll be late for my haircut."

She rose and walked beside him to their area's secure exit. "There was actually a reason I stopped by."

"Aside from to give me grief?"

"You know that's always just a side benefit." She bumped

her shoulder into his. "I'm staying on-island tonight in one of the cabins, and Esme's grilling steaks. Wilson, Carmichael, Gavin, and Bean are all coming. You're officially invited as well. You in?"

He shook his head as he typed his code into the door's keypad. The door swooshed open, and they stepped into the main lobby. "No can do. I invited Freya to dinner after the haircut thing."

Tash's eyebrow arched. "I thought you were *just friends*, Cassanova?"

"We are. It's simply a casual dinner between friends. A thank-you for cutting my hair if you will." At least, that's what he was telling himself it was. Yes, the woman had consumed an inordinate amount of his headspace these last few days. And he could admit that he liked her. However, he truly didn't know her. Freya seemed nice, but he'd been wrong countless times before. So this *was* a casual dinner between friends. If anything progressed beyond that, only time would tell. And he was still on the fence regarding whether or not he wanted that . . .

Tash smirked. "Sure. You keep telling yourself that. But do me a favor?"

He narrowed his eyes in mock suspicion. "Depends . . ."

"Don't be one of those assholes who ditches his friends for a chick, okay?"

Xander shook his head. He and his friends were a tight-knit bunch. They were his family. His only family. Any woman who'd ever tried to come between them—and a few had tried—were quickly kicked to the curb. "Never. Sparring tomorrow?"

"Of course. See you at five thirty." Her gaze drifted to his hair, and she smirked. "I can't wait to see what your lady does with that mop on your head."

Rolling his eyes, he gave her a salute and turned toward his car.

Five minutes later, he pulled into a parking space at the Pacific View Resort. With ten minutes to spare, he made his way to the main check-in desk. Scanning the lobby—occupational hazard—he saw Kwon and Carmichael off to the side. He gave them a chin lift and approached the counter.

As he waited for the front-desk guy to process his guest pass, a throat cleared behind him.

"If it isn't Xander Bonetti. What brings you to the Pacific View Resort this evening?" Kwon asked.

He took his guest pass from the front-desk man and thanked him before turning to Kwon and Carmichael, waving his key card. "Haircut. How are things going here?"

Carmichael snickered but wisely smothered his grin when Xander shot him a glare. The guy could give him as much shit as he wanted, but only during off-hours, and most definitely not in front of clients. Xander took some perverse satisfaction knowing that it was absolutely killing Carmichael to stay quiet.

"Good," Kwon said. He gestured to Carmichael. "We were just doing a final review of the training program for the front-desk and concierge staff."

Carmichael cleared his throat and was seemingly back in business mode. "We start training tomorrow. It'll be in phases so we don't disrupt the current schedule. We're looking at three to five days."

"Nice." Xander glanced at his watch. Five minutes. "I'll leave you guys to it."

Kwon's eyebrows rose in surprise. "Oh, you weren't kidding about the haircut?"

He shook his head.

"Are you with Lisa or Freya?"

"Freya." Again, his gaze shot to Carmichael. To anyone

else, the other man looked relaxed and professional. But Xander knew there was a smart-ass remark on the tip of his friend's tongue. When Carmichael shook his head, Xander smothered his own smirk.

"You should have her give you the scalp massage," Kwon said, glancing down at the tablet he held. "I'm telling you, the woman's hands are like magic."

Xander's eyes narrowed, and he bristled. A surge of something sour stirred his gut. The irrational hothead in him —the earlier version of himself that he'd worked damn hard to tame and beat—plowed forward. The urge to punch Kwon in the face was so damn strong. It didn't matter that the guy was a top-tier Muay Thai practitioner and would most definitely give him a run for his money. None of that mattered, because what the hell did Kwon know about Freya's damn hands?

As Kwon glanced up from his tablet, Xander took a step forward. To do what, he wasn't quite sure. Before he could find out, Carmichael stepped toward him, slapped a hand on his shoulder, and squeezed. Hard.

"Dude," Carmichael said in a low voice. "You're going to be late for your haircut."

Taking a deep breath, Xander stilled. What the hell was he thinking? He wasn't the damn hothead he used to be. He was one of the fucking heads of Hudson Security. He damn well needed to remember that and fucking act like it. Slowly exhaling, he met his friend's gaze and gave him an appreciative nod.

Schooling his features, he glanced at Kwon and nodded. "I'll see you again soon, I'm sure. Have a good night."

After slapping Carmichael on the shoulder, he muttered, "Thanks, brother." Then he turned and hustled out of the lobby.

When he arrived at the spa building, he scanned his key

card, waited for the tell-tale click, and pulled open the door. The eucalyptus and lemon scents washed over him, though it did little in the way of relaxing him. He didn't want to think too hard about why Kwon's seemingly innocent comment about Freya had sent a rush of jealousy surging through him and had him reverting to a damn Neanderthal.

"Hi! How can I help you?"

The chipper voice pulled him from his musings, and he glanced at the young lady behind the counter. The same one from two days ago. Donning a well-practiced smile, he stepped to the check-in desk. "Hi, Audrey. I'm Xander Bonetti. I have a four-thirty haircut with Freya."

"It's good to see you again, Mr. Bonetti. I have you all checked in." She waved to the salon's waiting area. "You're welcome to have a seat while you wait. If I can get you anything, just let me know." Audrey's grin took on a coy quality, and he recognized the interest flickering in the woman's eyes.

He toned down his smile. "I'm good, thank you."

He wandered into the salon's waiting area and took in the repaired space. At one end, at the sinks, a woman he assumed was Lisa spoke animatedly with her client. The other woman was laughing, her head resting in the sink while Lisa pulled foil strips out of her hair. At the opposite end of the room were four brand-new workstations complete with fancy leather chairs, expensive-looking lights, giant framed mirrors, and an array of tools and bottles.

Impressive didn't begin to describe the difference. Just days ago, bullet holes had riddled the walls. Every mirror had been shattered.

Glancing around, you'd never know it.

"It's pretty remarkable, isn't it?"

Xander turned at the melodic voice and smiled.

Freya.

The stress from earlier faded away at the sight of her. And what a sight she was. She was dressed in black from head to toe, the only color she wore was a sage-green canvas and brown leather apron with the Pacific View's logo on it. Her long black hair tumbled around her shoulders in waves. She had some kind of shimmery stuff on her eyelids that made her look fresh and bright like summertime, and her lips were painted a bright red that had him wanting to mess it all up.

Holy shit, Bonetti. Ease up.

"Hey, it's good to see you again." Heat rushed over his face as she approached, and he quickly looked away from her. "And yeah, the place looks great." He prayed his tone was casual, but holy shit, did his voice just crack?

Fuck. My. Life.

"Apparently, the crew worked around the clock to get everything ready," she said from beside him.

He glanced down at her, and a smile tugged at his lips, and some of his nerves eased. Even in her black heeled boots, she didn't even reach his shoulders.

She looked up at him and smiled. "You ready?" Her sparkling ice-blue gaze socked him in the gut, and he forgot to breathe.

He wasn't sure if he replied. If he actually uttered any words. But he must have pulled something out of his ass, because Freya was laughing as he followed her to her workstation. She continued talking—and apparently, so did he. He sat, and she placed a black salon cape around him and secured it behind his neck. His brain was finally catching up with their conversation—something about her running into Carmichael earlier. She gently pulled the hair tie from his customary man bun and finger-combed his hair, fanning it out around his shoulders.

Her warm hands brushed against his neck, and his mind

short-circuited. All thoughts fled. For a few moments, he could only blink as he watched her in the mirror.

A grin spread over her cherry-red lips. "Are you nervous?" she teased, absently running her fingers through the ends of his hair. "I promise I'll be gentle."

His mind—blank just moments ago—hit the gutter.

Yeah. This may not have been the best idea.

Head in the game, man. Head. In. The. Game.

Holy shit, the woman had him beyond distracted. He cleared his throat as he nodded. "I can admit that I'm a little nervous."

"You did mention it's been a while since you got a professional haircut."

Not at all why he was nervous, but he'd go with it. "I'm not quite sure 'professional' would describe any haircut I've ever gotten. I think the last person to cut my hair—who wasn't me—was my teammate Wilson back in the Army." He gave her a playful grimace. "Let's just say the end result wasn't pretty." But it sure had been necessary. He'd gotten caught on some barbed wire as they'd been crawling out of some jungle hellhole. It was either lose his hair or lose his head.

Freya placed her hands on his shoulders and squeezed, meeting his gaze in the mirror. "I promise I can do better. Now, did you have anything in mind?"

Loaded question. Because what was currently running through his mind had nothing to do with a haircut and everything to do with the woman with her hands in his hair. But he was an adult, dammit, and he pushed those inappropriate thoughts away. He aimed for a casual shrug.

Don't. Be. A fucking. Creeper.

"Not really. I'd like to keep it longish but cleaned up." He chuckled, shaking his head. "Not sure that's helpful. Obviously, I'm not familiar with the lingo." He held his hand flat at his shoulder and moved it up to his chin. "Maybe cut it to somewhere in this range, but so I can still pull it back."

He suppressed a shiver as she ran her fingers through his hair, pulled the top section back, and formed a bun. Damn, Kwon was right. Freya's hands were damn near magic.

"That looks really good. Not many guys can pull off a man bun," she said with a smirk before letting his hair fall back down. She quickly ran a brush through his hair, sectioned the top part again, but this time clipped it up. "What do you think about just trimming up the top? We'll keep it long to just above your shoulders, and then do a disconnected undercut here?" She ran her fingers along the lower section of his hair.

Goosebumps rose on his arms. He swallowed. Loudly. "I'm still not sure what disconnected undercut means, but if you think it'll look good, I'm game."

The smile she flashed him was brilliant. "It'll look really good. I promise. You've got the whole hot alpha thing going, and this will add a little oomph to it. Think of it as a modern-day Viking haircut. It'll also be easy to maintain, basically wash and wear, product if you're feeling fancy. Best of all, you'll still be able to pull it back into a bun since Carmichael told me that was kinda your thing."

A smirk lifted his lips as warmth filled his chest. "Hot alpha, huh?"

She chuckled and rolled her eyes. "That's what you got out of everything I said?"

He shrugged. "That and Carmichael has been blabbing his mouth."

"But his blabbing was all good things about you. Promise," she said with a grin before turning to grab the clippers. "Ready?"

"I'm all yours," he said with a wink, loving how her cheeks pinked.

"You're a flirty one, aren't you?" She flipped the clippers on as a smile tugged at the edges of her lips. "I'll cut first, then we'll wash. After, I'll do a final trim."

As she took down his sides, he watched Freya in the mirror. Her movements were precise and held a certain amount of grace that told him she'd been doing this for years. Contemplating her earlier words, he was hard-pressed to think of anyone who'd describe him as flirty.

Friendly? Absolutely. A jokester? Sure. A smart-ass? One thousand percent. But flirty? Nah, that wasn't his thing.

However, he was finding that the more time he spent with Freya, the more he enjoyed flirting with her. The way her skin would flush at his words. The way her lips would kick up. The way she'd shake her head like he was ridiculous. It fascinated him. And he wanted to learn more. Wanted to see how far the flush spread. Wanted to know if her lips were as soft as they looked.

But holy shit, that was *not* what he was looking for. He wasn't a relationship kind of guy, and Freya most definitely seemed like a relationship kind of woman.

Which sucked. Because that left him at an impasse. And holy fuck was he getting *way* ahead of himself. He hadn't even taken the woman out. He had no clue if this attraction was all one-sided. Yeah, he had a pretty good feeling she didn't think he was a troll, but that didn't mean she'd actually be interested in more.

Chastising himself for jumping the gun—big-time—he continued to watch her work. Once she turned the clippers off, he asked, "How are you settling into your new place?"

She swapped the clippers for a pair of fancy-looking scissors. "It's been really good. Now that I don't have to commute back and forth to Whidbey Island, I have a couple extra hours a day."

"What are you going to do with yourself?" he teased.

"Right?" She chuckled, pulling a section of his hair through her fingers and snipping. "I was thinking about taking up knitting. I live in the apartment above Knit Wits, and I've run into the knitting ladies a few times. They're all super nice and welcoming."

"I've heard a rumor that knitting night is more alcohol than yarn." He shrugged, mesmerized by how fast her scissors worked and how she didn't cut herself. "But no judgement here."

Freya snickered. "Oh, by the laughter coming from the shop on knitting group nights, I can say the rumor is most definitely accurate."

Her smile slipped a tiny bit. If he hadn't been watching her so intently, he'd have missed it. His brow furrowed as he asked, "Not your crowd?"

She shook her head. "Oh, it's not that. I was planning on joining next week with Hazel, but . . ." Her eyes darted around the salon before meeting his in the mirror. She leaned toward his ear and dropped her voice. "Hazel got let go."

"The interview she did?"

Freya nodded.

He wasn't surprised. Gabriel Ortiz ran a tight ship, and the Pacific View Resort wasn't world-renowned by accident.

Freya set down her scissors and ran her fingers through his hair again. "I haven't talked with her since she called me about doing the interview. And now . . . I don't know. It's awkward all the way around, so who knows. But enough about that." She moved his hair this way and that before meeting his gaze. "What do you think?"

Tearing his attention from her, he looked at himself in the mirror. His jaw dropped. Holy shit. He looked like himself but way cooler. "Damn, woman. You weren't kidding about the Viking cut." He turned his head to the left and then the right. "You're saying it's actually a thing?"

She nodded, and the hopeful grin she gave him warmed his insides. "There are only certain kinds of guys who can pull off this style. You like?"

"I do. The better question is, do *you* like?"

She tsked and rolled her eyes. "Fishing for compliments, mister? You know you're smoking hot. Now, come on." She patted his shoulder and gestured to the hair-washing station.

He'd relaxed through their conversation and reined in his wayward thoughts. However, once he leaned back, his head dangling in the sink with Freya's hands on him, her body hovering over him, all relaxation flew out the window. Was he imagining her hovering over him and her hands on him in a completely different scenario? Absolutely. Thank God the long black fabric cape was still draped over him, or else he'd sorely embarrass himself.

"Let me know if it's too hot," she murmured.

He knew she meant the water temperature, but he was having a difficult time keeping his thoughts out of the gutter. As she rubbed a citrus-scented shampoo into his hair that left his scalp tingling, all he could think of was just how hot *she* was.

Freya continued a steady chatter while she worked his scalp, rinsed the shampoo out, and repeated the process with a minty conditioner. The massage was equally erotic and relaxing. An odd combo that had all his nerve endings on alert, but he sure as hell wasn't complaining.

Warm water washed the conditioner out, and after she wrung the excess water from his hair, she squeezed the back of his neck. "You doing okay? You're pretty tense."

Woman, you have no idea.

"I'm good." He closed his eyes and made a production of

moving his head side to side. "The neck cradle thing is at an odd angle, I guess."

"Oh, I'm sorry. Let me see if I can adjust it."

"It's fine, Freya." He heard her moving above him, and he rushed on before she could adjust the perfectly fine contraption, "Are we still on for dinner after all this?"

She chuckled. "If you're not sick of me yammering on, then sure."

He opened his eyes and met her ice-blue gaze. "I could listen to you talk all damn day. Your voice?" He tapped his cape-covered chest with his fist. "So damn soothing, and I promise that's not a line." It was the truth—her soft, melodic voice calmed every nerve in his body. And yet at the same time, it set them all on fire.

The corners of her lips slowly lifted up, and that soft-pink blush that was quickly becoming his favorite stole over her cheeks. "That's sweet of you to say." Heat flared in her eyes before she averted her gaze and cleared her throat. "But now, it's time to close your eyes again."

Doing the opposite, his eyes widened in question.

"Hot towel time. Plus, a shoulder massage." Smiling, she lowered her voice to a cute conspiratorial whisper. "I've been told this is the best part."

Though his skepticism was high because the scalp massage had been fantastic and he doubted anything could beat it, Xander closed his eyes.

Ten minutes later, the warm towel had been replaced twice, and he was utterly relaxed and grinning.

Holy. Shit.

He'd thought Freya's scalp massage was amazing? Nope. The current massage she was giving him was ridiculous. She'd worked his shoulders and each of his arms until he was basically putty in her hands.

"Alright, big guy," she murmured, removing the damp, warm towel from his face. "Back to the chair."

He sighed, gazing up at her. "Do we have to?"

Softly shaking her head, she patted his shoulders. "Let's go, handsome."

Grinning, he rose, followed her across the salon, and settled back into the plush salon chair. Once situated, he opened his mouth to comment on the fabulous massage, but when he noticed what she was holding, his mouth slammed shut. He side-eyed her.

Noticing his expression, Freya laughed. Because of course she did.

"Relax," she said, waving the hair dryer in her right hand. "This doesn't revoke your man card. I need your hair dry to make sure it's even. Besides, it's cold outside, and you don't want to go out with wet hair." Glancing at him in the mirror, she arched an eyebrow. "You've trusted me this far, right?"

"Go for it," he said, nodding. In all honesty, she could do whatever the hell she wanted so long as she kept running her fingers through his hair.

Once his hair was dry, she brought out the scissors again, snipping here and cutting there. When she was done, he couldn't help but be a little disappointed. Not because of what she'd done to his hair, because it looked good. Really good. But because now she was done touching him. He wasn't embarrassed to admit that over the last forty-five minutes, he'd become addicted to her touch.

After brushing a damp towel over his neck, she unsnapped the cape and whipped it off him. "What do you think?"

Running his hand through his hair, he met her gaze in the mirror and grinned. "It looks great. A giant upgrade."

She grinned. "I'm glad you like it."

"Are you sure I can't pay you for this? I mean, what you did was way more than a haircut."

"Don't be ridiculous," she said, shaking her head. "It's my thank-you for coming to my rescue that first day." He frowned, and she laughed. "You can pay the next time you're due for a haircut. How about that?"

Letting out an exaggerated sigh, he stood. "I suppose. Can I take you to dinner now?"

"Yes," she said, chuckling. Then she inclined her head toward the waiting area. "But give me a couple minutes to clean up?"

"Take your time." Besides, it would give him more time to figure out how he could get her hands back on him. Yeah, he wasn't in the market for a relationship, but that didn't mean they couldn't have some fun together.

CHAPTER NINE

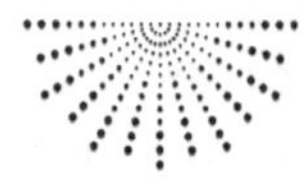

After sweeping up her area and putting her tools away, Freya hustled to the employee breakroom to retrieve her belongings. She had to admit that Xander's haircut had gone better than she'd thought. She'd been worried their conversation would be awkward and stifled, but it hadn't been. He was a genuinely nice guy who was easy to talk to. He had a flirty, sarcastic humor that she found endearing.

She frowned. *Endearing?* Nah, the man wasn't a sweet great-grandpa telling stories of days past. *Endearing* wasn't the right word at all.

She found the man attractive. Beyond his stunning good looks, she found *him* attractive—personality, humor, and all. Professionally speaking, he also had a great head of hair. Dark brown and slightly wavy with natural caramel highlights. Women paid good money for hair like his. She'd know because she'd done countless extensions that achieved that type of thickness.

Unprofessionally speaking, the man was ridiculously hot. Had she run her fingers through his hair a teeny tiny bit more than necessary?

One hundred percent.

But by the heated looks he'd given her, the man hadn't seemed to mind. So neither did she.

Freya wasn't one to flirt with her clients. Ever. With the few men who'd sat in her chair, she'd kept things completely professional. With Xander? Well, he wasn't *technically* a client. Not really. Besides, he made flirting easy. Which wasn't something she usually did.

She was an introvert who'd never made the first move with a guy. She'd never asked a guy out. Had never been bold and flirty. Her actions today proved that she still wasn't. Yes, she'd excessively run her hands through his hair, but not in an *obvious* obvious way.

But what had her timidness gotten her?

A string of cheating boyfriends. Guys who'd made her feel like crap about herself. Who'd gaslighted her into believing she was the cause of their relationship issues. If she'd paid more attention to them, if she'd worked less, if she'd put more effort into going out with their friends, they wouldn't have had to cheat. Rinse and repeat.

Four serious boyfriends in her twenty-nine years, and not one had remained faithful.

What was that saying about insanity? Doing the same thing and expecting different results? Yeah.

Maybe she needed to mix things up. Throw caution and her self-imposed dating rules out the window and just go with it. She wasn't sure she wanted a relationship, since those never seemed to work out for her, and she sure as hell had no clue what Xander wanted. If he wanted to do casual, she'd be cool with something like that. Granted, she'd never had a casual affair, but there was a first time for everything, right?

Catching her reflection in the employee lounge mirror, she paused and studied herself. Her long black hair still held a wave, though she wished she had time to refresh some of the curls. Leaning closer to the mirror, she grimaced. Swiping a finger under her right eye and then the left, she removed the mascara smudges. *Raccoon eyes. Excellent.*

She grabbed her purse from her employee locker, pulled out her compact, and powdered her nose. She reapplied her lip gloss, tossed it back into her purse, and grabbed her jacket. That was as good as it was going to get. Besides, Xander had just spent the last hour with her—raccoon eyes and all—and he still wanted to go to dinner.

She took a deep breath in, hoping it would bolster her confidence, and headed back to the waiting area. She slowed at the front desk and took a moment to just look. Xander sat in one of their oversized chairs. His large body and broad shoulders dwarfed the plush chair. He had his phone to his ear and was smiling and shaking his head at whoever was on the other line while running his free hand through his freshly cut hair.

"You going out with Hottie McHotterson tonight?" Audrey asked with a dreamy wispiness in her voice.

Freya glanced at the spa's receptionist and grinned. "Yeah, that's the plan. Have a good night."

"You lucky bitch," Audrey whispered with a dramatic sigh. "You better have a *really* good night. One I want to hear all about tomorrow."

"Not gonna happen." Freya shot her coworker a wink. "See ya!"

With Audrey muttering about helping a girl out, Freya chuckled and walked toward the salon's waiting area.

When Xander saw her, he murmured into his phone and quickly ended his call.

"Hey," she said. "Sorry I took longer than expected."

"You're good." He rose and gestured for her to precede him. "Ready?"

"Yeah." She waved at Audrey as they passed and then glanced up at him. "I assume you're parked in the main lot?"

"I am," he replied.

He held the door open for her, and the cool, crisp November air sent a shiver down her spine.

She zipped up her jacket and gestured in the opposite direction of the main building. "I'm parked in the employee lot, but I can drive around and meet you up front. Then I can follow you downtown. Or if it's easier, I can just meet you at Monty's."

"How about I walk you to your car, then you drive me to mine in the main lot?" He shrugged. "Not to state the obvious, but it's dark. I don't want you walking to your car alone."

Her insides melted the tiniest bit. A gentleman to boot.

"That works." Smiling, she fell into step beside him. "You should know that security installed some temporary lights in the parking lot yesterday. It's not pitch-black anymore, so me and the rest of the late-shift staff really appreciate whatever you said to Mr. Ortiz."

"Temporary lights?"

She nodded. "Mr. Ortiz sent an email out saying they'd be putting in new permanent light fixtures over the next week or so. Security cameras too."

"Good. I'm glad they've started implementing some of the security measures."

Entering the employee lot, she swept her hand in front of her in a ta-da motion. Along the perimeter were portable lamp posts every fifty feet or so. "You know, I don't think I realized just how dark it was back here until the new lights were put up. I mean, you can actually see all the cars now."

She led him to the back row, along the forest's edge, to where she'd parked. She noticed that as they walked, Xander scanned their surroundings. With her attention on the man beside her, she stumbled on the uneven gravel. She quickly righted herself, and heat washed over her face. *Graceful. Real graceful.*

"You okay?" he asked, placing his hand around her waist.

She didn't want to think too hard about how his casual touch had butterflies taking flight in her stomach.

"You should still have security walk you out at night. Even with lights and cameras, it would be safest to have an escort, especially if you're by yourself."

She also didn't want to think too hard about how Xander's attentiveness made her heart race and also enveloped her in a feeling of safety.

The man had her thoughts and emotions in a whirl. She cleared her throat. "I'm sure it'll be fine. I'd hate to inconvenience them . . ."

Freya's words died on her lips, and she came to an abrupt halt. She couldn't make out what she was seeing. Her trusty Kia was about fifty feet away, parked two spots down from one of the new light posts. However, something was off. Something wasn't right. But she couldn't figure out what.

Despite the confusion swirling her mind, she was aware enough to notice Xander had tensed beside her.

"What's wrong?" he asked, taking her elbow.

His tone changed. Became serious. What she imagined was his "work" voice. Whatever it was, the two words he'd uttered calmed her, tempered the unease brewing in her gut. She was grateful he was beside her.

"I don't know," she murmured.

She stood rooted to the ground and continued to stare at the back end of her Kia. The car was reflecting the light wrong, but she couldn't comprehend what she was seeing.

Until she did.

She sucked in a breath. "My windshield is smashed."

Through the back window of her sedan, she could see to

the front. There was a large circular hole on the passenger side, the glass sprouting like webs from it. The glass disappeared completely in the middle, its jagged pieces reflecting the light like a rainbow. The glass that was supposed to be in front of the driver's side was gone. It was completely shattered with only bits remaining in the frame, as if something had hollowed out the glass on that side of the windshield.

She took a step toward her car, but a strong hand clamped down on her arm.

Startled, she glanced at Xander.

Shaking his head, he kept his firm grip on her arm. His eyes scanned the parking lot as he moved her behind him. "Don't move. Not yet." With his free hand, he pulled his phone from his pocket, tapped the display, brought it to his ear, and after a moment, said in that assertive work-Xander tone, "Get Kwon on the phone. I need resort security to the employee parking lot immediately."

She pointed at her car. "But what about—"

"We'll take a look once backup arrives." He pocketed his phone, and with her still tucked behind him and his head on a constant swivel, he quickly crouched down. When he stood a couple seconds later, he had a wicked-looking knife clutched in his right hand.

Freya's eyes widened. *Where had that come from?*

"Just a precaution," he said, taking her hand with his free hand and pulling her back a few steps.

Confusion had her frowning. "But it's just a broken windshield." From as far away as she was, she couldn't see any other damage to her Kia. However, she'd bet good money that aside from the windshield, she was going to find body damage to either the roof or the hood. Or both. Something big must have fallen on her car to cause so much damage.

Then Xander's words registered.

Her frown deepened. "What do you mean by 'precaution'?"

Worry stirred in her belly, and her gaze swung back to her car. What else could have caused so much damage to her windshield?

"Just an occupational hazard, Frey. I won't investigate further until my client is secure. In this case"—he squeezed her hand—"you're my client."

She met his gaze. The steel and determination staring back at her both soothed her nerves and sent a heated zing surging through her. Completely inappropriate time and place? Absolutely. However, there was no stopping it. Or denying it. "I'm not in any danger. I'm sure it was just a branch or something—"

"I need you safe before we figure out what happened to your car. It's just you and me out here. We're not going near your car until we have more security with us."

Any other protests died on her lips, and that zing spread. She'd never been a fan of the damsel-in-distress thing, but if Xander was the one looking out for her, she'd go with it. Not only did the man work in security, but the protective vibe he was projecting was doing something to her insides. She'd follow his lead.

"Oh, okay. That makes sense." She internally cringed. Not her best response, but he had her fumbling for words.

Scanning the parking lot, he asked, "When were you at your car last?"

It took a split second for his words to register. "Um, this morning. I got to work just before nine."

"You didn't swing by your car during the day?"

She shook her head, grateful for his questions. She could focus on answering and not on how he made her stomach flip. Or how he was still holding her hand. And most definitely not on how she wanted to lean into him and let him take care of everything. "I had back-to-back appointments all day. This is the first time I've been back to my car."

"Mr. Bonetti," a voice behind them called out.

Xander turned, releasing her hand. While keeping her close, he angled himself in front of her.

She swooned a little. She couldn't help it. No one had ever been this protective of her.

He quickly crouched down and tucked his knife into some hidden holder under his pant leg, and when he stood, he retook her hand. As they strode toward one of the resort's security guards, she shook her head. *Focus. He's keeping you safe like a* client. *Don't read more into it.*

"Mr. Bonetti, I'm Andres Adam, head of evening security. Kwon is on his way." Andres's eyes glanced at their joined hands before he asked her, "Are you okay?"

She nodded, and as if on cue, Michael Kwon rushed into the employee parking lot.

After a quick greeting, she gestured to her car. "It looks like my windshield was damaged."

"We haven't gotten a close look at the car yet," Xander clarified. "I wanted her secure first."

"Understandable." Kwon turned to his colleague. "Call Croft and have him join us out here. The two of you can check the rest of this lot and the main lot for any other damaged cars."

Andres nodded and pulled his walkie-talkie from his hip. "Will do."

Kwon gestured to her car. "Shall we?"

Xander squeezed her hand, and she glanced at him. "Stay beside me. Please."

Nodding, she tightened her grip on his hand and followed his lead.

———————————◆———————————

Keeping Freya's hand in his, Xander walked toward her car. His eyes darted around, taking in the employee parking lot.

She'd mentioned the possibility of a branch falling onto her car, but he didn't buy it. The weather today had been surprisingly good for mid-November in the Pacific Northwest. It had been a rare sunny day. Crisp? Yes, but not at all windy. There was no debris in the parking lot from the surrounding trees. There looked to be some damage to the car to the right of hers, but none to the one on the left where the majority of the damage on Freya's windshield was.

Most importantly, a familiar twitchy feeling tickled his gut. He'd learned to trust that feeling. Hell, it had saved his life—and those of his friends—numerous times over the years.

Yes, he tended to immediately go to worst-case scenario —he wasn't lying earlier when he'd mentioned occupational hazards—but there was no denying things looked suspicious.

If he were being honest with himself, he hated that Freya was beside him. If it were up to him, he'd put her in a bubble and tuck her away so he knew she was completely safe. Then he'd figure out what happened to her car, determine if there was any remaining threat, and take care of everything for her. But Xander had enough strong women in his life to know that would be a dick move.

He didn't know Freya very well yet, but knew her well enough. She wouldn't appreciate the caveman routine. She'd want to be involved because she was a capable and smart woman. And it was her damn car. He'd just have to work extra hard to ensure her safety.

Stopping a few feet from the trunk of her Kia, he gave her hand one last squeeze before letting go. "Give me a minute to look?"

She nodded and crossed her arms over her chest.

From where he was standing, he took in the scattered glass on each side of the car. The safety glass sparkled against the packed gravel.

He caught Kwon's gaze, and in unspoken agreement, Xander walked to the passenger side while Kwon took the driver's side. The glass crunched under his boots, and he met Kwon at the hood.

The car beside Freya's sat next to the temporary light pole and had a similar circular hole in its windshield, identical to the one on Freya's passenger side. His first thought was someone had struck the glass with a hammer. That was the only damage to the neighboring car.

Freya's vehicle was another story entirely. The passenger side of the windshield had the hammer hole, but the glass on the driver's side was basically gone. As if someone had tried to knock the entire windshield out but had only gotten halfway through the job. The windshield frame on the driver's side had numerous dings. It had been something substantial, most likely metal, that had done the damage.

Taking a closer look into the Kia's interior confirmed his initial assessment. There was no tree branch inside her car. No large rocks. No indication that something natural had taken out her windshield. In fact, there was nothing in the interior of her car aside from shattered glass and a yellow Yeti tumbler in her cupholder.

His frown deepened, and that twitchy feeling in his gut intensified.

"Are you seeing what I'm seeing?" Kwon asked.

"More like not seeing." He exhaled and planted his hands on his hips. "Have cameras been installed yet?"

"Wouldn't that have been nice," Kwon murmured, "but negative. The cameras for this lot are scheduled for Sunday.

Permanent light poles for the following week." He sighed, glancing around. "I'll call the sheriff's department."

Leaving Kwon to make his calls, he rounded the car to where Freya stood worrying her lower lip, her arms still tightly crossed over her chest. He wanted to pull her into a hug but instead placed his hands on her shoulders and squeezed. "Kwon's calling the police. I'm sure they'll want to know if anything is missing. I wouldn't touch anything before they get here, but do you want to take a peek?"

She pursed her lips, and her gaze searched his. "It's pretty bad, isn't it? I mean, by the look on your face and Mr. Kwon's, I'm assuming it wasn't a fallen branch?"

Giving in, he ran his hands down her arms and tugged her close, pulling her into a hug. Her arms immediately encircled his waist, and she leaned into him, hugging him back. A feeling he didn't recognize swamped his senses. Protectiveness? Yeah, but it was more than that. It was something he couldn't quite define.

"No, sweetheart," he murmured, dropping his chin to the top of her head. "It wasn't a branch." What it actually was, he didn't know. But he was determined to stay beside her—if she let him—until they figured it out.

Running a hand up and down her slim back, he pressed a kiss to the top of her head before letting her go. "After the sheriff's department comes and does their thing, you still want to grab dinner with me? I figure you deserve an extra one of those blue drinks you said you liked after this mess. Or maybe three."

A smile lifted her lips, and his insides warmed. He'd done that. He'd gotten a smile out of her after all the chaos.

"That sounds great." Her eyes darted to her car and then back. "That is, if you don't mind driving me."

"Not at all. I can drive you home after too."

"Oh, that's okay. I live downtown, so I can walk."

"Ah, that's right." After a moment, she frowned, and he took a guess. "You have to work tomorrow, don't you?"

She nodded, and her forehead scrunched.

So. Damn. Cute. "Well, I don't, so I can give you a lift to work in the morning as well."

Her jaw dropped, and she was shaking her head before he'd finished speaking. "Xander, I can't ask you to do that."

"You're not asking. I'm offering."

Her lips pressed together again, but they tilted up at the edges. Like she was fighting a smile. "How about we grab dinner first. If you can still stomach me after food and multiple cocktails, we'll revisit this conversation."

He couldn't get a read on her self-deprecating comment. Was she being funny? Or did she seriously believe he'd be sick of her after he'd already spent the last however long with her? Or was she fishing for a compliment? He mentally frowned and nixed the last option. She wasn't the type. But if it were either of the first two, he was determined to show her how much he enjoyed her company. Fucked-up circum-stances or not.

"That's fair, I suppose." It wasn't, but he'd play along if it made her more comfortable. "We'll shelve this conversation as 'to be continued' then." He inclined his head toward her car. "Shall we take a peek?"

She grimaced. "May as well. The faster we get this over with, the faster I can get a cocktail in me."

He bit the inside of his cheek and kept his expression neutral. There was an inappropriate retort in there some-where. He was sure of it. But he dragged his thoughts out of the gutter and focused on the tasks at hand. They needed to figure out if anything was missing from her vehicle, get a police report filed, and then get her car towed and squared away.

Because he couldn't stand beside her and not touch her, he took her hand and walked her to the side of her car.

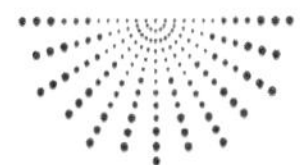

The waiter at Monty's Tavern placed a pint of beer in front of Xander. When he set the electric-blue concoction in a frosted, sugar-rimmed martini glass down in front of her, Freya couldn't help but smile. Holy crap, she was *so* looking forward to this drink. The last hour dealing with the sheriff's department and her messed-up car had been a lot. Though she had to admit that the man sitting across the table from her had been a genuine life saver tonight.

Xander lifted his glass, and when she did the same, he gently tapped his glass to hers. "To good days. Though I have to say—and don't kill me here—aside from your car getting vandalized, today's been a great day." He shot her a lopsided smile that had her stomach doing flips again.

She grinned—because how could she not? The man's charming smile was potent—then she took a sip of her drink. The blue-raspberry sweetness had her taste buds dancing. "The day is ending on a high note for sure."

She wanted to pat herself on the back. Who was this woman tossing out flirty comebacks? Usually in this kind of situation, her face would be in flames, and she'd be stuttering.

Oh, who was she kidding? She'd never been in a situation like this, and most definitely not with a man like this. The few men she'd gone out with in the past had been closer to her age and, well . . . safe. They'd had desk jobs and been regular looking. Not ripped security guys who looked like they'd jumped off the cover of a romance novel. And fine, maybe her face was getting a little hot, but that was probably due to the vodka in her cocktail.

Yeah, right.

Clearing her throat, she glanced around the crowded bar. Monty's Tavern, a fabulous gastro pub with an old-world nautical theme, was located in the heart of Hudson Island's downtown. The food was delicious, the cocktails were even better, and the atmosphere was upscale but not stuffy. The restaurant was packed, and the bar area was crowded with locals and tourists. They'd been lucky to arrive right when a group was leaving and had snagged a tall four-top.

She turned her attention back to Xander. "I really appreciate your help with the police report. I didn't realize how much I *didn't* notice until you gave your statement."

When the deputy from the sheriff's department had arrived, they'd taken her statement, which had been pretty basic. Then they'd asked for Xander's, and he'd provided so much more detail. From the damage to the car beside hers to the small dents in her windshield frame. She was sure it had been a branch that had fallen onto her car, but he'd pointed out the lack of any debris—aside from the shattered glass—inside her vehicle. When she'd been ready to write it all off as a freak accident, he'd pointed out that it was vandalism.

"Don't be so hard on yourself. Noticing the smallest details is what I do for a living."

"True." She wrinkled her nose. "But I still kinda feel like an idiot."

He shook his head. "Don't. The majority of people would have come to the same conclusion as you. One positive is that you're smart and don't use your car for storage, so nothing was stolen."

She winced. "That's only because I *used* to leave all my crap in my car. A few years ago, when I was living in Seattle, my car was broken into, and they took everything. Lesson learned."

"At least you learned. Most people don't. Another positive is that this happened at work, so the resort's taking care of it."

Freya was 100 percent thankful for that. Kwon had arranged for her car to be towed and said the resort would foot the repair bill since it had happened on their property. They were also arranging a rental car for her and were covering the costs of that as well. She was beyond grateful she wouldn't have to deal with either of those expenses.

"I do feel a little guilty though," she said after taking another sip of her drink. "I mean, with the damage to the windshield frame, who knows how long it's going to take to fix my car. And they're paying for me to have a rental car for the entire time? That's a lot."

His eyebrows shot up, and humor colored his face. "Freya, sweetheart, how much does one night at the resort cost for a basic room?"

She pressed her lips together to keep from laughing. The man had a point. "About nine hundred."

"And how much does a fifty-minute massage cost?"

She lost the battle and grinned. "Two-fifty."

He took a drink of his beer and then set his glass down. "Exactly. I'm sure they'll be okay footing the bill for your rental car. If anything, you should get an upgrade for shits and giggles."

She laughed. "I'll think about it, but if they question me about the upcharges, I'll be sure to point them in your direction."

He held his hands out. "By all means. In fact—"

Xander's words cut off, and his mouth fell open as the two empty seats at their table were pulled out.

Freya's eyes widened in shock as two women, wineglasses in hand, sat down. One in the empty seat next to her, and the other in the seat beside Xander.

"Um, can I help you?" Freya asked just as Xander groaned and muttered something that sounded suspiciously like, "Fuck my life."

Both women were smiling at Xander, wide toothy grins that screamed mischief. Though the woman beside Xander looked vaguely familiar, Freya had no idea who these women were or what they were up to. However, something told her they knew Xander, and whatever was about to happen was going to be entertaining. A slow smile spread over Freya's face.

Xander looked at both women and grumbled, "Aren't you two supposed to be grilling steaks tonight or something?"

They laughed, and Freya's eyes widened. The women were ridiculously pretty. Like unfairly so. The one beside Xander was probably around her own height, but in a million times better shape than her. She had long, wavy, jet-black hair and tan, sun-kissed skin. The other woman was no slouch either. Not at all. If Wonder Woman had a doppelganger, it was the tall, slim brunette beside her.

The familiar-looking woman next to Xander patted his arm like he was some cute little child. She didn't bother responding to him and turned her attention to Freya. "Hi, I'm Esme." She extended her hand across the table.

She shook the woman's hand and admired her firm but not obnoxiously hard grip. "Freya."

"I'm Tash," the woman beside Freya said, holding out her hand.

"Hi," she said, shaking Tash's hand.

Ordinarily, Freya would have been intimidated by both women, but the humor lighting their eyes immediately put her at ease.

"Great, you've all met," Xander said, leaning back in his seat. "Now you guys can leave."

Tash shook her head and tsked. "Where are your manners, young man?" She turned to Freya. "I apologize on Xan's behalf. He's usually much more charming than this."

She glanced across the table at Xander, who'd crossed his arms over his chest. He'd tilted his head back and was staring at the ceiling, slowly shaking his head.

"You know, this is your fault," Esme said, nudging him with her elbow.

He heaved a sigh as he met his friend's gaze. "And why is that?"

She flashed an innocent smile that Freya was sure was anything but. "Tash and I were just going to stop to say hi and then go about our way. But no. You had to immediately go all grumpy and irritated, so naturally, we have to stay longer now."

"Naturally," Tash chimed in with a bright smile.

Freya chuckled. Oh yeah. These two had to be close friends of Xander's.

"Esme, I have to ask," Freya said, curiosity picking at her brain, "have we met before?" She was certain they had. After all, the other woman was stunning and not exactly forgettable.

Esme's smile widened as she nodded. "I don't think we've

formally met, but I've seen you in passing. I'm a spa regular. I see Sergio every other Saturday."

"Ah! That's why you look so familiar." Freya turned to Tash. "I'm a hairstylist at the Pacific View Resort's spa."

"Oh, I know," Tash said with a nod. Before Freya could register the woman's cryptic reply, Tash asked, "How are things going over there? It must have been a crazy week with the shooting and everything."

"It's been hectic for sure. We reopened the salon this morning, and we're down a stylist, but it actually went a lot smoother than I expected." Freya took a sip of her drink and nodded at Xander. "This one was my last client of the day."

"That's what's different!" Esme said, slapping him on the shoulder. "I couldn't figure out why you looked different." She grabbed his chin and yanked his face to the left and the right.

He scowled at Esme, and Freya bit back a chuckle.

"Looking sharp, bud," Tash said, waggling her eyebrows. "Very Viking-esque."

Freya gave up the half-hearted fight and laughed. "See! I told you modern Viking is a thing."

"My apologies for doubting you." He winked at her.

Her stomach did that flipping thing again. She cleared her throat and turned to the women. "But thank goodness he was my last client, because when he walked me out to my car, we discovered someone had smashed in my windshield."

Before she'd finished speaking, both women straightened, their expressions going from relaxed to alert. It was as if the clouds had parted, and she knew *exactly* how these women were connected to Xander.

"Ah, *that's* how you two know Xander. You all work together, don't you?" Esme's brow arched, and Freya clarified, "You both went from laid-back to attentive and all alpha protector like that." She snapped her fingers and then nodded at Xander. "Just like him."

"Guilty as charged," Esme said, taking a sip of her wine.

Tash pointed her wineglass at Xander. "We've been teammates for what? Six years now?"

"Seven and a half." He shrugged and flashed Freya that lopsided smirk that was quickly becoming her favorite. "But, hey, who's counting."

Tash grinned and flipped him off, and Xander puckered his lips at her.

Freya laughed. They were just like her and her brothers.

Conversation halted when their waiter approached with a plate in each hand. "I have dinner, folks. The steak and mushroom flatbread for you, ma'am, and the grilled mahi for you, sir." He placed their plates in front of them. "Can I get you anything else?"

She shook her head. "No, thank you."

He turned to Esme and Tash and nodded to their near-empty wineglasses. "Ladies, would you like a top-off?"

"I'm good, thanks," Tash replied.

Esme shook her head. "No, thank you. We're heading out soon."

The waiter turned to Tash. "Would you like me to cork the bottle for you? I'd hate for it to go to waste."

"That'd be great, thank you," Tash said.

As the waiter left with a promise to return soon with Tash's wine bottle, Freya's gaze ping-ponged around the table. Xander was looking at the two women with suspicion, and they were both not so subtly avoiding his gaze and staring at each other with widening eyes and intense stares. Freya could only look on with amusement as a silent conversation, one she wasn't privy to, was happening around the table.

She missed that talk-without-words kind of friendship,

which these three obviously had. It had been so long since she'd had that.

Her mind flashed to the pictures she'd received the other day of Sarah, and her chest clenched painfully tight. But that was her own fault . . .

Pushing the melancholy thoughts away, she cleared her throat, gaining the women's attention. "Why don't you two join us for dinner? I'm sure we can snag a couple menus when our waiter comes back with your bottle of wine."

"Oh, that's okay," Xander said, giving the women a pointed stare. "They're leaving."

Chuckling, Freya shook her head. "Don't listen to him. You're more than welcome to join us. He'll survive."

Tash laughed and stood. "As much as we'd love to, we'll get out of your hair. God forbid, we turn your first date into a girls' night." She held out her hand. "It was nice meeting you, Freya."

"Likewise," she said, shaking Tash's hand.

Esme smiled at her. "It was nice officially meeting you." Her gaze shot to Xander and then back to Freya. "I'm sure we'll see you around."

"It was nice meeting you too. Have a nice night."

Both women slapped Xander on the shoulder as they left. Her gaze followed them as they made a pit stop at the bar to grab Tash's corked bottle of wine. After they were out of sight, she turned to Xander. "Well, those two are really sweet."

He coughed, choking on a bite of his fish.

After taking a sip of water, he cleared his throat and leaned back into his seat, amusement playing on his handsome face.

"What?" Smiling, she picked up a slice of her flatbread. She took a bite of the savory steak, earthy mushrooms, and the sweet and tangy caramelized onions, and her taste buds sang.

Wiping his mouth with his napkin, Xander chuckled. "Let's just say that those two aren't exactly known for being *sweet*. More like intimidating and intense."

She grinned around her bite of food. "Oh, believe me, I can definitely see that," she said after she'd swallowed. She set her flatbread down and shrugged. "But they also seem really nice. It's obvious you're all close."

"I don't have any family, not by blood anyway, but those two are my sisters through and through." The smile he gave her warmed everything inside her. It was soft and sweet and held a tiny bit of awe. Then, as if he'd realized what he'd said, he dropped his gaze and cleared his throat. "As Tash mentioned," he said, picking up his fork, his tone more playful and less reflective, "we're on the same personal security team, and Esme's our director of logistics. Both of those women are tough as nails, so it's amusing to hear someone call them sweet. Especially, Es."

Her heart squeezed, immediately missing the softer side of him, but she knew he hadn't meant to get sentimental with her. If he wanted to keep things light, she'd take it. Take *him* however he was comfortable. "Why is that?" she asked.

"Don't get me wrong, both of them are complete badasses. But Esme? She's got a little added scary in there as well. And she's damn proud of it. Believe me, I'm gonna love telling her that you thought she was *sweet* and *nice*."

Freya rolled her eyes. "God, you sound just like my brothers."

He grinned, pointing his fork at her. "Hey, family is family. Blood or not, right? And as her pseudo-brother, it's my right to give her shit."

It was her turn to point at him, but with her slice of steak and mushroom flatbread instead of a fork. "You are trouble, mister. Now eat your dinner."

"Yes, ma'am." He scooped some of his grilled mahi and chimichurri rice onto his fork and took a bite, shooting her a wink.

How that little gesture could be both sweet and sexy at the same time, she had no clue. All she knew was that the more time she spent with Xander Bonetti, the more she liked him. How could she not, really? The man was truly something else . . .

CHAPTER ELEVEN

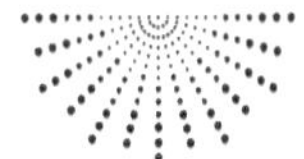

Xander stood at the side of the bar and waited for Freya. They'd been on their way out when Hazel had called Freya's name and rushed over. She'd enveloped Freya in a giant hug and pulled her off to the side to chat. From where he was standing, he could see Freya's forced smile. He was a heartbeat away from stepping in when she mouthed, "I'm okay" and held up a finger before turning her attention back to Hazel.

Hazel was beaming as she pointed to someone on the other side of the bar, and both women waved. Then they hugged once more before Freya turned back toward him with her to-go box in hand. She gave him a smile that conveyed her relief, and it socked him right in the gut.

Even though it had been a long-ass day, he didn't want it to end. And yes, it had been quite the day. From the budding anticipation of seeing Freya again, to the excitement and utter relaxation from that amazing massage when he got his hair cut, and then to the adrenaline spike of her car getting vandalized, his emotions had been all over the place.

Yeah, he'd nearly had a damn heart attack when Esme and

Tash had joined them at dinner, but it had turned out fine. Freya had rolled with their intrusion, and frankly, he'd been happy to see the women get along. He adored both Tash and Esme—he hadn't been lying when he'd said they were his sisters—but he knew they could be prickly as hell. They didn't tend to go out of their way to befriend other women. So it meant a lot that they'd all gotten along so well, and that Freya had liked them.

The thought had him stilling.

Shit. He was in trouble with this woman.

"Ready?" Freya asked, pulling him from his musings.

"Yup," he said, placing his hand at the small of her back and leading her toward the exit.

When they stepped onto the sidewalk, the cold air had him shifting closer to Freya. Her jacket, while pretty, looked to be more fashionable than functional.

"You said you're a few blocks away, right?" he asked, turning down the sidewalk.

"Oh, you don't need to walk me home." She gestured to his SUV, which was two vehicles in the opposite direction. "Your car's right here, and my place is out of your way."

She had to be out of her mind if she thought he'd let her walk home by herself. Yes, Hudson Island was a relatively safe community, all things considered. But she'd just had her car vandalized in the parking lot of an uber-upscale resort. Plus, it was dark, nearly nine at night. However, instead of saying any of those things, he simply arched an eyebrow at her. "Seriously?"

The corners of her lips twitched as she gazed up at him. Humor danced over her face. "Alpha protector. Right. Silly me, how could I have forgotten?"

Who knew he'd find sarcasm so attractive? "That's right, smart-ass, how could you possibly forget?" Unable to resist, he reached for her free hand and laced his fingers with hers. After a split second, he met her gaze. "This okay?"

He held his breath as he waited for her reply.

The smile playing at the edges of her lips broke free, and she nodded, squeezing his hand. "Yeah." Then she pulled him a few steps down the sidewalk. "Come on, I'm above Knit Wits."

"How's Hazel doing?" he asked, falling into step beside her.

"I'm not sure, actually. She was all smiles and raving about this new guy she was out on a date with but . . ." Freya sighed, shaking her head. "She said she was surprised the resort had fired her, and I genuinely think she was being serious."

"I'm assuming the resort explained to her why they fired her?"

"They did, but Hazel said she didn't think the whole do-not-talk-to-the-press thing applied to her." A look of disbelief colored her face. "I mean, how could she think it wouldn't apply to her when it was a company-wide message from the resort's *owner*?"

Because people were selfish.

But he bit his tongue. He wasn't about to badmouth the other woman. Regardless of what had happened, Hazel was still Freya's friend.

"We're going to meet up for coffee next week." She let out another weary sigh and frowned. "I just worry about her, you know?"

He squeezed her hand. "You're a good friend, Freya."

That frown on her pretty face was all kinds of wrong. As they continued down the quiet street, he was determined to change that. He told her a funny story from that morning at the gym. How an overly cocky Carmichael had gotten absolutely destroyed by Tash on the sparring mat.

After a block, Freya's laughter had him smiling. The lyrical sound did something he couldn't quite describe to his insides. Hell, her mere presence had his heart beating an erratic rhythm in his chest.

He liked her. A lot.

And that scared the shit out of him.

As shallow as it sounded, he didn't like women *and* sleep with them. He either liked them and enjoyed their company —like his female colleagues and some of the women who were in relationships with his friends—or he slept with them.

Not both.

Shallow? Absolutely. But that's what he'd always done. The women he'd slept with knew the score, and the arrangement worked for all parties involved.

But Freya? She was easy to talk to, funny as hell, got along with Tash and Esme—which was freaking unheard of—and so damn sweet. He liked spending time with her, and getting to know her was surprisingly fun.

And she was so fucking pretty.

He'd been half hard from the moment he saw her at the salon today. During dinner, he'd been pushing away thoughts of sinking his hands into her long dark hair. Of finding out if her lips held a lingering taste of that bright-blue drink she liked so much. Of whether the delicate curve of her hip was as soft as he thought it would be.

Yeah . . .

He liked her *and* wanted her in his bed. And he didn't know what the hell to do about that.

"Well, this is me," she said, yanking him from his thoughts. She'd stopped in front of a nondescript door to the right of the entrance to the Knit Wits knitting shop. Releasing his hand, she held out her to-go container to him. "Can you hold this?"

He took the box, and she dug through her purse for her keys. She unlocked the door and pushed it open to reveal a brightly lit staircase. "It's just me and a small storage unit for the knitting shop up here," she said, climbing the stairs in front of him.

He followed closely behind, and his eyes wandered. It was a damn shame her jacket covered her ass. However, it didn't stop him from admiring the flare of her waist, the sway of her hips, or the soft curve of her thighs.

They reached her apartment door, and before she could fit her key into the lock, he bent down and placed her to-go box on the ground. His actions had her stilling. She looked at him with her head cocked slightly to the side in question. Amusement danced across her face, and his gut tightened. Yeah, she was stunning.

Taking advantage of her surprise, he shot her a small smile as he slowly rose. When they were eye level, he searched her gaze, and the heat he saw in her blue eyes had his insides humming. As he straightened to his full height, he cradled her face in his hands. Her skin was so damn soft against his palms. She took in a sharp breath, and her exhale had her lips slightly parting.

He had to taste.

His gaze never left hers as he ran his thumb over her plump lower lip and leaned down. Her pupils were blown, and anticipation zinged through him.

When his lips were inches from hers, she rose onto her tiptoes and sealed her lips to his. Surprise had him freezing, and he vaguely heard her keys hit the ground. A split second later, she nipped at his lower lip.

An inferno engulfed him, and he slanted his mouth over hers. Her lips parted, and he tangled his tongue with hers. A low groan rattled his chest. She tasted even better than he'd imagined. Sweet with a hint of that candy drink and a sexy something that was uniquely Freya. It was a potent combination, and he pulled away only to change the angle before he tasted her mouth again.

So. Fucking. Perfect.

He kept his hands in her hair, and time stood still. It was just the two of them. Right now was all that mattered.

When he felt her arms tighten around him and her soft body press against his front, another growl left his throat. Though she was so much smaller than him, she fit him perfectly.

Letting out a shaky breath, he pulled away again and rested his forehead against hers. "Damn, woman. You're killing me." His heart thumped hard in his chest. "I better get going. Or else I won't."

She ran her hands up his sides, and he couldn't hold back a shiver. "I wouldn't be opposed to that."

He smothered another groan. He'd do anything to be with this woman, taste her, explore her. But by the pink flush brightening her cheeks, he knew they were moving too fast. He ran his thumb over her jaw and dropped a quick kiss to her lips before straightening. "Believe me, there's nothing I want more, but . . ." He shook his head.

The blush on her cheeks deepened, and she dropped her gaze like she was embarrassed.

Oh, hell no.

"Freya, sweetheart. It's not that I don't want you, because I sure as hell do." He wrapped his arms around her and ensured there was zero space between them. Rocking his hips into her, his hard length pressed into her abdomen. Her eyes widened, and her breath hitched. "Do not doubt for a second how much I want you. Trust me, baby, you have no idea what you do to me."

She arched an eyebrow, and any lingering doubts clouding her face were gone. The look she gave him was pure sex. Her blue eyes dared him to look away as she rubbed against him.

He groaned and then chuckled. "Okay. Maybe you do have an idea."

She smiled. "I'm getting a hint."

He kissed her again—because how could he not?—but before it could get too heated, he straightened. "I want to take my time with you, and it's already late. You have to work tomorrow. I'll be by at eight to pick you up. That time still work for you?"

She pursed her lips and narrowed her eyes. "You're not sick of my company yet?"

He tilted her chin up with his finger and claimed her lips again. His tongue swept into her mouth, exploring. He couldn't get enough of her. A low moan sounded—he didn't know if it was his or hers—and once again, he pulled away, this time putting space between them.

"That answer your question?" He dropped another kiss to her lips before straightening. "To be continued, okay?"

She nodded, and her eyes were hazy with desire. She rose on her tiptoes and pressed a kiss to his lips. "To be continued."

Unable to resist, he deepened their kiss but kept it quick. He wasn't sure he'd be able to walk away otherwise. "I'll see you tomorrow morning." He nodded to her door and then bent down to retrieve her to-go box and keys. Holding them out for her, he said, "I'll wait until you lock up."

After unlocking her front door, she took the box from him, paused in the threshold, and turned back to him. "Thank you for dinner, Xander. I had a lot of fun with you today."

His name on her lips had goosebumps rising over his arms. "I did too. How about a repeat tomorrow night?"

Her smile widened, and something loosened in his chest.

She stepped into her apartment and looked at him over her shoulder. "I'd like that. See you tomorrow, and thanks again for everything today. Goodnight."

She closed the door, and he waited until he heard the turn of her deadbolt. For a few silent seconds, he simply stared at her shut door. Part of him wanted to knock on her door and take her up on her earlier offer, but the other part—the one that was completely twisted up in a knot—screamed at him to march his ass home. He spun on his heel and quickly made his way down the stairs.

Tomorrow. He was going to see her again tomorrow.

Hopefully, his mind would no longer be racing by then. As it was, he didn't know what the hell he was doing.

However, he now knew a few things for certain. Freya's inky-black hair felt like the smoothest silk between his fingers. Her lips held the tiniest hint of that blue-raspberry drink she loved. The gentle curves of her hips were soft and fit perfectly in his hands.

While he wasn't quite sure how to proceed, he knew he wanted more . . .

CHAPTER TWELVE

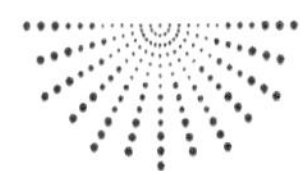

"Nice," Xander said, slapping his punching mitts together. He wiped the sweat off his brow with his forearm and lifted his chin at Tash. "Just so you know, after the last couple combos, you were lowering your guard a little."

Tash's right eyebrow arched, and she crossed her gloved hands over her chest.

He held up his hands. "I said *a little*. Nothing to kick my ass for, just something to keep an eye on."

She rolled her eyes as she used her teeth to loosen the strap on her right sparring glove. "What's on the docket for today?"

"Not much. Frazier wants me to sit in on a potential client meeting. A-list celebrity has a stalker, and she isn't happy with her current security team. But that's not until noon. What are you up to?"

"It's a rare Saturday off," Tash said, sitting on the bench and rolling her neck side to side. "Wilson and I are gonna swing into town and grab some breakfast before I head back to Seattle. Want to join?"

For a moment, he simply stared at her. Did he want to tell her? "Uh . . ."

That damn eyebrow of Tash's arched again. *"Uh . . .?"*

Act. Casual.

"I'm picking up Freya at eight and giving her a ride to work," he said, his words coming out in a rush. "You know, since her car's in the shop after all that shit yesterday. She lives downtown, and the resort hasn't figured out the rental car yet." *Stop. Fucking. Talking!* He cleared his throat. "So maybe next time."

For a full ten seconds, Tash simply stared at him. It took everything he had to not squirm. Holy shit, he'd forgotten how intense the woman could be.

Then Tash laughed. Not a quiet, reserved chuckle. No. It was loud, boisterous, people-were-starting-to-stare laughter.

Fucking hell.

He scrubbed his hand over his face and heaved out a sigh. "For fuck's sake, Tash, it's no big deal."

"Oh, I beg to differ, my friend." The irritating woman made a production of swiping away a tear. "You think if I mentioned your plans to Wilson, he'd think it was a big deal?"

She wouldn't dare. He pressed his lips together and shot her his best glare. The last thing he needed was Wilson giving him shit.

Tash snickered, pointing her finger at him. "Exactly."

He frowned. "Didn't you say yesterday that you were going to butt out?"

"Yeah, but I lied. Plus, that was before I met her." She tossed her gloves into her gym bag and stood, slinging her bag over her shoulder. "For what it's worth, she seems nice."

"Funny you should say that," he replied as he tossed his punching mitts into his bag. "Because that's exactly what

Freya said about you and Esme. That the two of you were nice and *sweet*."

He grinned when Tash's face scrunched in offense.

"Well, I suppose she may not be the brightest bulb," Tash grumbled. "But she's nice. So there's that."

"You're so full of shit." Chuckling, he shook his head, knocking his shoulder into hers. "But seriously, it's no big deal. Freya needed a ride. I have the morning off and am free to take her."

"And you say I'm the one who's full of shit? Please."

"I don't know what you're talking about." And he didn't. Not really.

He didn't know why the thought of picking up Freya in—he glanced at his watch—forty-five minutes had him on edge. Not "on edge" in a bad way. However, he wouldn't exactly say it was in a good way either. It was more unfamiliar than anything. Whatever the feeling coursing through him was, it leaned more toward nervous and restless than warm and fuzzy.

The thought had him nearly halting mid stride. *Nervous? Restless?* He sure as hell couldn't remember the last time he'd been either over a woman. But he undoubtedly was.

From the moment he'd left her doorstep last night, he hadn't been able to get Freya out of his mind. The way she'd run her fingers through his hair at the salon. How strong she'd been with the chaos of her car getting vandalized. Their dinner together. Holding her hand when he'd walked her home. And yeah, that mind-blowing kiss that was still on repeat in his mind. It had been *that* good. Hell, the entire time he'd spent with her had been that good.

At least it had been for him. Would she have second thoughts when she saw him this morning? Holy shit, what if that kiss they'd shared had done nothing for her? What if—

"Sure you do. You were actually normal for once."

Tash's words pulled him back to their conversation, and he frowned, glancing at her. "What are you talking about? I'm always normal."

"Oh God, you don't even know, do you?" She let out a dramatic, long-suffering sigh.

Trepidation stirred in his gut, and his worry about what Freya had thought of their date was momentarily shelved. "Apparently not, but I'm sure you'll enlighten me."

She stopped and faced him.

The trepidation grew. Tash was one of his best friends, but he wasn't sure he wanted to hear what she had to say.

"You're an absolute great guy, Xan."

He cringed. "Shit. I hear a *but* coming."

The look she gave him was one you'd give to an old, arthritic dog—a look full of sympathy, sadness, and a touch of pity. "We've known each other forever, and I've seen firsthand how you go into pick-up-a-chick-to-bang mode. I'll give it to you that it's been highly effective for you. I mean, whenever I've seen you morph into *that guy*" —Xander's eyes narrowed when she air-quoted the last two words—"you've never failed. However, as someone who knows you and cares about you and has zero interest in you getting into my pants, seeing you act like that when I know you're a stand-up guy is gross and sleezy."

Surprise had him rearing back. "What the hell, Tash? I don't have a pick-up-a-chick-to-bang mode."

Wait, did he?

She scoffed. "You do. Yeah, it's been a while since I've witnessed you deploy it, but seriously, when was the last time you took a woman out to dinner and stuck around the next day?"

He glanced around the crowded gym, leaned closer to Tash, and dropped his voice. "Not that it's your business, but

I did *not* sleep with Freya last night." They'd only shared the hottest kiss of his damn life.

Tash patted his chest. "That's exactly my point. If you take a woman out, you're banging her. Then you're done. Am I wrong?"

Christ, when she put it that way, he sounded exactly like she'd described: gross and sleezy.

"Look, I'm not judging, Xan. You know I'm a big fan of casual relationships and mutually agreed upon hookups. My point is that you weren't like that with Freya last night. You were . . . you. You weren't doing that"—her nose scrunched, and she waved her hand at his face—"schtick you guys all do."

He shook his head. Did he really act like that when he went out to pick up a woman for the night? He internally winced. The fact that he'd mentally phrased it as *pick up a woman for the night* probably said it all.

"I mean, Carmichael's the same," Tash said. "He's like the younger version of you."

Xander groaned. "Holy shit, please don't compare me to him."

"Wilson . . ." Tash shook her head and chuckled, continuing as if he hadn't spoken. "Well, Wilson just avoids people in general, so I don't have to witness him picking up women or anything. Trust me on this one. Being yourself is a good thing. When you weren't being all douchebaggy last night, it was surprising for sure, but it was also really nice to see. From what I saw, Freya wasn't running away screaming or kneeing you in the balls. Want my advice?"

He winced. "Pretty sure you're going to give it to me whether I want it or not."

"You know me well, friend." She grinned, crossing her arms over her chest and eyeing him up and down like he was some new mission to figure out. "Freya doesn't fall into your one-night-stand category, and you're going out of your way to pick her up and take her to work on your day off. I'm also assuming you're going to do something nice like pick up her favorite coffee on the way to get her. Correct?"

He frowned and shot Tash his most ferocious glare. It was that or stare at her dumbfounded. It was irritating when your friends knew you so damn well.

She ignored his glare and arched an eyebrow. Because that's how Tash rolled. "Am I correct?"

"Fine. I was going to swing by and get coffee for *both* of us. It's not a big deal though. Everyone needs coffee to start their damn day." He huffed out a sigh. "Is that supposed advice you're gonna give me in there somewhere?"

She rolled her eyes. "My advice is for you to stop thinking you aren't good enough for her. For once, allow yourself to like her."

He froze. *What the fu—*

Tash's eyebrow arched higher, silently daring him to argue with her. He couldn't, though, because he *wasn't* good enough for Freya.

"She obviously likes you, Xander. For once, just go for it. Be the good guy that you are and see where it takes you. Hell, look at Frazier. He shot his damn shot and is now all blissed up with B." She shrugged. "You never know. You could have something like that."

"I'm not sure that's what I want."

He was happy for Frazier and Bean. His friends were indeed blissfully happy, but he wasn't sure it was possible for him to have something like that. Especially not with Freya.

They were so different. She was sweet and kind. Him, on the other hand? He was a good friend but was shit at relationships. He'd had zero success as a boyfriend, and up until this point, that hadn't bothered him.

On top of that, Freya came from a big family. He could tell her brothers annoyed her, but when she spoke about them, he saw the warmth in her gaze. She not only loved them, but she liked them too. He had nothing to offer on that front.

Yes, they had insane chemistry, but that wasn't something to base a relationship on. The fire between them would inevitably burn out.

"Liar." Tash's finger jabbed him in the chest. "You want that. You just don't think you deserve it."

The muscle in his jaw twitched. It was the only indication she'd hit the nail on the head, but damn if he'd admit it out loud. "Yeah, well, what about you?"

She made a face. "I don't do relationships. You know that."

He sighed. "Neither do I, T."

"Yeah, but you've actually got a shot at one. A good one." She shrugged. "You should take it. If not for you, then for the rest of us dumbasses at Hudson Security."

He frowned.

Her eyes rolled. "You have to admit that we're an emotionally stunted lot. But, Xan, you're the best of us. If *you* can't have a good relationship, then there's no way in hell the rest of us can either. And that's fucking depressing."

He ran his hand over his jaw, shaking his head. "Shit, T. No pressure or anything."

She chuckled as Wilson approached, a gym bag slung over his shoulder. "You fuckers done deep-talking yet?" He lifted his chin at Xander. "You coming to breakfast with us?"

He shook his head. "Nah, I've got plans."

"Catch you later then," Wilson replied—well, more like grunted—before he headed toward the exit.

"Look, Xan, I know we've all seen too much, done too much . . . but at the heart of it, you're a good guy. Don't forget that." Tash slapped him on the shoulder. "Besides, we do the hard shit, remember? Don't wimp out now."

He let out a breath. They *did* do the hard shit. They took on dangerous assignments to not only protect but also rescue clients. He'd lost track of how many times he'd been shot at, and he'd been injured countless times. As Tash had said, he'd done too much and seen too much. They all had. But did he have the courage to try and pursue something he knew nothing about? With a woman who was starting to matter more to him with each minute he spent with her?

"Thanks, Tash," he said as she turned toward the exit.

"Stop overthinking things," she called over her shoulder. "Call me later. I want a sitrep."

CHAPTER THIRTEEN

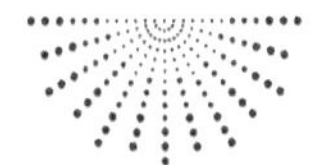

Freya glanced at her reflection in the full-length mirror and frowned. In five minutes, Xander was scheduled to show, and she was 99 percent sure the man was the punctual sort. She skimmed her hands over her hips and turned to the side. Did she have time to change?

Stop! You've changed three times already!

It was ridiculous. Her options were all variations of black clothes. The first outfit had been leggings with a loose tunic top, but it had looked too shapeless and frumpy. The second was ripped black jeans with a baby tee. While cute, it definitely gave off trying-too-hard vibes. The outfit she'd settled on was wide-leg pants with a simple long-sleeved, scoop-necked bodysuit. It was classic and cute, but was it *too* simple?

Ugh! You look fine. Stop being so nervous.

She snorted. Yeah, right. Easier said than done.

Last night had been . . . epic. No, beyond epic.

Their date had been like something out of a romance novel. Their conversation had been easy and flirty. He'd kept his attention on her with zero wandering eyes. That said a lot since a *lot* of women at the bar had checked him out. But he'd kept his focus on her, and it had been wonderful. Then his friends had joined their table, and his obvious initial discomfort had been so cute. Well, if you could describe such a large, muscular man as cute. How he'd talked about the two women after they'd left had nearly made her swoon. The man was so freaking sweet.

And that kiss? Her face heated.

Beyond hot.

She'd initially been surprised when he'd declined her invitation to come in, but right when all the doubts had started to bubble, his words had melted her into a puddle of goo. He wanted to take his time with her.

Holy shit. Who the hell said that?

Face flaming at the memory, she let out a breath. God knew, she was looking forward to their dinner later tonight and was definitely ready to follow Xander's lead. So far, she was enjoying every moment of it.

The brisk knock at her door startled her. She glanced at her watch and smiled. Eight o'clock on the dot. After one last glance at her reflection, she hustled to the door, muttering, "Calm down. You look fine. Obviously, the man likes you."

Her hand stilled on the doorknob. At least he had last night. What if he'd gone home, reevaluated the entire evening, and regretted their kiss. Found her lacking.

A new batch of nerves sprouted in her belly, and she wanted to bash herself over the head. *Stop! Relax and just follow his lead.*

If Xander had second thoughts about yesterday, she'd deal. It would suck, but she'd deal.

She took a breath for courage. Hoping her smile wasn't as nervous looking as it felt, she swung the door open with a chipper, "Good morning!"

She was momentarily struck dumb. All thoughts fled.

Xander took up the doorway. He was dressed casually—a light-gray henley under a distressed dark-brown leather jacket that looked buttery soft, faded jeans, and scuffed work boots. His hair was pulled back into a bun, and his sharp jaw was clean-shaven.

Delicious. The man looked utterly delicious.

She sent a prayer up to the universe that he wasn't having second thoughts about going out with her again.

It took a moment for her to realize he was holding two drinks in his hands. The smaller to-go cup was engulfed in his hand, but she could make out the familiar logo of Comfort Food, one of her favorite local cafes, on the larger plastic cup. Her eyes narrowed, and she tilted her head to the side. She didn't want to get her hopes up, but . . .

She shifted on her feet and nodded at the drink. "Is that for me?"

He held the plastic cup out to her, and a small smile played at the edges of his lips. "Iced sugar-free vanilla latte with oat milk."

Her jaw fell open in surprise. "How did you . . ."

"You mentioned you liked them when you were cutting my hair." He shrugged. "Hope I got it right."

Oh my God, this sweet man.

She took the latte from him and smiled. "Thank you. That was sweet of you. And yes, that's my favorite, even down to the oat milk." She took a step back and held the door open. "Come on in, and I'll grab my jacket."

He didn't move. Instead, he gestured to the stairs with his coffee. "Did you know the door downstairs was wide open?"

Her brows rose at the sharp edge in his voice. Nerves bloomed anew as she easily recognized the work-Xander tone. "Um, yeah. I wasn't sure what time you were showing up, so I propped it open. Is there a problem?"

She took a sip of her latte as she watched a flurry of emotions flash over his face.

After a moment, he cleared his throat and stepped into her apartment, his shoulder holding the door open. "There's no buzzer?" His tone lost that business-mode sharpness.

"No. Like I mentioned last night, it's just me and a storage unit up here," she said, grabbing her jacket and purse from the couch before making her way back to him. "A buzzer system isn't really necessary. I just use the brick to prop the door open when I'm having company over."

"Are they planning on installing a buzzer?" he asked, taking her purse and coffee from her.

"Thanks," she said and donned her jacket. She ushered him into the hallway and turned to lock her door. "I don't think so. Since it's just one apartment up here, I don't think it would be cost effective." She turned to him and shrugged. "It isn't that big of a deal."

"Do me a favor?"

She arched her eyebrow and eyed him up and down. "Depends on the favor."

The corners of his lips kicked up, and he shook his head. "Don't prop your door open. Just have your guests text you when they get here instead." She opened her mouth—not to argue, per se, but he continued before she could say anything. "Please, Freya. It's not safe." He gestured to her apartment door. "There's no peephole, so you can't even check who's at your door without opening it."

She took in his serious face, his tense jaw, and her teasing reply of him being all alpha caveman died on her lips. He really was concerned about her. And damn if that just didn't warm her insides right up. Xander Bonetti was more than just a handsome and sexy guy. He was a good man.

Taking her purse back from him, she tucked her keys inside and set it in the crook of her elbow. "Okay."

"Okay?" He narrowed his eyes, as if he was surprised she'd acquiesced so easily.

She nodded. "What you said makes sense. I'm a single woman living alone. It would be dumb of me not to listen to you. After all, you do work in security."

"That I do," he said, standing straighter with a smug smile growing on his lips.

She plucked her coffee from his hands and gestured to the stairs. "After you."

"Hang on."

She glanced at him and couldn't help but smile at the mischievous twinkle in his brown eyes. What was he up to?

He stepped close and gently tilted her chin up with his finger. Her breath caught, and her heart thudded in her chest as he lowered his head. His lips met hers and tingles shot down her spine.

She sighed into the kiss and reveled in the soft tease of his tongue. After a few glorious seconds, he pulled away.

"Good morning," he whispered.

She knew the grin on her face was dopey. Did she care? Not one bit.

He dropped a kiss to the tip of her nose before straightening. "You look beautiful. I should have started with that instead of going on about your door. I'm sorry about that."

She shook her head. "Xander, you have nothing to apologize for. You were looking out for me."

"I'm glad you think so." He took a sip of his coffee before making his way down the stairs. "I've been told I can be a little overbearing at times."

Following him, she fanned her face and took a huge gulp of her iced latte, hoping it would cool her off. "Like I said, you were looking out for my safety. Nothing wrong with that."

When they stepped onto the sidewalk, she waited while

he closed the door behind them and made sure the lock was engaged. "You know, if it would make you feel safer, I can have my company install some security cameras at the entrance."

She shrugged. "You'd have to check with Mrs. Nagy. She owns the building. I'm just renting."

"Yeah, but if it made *you* feel safer—"

"I'm fine," she said, nudging her shoulder into him as they walked toward his Rover. "I promise."

"Well, it's an open invite." They reached his vehicle, and he opened the passenger side door for her. "If you ever want extra security, just let me know, and I'll work it out with Mrs. Nagy. It's not a problem."

Once she was situated, he closed the door and rounded the hood. She placed her purse on the floor and her drink into the cup holder and waited for him to get settled. Before he started the SUV—and before she could second-guess herself—she reached out and caressed the side of his face.

He stilled completely, and his gaze locked with hers.

She ran her thumb over his cheek, mesmerized with how soft his skin was over the sharp cut of his jaw. "I appreciate you looking out for me. It means a lot."

She held her breath as Xander turned his face, and without taking his gaze from hers, pressed a kiss to her palm. Her heart pinged, and heat curled low in her belly.

"Spend the weekend with me, Frey? I know we talked about dinner tonight, but I don't think that's going to be enough. Spend tomorrow with me too?"

The desire in his eyes was mixed with another emotion she couldn't define. All she knew was she wanted this man. She wasn't going to concern herself with overanalyzing where this was going or whether things were moving too fast. She'd been cautious her entire life and it had gotten her nothing, just dead-end relationships that were all variations of the same dysfunction.

Go with the flow. That was the mantra she was embracing. Forget the rules she'd made for herself, and all the *proper* steps of dating she'd set.

Moving her hand away from his mouth, she raked her fingers through the hair along his nape and tugged him closer. Without giving herself time to think, she pressed her lips to his, kissing and nipping at his lower lip.

He let out a low growl before he deepened their kiss. Her heart raced as his hands ran up her sides. When his fingers gently traced the edges of her breasts, heat pooled between her thighs. What she'd do to have him touch her . . .

A loud honk had her pulling away, breathless.

She chuckled with her hands still buried in his hair, and Xander looked out the driver's side window and flipped off a passing car that was inching by.

In the passenger seat, smiling and waving at them, was a familiar face. Xander's friend Tash.

"It's like I work with a bunch of fucking middle schoolers," Xander muttered, shaking his head as the other car drove away. With a sigh, he took her hands from around his head and pressed a kiss to both of her palms.

Her stomach flipped at the gesture.

Releasing her hands, he leaned back in his seat. The uncertainty in his expression was adorable. "Can I assume that kiss was a yes to spending the weekend together?"

Confident-and-in-control Xander was sexy and had her lady parts tingling. But uncertain Xander? Bullseye straight to the heart.

"You assume correctly," she replied. The relief that flashed over his face had her chuckling again. "Now, we better get going, mister, before I'm late."

·   ·   ·

Twenty minutes later, Freya waved at Audrey as she entered the spa. The soothing scents did nothing to calm the zip of energy coursing through her. A buzz that had nothing to do with the iced latte in her hands, and everything to do with the man who'd gotten her favorite drink.

Their quick drive to the resort had been filled with comfortable chatter. She'd told him more about her brothers, and he'd told her about Tash and Wilson, the guy who'd been driving the honking car. When he'd pulled up to the resort, he'd waved off the valet and waited until they'd gone back into the building before blowing her mind with another smoking-hot kiss. She wasn't embarrassed to admit that her legs had been jelly when she'd stepped out of his SUV.

"Well, aren't you a morning person," Audrey said, smiling at her. "That must be some magical latte because—not that you're a grump or anything—you're not usually this smiley. I mean—" Audrey gasped, shot to her feet, and rounded the front desk. "Oh my God," she whisper-squealed, "did you get lucky with Hottie McHotterson last night?"

If only . . .

"Down, girl." At Audrey's dejected face, Freya laughed. "I don't kiss and tell, you know that. But no, he did not spend the night, though we had a wonderful time."

"That must have been some wonderful time if you're still walking on air," Audrey said, flopping back into her chair. "But I'm glad to see someone other than Hazel getting a hottie."

She shook her head. "Xander's more than just a hottie. He's sweet too." She held up her latte. "He brought me this when he picked me up for work this morning."

Audrey's eyes widened. "Oh my God, that's right! I heard about what happened to your car. Are you okay?"

"I'm good. My car?" She grimaced. "Not so much."

"I'm sorry to interrupt," Miriam said, approaching the front desk. "Freya, I know you still have a few minutes before you clock in, but can I talk with you in my office?" She turned to Audrey. "Since it's still quiet, could you restock the snack bar?"

"Of course," Audrey replied. "Catch me during your break, Freya. I need to know more."

Shaking her head, Freya chuckled and followed Miriam into her office. Taking a seat, she asked, "Everything okay?"

"I hope so," Miriam said, sliding a piece of paper across the desk. "This is the proposed schedule for the rest of the month. I kept your day off tomorrow, but I have you working every day with only next Sunday off this coming week. The following week is Thanksgiving, and Lisa will be off on her two-week cruise. I have you and Sophie working Monday through Wednesday, and as you know, we're closed Thursday. So far, the schedule is pretty light for Friday, but it picks back up Saturday and Sunday. Sophie said she can work all those days. Would you be able to come back Saturday and work the weekend?"

Freya glanced at the color-coded schedule. "That shouldn't be a problem, but let me check in with my brothers. Can I get back to you?"

"Of course, and thank you, Freya. I know this entire schedule upheaval isn't ideal, especially with Thanksgiving coming up, so I appreciate your flexibility." Miriam let out a sigh and leaned back in her chair. "The good news is I've already had nearly a dozen applicants send in their portfolios for the open stylist position. Unfortunately, none of them have a whole lot of experience." Her gaze shifted to her monitor. "Make that a dozen."

"Well, good luck. I hope one of them works out," Freya said, waving the schedule in the air. "And soon."

"Me too. For all our sakes. When I get down to the final

candidates, I'd like you, Sophie, and Lisa to meet with them as well. As you know, our team vibe is important."

"Whatever you need, Mir." Freya rose from her seat.

"Oh!" Miriam exclaimed, halting Freya's steps. "Michael Kwon updated me this morning on what happened with your car. I'm so sorry. You're okay, right?"

She nodded. "It was just shocking."

"I can't imagine. I'm glad Mr. Bonetti was with you."

"Xander's presence was definitely helpful." She was sure she would have figured out what to do had she been by herself. However, she wasn't going to lie. Having Xander there had been beyond reassuring.

Miriam winced. "Well, to add even more inconvenience to an already inconvenient situation, there was a snafu at the rental car company, and they won't be able to deliver your rental car here until Monday midday."

"Oh, okay. Um . . ." She frowned.

"If you need transportation," Miriam rushed on, "I can arrange for the resort shuttle to take you home after your shift."

"You know, Mir, I may be able to get a ride home." Part of her was hesitant to reach out to Xander for a lift home, but if that goodbye kiss was any indication, she didn't think he'd mind. "But I'll let you know if it falls through."

"I'm here all day, just let me know. Thanks again for your flexibility, Freya."

With a wave to her boss, she made her way to the employee lounge. She donned her Pacific View apron, slipped her phone into her pocket, and snagged her coffee and the proposed schedule.

On her way to her station, she waved at Sophie, who was creating an intricate updo on a client. Glancing at the month's schedule, she grimaced. Losing Hazel had thrown a wrench into everyone's plans. The next two weeks were going to be hectic. Not to mention her brothers were probably going to kill her for not staying the entire Thanksgiving weekend.

A printout of her Saturday schedule was laid on top of her workstation. Her first client was a cut, color, and style. Glancing at the time, she saw she had five minutes before the woman would arrive. She pulled out her phone, took a deep breath in, and tried—unsuccessfully—to calm the growing nerves in her belly.

> Bad news. The rental car isn't going to be ready until Monday. If you're not busy, would you be able to pick me up after work?

XANDER

Of course. What do you say to dinner at my place tonight? We can relax and maybe watch a movie after?

She glanced at her packed schedule and cringed.

> That sounds really nice.

Wait—are you a rom-com or action-flick woman?

She couldn't help but grin.

> Both. Though I wouldn't be opposed to watching some classic action flicks. Aliens, Commando or Predator would be my top suggestions.

The dots on the bottom of her screen danced, stopped, and then danced again. Until finally . . .

Holy shit, you're perfect.

> Deal. Let me know what time you think you'll be done and I'll come and get you.

She glanced at her schedule again.

> I should be done by 4:30. And thank you, Xander. I really appreciate the chauffeur services today.

> Trust me, Frey. It's not a hardship driving a beautiful woman around. See you later.

Warmth heated her insides, and that giddy, floating-on-air feeling threatened to engulf her. This time, she embraced it.

Yeah, she was a fan of this new go-with-the-flow thing. It definitely had its perks.

She glanced at the clock and wanted time to move faster. A smile crept over her face thinking about his texts. The end of her shift couldn't come fast enough.

CHAPTER FOURTEEN

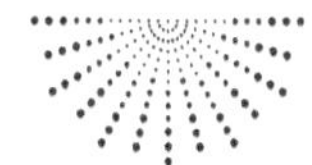

Xander glanced at his phone one last time before cutting his engine. Easing out of his SUV, he pocketed his phone and clicked the lock button on his key fob. He had no clue what was going on between him and Freya aside from their intense chemistry and the fact that he genuinely liked her. He sure as fuck knew nothing about relationships, but he could honestly say he wasn't sorry that Freya's rental car wasn't going to be ready until Monday. Though he didn't know what was happening between them, he knew he enjoyed being with her. Kissing, talking, hanging out, all of it. Now that he'd had a taste of her, he wanted more.

Maybe he needed to take Tash's advice and stop over-thinking things.

He'd simply go with it. No expectations. The attraction between them was crazy, and he was pretty sure they were going to end up in bed. Or on the couch. He wasn't picky. The edges of his lips twitched. Hell, he'd have her however she allowed.

In all honesty though, the connection he had with her was more than just physical. More than wanting a quick fuck. He'd had that before, and this—with Freya—wasn't that. He couldn't quite define it, but it was more.

Tash's words echoed in his head.

Yeah, he needed to stop being a coward and just embrace the unknown. Enjoy it while it lasted. Because he was pretty sure Freya would wise up sooner or later and kick him to the curb. He only hoped it was later rather than sooner. Because that earlier unsettled feeling had turned into a good kind of unsettled. Was that even possible? Did that even make sense?

He blew out a breath and shook his head. Holy shit, he was thinking in circles. The woman most definitely had him all tied up in knots.

His eyes narrowed as a company-issued Range Rover identical to his pulled into the Hudson Security parking lot and parked beside him. Xander crossed his arms over his chest as he waited for the driver to emerge.

"What?" Xander asked as Wilson slammed his door shut and gave him a shit-eating grin. "No honking this time? No partner in crime doing that stupid eyebrow wag?"

Wilson beeped his doors locked and met him at the front of their SUVs. "Public street, dude. You were parked in the middle of down-fucking-town. Pretty sure you traumatized the breakfast crowd by devouring that poor girl's face. God knows, both T and I almost puked watching all that PDA."

"Fuck off," Xander said with a chuckle and then glanced back at Wilson's vehicle. "Where's Tash?"

"We were having breakfast at Comfort Food, and Esme showed up. They started yammering about you and the chick you were sucking face with, so I left." Wilson shrugged. "They're both heading back to Seattle today, so I figured Tash could be Esme's problem until their ferry arrived."

As they entered the building, Xander slapped his friend on the shoulder and laughed. "Ah . . . still bitter that Tash handed you your ass on the mat this morning, I see?"

Wilson shook his head and groaned. "I don't get it, man. I outweigh her by at least sixty pounds. We're both trained in krav and jits, but I swear to God, she has me on the ground and tapping out before I can blink. The girl's a fucking beast."

Xander chuckled as he entered his code to access their secure offices. Well, the entire building was secured, but their actual work area—offices, bullpen, conference rooms, weapons cache—were *secured* secured. "Good thing Tash's on our side, huh? You should have seen what she did to Carmichael the other day. The dumbass didn't tap."

"Fucking idiot," Wilson muttered and lifted his chin at the man in front of them. "What's up, Frazier?"

"Waiting for B to get off a call. You know, just another lovely Saturday morning." Their friend gestured to Bean's closed door. "What are you guys up to?"

"I'm helping Buchanan plan a search and rescue op for Tactical. They have a group coming in next week for training." Wilson nodded to Xander. "This one was busy making out with some chick on Main Street for all of Hudson Island to see."

"For fuck's sake," Xander muttered, running a hand over his mouth. He glared at Wilson. "Seriously?"

The man shrugged and turned his attention back to Frazier. "Apparently, he even took her out last night to dinner, *didn't* fuck her, and then picked her up this morning to take her to work. If it weren't for me and Tash honking, they probably would have gotten arrested for something indecent."

Frazier nodded, crossing his arms over his chest. "That was good of you. If you and T hadn't done that, the lady probably would have been really late to work, and I'm sure that's the last thing the resort spa needs right now. I mean, I'm assuming we're talking about the same lady who gave him that dashing new haircut."

Xander's jaw dropped. He could only stare at his two *supposed* best friends. "You fuckers done?"

Wilson shook his head and held up a finger. "I also have it on good authority that on his way to pick her up, he stopped and picked up her favorite drink. All gentlemanly and shit."

Frazier's face scrunched. "And you're saying he *didn't* fuck her last night?"

"Holy shit, you guys suck," Xander muttered, dropping his head back. He stared at the ceiling and counted to ten. It was that or strangle them both.

"Oh my God, you two, stop," Bean said, stepping into the hallway. Wilson and Frazier cackled like two demented hyenas, and Bean smacked them both in the gut. "Leave the poor guy alone, jerks." She turned to him. "Good morning, Xan. Ignore them. Are you seeing her again?"

Frazier opened his mouth, no doubt to spew more shit Xander's way, but Bean shot him a death glare. "Not one peep, mister. Same goes for you." Wilson held up his hands in surrender, and Frazier wisely shut his trap, though it looked like both were struggling to not laugh. Bean turned her attention back to him. "This is the hairstylist from the Pacific View spa, right?"

He nodded. "Yes, on both counts. We're having dinner tonight at my place."

"Nice. You're a great cook."

Frazier's eyes narrowed. "Wait. How do you know he's a great cook?"

Bean shrugged and a smirk played at the corner of her mouth. "Xan has made many meals for me. God knows, he was cooking for me long before you started to."

He grinned at Frazier, happy to see his friend's smarmy smile was gone.

Bean wasn't wrong. They'd been friends and neighbors for years. They were both workaholics and often worked closely together. Bean also had the appetite and culinary skills of a twelve-year-old boy, so if he wanted any food of substance and nourishment, he was the one doing the cooking. "What do you suggest, B?"

Her lips pursed in thought. "You make a mean chicken parmesan."

"You make chicken parmesan? Since when?" Frazier frowned and glanced at Wilson, who shrugged.

"Since forever, boss man," Bean said, rolling her eyes. "It's my favorite thing Xander makes." She pointed her thumb at Frazier and gave Xander a can-you-believe-this-guy look.

Xander bit back a laugh and held up his hands in a timeout gesture. "I'll take your advice, B, thank you. And if you ever want me to make you some chicken parm, just let me know. You know I'm always at your service." He caught Frazier's gaze, waggled his eyebrows, and then laughed when Frazier flipped him off. "I'm going to help Wilson with the search and rescue scenarios. Call me if you need me back before noon for that security detail meeting."

"Will do." Frazier grimaced. "Though this client may be more high maintenance than we want to deal with. Esme sent me some new intel, and the current issues the client is having with her security team have more to do with her own actions than with the actual security detail."

Xander nodded. "Ah, let me guess. Another celebrity who thinks they know better than the security personnel they hire."

Frazier tapped the tip of his nose. "Got it on one."

"Well," Wilson chimed in, "if you do end up taking the job, I'm pretty sure Team One is going to be busy." He elbowed

Xander in the side and then headed for the exit. "Right, Team One Leader?"

"Right." Xander chuckled and lifted his chin at Frazier and Bean. "Catch you two later."

CHAPTER FIFTEEN

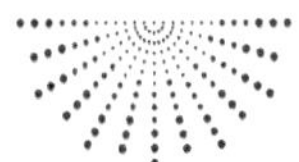

After loading the grocery bags into the back of his SUV, Xander glanced at his watch. He had an hour before he had to pick Freya up from work. He swung by his house to drop off the groceries and then made his way to the Pacific View Resort. Entering the main lobby, he made his way to the reception desk.

"Good afternoon, Mr. Bonetti," the man at the front desk said. "I'm Drew. We met briefly the other day. How can I help you?"

He appreciated that the other man recognized him. Not that Xander thought he was special enough to be recognized on sight, but rather because it boded well for the front desk. It was more than just greeting guests. Situational awareness and facial recognition were critical to the position. It not only would set them apart in terms of customer service, but also in security as the front-desk staff were the first line of defense. Hudson Security had recommended additional training for both the security and front-desk staff, which included tactics on reading body language.

"Hello, Drew. It's good to see you again," Xander said. "Is Sam Abbot from Hudson Security here?"

"Yes, sir. Miss Abbot is in the security office. Feel free to go on back." Xander arched a brow, and the man rushed on as he placed an access card on the counter. "Mr. Kwon let us know that you have full access to the resort, sir."

"Appreciate it," Xander said with a nod. "Have a good day."

Stepping away from the front desk, he made his way to the frosted glass door at the edge of the reception area. Before he could scan his access card, a discreet buzz sounded, unlocking the secure entrance to the resort's management offices. He pulled the door open and stepped into a smaller reception area. This time, the desk sat unattended.

"What's up, dude?" a voice called out from the office to his right.

"Hey, Abbot," he said, stepping into the resort's security room. It was a large room and was as frigid as a damn meat locker. His colleague was seated at a long desk with a slew of monitors in front of her, all showing various feeds from around the resort. How she kept track of everything, he had no clue. But given the resort's setup was smaller than Abbot's setup at Hudson Security, this was probably child's play to her. He tilted his head toward the empty reception desk. "Isn't that supposed to be manned?"

She spun in her chair to face him and rolled her eyes. "Ortiz's assistant is allowed to step away from her desk to pee, you know."

He held up his hands. "Hey, I'm just making sure."

"*Right*. What brings you to the resort? In need of another haircut, Viking boy?"

"Holy shit," he muttered, running a hand over his jaw.

"Hey, what can I say? Our office loves to gossip. You should probably stop cutting your own hair, because you always make it look like shit." She grinned at him and made a circular motion with her hand. "That haircut makes you look good. Still tough-looking and definitely more put together, but way less DIY."

He furrowed his brow. "I don't know what that means, so I'm just going to say thank you. I think. Anyway, as you probably already know, I'm picking up Freya—"

She snorted. "Of course, I already know that."

"But I wanted to check in with you first." Yeah, Abbot was definitely trying to give Tash a run for her money on giving him shit. "How's the security camera installation going?"

"Fine, we'll talk about work. You're no fun," she grumbled before waving at the monitors. "Good. No issues. Ortiz gave the go-ahead on all our suggestions including the upgrades. The install for the perimeter security fencing is about two weeks out, and when that goes up, so will the perimeter game cameras. Within the resort, the only cameras left to install are the ones around the meditation center and yoga facility on the north side and the ones at the outdoor challenge course. Those are all on Witherspoon's docket for tomorrow."

Xander nodded. "Great. Any new info on the vehicle vandalisms?"

Abbot wrinkled her nose. "One, I'm sorry to hear that happened to your lady's car. And two, unfortunately not. Cameras are up in the employee parking lot now, but the old cameras didn't pick up anything. Just to be sure, I sent the footage from all the nearby cameras to Bean. She has some program that . . ." Abbot shook her head. "You probably don't care about specifics, but basically, B can pull all the faces off the security cameras and cross-check them against the resort guests and staff. She can see if there was someone at the resort who wasn't supposed to be here and also see who was anywhere near the employee parking lot yesterday. It's a long shot, but you never know."

"I appreciate that." It was indeed a long shot, but it was all they had at this point. He nodded at the monitors. "Want to run through the cameras that were installed today?"

"I was hoping you'd say that. Have a seat, my friend," Abbot said, kicking out the rolling chair beside her. "You know I love this shit, but I've been staring at these feeds all day. I could use another set of eyes."

For the next thirty minutes, they went over the new video feeds, making slight adjustments to the angles to ensure there were no blind spots.

"Thanks for the assist." Abbot leaned back into her chair and stretched her arms over her head. "Now get out of here. You don't want to be late picking up your lady friend."

When she chuckled, he pursed his lips, his eyes shooting to the monitors. "Please tell me you aren't going to spy on me."

Abbot's eyes widened in shock. Clarification: fake shock that was so obviously full of shit it was ridiculous. "*Moi?*"

With a resigned sigh, he stood. "I take it there's no point in asking you not to?"

"You'd be absolutely fucking correct, buddy."

Abbot's wide, gleeful grin had him shaking his head as he made his way to the door. "At least tell everyone I swept her off her feet with my charm or some shit."

She chuckled. "You got it. See ya, Viking boy!"

It was a short walk to the spa building, and with each step Xander took, anticipation had his nerves humming. Using his access card, he let himself into the building. The euca-lyptus scent held a hint of lavender today.

A handful of women milled about in the spa waiting area, and another two guests stood at the front desk. Waving at Audrey, he stepped into the salon's waiting area and came to a halt.

Freya stood a few feet away with a black salon cape in her arms. She grinned up at him, and it was like a punch to the head. Her smile left him dazed every damn time.

"Hey, Freya." Holy shit, did his voice just crack? He inter-nally cringed.

Clearing his throat, he shoved his hands into his jeans pockets. More than anything, he wanted to pull her into his arms, but he was pretty damn sure that wouldn't be appro-priate. It was one thing kissing her in his car—even if his friends heckled him. It was another thing entirely to kiss her at her place of employment. "I'm a little early, so whenever you're ready."

Hours had passed since he'd dropped her off, and he knew she must have been on her feet nearly the entire time, but she still looked fresh and bright. Not a hair was out of place, and she damn near glowed.

"I'm almost done." She raised the cape in her hands. "Let me just put this away, clean up a little, and I'll grab my things."

"Take your time," he said as she spun and hustled to the employees-only area. Turning, he caught Audrey's gaze. "How're you doing?"

She was grinning from ear to ear. "Good. It's nice to see you again, Mr. Bonetti."

"Please. Xander is fine." Mr. Bonetti made him feel ancient. Well, he supposed in comparison to Audrey, he *was* ancient.

"So, Xander," Audrey said with a mischievous look crossing her face. "Isn't Freya just the best? Did you know that in the entire time she's worked here, she's never had—"

"Oh no. Don't believe a thing she says," Freya interrupted, giving the young woman a stern look.

Audrey simply laughed and waved at them in a shooing motion. "Have a good night, you two. Enjoy your day off tomorrow, Freya."

With his hands still tucked in his pockets, he nodded at Audrey and popped his elbow out for Freya to take. Once they were outside, she squeezed his arm. "Hi," she said, glancing up at him with that sweet and slightly shy look coloring her face.

He couldn't resist.

Stopping in the middle of the empty walkway, he turned to face her and framed her face in his hands. Pure male satisfaction surged through him when her breath hitched. He lowered his head and pressed a soft kiss to her lips. He would have given anything to deepen the kiss, but he was conscious of where they were. Not only could anyone walk by, but he knew there were at least two cameras on them.

Easing away, he kissed the tip of her nose. "Hi." He dropped another kiss to her forehead. "You look beautiful."

She shook her head and started them down the walkway again, but not before he saw her smile and the soft blush staining her cheeks. "Thanks again for picking me up."

"Anytime, Frey." When she linked her fingers with his, he wanted to beat his damn chest like a caveman. "How was your day?"

"Oh, it was a day," she replied with a chuckle.

As they walked to his SUV, with a stop at the front desk to drop off his access card, Freya told him about a couple of fun clients she'd had. When they were seated in his car, she spilled the beans on a very demanding, high-maintenance client.

"Luckily, the woman checks out tomorrow." Freya frowned as she buckled her seat belt.

He grinned and started the vehicle. "Do I sense a but?"

She scrunched her nose, and it was so damn cute.

Letting out a sigh, she said, "She mentioned that she really liked the color I gave her and is now hoping to get on my monthly schedule. She lives up in Vancouver and has to figure out how to break up with her current stylist first, so who knows."

"That's quite the trek for a haircut," he murmured, pulling out of the parking spot. "And couldn't she just not make another appointment with her current person?"

Freya chuckled. "Oh no. When you've been with your stylist for a while, you can't just start seeing someone else. There's a breakup process."

He glanced her way. "Seriously?"

"It's a thing." She shrugged. "And the distance isn't a problem for this woman. She gets to and from the resort in a private helicopter."

"Ah, I assume that's part of the high-maintenance bit?"

"You assume correctly." She grinned at him. "So what do you have in mind for dinner?"

A sudden onslaught of nerves had his hands tightening on the steering wheel. He was usually calm and even-keeled, but this beautiful woman had him off-kilter. "Do you like chicken parmesan?"

Holy shit. If he could slap himself upside the head, he would. He really should have checked with her before he'd gone grocery shopping. What if she hated it? What if she had food allergies? What if—

"Uh, who doesn't?"

Relief washed over him.

"Seriously, Xan, I'm not picky, so whatever you have planned will be great." She quickly squeezed his arm before letting go.

He missed her touch.

Fuck.

He didn't want to think too hard about that wayward thought.

Thankfully, his turn was coming up. He pulled into his private road and gestured toward his house and the neighboring houses farther down the road. "This is all technically company housing. When Gavin Frazier started Hudson Security—which we passed back down the main road by De La Rosa Gym—he bought eight acres out here and built five houses. My place and the next three all have the same floor plan. The biggest one at the end is Frazier's house. Our head of cybersecurity used to live in the place next to his, but they ended up getting together, and she just moved in with him. The two houses in the middle are used by various staff who don't live on the island. Tash and Esme tend to use them the most."

"Oh, they don't live on Hudson Island?"

Xander shook his head. "No, they both have places in Seattle, but they're here at least a couple times a month."

He pulled into the garage and cut the engine. The swarm of nerves were back—hell, they'd never really left—and he cleared his throat. "Um, it's not the biggest place or anything," he began as they got out of the SUV, "but it's comfortable."

It was comfortable, but it sure as hell wasn't fancy. Furniture-wise, he had the basics. His decor was lacking, as Tash was always happy to point out. He didn't know the first thing about decorating and had never really cared. Until this very damn moment . . .

What if she thought his place was a shitty bachelor pad? What if cooking dinner for her was a horrible idea?

Freya chuckled. She met him at the front of the SUV and looped her arm with his. "Xander, I'm sure your place is great. I live in an apartment the size of a shoebox. I'm not gonna judge. Trust me."

Too late to back out now.

He let out a breath and nodded. "Don't say I didn't warn you," he muttered, shooting her a wink.

The man was ridiculous. So stinking cute, but ridiculous nonetheless. Who would have thought the tall, muscular man who sported a deliciously hot man bun and basically screamed *alpha* with every fiber of his being would be nervous to show her his home?

She wasn't going to lie. That little crack in his macho armor was endearing. Sweet. And sexy as hell.

Focusing back on the tour, she followed Xander down a hall and glanced around. His house was really nice. Sure, it wasn't gigantic, but it was big enough. The comfortable space had two bedrooms and two and a half bathrooms with a living room and kitchen combo that was open and airy. There were a ton of windows and high ceilings, so it didn't feel cramped. At the far end of the great room was the most gigantic television Freya had ever seen mounted on the wall —and she had four brothers, so that said *a lot*.

The dark-brown leather furniture was equally gigantic and plush looking. Granted, the walls were bare, but with so many windows, it wasn't noticeable. There also wasn't a knickknack in sight. However, Xander didn't strike her as a knickknack type of guy.

"And that's the place," he said, leading her back into the

kitchen. He shoved his hands into his pockets, rocked back on his heels, and gave her a sheepish smile.

She probably shouldn't find his uncertain smile so attractive, but she did. "Your house is great. Pretty sure my entire apartment can fit in there." She gestured to the living area. "Now what can I do to help with dinner?"

He pressed some buttons on his oven, turned to the fridge, and began pulling food out and placing everything on the island. "It pretty much makes itself. Can I get you something to drink? Beer, wine, soda . . ." He looked in the fridge and bent to dig deeper. "I think I have some juice hiding somewhere."

"Oh, a glass of ice water is fine." Though not as fine as the denim-clad ass she was currently checking out. Pressing her lips together, she averted her gaze when he straightened and turned back to her with a bottle of beer in his hand.

He placed it on the counter and pulled a glass from the cabinet. After filling the glass with ice and water from the dispenser in the fridge door, he placed it in front of her and grabbed the bottle of beer. "Do you mind?"

She shook her head. "Not at all. As you know, I'm not opposed to alcohol, but if I have a drink tonight, I'll probably end up falling asleep on you."

"Wouldn't want that." A sexy smile played at the edges of his lips before he took a swig of his beer. "I have plans for you."

She eyed him up and down, taking her time. "Do you now?" Her heart galloped in her chest. Uh, who was this flirty woman? It couldn't actually be *her*, could it? But the heat in his gaze made her bold, made her confident that he wouldn't turn her away. Rounding the island, she moved to stand in front of him.

His hands settled on her hips. "Yes, ma'am, I sure do."

"Well." She placed her palms against his solid chest. The

racing beat of his heart had her insides melting a little more for him. "In case I forget to say it later, Xander Bonetti, thank you for inviting me over for dinner tonight. I had a really great time." She fisted her hands in his shirt and tugged.

As Xander lowered his head, she rose onto her tiptoes and met him halfway. His lips were soft against hers, but everything intensified after a heartbeat. His tongue traced the seam of her lips, and she eagerly opened for him. He deepened their kiss, pulling her flush against him. He tasted of beer and something uniquely him. She wanted more.

He wrapped his arms tightly around her, and she moaned when she felt the hard press of him against her belly. She delved her fingers into his hair, and satisfaction tore through her when he growled.

Then another growl sounded. Loudly. A growl that had them stilling.

It sounded again, and she cringed.

Her stomach.

"Oh my God," she murmured, dropping her forehead to Xander's chest.

She felt the rumble of his laughter. "I take it that's my cue to get dinner started?"

Glancing up at him, she grinned and marveled that his arms were still around her, that whatever this was, it wasn't awkward, and she probably could stay like this with him all day. "I didn't get to finish my lunch."

He arched an eyebrow in question.

"I was halfway through my smoothie—"

"A smoothie isn't lunch, Frey."

She rolled her eyes. "It was a really *big* smoothie." His eyebrow arched higher, and she chuckled. "Trust me, the resort does smoothies right. But anyway, Angelica—Mrs. High-Maintenance—showed up early and didn't want to wait, so I never got around to finishing my lunch."

"Well then, it's a good thing this chicken parm recipe is quick." He tipped her chin up with his finger and kissed her. A soft, swoony kiss that made the butterflies in her stomach dance. "To be continued."

"Yes, please," she whispered against his lips.

He growled again, deep in his throat, as he stepped away. "Why don't you grate the parm?" He pushed a plate with a wrapped hunk of parmesan on it toward her. "There's a microplane grater in the drawer behind you."

As he stepped away and turned his back to her, she fanned herself. Cheese. Right. Grate cheese. *Not* jump the man. At least not until after dinner . . .

Smiling to herself, she grabbed the fancy grater and unwrapped the cheese. For a moment, she simply watched him. When he said he'd make her dinner, she wasn't quite sure what she'd been expecting, but it wasn't this. She'd expected stilted conversation with a dose of awkward. Not that any of the time they'd spent together had been like that, but because . . . Well, that's how things tended to end up with her. Things started out good but then devolved. But Xander? He was unlike anyone she'd ever met before. The more time she spent with him, the more she was appreciating it, appreciating *him.*

Watching him move around the kitchen calmed her. For such a large man, he moved with ease and grace. For as long as she could remember, her brothers had teased her, saying that they always knew where she was because she walked like a stomping elephant. Even though she was barely over five-two, they weren't wrong. Delicate walking had never been her thing.

As Xander swiftly laid out his ingredients on the island, it was obvious this wasn't his first time making this meal. In one glass dish, he quickly combined the breadcrumb concoction with an array of spices—with no measuring spoon in sight. He broke two eggs into another dish, expertly breaded the chicken pieces, and laid them into a third dish. Finally, he popped the chicken dish into the preheated oven and set the oven timer.

She grinned as he washed his hands, then pulled out a chopping board, some fresh herbs, and a few zucchinis. "Mr. Bonetti, I'm going to go out on a limb and assume this is not your first chicken parmesan rodeo."

"Your assumption is correct, Miss Hansen. And for the record, adding in panko is the secret," he said, winking at her. "I can make a handful of dishes, but it was heavily suggested that I make this for you tonight."

Her eyebrow rose. "Oh?"

"My friend Bean says this is the best meal I make, and since the woman's a certified genius, I take her advice seriously."

"Smart man. So you can cook—"

"Only a handful of dishes," he said with an easy grin. "Don't want to set the bar too high, you know."

From where she was standing, the bar was looking pretty damn impressive. The guy was something else.

"Hmm . . ." She stared at him with narrowed eyes and pursed lips. There had to be a fatal flaw somewhere.

He cringed. "I'm afraid to ask what that 'hmm' means."

"There's gotta be something you do that's annoying."

He barked out a laugh. "Baby, I can get Tash and Wilson on the phone. They'll be more than happy to list my annoying qualities."

She highly doubted that. The way he talked about his friends, she was certain that after some initial teasing, they'd be listing his accolades. "Do you talk during movies?"

"I don't know," he hedged. "What's your opinion on talking during movies?"

She shook her head and tsked. "Uh, uh, uh. Looks like we'll find out later during the movie portion of our evening."

"Yikes. No pressure or anything." He made a face that was equal parts adorable and sexy.

Yeah, this guy was too much.

A nagging voice whispered in her brain, reminding her that she had strict dating rules for herself. Rules she'd established to protect herself. No kissing until date two. No rounding the bases until seven dates. No sex until after two months of dating.

Another voice—a louder, disarmingly confident one—scoffed. Where had those damn rules gotten her? Nowhere.

Actually, no.

Those ridiculous rules had resulted in one disastrous relationship after another. But it had all led her to this moment. Standing with a man she'd technically already kissed before they'd had their first date. A man who, after their first official date, had given her a panty-melting kiss. A man who'd not only gone out of his way to chauffeur her to and from work, but who was a bona fide gentleman.

She was chucking those rules out the window, because they'd done the job. They'd led her to this exact moment, and while every part of her wanted to forget dinner and get back to kissing the man, she knew there was no rush. Because the way he was looking at her left no question that they'd get there, probably sooner rather than later. In the meantime, she was going to focus on the now. On the man who was making her dinner and who she was determined to get to know better.

Anticipation zinged through her, and she remembered a question she'd wanted to ask when they'd arrived at his house. "When we pulled in earlier, was that a motorcycle I saw in your garage?"

The way his eyes lit up had her stomach fluttering. The man truly was ridiculously handsome.

"It is. It's a Panigale. Do you ride?"

She shook her head, racking her brain for any sort of information she knew about motorcycles. She internally winced. Not the best conversation starter since she didn't know much. "No, but one of my brothers does. He has a Ninja H2-something—at least that's what I think it is—and to hear him talk about it, you'd think it was his baby."

"I don't blame him. That's a nice bike. Has your brother taken you out?"

She shook her head again. "I've actually never ridden. Too scared."

Understatement of the century. It had taken her years to get behind the wheel of a car after the . . . accident. Such a simple word for something so horrific.

Her mind shot to the past. Crushed behind her steering wheel, unable to move, unable to call for help, unable to do anything. But she shoved the memory away. Not the time or the place.

To this day, she was still a nervous driver. She couldn't begin to imagine being on a motorcycle.

"In all honesty," Xander said, his attention thankfully on prepping dinner, "I haven't ridden much lately. I was in a car accident back in March and had to do some PT. Once I was good to go, things got busy at work." He shrugged. "When the weather gets nicer, maybe I can convince you to join me."

She injected as much levity into her voice as she could muster. "I wouldn't hold your breath." Clearing her throat, she asked, "So are you originally from Hudson Island?"

Not the most subtle change of topic, but Xander didn't seem to notice. Or at least, he pretended not to, which she was grateful for.

"No. I'm originally from Oregon. Grew up all over the

Portland area," he said, adding the sliced zucchini chunks onto a sheet pan. "I joined the Army right after high school and did that for thirteen years. I served with Frazier my last four. We left the Army around the same time, and a few months later, when he started Hudson Security, he called me. Dude's a stand-up guy, so it was a no-brainer to join him here. Back then, the company was just me, Frazier, Bennett Wilson—who was also in the Army with us—and Oliver MacKay, Hudson Security's number two. He's based in London."

"Is it bodyguard type stuff or like the security stuff you did at Pacific View?" She winced. "Sorry, I guess I'm not quite sure what it is you do."

"That's absolutely fine. Hell, half the time I don't know what I'm doing either." He grinned, and it wasn't lost on her that he hadn't clarified what it was that he actually did. But she'd go with it. "When we first started out, between Frazier's and MacKay's contacts, we had a good number of personal security jobs—the bodyguard type of work. Corporate executive big-wigs, politicians, celebrities, that kind of thing. Esme and Tash came on board next, and with them, we were able to expand to add corporate security and consulting to the mix. Then Bean came on and added the cybersecurity element to the company, which was a game changer. The woman's brilliant, a bona fide genius. From there, we just grew."

There was a lightness when he spoke about his work, a fondness when he mentioned his colleagues. She was glad he had that. "You love what you do and the people you work with."

"I do. The crew we have is great. We're looking at adding personnel, and it's been tough. More like a headache, actually." He chuckled as he cut thin slices of mozzarella and set them aside. "We're a tight-knit group and have a lot of common ground between us. I'd go to bat for any of them, but I'll admit, there are a handful in particular who are like my family. Almost all of us are former military or alphabet agency, and we did a lot of shit, saw a lot of shit. We're all highly trained in very specific skills that don't translate well to civilian life. So when Frazier offered me a position at Hudson Security . . ." He shrugged. "I get to do what I'm good at. Not only that, but it's with a group of people I completely respect and without a bunch of bureaucratic red tape."

A dark shadow flashed over his face. There was a story there, she was sure of it. But everything inside her told her it wasn't a happy one. The last thing she wanted was to prod and have him rip open old wounds. "If you ever want to talk about any of that, get any of it off your chest, I've been told I'm a good listener."

The oven beeped.

"I appreciate that, Frey. And who knows? I may take you up on that." Removing the dish of chicken from the oven, he quickly flipped the pieces and took the parmesan she'd grated and sprinkled a thin layer over the top. He placed the chicken dish back into the oven, added the sheet pan of seasoned zucchini to the lower rack, and reset the timer.

After setting the small plate of sliced mozzarella and a bowl of marinara to the side, he quickly cleaned the kitchen and shooed her away when she tried to help. Once he was done, he rounded the island, took her hand, and pulled her toward the couch. "To echo your earlier comment, thanks for having dinner with me tonight."

She took in the cut of his jaw and the five-o'clock shadow, the lines of his strong back beneath his long-sleeved shirt, and the feel of his calloused hand in hers. "Believe me, the pleasure's all mine."

"Doubt that, Frey." He shot her a wink before glancing back at the oven. "We have twenty-five minutes until the chicken's ready," he said as he sat on the couch and tugged her down so she sat across his lap. He snaked his fingers into her hair, and her breath caught. "May I please kiss you until then?"

She may have nodded, she wasn't quite sure. She could only focus on his hypnotic brown eyes and the way his thumb gently caressed her cheek. Then his lips were on hers, and she couldn't focus at all. Her pulse went from zero to sixty within a heartbeat.

Her hands found his solid chest, and gripping his shirt, she sank into the kiss. Electricity shot through every nerve as she tangled her tongue with his. Her body was on fire, but she wanted more.

"Hang on," she murmured, pushing against his chest.

Xander immediately stilled and pulled away slightly. She could see the apology in his gaze, and she shook her head. Quickly untangling herself from his arms, she stood.

"Freya, sweetheart," he began, worry and regret warring on his face. "I'm so sor—"

She pressed her finger against his lips and quickly straddled him. Her knees sank into the plush couch on either side of his hips, and she replaced her finger with her mouth. "I'm not going anywhere," she murmured, nipping at his bottom lip. "I just needed to get a little more comfortable." Pressing her chest flush against his, she rocked her hips. "Hope you don't mind."

His hands squeezed her hips and rocked her harder. "Not at all."

She lost track of how long they made out. Her focus was entirely on Xander and the explosions he set off within her. His mouth was downright magical, and while his gentle hands explored her, he kept everything over her clothes, not rushing. The hard bulge she rocked against told her they'd get there in due time.

"I feel like I'm back in high school," he said when they came up for air.

She tsked. "Naughty, naughty boy."

"Like you didn't make out with dudes in high school?"

She scoffed. "I'll have you know, mister, I never even dated in high school."

He rolled his eyes. "Yeah, right."

"It's true. My brothers didn't let me date, and besides, I was a late bloomer." She shrugged. "However, you're definitely making me reevaluate the merits of a good ole make-out session."

He laughed. "I don't know if that's a good thing or a bad thing."

She rocked her hips once more and was rewarded with a deep, throaty groan. She arched a brow.

"A good thing. Definitely a good thing." He grinned, and for a moment, he simply stared at her. He tucked a stray lock of hair behind her ear and murmured, "You're so damn pretty, Freya."

She melted at his words. "Thank you."

"And I hope you don't think I'm being presumptuous, but I don't want our first time to be a quickie on the couch before dinner. Hence"—he ran his hands up and down her back—"keeping things above the clothes."

She desperately wanted to feel his hands on her skin but agreed. Something told her the man would make the wait worth her while. Grinning, she laced her fingers behind his neck and nipped at his lower lip. "That's fine with me so long as you promise we'll get there sooner rather than later."

His hands met her hips, and he lifted up, rocking her against him. His hard bulge hit her in the perfect spot, and she gasped.

"You were saying?" His mouth was back on hers, and he

found a spot along her neck that sent shivers tearing through her.

"Don't remember. Just don't stop doing that."

"I want you to get yourself off on me." His hands cupped her ass as he guided her, grinding her against his hard length. "You feel so good, Frey."

The heat surging through her grew as she continued to rub herself against him. The tension within her built, and her breaths became erratic.

"That's it, baby. I want to watch you come."

His hips pressed up again, and she ground down hard against him. Moments later, she detonated. Spasms rocked her body, and she fused her mouth to his. God, this man . . .

"That was so fucking hot," he murmured against her lips. "Can't wait to see that again."

She met his gaze, and the desire staring back at her had her reaching for the button on his jeans. "I'm sure that can be arranged—"

The oven timer sounded.

She frowned when he covered her hands, stilling her movements. Xander had just bestowed her with her first non-self-administered orgasm in forever, and she was feeling all kinds of good, but the large bulge she'd been rubbing against was still prominent. "But you didn't—"

He kissed her words away. "Don't worry about me. You're fucking beautiful and watching you come was worth every second." He kissed the tip of her nose. "Dinner first." Wrapping his arms around her, he quickly stood, making her yelp.

When her feet hit the ground, she chuckled. "Holy moly, you're strong."

"It helps that you're a tiny little thing." He playfully slapped her on the rear and made his way to the kitchen.

He removed both items from the oven and set them on the stovetop. He added the marinara and the thinly sliced mozzarella atop the chicken pieces and placed it back into the oven to broil. While he waited for that, he scooped the perfectly blistered zucchini chunks into a serving dish and topped it with a little of the grated parm.

The savory aroma filling the kitchen made Freya's mouth water, and her stomach let out an angry growl. Yeah, they could get back to the make-out session after dinner. Something told her she'd need all the energy she could get to keep up with the potent man.

Once Xander pulled the finished chicken parmesan from the oven and plated their food, they settled at the small dining table and dug in. The chicken had maintained its perfect crispiness while the mozzarella provided just the right amount of gooey goodness. The parm gave it a kick of saltiness, and the marinara tied it all beautifully together.

"Oh my God, Xander." She moaned around a bite of food. "This is heaven."

He chuckled and sent her a heated look. "Not gonna lie, baby, I was hoping to hear those words under different circumstances."

She grinned and popped another bite of food into her mouth. "You never know," she teased. "The night is still young."

"Indeed it is." He winked at her, and for a few moments, they focused on their food. "So, Freya, tell me about this big family of yours. Are your folks having a packed house this Thanksgiving?"

Her chest squeezed. Even after all these years, there were times it felt like yesterday. "My parents actually passed when I was in middle school."

"Oh shit, I'm so sorry."

She shook her head. "Thank you. Even though my parents aren't with us anymore, it'll still be a packed house. I grew up in Blanchard Bay. It's a little coastal town about a dozen miles south of the Canadian border. My oldest brother lives in our childhood home with his twin girls. We all go there for Thanksgiving, and it's absolute chaos."

"I'm sure." He ate another bite before asking, "Is it okay to ask how they passed?"

Her mind flashed to all those years ago. Being called out of English class and seeing Axel waiting for her in the principal's office. The devastation on his face. He'd only been a young man himself, and yet he'd been her rock. He'd been the rock for all their siblings.

Xander squeezed her hand, and she swallowed past the lump in her throat. "Plane crash. It was their twenty-fifth wedding anniversary, and they'd chartered one of those little Cessnas over to Victoria."

"Freya, baby, I'm so sorry."

She turned her hand and laced her fingers with his. She wasn't going to question the comfort she found in his touch. Instead, she was going to embrace her new mantra and just go with it. "Somehow, we made it through, but it was a rough few years." She lowered her voice in an exaggerated whisper. "Believe it or not, I wasn't exactly the easiest teenager."

Understatement of the century. Her biggest act of rebellion had had devastating consequences. It was something she'd never forgive herself for.

"Even though I know my brothers mean well, they drive me crazy. Especially Axel, the oldest. He was twenty-three when our folks passed. The twins were nineteen, and my other brother was eighteen. Axel became my legal guardian, so I didn't have to go into foster care. He took on the father-figure role as best he could, and I'm sure you can imagine how smoothly—or not smoothly in my case—that went." The edges of her lips tipped up in a bittersweet smile. "With hindsight, I can see that Axel sacrificed the most for all of us. Even so, he's also the one I want to strangle the most.

Considering he's a detective with the Blanchard Bay PD, that would be frowned upon."

"I'd say so." Xander chuckled. "And your other brothers?"

"The twins—Oscar and Jasper—are four years younger than Axel and run the construction company our dad started years ago. Then there's Finn. He's an EMT and probably the one I'm closest to." She smiled. "I'll be staying with him for Thanksgiving so Axel and I don't kill each other."

"Is it that bad?"

"Yes and no. He treats me like I'm an irresponsible teenager, and so I revert to said teenager to piss him off." She shrugged. "Rinse and repeat."

It was on the tip of her tongue to tell Xander *why* Axel treated her the way he did. That she had, in fact, been the most irresponsible of all teenagers and had hurt so many people. Destroyed so many lives. But that wasn't a conversation she wanted to have. Ever. She enjoyed how Xander treated her—like she was special and good. If he knew what she'd done all those years ago . . .

She cleared her throat. "What about you? You mentioned joining the Army and then Hudson Security? What about your family? Are they still in Oregon?"

A look flashed over his face before it settled into a carefully blank expression, one that was similar to his work-Xander look. "No family. Apparently, my mom was a junkie who OD'd when I was three. I went into foster care and bounced around until I ended up at a group home at fifteen. I got into a lot of trouble, was a hothead who knew everything." He gazed off to the side, as if carefully choosing his words. "A couple guys I hung with got picked up for robbing a convenience store. I was supposed to be with them but got the meet-up time wrong. One of the guys had just turned eighteen. He was armed and got nine years. That was a big wake-up call."

Her heart went out to him. "I'm sorry. That must have been tough."

"It was what it was." He shrugged. "After that, I did my best to keep my nose clean until I could enlist."

"Was joining the Army what you'd hoped it was going to be?"

"It was definitely different than what I'd expected." A small smile lifted the edges of his lips, softening his guarded look. "It was good. It gave me structure I didn't know I needed. Gave me brothers I didn't know I wanted."

Her chest squeezed. The man was remarkable. "Well, you should be proud of yourself."

His eyes narrowed in question.

"My brothers and I had our folks as role models. We had them for shorter than we wanted, but we saw the kind of people we wanted to be. My brothers are giant pains in the ass, but they're stand-up guys. And you, Xander Bonetti, are a good man, and you did it all on your own. That's beyond admirable." She held his gaze and silently dared him to look away. He didn't. "I can see in your eyes you don't believe me. But trust me, Xander. It's impressive. *You're* impressive."

He shook his head and brought their still-joined hands to his lips. He pressed a kiss to the back of her palm and stood. "You're too sweet. Now, how about that movie?"

He didn't believe her, but that was okay. She was persistent and could be patient when she wanted to be. And with Xander, she wanted to be. "Sure," she said, rising. She grabbed their empty plates and brought them to him at the sink. "I can load the dishwasher since you cooked."

"No way in hell, baby." He dropped a kiss to her forehead. "Why don't you go pick a movie, and I'll clean up here."

Wrapping her arms around his waist, she pulled him into a hug. His arms went around her, and she propped her chin on his chest, looking up at him. "Thank you again for dinner.

For the conversation. For the make-out session. For being so good to me."

His hands framed her face, and his lips found hers. "Thank *you*. You make everything easy. Now go find us a good movie."

It took her a few minutes to figure out Xander's television. What was the male obsession with televisions and receivers and countless remote controls? She was a point-and-click kind of girl. After going through a few different streaming services, she was able to find one of her favorite movies. *Aliens*.

Grabbing a blanket from the back of the recliner, she curled up on the couch. Her eyes were heavy when Xander approached. "You have room for another?" he asked.

She scooted to the front edge of the couch and patted behind her. "You're in luck."

He climbed in, and her heart skipped as she settled against him. His arm wrapped around her waist, and he pulled her close.

This. She could get used to this.

After the movie started, she whispered, "Is it weird that this is a comfort movie for me?"

He chuckled. "Same. Pretty sure I can recite every line."

She smiled. It was the same for her. She even knew all the words to the director's cut. The movie had been one of her parents' favorites.

When Ripley and the Marines were shooting up the aliens, Xander's phone rang.

"Sorry," he groaned, reaching over her to the coffee table where he'd left his phone. "I have to take this. It's the boss."

"Go ahead," she said, stifling a yawn. She moved to get up, but he wrapped his arm around her waist, halting her. He tucked her close and brought his phone to his ear. As he answered, he pulled them back down to the couch.

"What's up, Frazier?"

"Sorry to be calling so late," Freya heard the other man say. "I just got off the phone with Esme. There's a problem with one of the candidates we declined."

Tuning their conversation out, Freya shifted so she was better cocooned against him. She tried to focus on the movie, but Xander's cedar-and-soapy scent filled her nose. As he spoke, his voice was a quiet, soothing rumble. Each blink became a chore, and with her head against his chest, the vibrations of his deep baritone lulled her to sleep.

CHAPTER SIXTEEN

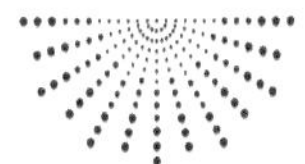

X ander had been awake for the last couple of hours. He was used to waking up at the crack of dawn to work out, and Sundays were no exception. But this morning, he didn't move. In fact, he'd lain as still as possible. The last thing he wanted was to disturb the warm weight pressed against him. He took a deep breath, and the soft floral scent of Freya's shampoo filled his nose.

Thank God he'd listened to Esme years ago and had gone with the oversized and overpriced couch, because he and Freya fit it comfortably. Well, *he* fit it comfortably, she was tiny enough to lie completely sprawled over him.

The corners of his lips lifted.

Who was he kidding? Even if he'd had the world's most uncomfortable couch, there was no way he'd move a muscle. Because this? Freya sleeping comfortably on top of him? It was everything.

Over the last couple of hours, as he'd lain there listening to the early morning quiet, he'd had time to think. Or rather, he'd had time to go down the what-the-hell-are-you-doing rabbit hole. However, he'd also had time to crawl back out of said hole.

Freya, the intoxicating woman who'd been a stranger only a handful of days ago—holy shit, had it really been less than a week?—made him want things he'd never thought possible. Sex aside, he wanted this. Having dinner together and talking about their days. Falling asleep together and waking up with her in his arms.

Hell, Xander wanted to meet her brothers. He wanted to see for himself the men who'd banded together to raise their little sister. He wanted her to meet Wilson and Frazier and Bean. Wanted her to get to know Tash and Esme better.

He sure as hell didn't deserve her—she was so damn good—but if she was willing to give him a chance, he'd take it. For the first time ever, he was thinking of a future. Of sharing his future. With her.

It scared the shit out of him, but what the hell did he have to lose? If she kicked him to the curb, he'd still be where he currently was. Living a quiet life with his chosen family. But if she didn't . . .

He could have something he'd never allowed himself to dream of. With a woman who filled something inside him he hadn't known was missing.

Freya was a kind of peace. A calm. But she was also an excitement he'd never known.

Without thought, he pressed a kiss to the top of her head. Nerves rumbled in his belly and left him unsteady. He hoped to hell she felt an inkling of what he did.

She shifted, letting out a soft sigh, and his breath caught in his chest. He braced himself, unsure how she'd react when she woke.

When he'd gotten off the phone with Frazier last night, he hadn't expected to find her asleep. When he'd tried to wake her, she hadn't budged. The woman had been out cold. Self-ishly, he hadn't woken her. He liked how she fit against him. Then before he knew it, he'd fallen asleep as well.

So this morning was a crapshoot. It took another minute for Freya to fully awaken, but he knew the exact moment she did, the exact moment she realized where she was. Her body tensed, and he ran a hand gently over her lower back.

"Morning," he murmured. "Sleep okay?"

When she relaxed against him, he let out the breath he hadn't realized he'd been holding.

"I did." She propped her hands on his chest, rested her chin atop them, and met his gaze. "Sorry I fell asleep on you last night." She chuckled and patted his chest. "Literally."

The slow, sleepy smile she gave him had his mouth going dry. Yet he somehow managed to respond. "Not a problem. Though I can't imagine I'm the best pillow."

"You won't hear any complaints from me." She tucked her hands against his sides and dropped her head back onto his chest. But not before he saw a soft flush cross her face that warmed his insides and quelled some of his worries.

He traced little circles over her soft skin, and she snuggled into him. Holy shit, he could stay like this forever.

"Still want to hang out today?" she asked.

He heard the hesitation in her voice and ran his hand up her back until it was buried in her hair, cupping the nape of her neck. "I'd love to spend the day with you. Would you mind going over to Whidbey Island with me?"

She shifted positions, sliding to the side so she was no longer lying atop him. She wedged herself between him and the couch back and slung her leg and arm over him. While he missed her weight, he could see her better now. Even with her mascara a little smudged beneath her eyes, she was stunning.

"Sounds good to me," she said. "Anywhere in particular you need to go?"

He nodded. "I have to pick up Daisy's birthday present."

She grinned. "What did you get her?"

"This indoor playhouse tent thing."

Her eyebrow arched, and a smirk lifted her lips. "Why do I have a feeling it isn't a simple playhouse you're going to pick up at a big box store?"

Xander shrugged and bit back a grin. "No clue."

Internally, he scoffed. A standard, boring playhouse? For his little buddy? No way in hell.

"Right." She snorted. "Do you mind if we swing by my place first? I need to shower and change."

"Of course," he said just as his stomach let out a loud growl. He carefully sat up, pulling her with him. "How about this? I drop you at your place, and while you're doing your thing, I'll head over to Comfort Food, grab us some food and coffee, and meet you back at your apartment?"

She pressed a kiss to his T-shirt-covered chest. "I like your thinking."

"Excellent, but first . . ." He tipped her chin up with his finger and pressed a soft kiss to her lips. "Good morning, beautiful."

The sigh she let out had him wanting to pump his fist in the air. He refrained. Barely.

They got a later start than Xander had intended. After Freya had showered and changed, they enjoyed the coffee and pastries he'd picked up. He'd intended for them to take the ten o'clock ferry to Whidbey Island but had gotten distracted. Kissing Freya was quickly becoming his new favorite thing. Instead, they had to wait an hour for the next ferry. Not that he really minded since it gave them more time to make out and ensure he got her off. Dry-humping was so damn underrated.

It was a twenty-minute ferry ride to Whidbey, and a short drive from the Keystone Ferry Landing to the town of Coupeville. Usually, parking wasn't an issue in the quaint little town, but the place was packed. Bright-orange traffic cones indicated multiple street closures. After circling the town's residential streets, he eventually found a parking spot and cut the engine.

"Wow," Freya said, glancing around. "I don't think I've ever seen it this crowded."

"I know. I wonder—"

His words cut off as a group of teenagers dressed in marching band uniforms raced past his vehicle. The plumes in their shako hats waved wildly as they sprinted around the corner, screaming for someone to wait for them.

"You know," Freya said, "Veterans Day is this week. I bet they're having their parade today."

"Well, that explains . . ." He gestured out his window as three more teenagers raced past laughing and hollering. "The toy store is right downtown. Care to take in a parade with me today?"

She grinned at him as she reached for her door handle. "I love parades."

Walking hand in hand, they passed the group of teenagers at the band's staging area. As they approached the heart of the small downtown, Xander's brows rose at the crowd. "Holy shit," he muttered. "There's a lot of people here."

"Before I moved to Hudson Island, I used to live here on Whidbey, but up in Oak Harbor." She gestured ahead of them. "Coupeville has the best parades."

From the rows of occupied camping chairs lining the streets and the number of people milling about, it must be a fantastic parade. As a resident of Hudson Island for nearly the past decade, he had to admit that the Pacific Northwest's small-town Americana indeed had its charm. "The toy store's down on Front Street. Want to see if we can catch some of the action from there?"

She squeezed his hand. "Lead the way."

Xander led her through the crowds, crossing the streets in between floats and decked-out pickup trucks. As they neared Front Street, the hairs on the back of his neck rose. Under the guise of waving at a group of kids in a passing float, he pulled them to a stop on the sidewalk. He glanced around, grateful he was wearing sunglasses, and scanned the crowd.

Nothing. No one seemed out of the ordinary.

But he knew that didn't mean a damn thing. He couldn't see who it was, but someone had eyes on him. He'd learned long ago to trust his gut. Hell, it had saved him and his teammates numerous times.

Letting go of Freya's hand, he wrapped his arm over her slim shoulders and tucked her close. "Let's watch the parade for a little bit," he said, studying everyone around them.

"Oh, look how cute they are." She waved at a passing float with about a dozen little kids dressed as rubber ducks. Following the float was a group of square-dancing seniors swinging their partners down the street. Then came a slew of classic cars with people tossing candy to the children lining the sidewalk.

Xander continued to discreetly scan the crowd, but he didn't see anything amiss. However, the hinky feeling remained. Something was off, and he needed to get them moving. Retaking her hand, he gently pulled her in the direction of the toy store. "Let's pick up Daisy's gift before it gets too crowded."

He bit back a wince. As far as excuses went, it was pretty

weak, but thankfully, Freya didn't seem to notice and followed him to the nearby toy store.

A soft bell chimed as he pushed open the store's front door. Once they were inside, that feeling of being watched disappeared. He frowned.

"Oh, this place is so cute," Freya said, grinning up at him. "I'm going to pick up a little something for Daisy too."

Before she could release his hand, he pressed a kiss to the top of her head. So what if he also took another peek outside the store's front window. Again, nothing was obviously amiss. And again, that meant jack shit. "I'm going to pick up my order at the register. Do me a favor and don't leave the store without me."

She met his gaze, curiosity evident on her face. "Everything okay?"

He nodded. "It's crowded. I don't want to lose you out there." Not a lie. Not at all. Especially with that sixth sense screaming at him that something wasn't right. He gave her his most charming smile. "Humor me?"

He relaxed the tiniest bit when she returned his smile. "Of course. You're sweet, you know that, Xander Bonetti?"

Sweet? With Freya, perhaps.

He knew with certainty that he wanted her safe. Until he could determine what had triggered that feeling of being watched, he was planning on keeping the woman close. Not that it was a hardship. Not at all.

***

Freya did a full loop of the store before she returned to the small clothes section. The store was adorable. She'd passed by it numerous times when she'd visited the cute little town before, but she'd never gone in. The gifts she'd gotten for her twin nieces tended to come from the big box stores, but she was quickly rethinking that.

After hemming and hawing over a few different designs, Freya finally settled on an adorable pajama set for Daisy's birthday and a pair of sleep dresses for her nieces for Thanksgiving. She made sure she had the correct sizes and went to look for Xander and found him with a store employee who was showing him how to operate the elaborate playhouse tent.

As she approached them, Freya's jaw dropped. *Tent* was an understatement. While technically the walls were made of a tent-like material, and one entire side was rolled up, the interior was as far from tent-like as it could get. Fairy lights twinkled along the ceiling panels, which looked to be high enough for her to stand upright in. Granted, she wasn't the tallest person, but still. On top of that, the interior was decked out with a fully functioning inflatable mini living room set—a couch, two end tables, a recliner, and coffee table.

Yeah. It was *fancy* fancy.

"Wow," Freya chuckled. "That is quite the 'indoor playhouse tent' thing."

The saleswoman waved at the inflatable mini couch, which would be the perfect size for Daisy and two friends. "Believe it or not, the couch can hold up to two hundred pounds."

Freya grinned at Xander and shook her head. "What? No dining room set?"

"I already got her one over the summer." A soft flush colored his cheeks as he gestured to the opposite end of the tent. "It should fit between the two windows."

Freya laughed. "Of course you did."

He cleared his throat and turned to the saleswoman. "Great, I'll take all of it. I'll get those small unicorn decorative pillows you showed me too." He caught Freya's gaze and shrugged. "Daisy likes pillows."

Good freaking God, the man was cute.

"Excellent," the saleswoman said with a smile. "I'll run to the back and grab you some new ones. Give me a few minutes, and I'll meet you at the register."

As the woman hurried off, he turned to Freya, nodding to the items in her hand. "Find something?"

She showed him her loot as they made their way to the register. "I figured Daisy could use some rainbow-sloth-unicorn-narwhal pajamas for her birthday."

"Nice. Those are just her style."

She bit back a laugh at Xander's serious expression. "And since I'm here, I picked up these jammies for my nieces."

He glanced between the two nightdresses and nodded in approval. "Donuts and bacon. Popcorn and pizza. Looks like your nieces are my kinda people. They're Daisy's age, right?"

She nodded. "Only about six months older."

"Well, I hope to meet them one of these days." The warm smile he gave her had her belly fluttering.

"I'm sure they'll adore you." There was no doubt about it.

She could easily picture him hanging out with her nieces, fitting in with all her loud brothers. And if she allowed herself to get dreamy, she could see the two of them together months down the road in a relationship that was both comfortable and passionate, maybe even—

"I can help the next person," a voice called out.

Exhaling, Freya tore her gaze from the man beside her—and from her fanciful thoughts—and turned to the lady behind the counter. "Hi there," she said, setting her items onto the counter. Clearing her throat, she glanced at Xander. "Are the playhouse and furniture the only things you got Daisy for her birthday?"

He shrugged, but the way the edges of his mouth quirked suggested she was onto something.

She chuckled as she paid for her items and then waited for Xander to pay for his gifts—which they'd kindly wrapped for him in a trio of giant bags with tons of pink and lavender tissue paper.

As they made their way out of the shop, she asked, "So what else did you get Daisy?"

Glancing at her, Xander's innocent who-me expression didn't fool her. "What makes you think I got her an additional gift?"

"Your face," she replied, deadpan.

That handsome face broke out into a wide grin. "Touché."

God, was he seriously this cute? "Well?"

"It's just a little something—an adventure, if you will—that'll ensure I stay Daisy's favorite. But I'm not revealing anything yet since I'm still waiting for a couple details to be finalized. Don't want to jinx it, you know." He took her hand, wagging his eyebrows, and she couldn't help but laugh.

Yeah, he was seriously that cute.

As they made their way up the busy sidewalk, Freya spotted a break in the crowd. Tugging on his hand, she pulled them to the edge of the curb. A group of school-aged Irish dancers were high-stepping by, followed by a float carrying a Little League team decked out in their uniforms. She and Xander clapped and cheered when the team's catcher hoisted a shiny gold trophy that was nearly as big as him.

As the float passed, a buzz of excitement zinged through the crowd. A group of nine dirt bikes were coming down the street. The kids along the parade route shouted their approval of the tricks and wheelies the riders were performing. While impressive, it was *loud*. But from the expressions of those around her—Xander included—she seemed to be the only one who thought so.

Her eyes widened as two of the dirt bikes popped up onto their back wheels and spun in a tight circle while the other bikes whizzed up and down the street in some sort of synchronized chaos. Okay, fine. It was impressive. Had she been on any of those bikes, she would have crashed within—

She gasped as she was shoved forward.

Hitting the ground hard, her breath seized painfully in her chest. Dazed, she glanced to her right, and her insides froze. Time slowed. A pair of dirt bikes was bearing down on her. She didn't have time to curl into a ball, didn't have time to throw her hands over her head. She could only slam her eyes shut and brace for impact.

Tires squealed, and a heavy weight landed on her. The smell of burning rubber filled her nose. She heard shouts and screams, but the sounds were muffled, like a hazy noise behind the loud drumming of her heart.

Then Xander's cedar-and-soapy scent was there, competing with the burning rubber. She peeked her eyes open, and there he was. Lying over her on the ground.

"I've got you, baby," he murmured. He moved to his knees but remained hovering over her.

She started to move, but he placed a hand on her back, stilling her. From the ground, she saw people rushing toward them. Numerous people asked if she was okay.

Unsure of what had happened, she closed her eyes and focused on Xander's deep voice responding to the questions coming at them, on his familiar scent that soothed her nerves, on his warm hand on her back that kept her grounded.

"Alright, sweetheart, let's get you sitting, okay?"

She met his gaze and nodded. He helped her to sit, and she tried her hardest not to wince but failed. As she sat on the pavement, every muscle in her body screamed. She sucked in a breath when she saw her scraped-up palms. A whimper escaped when she straightened her legs. Her left knee was throbbing, and her jeans sported a new hole.

Glancing past Xander, a sea of concerned faces stared down at her.

"I don't know how the hell we didn't crash into you," a man said from atop his dirt bike, a disbelieving look in his eyes. "You alright?"

The tires racing toward her flashed in Freya's mind. She'd been so sure they were going to run her over. She nodded, unable to say anything past the lump in her throat.

"Well, I'm glad you're okay." The second biker turned to Xander. "You need us to send the paramedics over?"

Xander shook his head. "We're good. If you both hadn't swerved, it'd be a different story, though. Appreciate the quick reflexes."

"Me too. Take care." The men on the dirt bikes gave them nods before continuing down the street to their waiting group.

"Here you go, honey."

Overwhelmed, Freya startled at the woman crouched beside her holding out a wet wipe.

"You poor thing, you're all scraped up." Xander took the wipe from her, and she rummaged through her large diaper bag. "I have more wipes if you need them, and I'm sure I have some Band-Aids somewhere in here."

"Thank you," Xander murmured, gently pressing the wipe against Freya's scraped palm. She bit her bottom lip to keep from hissing. "Don't worry about the Band-Aids, ma'am. I have a first aid kit in my car."

"Well, aren't you just the Boy Scout," the woman said with a smile as she rose. She turned to Freya and held out a couple more wet wipes and a small pack of tissues. "I have four boys under five, so I'm no stranger to scrapes and bruises. You'll want to make sure they get cleaned out. That was a nasty fall you took."

"Thank you," Freya said, finally finding her voice as she took the offered items. "I appreciate these."

"Of course. I hope it's nothing too serious. I mean, that's quite the tumble you took." The woman glanced at Xander, who'd subtly repositioned himself between her and the woman. "It appears you're in good hands though, so that's a plus. I hope you're able to enjoy the rest of the parade."

"Thanks again," Freya called out as the woman stepped away.

"Let me help you," Xander said, reaching for her. When his arms wrapped around her, her breath caught. An uncomfortable twinge along her left side flared to life.

"Easy," he murmured, effortlessly bringing her to her feet, careful of her side. For such a brawny man, it amazed her how he could be so gentle.

"Tell me what hurts." His arm was still wrapped around her, like he was her own personal protective bubble.

A week ago, she would have smarted. She would have most likely insisted she didn't need his help. But there was something about Xander. Something that filled her with warmth. Something that had her leaning into him. She'd never felt so safe before, so protected.

"I'm okay." As much as she wanted to completely lean on him, she really was fine. Aside from her stinging palms, a minor twinge along her left side where she'd landed, and her sore left knee that had taken the brunt of the fall, she was okay. A little shaky still, but good. After all, she'd suffered worse.

"Are you sure, Frey?"

"I'm fine. I'm not really sure what happened, but it's just some minor bumps and bruises. I promise."

She gave him what she hoped was a reassuring smile, took one of the baby wipes, and gently patted her left palm. Fire lit her skin, and she winced.

"Still fine, Frey?" Humor laced his words.

Frowning, she blew on her stinging palm. "Okay, fine. It stings a little." More like a lot.

With a soft chuckle, he kissed her forehead. "I wasn't lying when I told that lady I have a first aid kit in the car. You want to head back so I can properly clean that out?" His eyes narrowed as he peered down the street where more floats were making their way toward them. "Unless you want to stay for the rest of the parade. I can't imagine they have that many more groups lined up."

"We can head back. I think I'm all paraded out." As much as she loved a good small-town parade, her knee was beginning to throb.

"Are you okay to walk?"

She nodded. For now, anyway. The faster she could sit down, the better. She had no doubt that Xander would have no problems carrying her to the car, but she still had her pride.

Glancing to her right, she spotted her purse on the ground, along with their toy store bags. "Don't forget Daisy's gifts," she said, gingerly stepping toward their things.

Before she could bend down, Xander had her purse slung over his shoulder and all their bags in his hand. He wrapped his free arm around her shoulders and tucked her against his side.

Noise and people surrounded them once again, but as Xander led them through the throng of bodies, not a single person bumped into her. Yeah, being wrapped in the man's protective bubble wasn't a hardship. His physical strength steadied her. That cedar-and-soapy scent that was distinctly his calmed her. Those two things, along with his mere presence, all added up to a wonderful feeling of safety. It was new, and while it left her feeling a little uncertain, she could admit to herself that she really liked it. Really liked *him*.

Leaning into his side, a smile lifted the corners of her lips as his arm tightened around her. She took in a steadying breath, and her resolve solidified. She was determined to go for it. To not self-sabotage. To not let that little bit of uncertainty freeze her. To not push him away.

For once, she was going to go after what she wanted. And that was Xander Bonetti.

CHAPTER SEVENTEEN

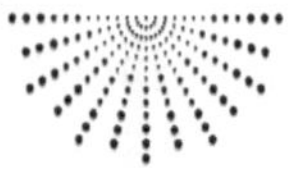

"Holy crap," Freya hissed. "This is not what I imagined playing doctor with you would be like."

"Is that so?" Xander's eyebrows rose. He chuckled as he tipped the water bottle over her palm. The glare she shot him was fucking adorable. "Trust me, Frey, I'm up for playing doctor later. *After* I get this cleaned up."

He inspected her wounds. Minor injuries—two scraped-up palms that should heal just fine. Taking the gauze and tape from his vehicle's first aid kit, he made quick work of dressing her palms.

"I was going to suggest lunch out here," he said, "but what do you say we head back to Hudson? We can pick up some food, head back to my place to eat, and then hit the hot tub. It'll help your side and knee."

Her narrowed gaze shot to his, and her brow furrowed.

Yeah, fucking adorable.

Unable to help himself, he pressed a kiss to said furrowed brow. "Baby, did you think I didn't notice you limping? Or that you're favoring your left side?"

She frowned. "I thought I did a good job walking normally."

"You did, but what can I say?" He shrugged, shooting her a smile. "I'm observant."

"I'm beginning to see that." The edges of her lips quirked, and she arched an eyebrow at him. "A hot tub, you say? You wouldn't happen to be trying to get me into a bathing suit, now would you?"

He gave her his most innocent smile. "Who, me? Sweetheart, bathing suits are completely optional. If au natural is your thing, then by all means, please don't let me get in your way."

She chuckled. "How magnanimous of you."

Shrugging, he packed up the first aid kit and returned it to its spot in the cargo area. After helping her down from the back, he pressed the button to close the liftgate and led her to the passenger side. He pulled the door open, guided her into her seat, and waited until she was situated before shutting her door and rounding the vehicle.

"Seriously, Xander," she said once he'd started up the Rover, "thank you for helping me. Not only when everything happened, but for also bandaging me up and taking my mind off things."

"No need to thank me, Frey. I'm happy I was there." He didn't even want to think about what might have happened if she'd been by herself when she'd fallen.

"Well, I'm thanking you anyway," she said with a soft smile. "Do you mind if we stop by my place first? I need to pick up a bathing suit for the hot tub."

"Bathing suit? Are you saying it's too early in our relationship for naked hot tub times?" He shot her another wink to let her know he was teasing. Well, sort of.

"I don't know, Xander. The day is young. I wouldn't exactly count that out just yet."

Her wicked grin had his mouth falling open.

Forget fucking adorable. The woman was fucking hot.

She chuckled and gestured at the windshield. "Uh, are you gonna drive us back to Hudson or are we just gonna sit here?"

Drive. Right. Shit.

Quickly checking his blind spot, he peeled out of their parking space. Her laughter filled the SUV as he got them on the road to the ferry terminal. Within seconds, though, he dropped his speed to within the limit.

"Looks like someone's *not* in a rush to get home," she said, humor lacing her words.

"Just the opposite, actually. The road back to the ferry terminal has two speed traps. If I got pulled over"—he made a production of glancing at his watch—"we'd miss the next ferry back to Hudson Island, thus postponing the possible future naked hot tub times. And that, my beautiful girl, is unacceptable."

"True. That would be a damn shame." A grin lit her gorgeous face. "But to clarify, it's a stop by my place, a stop to pick up lunch, and *then* hot tub. Possible nakedness is to be determined."

"You know I'm just teasing, right, Frey?" The last thing he wanted was for her to feel any kind of pressure. She'd been right earlier, he was trying to lighten the mood, trying to keep her mind off what had happened, of how close she'd come to disaster. Knowing she'd gotten hurt—*seeing* her hurt, no matter how minor—tore him up. He should've protected her. "I think the hot tub will really help your knee. When I was washing it out, I could already see the bruising. I'm sure your side is the same. And if you so happen to decide to wear a skimpy bikini in the hot tub, who am I to stop you?"

She laughed—as he'd intended—and playfully slapped him on the arm. "You're ridiculous."

"Seriously, though, you have to know that I'm all in with you, with whatever this is that's going on between us." Driving with one hand, he took her hand and brought it to his lips. "You're in charge. Always. You set the pace for whatever's going on here, okay?"

"I know. And I'm all in too." His heart squeezed when she kept his hand in hers and brought it to rest on her lap. "We'll just see where things go."

"Deal." He glanced at her and grinned, arching his eyebrow. "So is that a yes on the skimpy bikini?"

She chuckled, and for a few moments, a comfortable silence filled the vehicle. He peeked over at her and noticed her shifting in her seat. "How's the side and knee? For real?"

"A little uncomfortable. Truthfully, the hot tub will probably help a lot." She frowned. "I landed hard."

His mind flashed to what had happened, and a feeling he couldn't quite describe twisted his gut. One second Freya had been standing beside him, and the next she was flying toward the ground. With fucking dirt bikes racing her way. He hadn't been lying earlier when he'd spoken to the riders. Had they not been as skilled as they were, had they not swerved at the very last second, their day would have taken a tragic turn.

A prickle of unease ran down his spine. It didn't make sense. "Can we talk about what happened? About how you fell forward?"

She remained silent for a moment, and he could see the wheels turning in her mind.

He hadn't wanted to ask her while they were in the street. Immediately after she'd fallen, his priority had been her safety—to keep her close and tend to her injuries. He hadn't seen anyone lingering, didn't observe anyone who'd set off any alarms in his gut. Regardless, he had a feeling he knew what had happened, but he wanted to hear what she had to say.

"Frey?" he prodded when she still hadn't said anything after a minute.

"I'm not sure. It happened so fast." She shrugged. "I must have tripped."

One glance in her direction, and he knew she didn't believe that for one second. He gently squeezed her hand and stated the obvious. "Freya, baby, you were standing still."

A couple of seconds of silence ticked by. Then she sighed and whispered, "I know."

He felt a shiver tear through her, and he wanted to pull the car over and yank her into his arms.

Before he could do exactly that, she cleared her throat. "I felt something hit my back really hard. I think someone pushed me."

"I think so too." He recalled that earlier feeling of eyes on him when they'd first arrived in town, and he bit back a curse. "Would you be okay if I look into it?"

"Um, I'm not exactly sure what that means or entails, but okay."

He glanced at her, and the worry on her face made him want to howl. His fingers on his left hand flexed on the steering wheel, and he made a conscious effort to loosen his grip. *Relax, dammit. The last thing she needs is for you to lose your fucking shit.*

Releasing her hand, he pulled up the phone function on his on-dash display. Clearing his throat, he looked over at Freya once again. "Trust me on this. If there's anything to be found, my team will find it. If it's alright with you, everything you hear needs to be kept between us."

Her eyes widened, but she nodded. "Of course."

With a couple taps on the display, a ringtone sounded

over the SUV's speakers. Seconds later, a familiar voice answered. "What's up, Xan?"

"Hey, Bean. I'm in the car with Freya, and you're on speaker." He gave his colleague a quick recap of what had happened at the parade. "Not sure what's available, but can you pull any security cameras in the area? I'd like to see if we can get a visual of who pushed her into the street."

The sound of typing filled the vehicle. "On it. I'll give you a call on your cell if I turn up anything. Fingers crossed it was just some oblivious dumbass not paying attention."

Exactly. Because the alternative would be . . . Holy shit, it would be completely fucked up.

"Thanks, B."

"Of course. I'll loop Gavin in too. Later."

He disconnected the call, and Freya let out a breath.

"Xander?" she asked after a moment. "What if it wasn't some oblivious dumbass not paying attention?"

As he pulled into the ferry line, he gently retook her hand and brought it to his lips again. "Let's not borrow trouble, baby."

She sighed. "Easier said than done."

"I know, but there's no need to worry—"

"Until there's need to worry."

"Exactly," he murmured, pressing another kiss to her bandaged palm. He would do whatever he could to lessen that worry. To mitigate the problem should any arise. Because keeping Freya safe was the top priority. He wasn't going to fail her again.

CHAPTER EIGHTEEN

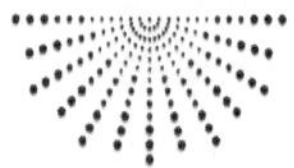

Freya was lacking in the skimpy bikini department. During her rebellious early high school years, string bikinis had been her go-to, much to her older brothers' dismay. However, since the accident, it was only one-piece bathing suits or tankinis. She was self-conscious of her scars. They'd faded over the last decade, but the sight of them still turned her stomach.

She rummaged through her dresser drawer, grabbed a simple teal tankini top and black bikini bottoms, and added them to her tote. Her lips pressed into a tight line as she eyed her closet. Should she pack a change of clothes? Would that be too presumptuous? Or would it be good just-in-case planning?

She heard the key in the front door, and the soft creak as it opened—Xander had double-parked to help her up to her apartment before heading back out to find parking—and she made her way to her bedroom door.

"Hey," she called out, leaning against the doorframe. She nodded at the brown paper bag he held, which sported the logo of her favorite bakery, and grinned. "What'cha got there?"

He dropped his keys and the bag onto her small dining table. "I had to park a few blocks down, and since I had to walk by Comfort Food, I figured I may as well get us some post-lunch desserts."

She made her way to the dining table and reached for the bag, and he tsked, snatching it away and hiding it behind his back. "Uh-uh. Pack first. Lunch second. *Then* dessert before the hot tub."

She pouted. "Not even a hint?"

His eyes narrowed as he playfully contemplated her question. "It's pie-ish," he finally said.

Her stomach let out a loud growl, and she grinned, clapping her hands in excitement. "Oh my God, Xander. If you got us any of their mini fruit cobblers, I swear, I'll love you forever."

"Duly noted." He chuckled and nodded toward her room. "Pack."

"Bossy," she muttered, but her lips tipped up in a smile. Heading back to her room, she called over her shoulder, "I'll only be a few more minutes, but the TV remote is on the coffee table. I think there are some magazines too if you're bored out of your skull waiting for me."

She heard his soft chuckle from the living room. "I'm good. Take your time, baby."

Her stomach fluttered. She'd never been one for pet names. But Xander calling her baby? With that deep, sexy voice of his? Yup, she could get used to hearing that.

She opened her closet and grabbed a change of clothes to add to her tote—a casual, comfy post–hot tub outfit. Before she could overthink it, she grabbed another outfit, carefully folded it, and added it to her bag. So what if that second outfit happened to be all black and one of her favorite work outfits?

Chuckling to herself, she filled a small toiletry bag with some makeup and skincare essentials. Not that she was expecting anything to happen between them tonight, but it was better to be prepared, right? Besides, if she accidentally fell asleep on him again, she didn't want to be a giant inconvenience. His place was closer to her work, and it would be easier to just go from his place than for him to drive her all the way back to her apartment and *then* back to the resort . . .

Yeah, that's it. She was simply being courteous. Just in case.

Oh, who was she trying to fool? She definitely wouldn't be opposed to something more happening between them. As he'd said earlier, she was in charge. Yes, their make-out sessions both last night and earlier this morning had been mind-blowing, however, she wasn't sure she was brave enough to actually push things forward more.

Shaking her head, she blew out a breath. *Relax. Just go with it. One step at a time.*

After double-checking she had everything she needed in her tote, she slung it over her shoulder. Entering the living room, she turned toward Xander.

And froze.

The words "I'm ready" locked in her throat. Right beside her breath.

She couldn't believe what she was seeing.

Xander. Sitting on her couch. With the photos she'd received in the mail laid out on the coffee table in front of him. The photos she'd forgotten to put back into the white envelope.

Her heart hammered in her chest when he met her gaze, all the earlier teasing and flirtation were gone. His dark-brown eyes swirled with an intensity she couldn't interpret.

He held up a photo by the corner. The one with her eyes blacked out. The one with the familiar scrawl that never failed to make her stomach heave.

"Freya, what the hell is this?"

<hr>

Xander wasn't sure what he was looking at.

When he had picked up the *Vogue* on her coffee table, he'd caught sight of the photos beneath the magazine. At first, he'd seen a photo of a young Freya. She looked very much the same. Sweet and beautiful. Even back then as a teenager. But the last two photos had the hairs on the back of his neck rising.

Her xed-out image.

Her blacked-out eyes.

The ominous words: "It should have been you."

What the fuck?

Her footsteps had him turning, needing an explanation.

Freya stopped in her tracks. The way her eyes widened and mouth fell open had worry and unease swirling in his gut.

He carefully picked up the photo with her eyes blacked out. "Freya, what the hell is this?"

She sucked in a breath and blinked, simply looking at him. Silence filled the room for two long heartbeats. Then she cleared her throat and was suddenly in motion.

"Oh, um. Those are nothing." She rushed over, plucked the photo from his hand, gathered the remaining pictures, and stuffed them into a white envelope.

"Freya?" His gut was screaming that something was wrong, that he needed to demand answers, but he needed to proceed with caution. "I didn't mean to snoop. They were in between the magazines."

"Oh, it's fine," she said, flashing him a giant smile. A giant, fake smile. "No worries. I forgot to put them away. You about ready to go?"

Everything in him wanted to push, to ask what the hell was going on, but he'd follow her lead. For now.

Rising, he took her hand before she could turn. He could see the flutter of her pulse in her neck. "Freya, baby." He waited until she met his gaze. The worry shimmering in her blue eyes made him crazy, made him want to slay all her dragons. "If someone's bothering you, or if you're in trouble, you know you can tell me, right? Even if I didn't work for Hudson Security, I'd still help you in any way I can."

"I know," she whispered before surprising the hell out of him and wrapping her arms around his waist. His arms automatically went around her. "I appreciate your concern, but those photos aren't a big deal. Just a prank, I'm sure. Can we just get out of here?" She glanced up at him. That fake smile of hers was beginning to look painful.

He was about to protest. Until he saw the unshed tears shimmering in her eyes. It was like a punch to the gut.

"Okay, baby, if you say so." Pulling her close, he pressed his lips to her hair. They'd talk later. Because no way in hell were photos of her face and eyes scratched out *no big deal.* "Lunch and hot tub?"

Exhaling, she nodded and blinked back her tears. Her smile was shaky and tugged at his heart. "My knee is starting to hurt, so that hot tub actually sounds really good."

CHAPTER NINETEEN

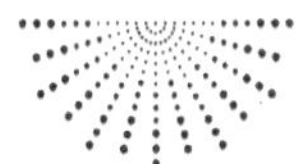

Xander pulled into an open parking space in front of Ray's Diner. After putting his SUV in park, he turned to her.

Freya held her breath, and her chest squeezed painfully tight. Her gaze fixed on the vehicle's on-screen display that announced the next song on the radio. Her stomach churned with nerves, and her hands twisted in her lap. Holy crap, she'd do anything to have the seat swallow her whole.

This was it. This was where Xander would make his gracious exit. Not that she blamed him. Not at all. She'd completely frozen back at her apartment. She wasn't even sure what idiotic excuse she'd used to brush off the pictures.

No, she'd flat-out lied to him. To his face. And the worst part? He knew it.

"Frey, can you look at me, please?" His soothing tone had her frown deepening. Of course he was going to let her down easy. Politely. He was nice like that.

With a resigned exhale, she turned to him and reluctantly met his gaze. When he took both her hands in his and squeezed, her eyes widened in surprise. Not what she was expecting.

"Relax, baby. We don't need to talk about anything you don't want to. How about I go in and pick up some food for us to bring back to my place. If your knee's still hurting, I can go in, and you can stay in the car. Want anything in particular?"

For a moment, words failed her. The last thing on her mind was food. Clearing her throat, she stammered, "Um, a salad?"

He nodded, still holding her hands. "I was going to get a chicken cobb with extra chicken and balsamic on the side. Want the same?"

Why was he being so nice to her? There's no way he'd bought her story about the photos being a prank. Right? "Sure, that sounds good, but no extra chicken and the white wine vinaigrette instead. Um, please."

"You got it," he said, giving her hands a soft squeeze before releasing them.

As he reached for his door, guilt rushed over her. She may not be ready to talk about the photos, but he didn't deserve her blatant dishonesty.

"I lied to you," she blurted as he pushed his door open. He turned back to her with raised eyebrows, and the words tumbled from her mouth. "Back at my apartment. When I said the photos were no big deal, I lied. They *are* a big deal." They terrified her. "But I don't know what they mean or who they're from, and I'm scared to tell you about it." Because he'd look at her differently after he found out what she'd done. And, dammit, she loved how he looked at her.

Closing his door, he faced her. Her heart tripped when he gently pushed a lock of hair behind her ear and cupped the side of her face. "I know you lied, baby, and it's okay—"

"It's not," she protested, shaking her head.

"You may have lied with your words, but I could see the truth in your eyes." His thumb caressed her jaw. "I promise, it's okay. So long as you're safe, we can talk about those photos whenever you're ready, whenever you're comfortable. I meant it earlier when I said I'm all in, Freya. I'll use every resource I have to find out what's going on and to keep you safe. You can trust me. When you're ready."

"I do trust you," she murmured. "I just don't know . . ." Where to even start or *how* to begin explaining.

She leaned into his hand, closed her eyes, and exhaled.

Her eyes flew open when he pressed his lips to hers. "Whatever's going on, we're in this together. But when you're ready." He flashed her the sweetest grin. "Now, how about we table the heavy talk, and I'll go get our food. Did you want anything to drink?"

Forty-five minutes later, they were unloading their food onto Xander's dining table. Delicious-looking salads and a trio of mini cobblers—blueberry, peach, and strawberry-rhubarb.

Balance, right?

Her stomach growled loudly, and she slapped her hands over her stomach as heat washed over her face.

"Well, that answers my question," Xander said with a chuckle. When she tilted her head, he clarified. "I was going to ask if you wanted to hit the hot tub first."

She shook her head, pointing at the cobblers. "I'm tempted to eat those before the salad."

"I don't blame you, but either way, you have to share them with me."

"Share?" She tapped her lips with her finger as she eyed him up and down. "What's in it for me?"

He closed the distance between them and hauled her

against him, all the while being careful of her sore left side. "Whatever you want, baby," he said with his lips inches away from hers.

Grinning, she pressed her lips to his in a soft kiss. This was a million times better than the nerves and doubt, than the fear that he was going to call things off because she was too much. Granted, the worry still lingered deep in her gut, but Xander's earlier words, not to mention his firm lips on hers, went a long way to reassure her.

Before things could get too heated, before she could sink into him and get lost in their kiss, she pulled away and shot him a wink. "Oh, I'm sure I can think of something." Her stomach rumbled again, and she cringed. There went her attempt at being sexy. "But food first."

***

While they ate their salads, Xander kept their conversation light. He knew she'd been rattled by the pictures, of him seeing those fucked-up photos, but he didn't want to push, didn't want to rush her. However, that didn't mean his mind wasn't whirling with every conceivable scenario. But he'd be patient.

They'd both been stuffed after lunch and shared the peach cobbler, saving the other two for later. Now, after quickly changing into his swim trunks, he double-checked the temperature of the hot tub while Freya changed.

One hundred and one degrees. Perfect.

He found a mellow playlist on his phone, connected it to the outdoor speakers, and set the volume to low. He placed a couple of bottles of water on the table beside the steaming hot tub and climbed in.

He groaned as he lowered into the water. Aches he didn't know he had screamed in relief. He leaned back against one of the jets and sighed. Closing his eyes, he sank down and let the water work its magic.

After a few moments, he heard the sliding door open and close, and he peeked his eyes open.

His jaw dropped, and he was struck dumb. Hell, he may have even drooled a little.

Holy shit, she's stunning.

Her bathing suit was one of those tank top two-pieces. The top was an ocean blue that made her eyes pop. The bottoms were simple black bottoms. Everything was covered, nothing crazy low cut, no ass cheeks hanging out. Not even a sliver of her stomach showed. Yet Freya was hands down the hottest woman he'd ever seen.

"Sorry. Looks like my closet was all out of skimpy bikinis." A sheepish smile lifted her lips.

He shook his head as his gaze took in every inch of her. From the top of her raven-black hair to the tips of her hot-pink-painted toes. His dick twitched. "You're gorgeous, baby. Pretty sure you could wear a garbage sack and still be the prettiest woman in the room."

A soft blush stole over her cheeks as she stepped toward him. "Charmer."

Rising, he gestured to the opposite side of the hot tub and held out his hand. "Steps are over here."

After helping her into the hot tub, he showed her where the various jets were and happily watched as she tried each out. Apparently, when you were five-two, finding the optimal seat and jet configuration was tricky. At six-four, he'd never given it much thought. Sitting too low in the water was never a thing.

Once Freya had found her spot—the corner opposite him —she leaned back, closed her eyes, and sighed. "Holy moly, Xander. This was a great idea. Thank you."

She was too far away, but he couldn't complain about the

view. Not at all. She was utterly relaxed. And so damn pretty. "How's the knee?"

"It was getting achy, but this feels lovely."

"And your side?"

Her eyes were still closed, but the edges of her lips twitched up. "It's good. Promise."

A comfortable silence fell over them. The sounds of the swirling water and the soft music provided a calming backdrop.

After who knows how much time passed, he asked, "What's on your docket this week?"

"Just work." She sighed, opening her eyes.

He grinned at her drowsy look. "You hanging in there?"

She nodded and moved to the seat on her right, which was higher and had her shoulders and tops of her breasts peeking out of the water. "Thought I was going to fall asleep on you there." She chuckled. "Again."

"Go for it." He spread his arms out. "I'll happily volunteer to be your pillow anytime."

"I may take you up on that." She grinned as she stretched her legs out in front of her. "With Hazel gone, Miriam redistributed her clients to the rest of us, so this week is going to be crazy. But the good news is that my rental car is supposed to get dropped off at work sometime tomorrow afternoon, so you won't have to keep driving me around." She grimaced. "Speaking of, if it's not too much trouble, would you mind taking me to work one more time tomorrow morning?"

"You know I don't mind."

"That's because you're a sweetheart."

Again, that soft smile that did him in bloomed on her face. "What time do you need to be at work?"

"Eight."

Sitting up, he raised his arms and rested them along the

hot tub's edge. The cool air was refreshing, and goosebumps covered his skin. "Want to join me at the gym beforehand?"

Her brow furrowed and she side-eyed him. "What time?"

Goddamn, she was cute. "Five thirty."

"In the morning?" Her eyes went owl wide.

He chuckled. "I take it that's a no?"

"You better believe it." Her gaze traveled over him. "How often do you work out?"

He shrugged. And so what if he also flexed a little? "Most mornings."

She snickered while her eyes continued to wander over him. "So you're saying today was the first morning you missed in how long?"

"I'd say at least a month." He grinned. She had his number. "But, Frey, waking up with you this morning was worth it."

She met his gaze, and her eyes heated. "Yeah?" The one word was breathy and sent a bolt of desire through him.

"Hell yeah, baby." Holding her gaze, his pulse kicked. Lowering his arms back into the water, he murmured, "Come here. You're too far away."

She moved one seat down, still out of arm's reach, and sent him a saucy smirk. Minx.

He tsked, shaking his head. "Nope. Still too far away."

She moved one more seat closer.

He crooked his finger at her. "Get over here."

Grinning, she pushed off her seat, and he snagged her by the waist, hauling her to him and across his lap.

Water sloshed over the side of the hot tub, and she laughed. "Look what you did!"

With her perched on his lap, he framed her face with his hands. "Totally worth it," he murmured before claiming her lips.

CHAPTER TWENTY

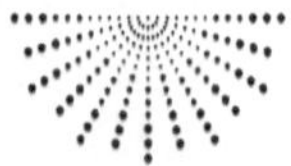

Freya moaned into their kiss. Tiny explosions fluttered through her with each nip of Xander's teeth, with each slide of his tongue. His hands began to roam, and when he slipped a hand beneath the fabric of her tankini and cupped her breast, when he pinched her nipple between his fingers, the explosions grew.

"More," she groaned, clutching his neck. The heat within her was building, and she squirmed. "Please, Xander. More."

A low growl sounded from his throat as he began peppering kisses down her throat. Her racing heart kicked when his fingers slid under the shoulder straps of her bathing suit and began pulling them down.

"Yes," she murmured, yanking her arms free. The warm water raced over her chest when he shoved her top to her waist. Throwing her head back, need raced through her as his hands molded her breasts.

Her eyes flew open, and she gasped when she was suddenly hoisted higher. The cold air had her already hard nipples aching, and then his mouth was on her. He sucked on her breasts, pulling on one nipple while his fingers worked her other. Her core throbbed, and she threaded her fingers through his hair, clutching his head to her chest. *God, yes . . .*

Her heart hammered as she felt one of his hands skim her side. His thumb hooked the edge of her bikini bottoms, and he tugged.

She leaned back, pulling her breast away from his mouth. He groaned in protest, but she gripped his shoulders and lifted.

A sexy smile flittered over Xander's face as he quickly pulled her bikini bottoms off and then crashed his lips to hers.

Clutching his neck, she dueled her tongue with his. His hand trailed along her front, over her breasts, and down her stomach. She sucked in a breath when his fingers found her center.

"So fucking soft," he murmured against her neck while his fingers teased her. "So fucking pretty."

She gasped when his fingers slipped between her folds and moaned when he rubbed her clit in tight circles.

"You're all fucking mine." He swallowed her cry and slipped two fingers into her.

Sensation after sensation bombarded her. She pulled away from their kiss to gasp for air as he finger-fucked her into oblivion. She rode his hand, not caring that she was chanting, "Yes, yes, yes!"

Tingles raced over her body, and she grabbed his shoulders in desperation.

"That's it, baby. Your pussy feels so good. I want you to come on my fingers. Then I want you to come on my face. Then on my cock." His guttural words sent her over the edge. Her body tensed, and she slammed her thighs together, trapping his hand that kept working her. She cried out, and her body convulsed.

"So fucking beautiful, Freya." His mouth claimed hers, and though her body was reeling, she needed more.

She gripped his hair and yanked him away. "More, Xander. I want more." She stood. Water sluiced down her body. She moved to a spot at the edge of the hot tub where the water came up to just over her knees. She was dimly aware she was standing there with her top bunched at her waist. And that was it. But with the way Xander was looking at her, she didn't care. The way his impressive erection was tenting his swim trunks, she didn't care.

She needed him. Now.

"I'm on the pill, and I'm clean." She turned away from him and leaned toward the edge. She glanced over her shoulder. The naked desire in his gaze sent a flood of heat to her pussy and emboldened her. "I need to feel you inside me. Please."

Within seconds, Xander was out of his swim trunks. She didn't have time to appreciate his sculpted abs or his thick cock before he was behind her. His hands ran over her ass, squeezing. His lips and tongue trailed up her spine.

"You're so damn perfect, Freya."

Before she could respond, he slid into her in one long thrust.

She groaned as he stretched her, and wetness flooded her. She was so full. "So good," she murmured. "You feel so good."

"Holy fuck, baby," he growled as he began to move.

Fireworks sparked within her, and she gripped the edge of the hot tub. Her knuckles turned white as he worked her, her pussy fluttering around him. In and out he thrust, driving her wild. Water sloshed over the sides of the hot tub, but she didn't care. When he reached around and his fingers rubbed hard circles over her clit, she exploded. Her pussy clenched his cock and he pounded into her, his rhythm becoming erratic as he came.

"Oh my God," she said on an exhale, dropping her forehead to the edge of the hot tub. The movement pushed her hips back, and he groaned, still buried within her.

His hands squeezed her hips and smoothed over her cheeks. "Oh my God is right." He slowly pulled out, and she immediately missed him. She felt his come trickling out of her, and she glanced over her shoulder.

His gaze was locked between her thighs, a renewed hunger sizzling in his expression.

"See something you like?" she teased, wiggling her hips.

His dark eyes flickered to hers and then back between her legs. "You have no idea, baby."

She grinned. There was something about this man that had her throwing her inhibitions—and every rule she'd set for herself—out the window.

His hands moved to her waist, and he squeezed.

She yelped when he pulled her against his chest and sank back into the water.

With her back to his chest, he wrapped his arms around her and pressed a kiss to her temple. "Well, that was fun."

She chuckled and dropped her head against him. "Sure was." Yeah, she could get used to this.

He let out a sigh. "If you give me twenty, we can go for round two but . . ." He glanced around them and chuckled. "I think we should try out a bed."

"I wouldn't be opposed." She grinned and tilted her head to look at him. "Don't get me wrong, this was amazing, but a bed would be nice."

He plucked at her top that was rolled up and scrunched around her waist. "This is cute, though."

Rolling her eyes, she adjusted her top so it was back on and then leaned back against him.

"You know what, Frey?" he asked, his hands running over her thighs.

Excitement began to brew anew as he pulled her legs apart. "What's that?"

"Since I'm gonna have to add a shit ton of chlorine to the hot tub anyway . . ." His fingers played between her thighs, and she moaned, rocking against the growing erection tucked against her bare ass. "We may as well go for round two right now. Don't want to waste all the chlorine, right? What do you say?"

He slipped two fingers into her, and she groaned. "I really like the way you think, Xander Bonetti."

He nipped at her neck and his fingers pumped in and out of her. "Well, I really like you, Freya Hansen."

CHAPTER TWENTY-ONE

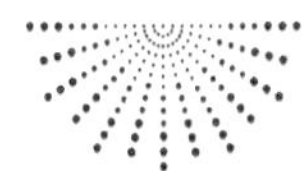

They'd ended up going three rounds in the hot tub. Or was it two and a half? After Freya had ridden him reverse-cowgirl-style, she'd given him some time to recover before she commanded he sit on the hot tub ledge. Yeah, that's right. *Commanded.* His sweet girl was a bossy little thing. Not that he minded. Not at all. Especially since she'd eagerly taken him down her throat. It had been so damn hot, and she'd sucked him so fucking good, he'd seen stars and come within minutes.

After their hot tub naked times, he'd added extra chlorine to the water because, well . . . bodily fluids, right?

While he'd grilled up some steaks for dinner, he'd made a mental note to not only check the pH levels in the morning, but to also delete the security video footage overlooking his back deck. After dinner, they'd shared the two remaining cobblers. Though truth be told, he'd probably gotten one bite of the blueberry and maybe three bites of the strawberry-rhubarb. Not that he cared. He loved finding out these little things about her. She didn't like sharing her dessert. And when she was bossy, it was sexy as hell.

They'd gone one more round after dinner. While their time in the hot tub had been wild and fun and raw, this last time may have been his favorite. In his bed, face-to-face, slow and sweet and gentle. He'd taken the time to explore every part of her body. Kissed every silky, soft inch of her skin. Every scar.

And there had been scars. Jagged scars along her ribs that had piqued his curiosity, but he'd shelved his questions. It hadn't been the time or the place. Especially since she'd tensed when he'd kissed them. At the time, her apparent anxiety had made him even more determined to get her to relax again, to put her at ease in his arms, to make her boneless. To give her his all.

A small smile lifted his lips. It was nearing ten at night, and they were still cuddled in bed. Still spent. Still naked.

Mission accomplished.

She was sprawled over him, and as he'd been doing for the last handful of minutes, he traced his fingers up and down her spine. He loved how she sank into him, utterly relaxed. Her hair was draped over his chest, and he wasn't embarrassed to admit he'd buried his nose in her hair countless times to inhale her soft floral scent. In a ridiculously short amount of time, this woman had slipped under his skin, under his defenses, and deep into his heart. And he had no intention of letting her go.

With the only light in the room coming from the fireplace, he traced his fingers over her shoulders and then dipped them lower and traced the scars along the left side of her ribs. For a split second, she tensed. A warm satisfaction coursed through him when she relaxed a moment later.

He knew it probably wasn't the wisest idea, but his curiosity nagged at him. "Tell me about these?"

Tension returned to her body, and he wanted to smack

himself upside the head. *Holy fuck. What the hell is wrong with you?*

He hugged her tightly, pressing his lips to the top of her head. "Shit, I'm sorry, baby. I shouldn't have asked."

"No, it's alright," she murmured as she shifted off him.

She lay on her left side—with her scars no longer in view—and he rolled onto his side so they faced each other. The sorrow coloring her beautiful face punched him in the gut.

"Freya, sweetheart, what's wrong?"

She shook her head and let out a breath. "They're from a car accident." He didn't think her expression could get sadder, but it did.

"Frey?" He gently brushed a lock of hair behind her ear. Worry churned in his gut as her eyes glistened, filling with tears. His heart ached when a single tear escaped and dripped onto the pillow.

It took her a few moments to find her words, but he remained patient. When she finally spoke, his heart stopped.

"I killed my best friend."

CHAPTER TWENTY-TWO

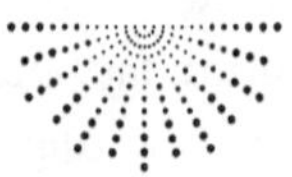

oly shit. That wasn't how she'd planned on telling him. But it was the truth. The god-awful truth. And now the words were out there.

After she'd blurted out those five words, she'd dropped her gaze to his chest. She watched the rhythmic rise and fall of his breath, analyzed every detail of the golden skin that she'd kissed not too long ago.

Because she didn't want to see his expression. Didn't want to see him look at her with horror. With disgust.

Today had been spectacular. While getting pushed and banged up had been awful, she didn't regret any of it, because it had led to this. Being with Xander. Wild sex and making love and all the intimate, mind-blowing moments in between. Starting the day and ending it in his arms had warmed parts of her soul that she hadn't known existed. It had been a truly wonderful and life-changing day.

Then he'd asked one simple question, and she had to go and ruin it.

She could have easily evaded and given him a watered-down version of the truth. But he didn't deserve that. Hell, he deserved so much better than her.

God, this sucked.

Awkward seconds ticked by, but she couldn't bring herself to meet his gaze.

Then he gently pressed a finger under her chin and tilted her head up. "Freya," he whispered. "Please look at me."

When she met his eyes, her heart squeezed with surprise. There was no horror. No disgust. Only concern. And so many unanswered questions.

"Talk to me, Frey. Please."

For a moment, she froze. God help her, she wanted to, wanted to tell him everything. But fear held her back.

He pressed his lips gently against hers. A quick kiss that was feather-light and calmed her heart with its simplicity.

His earlier words echoed in her mind: *You can trust me. When you're ready.*

At the time, she'd told him that she did trust him, and that still held true. She just prayed that when he knew the full truth about what she'd done, that he wouldn't walk away.

She took a deep breath in for courage and then slowly exhaled. His brown eyes remained locked on hers, remained steady.

"I'd just turned sixteen," she began. Her stomach twisted with nerves and gut-wrenching memories. "At that point, Axel had laid down some pretty strict rules for me, and I was pushing every boundary I could." Looking back, the rules were simply a big brother trying to keep his youngest sibling safe. But at the time, they had been stifling and unfair. "It was the weekend before Halloween, and there was a party I wanted to go to. Axel said absolutely not. When he went to his room for the night, I snuck out. Earlier that day, I'd parked my car on the street so no one would hear it start up

—I thought I was so damn smart—and went to pick up Sarah, my best friend."

Her insides squeezed, and she blinked back tears. So much heartbreak. So much regret. "In the back of my mind, deep in my gut," she continued, "I knew it wasn't a good idea. I'd just gotten my driver's license, so I knew I wasn't supposed to have passengers for the first six months, but I didn't care. I was so tired of all of Axel's rules. Be home by ten. Dress like a nun. No boyfriends. No makeup. No fun."

Idiot. She'd been such a fool.

"Sarah and I made it to the party—some house in the middle of nowhere between Blanchard Bay and Bellingham." She recalled some Maroon 5 song blaring on the speakers, and the smell of too many clashing perfumes and colognes and spilled beer combining into a nauseating aroma. It should have been an omen. "There were kids from our high school there, and a ton of kids we didn't know. We were there for about an hour when my brother texted me."

Goosebumps rose over her skin at the memory.

AXEL

If you don't get your ass back home this instant, I will drive out there and pick your ass up my damn self.

He'd included a screenshot of her location on their phone tracker.

Shit, shit, shit!

And just so you know, Sarah's mom called me and asked if she could drop anything off for brunch tomorrow. You know, since Sarah is apparently here for a sleepover. What the fuck, Freya?

Oh, shit! Bile rose in her stomach, and she frantically glanced around looking for Sarah. Spotting her across the room with a couple seniors from their school, Freya rushed over.

"What's up, girl?" a familiar-looking guy said, handing her a shot glass of who knows what. "Bottoms up!"

Setting her can of beer on a table, she slammed back the shot and winced. *Ugh. Whiskey. Gross.* "Thanks," she said with a pained smile and grabbed Sarah's hand. "I need to talk to you."

Pulling her friend to the side, she showed Sarah the texts from her brother.

Sarah's green eyes widened. "Shit. Did Axel say I wasn't at your place?"

She shrugged. "You know as much as I do."

"Shit, we have to get out of here." Sarah pulled her toward the front door and stumbled.

Freya grabbed her friend by the waist, concerned. "How much did you have to drink?"

"Just a beer and a couple shots." Sarah frowned. "Are you okay to drive?"

Freya nodded. "Only had that shot just now. The beer was nasty, so I was only holding it."

"Oh no," Sarah grumbled, hesitating in the doorway.

Crap. The rain had started to really come down.

Grabbing Sarah's hand, she squeezed. "Ready?"

With a squeal, they raced to her car and jumped inside. Freya quickly started it up, cranked up the heat, and grabbed her phone.

We're heading back now. I'm sorry.

Have you been drinking?

She grimaced. They were in the middle of nowhere and it would take at least half an hour to get back to Blanchard Bay.

No. Can Sarah spend the night?

No. Take her ass home.

But she's been drinking! And you know how her mom is . . .

For fuck's sake, Freya.

Fine. Sarah can spend the night. But I swear to God, you and I are gonna have a serious fucking talk when you get home.

She could feel her brother's frustration through the phone, and guilt swamped her. Along with a slightly warm and hazy feeling from that stupid whiskey shot.

I'm sorry. On our way back now.

Huffing out a breath, she tossed her phone into the cup holder. She had to get them home.

She glanced at her friend. "You ready?"

"Yeah," Sarah replied with a sigh, sinking into her seat. "My mom's gonna kill me."

She pulled her car into the street. "Axel said you could spend the night. I hope *you* don't kill *me*, but I told him you've been drinking."

"What?" Sarah shot up in her seat.

Freya held up a hand as she turned onto the two-lane highway that would lead them back to Blanchard Bay. Her eyes narrowed. The rain made the lines on the road hard to see. "I asked him if you could spend the night, and he said no. So I told him you've been drinking and that he knows how your mom is, and so he said yes. Wouldn't you rather have my brother know than your mother?"

Sarah flopped her head back into the seat. "Ugh, God. My mom threatened to ground me until— Look out!"

A deer stood in the middle of the road, frozen in her headlights.

With a panicked scream, she yanked the steering wheel to the right. The car jerked and dipped as they hit gravel and then grass.

Trees filled her windshield.

Crying out, Freya pulled the steering wheel to the left. With her heart threatening to beat out of her chest, the road came into view. She tried to readjust but lost control. The car crossed to the other side of the road. Lights blinded her, and someone screamed. Her? Sarah? She wasn't sure.

There was a deafening crash.

A tight pressure against her chest had her breath seizing. Glass shattered. Metal crunched. An awful burning scent overwhelmed her.

Her ears rang, and she blinked.

Silence.

Sarah came into focus. She was still in the passenger seat, but her head lay at an odd angle against the dash. A trickle of blood ran down her friend's forehead. Sarah's green eyes stared off in front of her.

"Sarah?" she whispered, her throat burning.

Nothing.

Why isn't she blinking? Why isn't Sarah blinking?!

Freya's racing pulse hit panic mode, and she screamed her friend's name again, begging her to blink.

Another deafening crash exploded, and her body was painfully in motion.

Then everything went black.

***

"I'd swerved to the right to miss the deer, and we went off the road. I swerved back to the road to avoid the trees but overcorrected. An oncoming pickup truck slammed into my passenger side. Everything was hazy and everything hurt. I remember seeing Sarah in the passenger seat. There was metal all around her, and her eyes were open. She looked shocked, but all the light was gone from her eyes." Freya's chest squeezed painfully tight, like someone was ripping out her heart, like she was back there trapped in her car. "The last thing I remember thinking was 'Blink. Please blink.' But there was nothing. Then another car hit us, and everything went dark." She sniffed and swallowed past the rock lodged in her throat. "I killed her. I killed my best friend."

A sob tore through her. She was vaguely aware of Xander wrapping his arms around her and pulling her close. All she could focus on were her memories. Her heart was breaking all over again.

And it was all her fault.

CHAPTER TWENTY-THREE

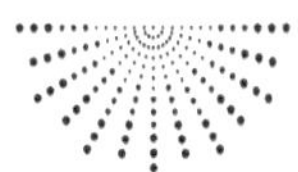

Freya's tears shattered his heart. The anguish of her sobs tore at his soul. He couldn't imagine the amount of guilt she carried. He would do anything to protect her from this devastation, but there was nothing he could do. It had happened, and there was no bringing her childhood friend back. No way to turn back the clock. So he did the only thing he could. He held her as she cried.

He smoothed his hand up and down her back. No empty platitudes. No words promising everything would be okay. He simply held her as she sobbed.

After a while, her tears eased, and she sighed. "I'm sorry. I didn't mean to lose it all over you."

He tightened his arms around her. "You have nothing to apologize for, baby. I'm so sorry about what happened."

"They said Sarah died on impact." She sniffed, and her next words were in a heartbreaking whisper. "So at least she didn't suffer. The man driving the pickup lost a leg, and the woman driving the second car that hit us ended up paralyzed from the waist down. She was a grandma of seven driving home from vacation."

He closed his eyes. Holy fuck. "I'm so sorry."

"Me too." She was silent for a few more moments and then cleared her throat. "They deemed it an accident, but . . ."

Shaking her head, more tears spilled over, and he tightened his arms around her. He didn't know how much time had passed, only that her tears finally subsided. Her breaths finally calmed. If it weren't for her fingers feathering over his skin, tracing over a scar at the edge of his waist, he would have thought she'd fallen asleep.

After a few more moments of silence, she asked, "What's this from?"

Sensing her need for a subject change, he followed her lead. "Army days. Bullet wound. In the jungles of some swampy hellhole. I was lucky it was a through and through. A couple more inches inside and it would have been a different story entirely." Both Wilson and Frazier had also been hit during that clusterfuck. Their team had been damn lucky to get out of there in one piece.

"And this? This one looks newer." She ran her finger over the scar that ran along the left side of his ribs.

"Because it is. About a year ago, I was driving with a client and got T-boned. Intentionally. By an asshole trying to get to my client. Driver's side door got me." He grimaced. "Pretty sure the steering wheel got me too."

She frowned and peeked up at him, meeting his gaze. "Was your client okay?"

"It was a little hairy—he took her while I was out cold— but our team came together, and she was pretty kick-ass herself. In the end, it all worked out, and she was fine."

He placed his hand over Freya's as she traced his scar. "But this was intentional." He moved his hand and traced the edges of her scars. "These? An awful, tragic accident. A deer. The rain and dark. An inexperienced driver. Alcohol. One hundred percent accident." He saw the denial in her eyes, and when she opened her mouth to reply, he kept on talking. "Were there some poor choices made on your part? Yes. But, baby, that doesn't make it any less of an accident."

Her eyes glistened, and she swallowed. "After the accident, my brothers made me go to therapy. For years. Logically, I know it was an accident. But . . ."

His hand moved to the center of her chest. "But it's taking longer for you to believe it here." He traced a heart over her heart.

She nodded, and another tear slipped from her eyes and dropped to the pillow. "Yeah. I'm not sure I'll ever forgive myself."

Not knowing how to reply, because guilt's a tricky bitch, he pressed a kiss to her forehead. "One day at a time, Frey. And I'm here to help you every step of the way. However you need."

A thought tickled the back of his mind. "Those photos you got in the mail, the ones I saw . . . Those aren't the only ones you've received, are they?"

—◆—

Freya took a deep breath, inhaling Xander's cedar-and-soap scent. Like every time before, it calmed her, grounded her. She'd already told him about the accident, and he hadn't responded as she'd thought he would. She'd never imagined he'd respond with kindness. With support. With words of reassurance that she wanted desperately to believe.

She'd underestimated him, but never again. So she'd trust him with all of it.

"I got the first photos two months after the accident. December fourteenth. Sarah's birthday." Her breath hitched, the giant lump in her throat threatening to suffocate her.

"Four photos. Three of me and Sarah, happy and smiling. One of me at her funeral, crying at her grave."

His hand squeezed her hip, and the steady look in his brown eyes gave her the courage to keep talking. "I didn't think much of them until more photos arrived the following year. They came on the anniversary of the accident and on Sarah's birthday again. And every year since. Even if I move, I still get a white envelope of four photos. All the photos are different, but there are always three of me and Sarah, and one of me at the cemetery, either from her funeral or from different times I've visited her grave. But then . . ."

A shiver tore through her. Xander ran his hands over her arms, but they did nothing to relieve the goosebumps. "And then?"

Tingles of unease crept up her spine. "Three years ago, on the tenth anniversary of Sarah's death, the photos changed. There were still four, but two were photos of me and Sarah smiling into the camera, and the other two photos were of me at the cemetery after her funeral. But my face was scratched out in them, and 'It should have been you' was written on one of them. It's been like that ever since."

She met Xander's gaze, and the anger that flashed over his face reassured her. For so long, she'd brushed off the unease she'd felt at receiving the photos, chalking it up to guilt. When the tone of the photos had changed, she'd convinced herself she was overreacting.

"This year," she continued, "when the anniversary came and went last month and I didn't get any photos, I thought it was over. I thought whoever was sending the photos was done."

Xander's eyes narrowed. "You'd just moved to Hudson Island, right?"

She nodded. "At the beginning of October."

"Because of the photos?"

"Kinda. I mean, it was, a factor." She shrugged. "My old landlord was a friend of my oldest brother. The one before that was related to my youngest brother's coworker. And the one before that was a friend of the twins. I wanted my move to Hudson to be a fresh start. For the first time, I was moving somewhere that wasn't tied to my family. I'm twenty-nine and figured it was well past time to do it on my own, you know?"

"It's understandable you wanted independence," he murmured.

"But I'd be lying if I said the photos had nothing to do with my move. I purposely timed it so it was right before the anniversary. Whoever the sender is finds me everywhere I go. So I kept my new address here on Hudson pretty quiet. I didn't even tell my brothers. There was that snafu with my new address and the post office, so my boss allowed me to use the Pacific View as my forwarding address."

His eyes narrowed. "The photos you got recently were delivered to your work, right?"

"Yeah, you were there." She sighed, defeat threatening to overtake her. "Whoever it was didn't forget. The package just got delayed in the post office's mail-forwarding process. I suppose the one positive is that they don't have my new address since it was originally sent to my old address on Whidbey."

"Did you keep the other photos?"

She cringed as she nodded. "I did. They're all in a box in my closet." Morbid, but true. "They'd arrive, and I'd look at them, cry, and then stuff them back into their envelopes and shove them into the box. I tried to throw them away once, but it felt . . . wrong." She'd held on to them as a reminder— not that she'd ever forget—of what she'd done. Of the pain she'd caused.

"You kept them to punish yourself."

It was like he could read her mind.

"Maybe," she whispered before clearing her throat. "But when the photos became scary, I kept them just in case . . ."

"In case?" he prodded.

"In case something happened to me," she admitted, her stomach twisting. "I've never told my brothers about the photos. If something happens to me, there'll be the photos to let them know why."

The wrinkle between Xander's brow popped. "You didn't tell your brothers? Not even the one who's a cop?"

She shook her head. "After the accident, I pulled away from them. The photos of me and Sarah were like a kick to the face. I was too wrapped up in my grief, and then my guilt, to realize how creepy the photos of me at the cemetery were. It didn't quite register that someone had been following me —especially the cemetery photos that were taken years later. When the photos took a darker turn, a decade had passed. I guess I felt stupid for not letting my brothers know earlier. They've always been overprotective, and I knew if I told them, it would turn into another fight. Another Freya-can't-take-care-of-herself thing."

His lips pressed into a thin line. "Yet you kept the photos in case whoever this person is comes after you. So your brothers would know—*after* something happened to you— that someone wished you'd died instead of Sarah."

She fought a wince. When he put it that way, she was a top candidate for being too stupid to live. "In a nutshell."

"When we go back to your place, can I take the photos and show them to my team? You mentioned putting them back in their envelopes, so maybe . . . I don't know . . . Maybe there's a fingerprint or something they can find."

Was that even possible? "Um, sure."

"I can't promise we'll find anything, but it doesn't hurt to check, right? Now, come here," he murmured, pulling her close and wrapping her in his arms. When her head was resting comfortably on his chest, he ran a hand up her spine. "Tell me about Sarah. What was she like?"

For the first time since their conversation had started, the image that popped into her mind of her friend wasn't from the car accident, of Sarah's vacant green eyes, or of her friend lying so utterly still in her casket. Instead, she thought of her kind best friend sitting beside her and holding her hand at her parents' funeral.

"Sarah was the best." The tip of Freya's nose tickled, and her throat grew thick. God, she missed her friend. She sniffed as a bittersweet smile lifted her lips. "We met on the first day of first grade. My mom had dropped me off, and I was so scared. Then this blond girl with bright-green eyes came right up to me, told me her name, and asked if I wanted to be best friends . . ."

CHAPTER TWENTY-FOUR

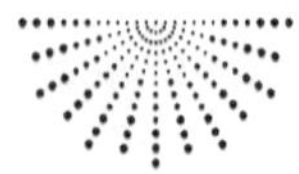

Monday morning came way too soon. Freya was struggling with an emotional hangover. Yes, waking up in Xander's arms again had been amazing—and yes, the man had once again skipped his early morning workout—but all the tears she'd shed as they'd talked into the night had left her with a raging headache.

She'd taken some Tylenol before she'd left Xander's place, but they'd yet to kick in. Regardless, as she placed her purse into her locker, she couldn't help but smile. The man was truly something else.

Yesterday, he'd given her the most pleasure—wild, sexy, sweet, and everything in between—and then he'd taken care of her heart, her soul. He'd listened without judgement . . . about everything. And through it all, he'd held her. He'd wrapped his arms around her, cocooning her until she'd felt safe.

How was it even possible that she trusted him so completely in such a short time span. It had only been a week. Granted, it had been an intense week, but still only a week. And yet she was falling for him.

"Now that's what I call a sappy grin," Audrey said, breezing by her and grabbing a banana from the basket on the table. "Please tell me you went out with Hunky Security Guy and had wild, crazy sex."

Freya choked out a laugh. "Wow. You got all that from my sappy grin?" Work gossip spread like wildfire, and she wanted zero part of it.

Audrey eyed her up and down. "I can't tell if you're evading or not. But throw me a bone. Did you at least kiss the guy?"

Chuckling, she grabbed a fresh apron and made her way to the door. "I don't kiss and tell."

Audrey squealed, following close on her heels. "So you admit there was kissing!"

She shook her head and wagged a finger at her colleague as they rounded the corner to the front desk. "I'm not admitting a thing. Now behave, miss!"

"You're no fun." Audrey sighed. "And FYI, your first appointment is here. She knows she's twenty minutes early but wanted to have some snacks first."

The next few hours were jam-packed with one appointment after another.

"Enjoy the cooking class tonight," Freya said as her client stood, fluffed her hair, and thanked her.

It was one o'clock, and she finally had a half-hour break. She was contemplating running over to the café when Miriam strode toward her holding a large to-go cup with a giant pink straw popping out the top.

"Here you go." Miriam handed her the cup. "A large peanut butter and strawberry smoothie."

"Oh my God, I love you." Freya took a grateful sip of the decadent goodness and sighed. Her stomach growled in approval.

"It's the least I can do for booking you solid until five thirty."

Freya's eyebrows rose. "Five thirty? The schedule said my last appointment was a four o'clock men's cut."

Miriam cringed. "I know. I just added a woman's cut and blowout at four thirty. The guest was a client of Hazel's that was originally down for tomorrow, but she wanted to change it to today. I'm sorry. I'll buy you whatever you want for dinner."

What was another hour, right? "It's fine, Mir, but I'll take a rain check on that dinner."

"I do come bearing good news too." Miriam pulled out a key fob with a valet parking ticket attached to it. "Your rental car is here. It's a gray Ford Explorer, which is nice since it's supposed to snow at the end of the week. This is the spare key and claim ticket. Valet has the other key."

"Thanks. Do you know how long the autobody shop is going to have my car?"

"I'll have to double-check with security, but I think I heard two to three weeks? And again, the rental is on us."

"Well, I appreciate that, and the car upgrade." It would be nice having four-wheel drive if it snowed. She wasn't the best at driving in the stuff, so she could use all the help she could get.

"Freya, out of curiosity, have you heard from Hazel?"

She noted the hint of unease on her boss's face. "I thought I saw a couple texts come in from her this morning, but I haven't had the chance to check them. Everything okay?"

"Well, just as an FYI," Miriam said, "she left a message on my voicemail saying she's planning on opening a salon downtown."

Freya's eyes widened. "Really?"

Miriam nodded. "I want to be completely transparent with you. Please know that we value you. If she offers you something at her salon, by all means, feel free to consider her offer, but know that we'll fight to keep you here."

Freya pulled her phone from her apron. Sure enough, there were three messages from her. "Hazel did text." She flashed her screen at Miriam. "I'm not going anywhere. This place is great. With everything that happened, not only with the shooting, but also my car getting damaged, it made me realize how lucky I am to work here."

"I appreciate you saying that, Freya."

"I'm sorry to interrupt," Audrey said, walking toward them. "Your next client is here, Freya."

Miriam glanced at her watch. "You still have ten minutes. Finish up your smoothie. Let me know if you need anything —another smoothie, snacks, or whatever, and I'll grab it for you. Thank you again for staying late."

"No problem," she said as Miriam walked with Audrey back to the front desk.

Taking another gulp of her smoothie, Freya pulled up her text messages.

HAZEL

OMG, I have some exciting news to share!
Do you have time to meet for coffee
tomorrow morning?

Freya checked her schedule and frowned.

I can't tomorrow. Staff meeting. But how
does Wednesday at 8AM work? Want to
meet at Comfort Food?

Three dots immediately appeared at the bottom of her screen.

Yes! I have so much to tell you! I can't believe how amazing the shooting turned out to be! See ya!

Freya cringed but gave her friend the benefit of the doubt. There was no way Hazel had meant it that way, there was no way she was that tone-deaf. Right?

Her phone buzzed again, and she glanced down. This time, a smile lifted her lips as she pulled up the new text.

XANDER

Still up for dinner? I can meet you at your place at 5. Or I can pick you up if you don't have a rental yet.

The rental's here! And yes, dinner sounds great. But I picked up another guest, so I won't be out of here until about 5:30. Want to meet at my place at 6?

Sounds good. Can I stay the night? Or is that too forward?

A blush stole across her cheeks, and she chuckled.

After yesterday, I'm pretty sure "forward" has gone out the window.

I'd love for you to spend the night.

Excellent. There's a whole slew of things I want to do to you tonight. See you at 6.

She hearted his last text and then fanned herself. Yowza. Six o'clock couldn't come fast enough. A smirk kicked at her lips. Well, at least *she'd* be coming plenty tonight.

· · ·

As it turned out, she had to wait an hour longer before she could see her handsome man. Yeah, that's right. *Her* handsome man. While she was waiting for the valet to pull around with her rental, she got another text from Xander letting her know the meeting he was in was running long. He'd meet up with her at seven.

Though a little disappointed at first, after parking around the corner from her apartment and trekking down the sidewalk, she was grateful for the delay. Her left knee was beginning to throb, no doubt a combination of being on her feet all day and yesterday's fall. She planned on using the extra time to take a piping hot shower and shave everything that needed shaving. Though she was pretty sure Xander wouldn't care one way or another.

Smiling at the thought, she walked by various shops that had just closed for the evening and unlocked the door to her building. Clutching on to the handrail, she winced as her knee protested each and every step. Maybe she'd forgo the shaving and just soak in the tub for the next hour. She let out a sigh when she reached the landing. Another two steps toward her apartment door and—

She froze.

A large white envelope was leaning against her front door.

Her eyes darted around the empty hallway and came to rest on the closed door across the hall—the storage room for Knit Wits. She glanced back at the envelope, and the feeling of spiders crawling over her skin had her shivering. Spinning on her heel, she hustled back down the stairs.

She spilled out onto the sidewalk, her heart hammering in her chest. There were a handful of people milling about down the street, but nothing out of the ordinary. Just people going about their evening.

Standing in the alcove of Knit Wits' entrance with her

back to the door, she pulled out her phone. Her fingers trembled as she called Xander.

It immediately went to voicemail.

She frowned, disconnected, and redialed. This time it rang.

It's just an envelope. You're overreacting!

Was she though?

Yes, it was the same type of envelope the photos were always sent to her in, but those types of white mailing envelopes weren't uncommon.

However, this didn't feel right.

She grimaced as the phone continued to ring. *Didn't* feel *right? Seriously?*

Right when she was about to hang up, the call connected.

"Hey, Frey, what's up?" Xander asked, his voice hushed.

For a moment, her words failed her. Holy crap, what if that stupid envelope was nothing?

"Freya, are you there?"

"Hey, I'm sorry to interrupt your meeting." She cleared her throat as heat washed over her face. "Um, when I got home there was an envelope and . . ."

And when you say that out loud, you can hear how ridiculous it sounds. You're an overreacting nutcase. It's a freaking envelope.

Letting out a sigh, she rubbed her temples and rushed on. "You know what, never mind. I'm so sorry I interrupted. I'll just see you when you get here."

"Hang on, Frey," he said, his voice louder. "Tell me what's going on."

If she could clobber herself over the head, she would. "It's nothing. When I came home, there was a large white envelope propped against my apartment door, and I freaked out. But I'm sure it's noth—"

"Did you open the envelope?"

Though he couldn't see her, she shook her head, feeling

like a fool. "No. Like I said, I got scared, so I ran back outside. I'm standing in front of Knit Wits."

"Don't move from there. I'm going to call you right back."

She frowned as he disconnected their call. Before she could question anything, her phone rang with an incoming video call. She tapped the button, and Xander's face filled her screen. Some of the tension in her body eased.

"Hey, beautiful, you okay?" A muttered curse sounded off camera, and Xander glared to the side before looking back at her. "I'm only a few blocks over, and I'm heading your way right now."

Guilt began to mix with the worry and uncertainty whirling in her gut. "It's okay, Xan, you don't have to rush over. Like I said, it's nothing and—"

"And it was an envelope that gave you a bad feeling. A feeling that had you calling me. Did your landlord call or text you that they dropped anything at your front door?"

She shook her head.

"Has anyone ever left anything at your front door before?"

Again, she shook her head, and that uneasy feeling in her stomach grew.

"Freya, baby, trust your gut. It told you something was off, so you got the hell out of there. That's smart."

His simple words had relief battling the doubt within her.

"If it turns out to be nothing," he continued, "which I hope to hell it is, then this will be something we can laugh about later. But if it's not—"

"It's best to be safe," a deep voice interrupted. Xander swung his phone to the side and showed the man driving—a broad-shouldered, thick-necked man with dark hair that was cut high and tight.

"That's Wilson," Xander said. The other man lifted his

chin, not taking his eyes off the road. "He's a man of few words."

"Whatever, dude." Wilson snorted before glancing at the phone. "Freya, I'm looking forward to meeting the woman who's had Xan blowing off the gym two days in a row."

Before she could respond, the phone jostled, and Xander's face filled the screen again. "Don't listen to a thing he says, baby. He's always full of shit."

She let out a breath, and a soft smile lifted her lips. "Thank you for coming over early."

"Of course. We're turning onto your street now." Xander's eyes narrowed. "I see you, Frey."

She glanced up. A familiar-looking SUV drove toward her and quickly and expertly parallel parked a few spaces down from where she was standing. She caught a glimpse of Xander through the windshield in the passenger seat, and the remaining tension and fear rumbling within her eased.

CHAPTER TWENTY-FIVE

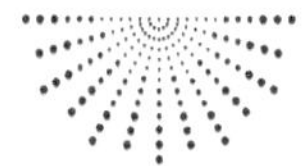

Xander was out of the Rover before Wilson was able to put it in park. He ate up the sidewalk in his rush to get to her, taking in her bright-blue eyes that were wide with both worry and relief. Reaching her, he enveloped her in his arms and let out a breath when she sank into him. A shiver tore through her as she exhaled, and a protectiveness stirred in him and clutched at his gut.

No one was going to hurt his woman. Not on his watch.

He kept his arms around her as he pulled slightly away. "Hanging in there?"

She nodded, but her eyes turned glassy. *No. Hell, no.* Cupping her face in his hands, he brought his lips to hers, unsure if he was reassuring her or himself. "We'll see what this is together, okay?"

She nodded again, buried her face in his chest, and hugged him tightly.

A throat cleared, and he glanced at Wilson who stood a few feet away from them with his hands tucked into the pockets of his dark-gray tactical pants. Despite the worry for the woman in his arms, Xander couldn't help but grin. His friend looked damn uncomfortable, and it was fucking hilarious. Nothing fazed Wilson. Or so he'd thought.

Before Xander could let some smart-ass comment fly, Wilson rolled his eyes and scratched the tip of his nose with his middle finger.

Smothering a chuckle, Xander released Freya but kept her tucked against his side. "This is Wilson. Wilson, Freya."

"It's nice to meet you," she said, extending her hand.

Wilson stepped toward her, and when he shook her hand, his friend's hand engulfed hers. He and Wilson were roughly the same height, and while Xander prided himself on staying in excellent physical condition, Wilson took it to the next level. His friend was a damn beast. He'd never been able to figure out how the man had stayed so stealthy when they were on ops. Not that he was complaining, because he was grateful to have Wilson watching his six.

On top of the man's operative skills, Wilson probably knew him better than he knew himself. The moment Xander had realized something was wrong with Freya, all it had taken was one glance at his friend, and Wilson was in motion. He'd made their excuses with Frazier, leaving their boss to handle the client meeting on his own. No hesitation. No questions. Wilson had simply grabbed his keys and asked, "Where to?"

And Frazier, who knew him as well as Wilson did, had met his gaze and given him a nod.

"Shall we do this?" Wilson asked, angling his head toward her building entrance.

Taking Freya's keys from her hand, Xander unlocked the main door and let Wilson in first. He ushered Freya in next, and after making sure the door was securely closed behind them, he followed her up the staircase.

At the landing, he scanned the hallway. No security cameras that he could see. On the left was the door to Knit

Wits' storage room. Directly across the hall was Freya's apartment. With a large white mailing envelope on the ground propped against the door.

He turned to Wilson, and as if the guy had read his mind, he pulled a credit-card-sized bug detector from the side pocket of his pants.

"Let's give him a minute," he murmured to Freya, who stood stock-still beside him.

Wilson walked up and down each side of the hallway before pulling a pair of gloves from another pocket and donning them. "Clear," he said, picking up the envelope.

"Thanks," Xander said as he stepped away from Freya to unlock her door. After Wilson silently entered her apartment, Xander turned back to her. "Hang tight."

"You think someone's in my apartment?" Her eyes widened, and her voice was a panicked whisper.

He wrapped an arm around her shoulders and squeezed. "No, I don't." That was the truth. Because if someone had gained access to her apartment, they would have left the envelope on the inside.

After a moment, Wilson's body filled the doorframe, and he glanced at Freya. "Why don't you look around to see if anything looks out of place."

She glanced up at him, and he gave her a reassuring nod. "We'll both be right beside you."

Pride surged through him when she took a deep breath, squared her shoulders, and followed Wilson inside.

After going through her small apartment, she said nothing was amiss. However, he could see her anxiety remained. He gestured to the envelope. "Want me to take a look first?"

She crossed her arms over her chest and nodded, clearly nervous.

Wilson held out another pair of gloves, and as he reached

for them, Freya chuckled. "Geez, Wilson, what else do you have in those pants of yours?"

Two seconds of silence ticked by. Then her eyebrows shot up, and she slapped her hands over her reddening cheeks.

Xander bit back a snort—and thankfully, so did Wilson.

"Oh my God, that sounded awful," she murmured. "That's *not* what I meant. Can we please erase that?"

Chuckling, Wilson ran a hand over his jaw. "I'd totally make an inappropriate joke right now, but I think your man would try to beat the shit out of me if I did."

"Not wrong, friend."

Wilson caught his gaze, and amusement danced over his friend's face. "Notice how the operative word there was *try?*"

He and Wilson were evenly matched, that was for sure. "Well," he began with a shrug, "if all else failed, I'd sic Tash on you for me."

Wilson held up his hands in mock innocence and gestured to the envelope.

He quickly pulled on the nitrite gloves, opened the top flap of the envelope, and peeked in. He shook the envelope to get a better look at the contents.

Fuck.

Lead filled his stomach. All the teasing and laughter from just seconds earlier was gone.

He met Freya's gaze and frowned. "You were right to be worried. It's more photos." The way the light in her eyes dimmed tore at his gut. "I want you to pack a bag, baby. Come stay with me for the rest of the week."

Her mouth fell open, and she sucked in a breath. "That bad?"

He'd only caught a glimpse of a couple of the photos, but that had been enough. He nodded. "Do you want to see them?" *Please say no.*

She worried her bottom lip. "I don't know."

He pulled her into his arms. How could he not? "Why don't you pack first?" As much as he wanted to protect her, he wasn't going to lie to her. "The photos aren't good, but we can look at them later. I don't want you staying here any longer than you need to, and most definitely not by yourself."

She gulped and squeezed his waist before she let go. "Um, how much should I pack?"

"At least for the week. We can come back this weekend and get you more stuff if need be."

"Holy crap, okay," she said on an exhale and hustled to her bedroom.

Wilson was beside him in seconds. "What were the photos of?" he asked in a hushed voice.

"The two of us from yesterday." With their faces scratched out.

Wilson's jaw clenched, and his eyes narrowed. "What shit have you stepped into?"

Anger simmered in his blood. "I don't know, but I'm gonna use every fucking resource we have to find out."

Wilson slapped him on the shoulder. "I'll round up the troops. Bean and Frazier, for sure. Want me to see if Alvarez is free to join?"

He nodded and handed Wilson the envelope. "Yeah. Tash and Esme too, if they're available. Between all of us, we've got to be able to figure out what the hell is going on."

Freya's hands shook as she folded the final black dress, placed it in her small suitcase, and zipped it up. She'd packed enough work outfits for the rest of the week, along with toiletries and makeup in record time.

She pulled her suitcase off her bed, set it on the floor, and pulled up the handle. She paused and sat on the edge of her bed, her shoulders sagging.

She should have asked to see what was in the envelope, should have demanded to see the photos. After all, burying her head in the sand was never a good idea. But after seeing the look on Xander's face, she'd chickened out. The anger radiating off him told her that whatever he'd seen had been bad.

It wasn't like she wasn't ever going to look at the photos, just . . . not quite yet. Because the fact he didn't want her to stay alone at her apartment said a lot. The fact that she'd gone and packed her suitcase, no questions asked, also said a lot.

She trusted him. Implicitly.

Knowing him a short time or not, she trusted him. With her safety, her body . . . her heart. She simply needed to focus on the now, not the what-ifs. Not only with them and whatever their intense relationship was, but with whatever danger seemed to be swirling around them. If she didn't focus on the now, she'd lose her mind.

"Hey."

She glanced up at the now-familiar voice.

Xander stood in her doorway with empty hands, and she frowned.

"I gave the envelope to Wilson," he said, answering her unasked question. "We're calling in the crew to try and figure out what's going on. If it's okay with you, I'd like you to talk with my team about the photos you've gotten over the years."

Her stomach twisted. She knew it was inevitable, but still . . .

She nodded toward her closet. "The blue box on the top shelf has the rest of the photos."

As he crossed the room to her closet, she asked, "What were the photos in the envelope of?"

"Us. Yesterday."

She gasped, and the blood drained from her face.

With the blue box tucked under his arm, he turned to her with narrowed eyes. A split second later, they widened. "Oh shit. No, baby. They were us from yesterday at the *parade.* Some by the toy store, not of us . . ."

Relief surged through her. She exhaled and slapped both hands over her racing heart. "Oh my God, Xander. I thought they were pictures from the hot tub." Heat scalded her cheeks.

He sat beside her, placed the box on the bed, and took both her hands in his and squeezed. "The photos I saw were from the parade. I didn't see all the pictures, but I highly doubt there were any of us from the hot tub."

"How can you be sure?"

"I can't. Nothing's impossible, but one of the reasons I want you to stay with me is that my house—hell, all the houses on Frazier's property—are secure. We have more cameras and security measures than Fort Knox."

But didn't that mean . . .

She frowned, and panic started to build anew. "So if you have all these cameras, what about—"

"I wiped the security footage of us last night, and I went into both the master file and backup and cleared it from there as well." He pressed a kiss to her forehead, and she felt him smile. "Not gonna lie, though, sweetheart. Seeing us was hot as hell, but don't worry. All the footage is gone."

She let out another breath. Holy crap, she wasn't sure she could take much more. Her emotions were all over the place —fear, relief, terror, completely inappropriate arousal. Rinse and repeat.

She could admit that picturing Xander watching the video of them in the hot tub had her heart rate quickening.

Again, completely inappropriate with what was going on, but it was the God's honest truth.

"The photos of us looked to be long-range."

And back to being scared. But long-range was good, right? Creepy, but good. It had to be better than up close and personal.

"Baby, we're going to figure this out. Your car, you getting pushed, all the photos. We're going to figure out how it's all tied together."

For a moment, she studied their linked hands. She knew he'd do everything he could to protect her, but it didn't stop the trickle of fear from inching down her spine. Then his words registered. "You think it's all connected? Even what happened with my car?"

"I do. Too many coincidences." He hesitated, and she tilted her head in question. "One of the parade photos I saw had our faces scratched out." He nodded to the blue box on the bed behind them. "Like those."

Her stomach dropped and filled with dread. *Holy shit, of course their faces were scratched out.*

His phone dinged with an incoming text, and the pessimist in her cringed. She didn't want any more bad news.

He checked his phone and stood, pulling her up with him. "Wilson's downstairs. Everyone's gathering at Frazier and Bean's place. We can take your rental, and Wilson will follow us."

She focused on the plan and nodded. "One step at a time, right?"

He tilted her chin up with his knuckle and pressed a kiss to her lips. "That's right."

As he picked up her suitcase, she grabbed the box of photos and placed it in a large tote bag. "Xander?"

He paused at the door and turned back to her.

"Thank you for helping me. I don't know what I would

have done if you hadn't shown up . . ." She'd probably be curled up in fetal position in her bed after having puked her guts out from fear. Like she'd done the last few times she'd gotten the ominous photos.

"There's nothing to thank me for, Frey. I'm here for you." He was once again in front of her, wrapping her in his strong arms. "I'm all in, remember?"

Again, he lifted her chin up with his finger, and the look he gave her—one of care and concern and something so sweet she didn't want to jinx it by naming it—had her chest squeezing. "I'm all in too. Let's go figure this out."

CHAPTER TWENTY-SIX

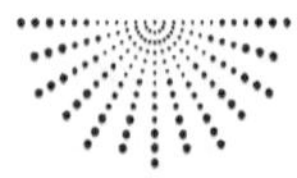

Tension gripped Freya's shoulders as Xander pulled into a driveway that was about half a mile down the road from his.

They'd left her apartment with Xander driving her in her rental and Wilson following behind in his Range Rover, which was nearly identical to Xander's. Apparently, Hudson Security had a fleet of eight armored SUVs—all black Range Rovers—which seemed like quite the job perk. Until he'd mentioned that all the vehicles were fully armored. What that exactly entailed, she wasn't quite sure, but it sent a bolt of unease through her. It was a reminder that what Xander did was dangerous, and the thought of him putting himself in more danger because of her didn't sit right.

As he led her from the rental car into the house, nerves sprang anew in her stomach. Not only from the thought of rehashing the worst day of her life, but also from meeting more of Xander's friends.

"Oh good, you guys are here," a familiar-looking brunette said as they entered the main room. The petite woman was seated at the end of a rectangular dining table with two giant men occupying the chairs on either side of her. She waved toward the kitchen. "Gavin made some chicken stuff if you two are hungry."

Xander glanced down at her. "Want me to grab you some food?"

Her stomach turned. Food was the last thing on her mind. "No, thanks. But if you're hungry, go ahead and—"

"I'm good." With his hand at the small of her back, he nudged her toward the dining table, and she quickly glanced around. Xander was right, this place was a larger version of his. However, where Xander's giant television sat in his living room, here it was a mammoth workstation with an intimidating number of screens.

"I'm Bean," the woman said with a wave, pulling Freya's attention back from the computer setup. "Wait, we've met before, haven't we?"

"We have." Freya nodded, trying to place the woman. "Ah, I did your hair about a month or so ago. You were going to a charity event, I believe." She quickly racked her brain for what she knew of the woman—from when she'd done her hair and from what she'd been told by Xander. And just like that, nerves bloomed. Because this unassuming, delicate-looking woman was, in reality, formidable. *Small talk, Freya. It's what you do. So what if the woman's a bona fide genius?* "Xander tells me you're in charge of the company's cybersecurity. I believe his words were 'brilliant' and 'game-changer.'"

In her line of work, Freya had learned that compliments never hurt.

The woman beamed. "Oh, did he now?" Bean turned her smile toward Xander. "I *knew* you were my favorite."

"Oh good God, don't get her started," the man to Bean's left grumbled before lifting his chin. "Gavin Frazier. Nice to meet you."

"You too," she replied as Gavin shot Bean a wink. "Thank you for helping—"

"Good to see you again, Freya," a woman's voice called out.

Frowning, Freya glanced around, but Bean was the only other woman in the room.

"Over there," Bean said, pointing to an open laptop that sat at the opposite end of the table.

She smiled when Esme and Tash waved from separate boxes on the screen. "It's good to see you both again."

"Wish it was under better circumstances, though," Tash said.

The man seated to Bean's left rose and turned to her with his hand extended. "Matt Alvarez."

"Nice to meet you," she said, shaking his enormous hand. The guy was just as tall as Xander, but even more muscular, and he had jet-black hair and tanned skin. The wave of intensity that he emitted was beyond intimidating.

"He's Daisy's dad," Xander said, pulling out the chair beside Alvarez and gesturing for her to sit.

"Daisy said she invited you to her birthday party." Alvarez shot her a bright smile that nearly had her jaw dropping.

Holy crap, the guy's smile transformed him. In one second, he'd gone from a tough-looking badass you'd be afraid to run into in a dark alley to an obviously doting father who was completely enamored by their child.

Freya's shoulders relaxed, and she grinned back at him. "She did. We met over ice cream last week. For the record, Daisy is an absolute darling."

"That she is, and she knows it too." Alvarez chuckled. "If you can make it to her party, I know she'll be thrilled to have you there. She was excited that 'Xandy's friend' liked ice cream and had black hair and blue eyes like her and her mama. I mean, no pressure or anything."

"Oh, I'm in," Freya said, smiling. "I work on Saturday, but Xander said it's at five, so I should be done by then."

"Great," Alvarez said. "And you don't need to bring a gift or anything."

"Too late," Xander said. "We picked up Daisy's gifts when we were in Coupeville yesterday."

"Speaking of which," Wilson said as he entered the room, took the seat beside Gavin, and placed the white mailing envelope on the table. "Someone had eyes on them."

"And there goes the kumbaya," Tash muttered.

After taking a pair of gloves from Wilson, Gavin opened the envelope, pulled out the photos, and spread them out on the table.

Her stomach clenched, and she sucked in a breath.

Gavin's gaze swung to her. "Fuck. You haven't seen them yet?"

Taking in the photos, she gave a slight shake of her head. "It's fine."

She rose and rounded the table to stand beside Gavin. Xander was immediately beside her, his hand warm on her lower back as he instructed Gavin to rearrange the photos so they were chronological.

Eight photos in total.

The first two were of them on the sidewalk watching the parade—well, she was watching. Xander had his sunglasses on, but the photos captured a tension in him, as if he were looking around for something. Or someone.

The next was of them entering the toy store, and then of them leaving the store with bags in hand.

The last four had her stomach turning. They were after she'd fallen. Two were with her on the ground, and two after Xander had helped her to her feet. In all of them, both of their faces had been violently scratched out, the black pen digging through the photo paper.

"Well fuck, Xan," Gavin murmured. "Someone's not happy with the two of you."

"The marks are similar to photos Freya has received in the past." Xander glanced at her.

Nodding, she rounded the table and retrieved the blue box from the tote bag she'd left by her chair. Setting the box on the table, she hesitated as she lifted the lid. "Do I need gloves?"

"You're good," Alvarez said as he donned a pair of black gloves. "Chances of getting prints are low, but yours are already on them."

A rock formed in her gut as the members of Hudson Security carefully picked through the envelopes in the box. Years of painful memories bombarded her, making it hard to swallow. "They're in reverse chronological order," she said, her voice suddenly scratchy. "The photos were fine until three years ago. That was the ten-year anniversary of the car accident . . ."

Strong arms wrapped around her from behind. She closed her eyes when Xander's lips pressed against the top of her head. She sank into him, grateful for his comfort. The rock in her gut grew, and her breaths became labored.

Glancing up at him, she fought back tears and shook her head. "I can't. I'm sorry, but I can't."

The tears shimmering in her eyes slayed him. Absolutely destroyed him.

He cupped her jaw and ran his thumb over her cheek. Then he sat back into his chair and pulled her across his lap.

"I've got you, baby," he murmured into her ear. "Do you want me to tell them what happened?"

She nodded, trembling in his arms.

Aware his teammates—his *family*—were watching them, he cleared his throat and tightened his hold on Freya. He recognized their expressions. Concern and determination.

Over the next twenty minutes, he recapped Freya's story. From her parents passing and her oldest brother taking over her guardianship, to the car accident and her best friend's death. From the photos that continued to follow her year after year, to her car getting broken into at the resort, and finally to her getting pushed down at the parade.

As he spoke, Freya slowly relaxed in his arms. Soon, she began interjecting and clarifying points here and there. By the time they spoke of the photos arriving at her door earlier this evening, her tremors had stopped. He was damn thankful for that, and damn thankful for his team.

With the exception of Bean, he'd witnessed each and every one of them interrogate people who were the dredges of humanity—fucking god-awful people—so he knew his teammates could be intimidating and scary as fuck. But the gentleness and care they'd shown Freya when they'd asked their questions? He'd never forget it. Ever.

Xander gestured to the photos on the table, which now included the ones from the last three years. "I mean, I'm not reaching, am I? It's connected. The scratched-out markings have a similar feel."

"I agree," Frazier said, leaning back in his chair. "The cars that were vandalized at the resort were all the same make, model, and color. So maybe whoever this was, wasn't sure which car was yours."

"I'd venture to guess they also didn't know you'd moved until recently," Alvarez said, glancing down at his notes. "You moved to Hudson Island on October first and wisely kept it quiet. The anniversary of the car accident is October twenty-sixth and the postmark from the envelope is October twen-tieth to your old address. It got lost in the mail, and I think it's pure coincidence that it arrived to your work when it did. However, these photos . . ." He gestured to the newest ones on the table. "These were dropped at your apartment. So the question is, how did they find you?"

For a few moments, the room was silent.

Until Tash said, "The shooting at the resort. Everything that happened—the escalation—happened after that."

Xander felt Freya's body tense, and he glanced at her. "Frey?"

"Hazel's interview with the news." Sighing, she rubbed her temples. "I'm pretty sure she mentioned me by name."

"On it," Bean murmured, her fingers flying over her laptop. Within seconds, she spun her computer around.

Hazel was on the screen, and Bean pressed play. They listened for about thirty seconds, and then Hazel said, "The lady was getting her hair done right next to me, and the guy just stormed in. He threw my coworker Freya Hansen to the ground and started screaming and yelling, trying to yank the lady out of the chair. My poor friend is all bruised. Freya and I both live here on Hudson. It's a quiet and wonderful small town, and the resort is the last place you'd expect that kind of violence. It was just awful . . ."

The clip cut back to the reporter, and Bean paused the video.

Chills skated down Xander's spine.

"The interview aired last Wednesday," Bean said.

"Freya's car was damaged at the resort on Friday." Xander's mind raced, desperate to find a link. He glanced at Bean. "What did you find on the security videos from Friday?"

She grimaced. "Unfortunately, not much. Our updated camera install for the employee parking lot didn't happen until the weekend. I ran the videos they had through my facial rec software. All the people that were picked up by the existing cameras around that parking lot were either employees or guests."

"But it doesn't really matter," Tash interjected. "That employee lot was accessible from the forest, and there were no cameras along that edge until our team installed them later."

Xander sighed in frustration. "So a whole lot of nothing."

Warm hands squeezed his forearms, and he glanced at Freya, who was still sitting on his lap. She framed his face in her hands. "It's okay. One step at a time, right?"

The rising tension squeezing his lungs released. He turned his face and pressed a kiss to both of her palms. "That's right, baby."

"Aww, you guys are cute," Tash said, grinning into the camera. "B, what about the parade? Any usable security footage from there?"

Bean rolled her eyes. "No. Let's just say that the security cameras on their buildings are about the same caliber and quality as the ones we have in downtown Hudson."

"So complete and absolute shit," Wilson muttered. "Got it."

Bean shrugged. "You're not wrong. They got just the crowds within three feet of the store entrances. Nothing showing the whole street, let alone Freya getting pushed."

Xander ground his molars together, and again, Freya's hands tightened over his forearms. He exhaled and worked his jaw side to side.

"Bean," Wilson said. "You should have your team install cameras in Freya's building tomorrow. Entrance and main hallway."

Bean nodded. "Will do. I'll have Abbot send one of her guys out."

"You should have him dress like a plumber or electrician

or something," Esme called out from the video screen. "In case there are eyes on her place."

"Do you think that's necessary?" Freya asked, worry tinging her words.

Before Xander could respond, Wilson turned to her. "Yes, I think it's absolutely necessary."

"You're completely secured at Xander's place," Frazier interjected. "But it's better to be safe."

"Do we have anyone still working at the resort?" Xander asked.

Bean nodded. "Abbot's on-site. She's still training their surveillance personnel on the new resort cameras and setups. Witherspoon and Torres are doing some final camera adjustments, and then they'll work on the perimeter and game-camera install since the security fence was actually delivered early."

"On that note," Esme chimed in, "I spoke with the security-fence company, and they *should* wrap up by the end of next week. But with the storm rolling in, it may push to the following week. However, they've assured me they'll finish before Thanksgiving."

"Carmichael is still on-site as well," Tash added. That news had Xander's brows rising, and she held up her hands. "What? You were busy this evening."

Xander frowned. "I thought he wrapped up training today."

"He did, but then he sent Owen in undercover this afternoon and wasn't impressed with the front desk's performance." Tash shrugged. "She basically walked right in, and no one stopped her."

"Right." He sighed and ran his hand over Freya's arm. "I don't mean to sound high-handed, but I'd like to have someone keep an eye on you. Until we know who's sending you these photos, I want eyes on you when I'm not around."

She nodded. "Okay."

He tilted his head in question, surprised she was readily agreeing.

"Xander, I'm not an idiot. All of you . . ." She gestured around the table. "This is what you do. You protect people. I'd be lying if I said I wasn't scared. The pictures alone make me want to puke. But knowing that this person knows where I work, where I *live* . . . If you want to have someone parked at the spa with me all day, I'm in." A tremor rocked through her, and he ran a hand up her back and squeezed her nape. "I can't help but feel like the other shoe is about to drop."

He pressed a kiss to her forehead. "Not on my watch, baby."

"Not on *our* watch," Wilson added, crossing his arms over his chest.

Frazier met his gaze and lifted his chin. "A-fucking-men."

CHAPTER TWENTY-SEVEN

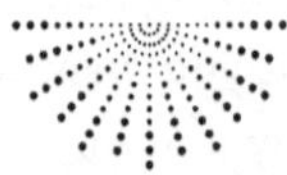

The week flew by in a blur. Xander drove her to and from work, and her schedule was jam-packed. From seven thirty in the morning to five thirty in the evening, it was back-to-back-to-back appointments. All the while, Xander's colleague, Bonson, had parked himself in the corner behind the spa's front desk, much to the delight of Audrey, the other front-desk girls, and many of the spa guests. To say the man was easy on the eyes was an understatement. Freya was beginning to think it was a Hudson Security job requirement to be charming, ripped, and stupidly hot.

The only morning she had a light schedule was Wednesday—she didn't have to start until nine thirty—but she'd met Hazel for coffee at Comfort Food. Xander had discreetly taken a small table by the entrance while she and Hazel had caught up on the opposite side of the café.

Meeting with her friend had been a huge disappointment. Hazel had talked her ear off, going on and on about her new boyfriend. How amazing he was, how handsome he was, how rich he was. Every question Hazel had asked her seemed to be just a segue to the next topic she wanted to talk about, which always had to do with her boyfriend.

Freya was happy for Hazel, she really was. She knew her friend tended to move from man to man, never quite finding what she wanted. But this guy seemed to check all of Hazel's boxes. However, when Hazel said he was giving her the money to open up her own salon downtown, she couldn't help but be skeptical, especially since their relationship was still so new. However, seeing as her own relationship with Xander was also brand spanking new and moving a million miles an hour, she couldn't say a thing.

As Miriam had warned her, Hazel had asked her if she wanted to work at the new salon. She'd declined, but it was like Hazel hadn't heard her and just continued to talk about how much fun they would have working together again.

While Hazel had taken a moment to text her boyfriend, she'd discreetly caught Xander's eye and sent him a pleading look. Within minutes, he'd rescued her from the painful meetup, and she'd given Hazel a vague promise to see her again soon.

It had been go go go since then.

A highlight was that Miriam had made good on her promise for dinner and had upped the ante. On Wednesday, Mir had treated her and Xander to an amazing dinner at the Orca Moon Lounge, where Mia—on a rare night off—and her boyfriend had joined them. The following night, her boss had surprised her with reservations to the resort's uber fancy Watermark Restaurant.

Freya's days were busy and exhausting, with a nervous edge that hovered over her like a storm cloud, but ending each night in Xander's arms made it all worth it.

On Saturday, after another long day of work, they headed to Daisy's birthday party, albeit a little late. Her feet were killing her, but she was looking forward to a mellow evening celebrating the darling girl. Apparently, Daisy wanted everyone to come over and watch her newest favorite movie —*Tangled*—in the backyard. Though the snowstorm the forecasters had anticipated had never materialized, at least not on Hudson Island, it was still twelve days until Thanksgiving, and the temperatures had dropped. So if anything, a backyard movie-night party would be interesting.

They pulled into a long driveway that led to an amazing house that overlooked the water, and despite the nerves blooming in her stomach, she chuckled at the number of all-black Range Rovers lined up along the side.

Over the past week, aside from work, she and Xander had spent every waking moment together. Talking, hanging out, making love. In all that time, it had been on the tip of her tongue to invite him to Thanksgiving. Each and every time, she'd chickened out.

Yes, they were together, but a holiday with her family seemed so official. Not that she wasn't there. She was. But was he? They hadn't had the official are-we-boyfriend-and-girlfriend talk, but, temporarily or not, she'd moved in with him, and it was fantastic.

Also, she knew her brothers would grill him. She wasn't sure she wanted to subject him to that. Hell, she didn't know if *he* wanted to be subjected to that. After all, they were still so new. So she'd hemmed and hawed all week, and now it felt like it was too late to ask.

Oh my God, you're spiraling. Stop!

Was she overthinking things? Most likely. Did that make inviting him any less nerve-racking? Nope.

Xander cut the engine, and her pulse picked up speed. *Now or never.* As he reached for his door handle, she blurted, "Will you come home with me for Thanksgiving?"

He released the door handle and turned to her with questioning eyes.

Oh no. Words spewed from her mouth. "I mean, if you're not busy. It's totally okay if you can't. I mean, Blanchard Bay is a long drive from here. I just thought maybe it would be nice and—"

He kissed her quiet, and some of the built-up tension within her released.

"I'd love to spend Thanksgiving with you. Honest question, Frey," he began, pushing a lock of hair behind her ear. She held her breath. "Were you thinking about asking me the entire drive here?"

She squirmed and gave him a sheepish smile. "Maybe."

He exhaled and mimed wiping sweat from his brow. "Well, that makes me feel better. You were so quiet, I'd thought you were having second thoughts about coming to the party. *Then* I thought maybe you were having second thoughts about us."

Shaking her head, she chuckled. "If you could have been in my head a few minutes ago, I was going down the rabbit hole of whether we're *together* together or just kinda together."

The smile he flashed her had her insides lighting up. He leaned over the console and pressed another kiss to her lips. "*Together* together. For the record, boyfriend and girlfriend feel a little juvenile to me, and partner feels too formal. And since lover just gives me the creeps, my vote is to go with boyfriend and girlfriend. Thoughts?"

For a second, she could only stare at him in wonder. This amazing man was constantly surprising her. "I'm in agreement on the term lover. It's . . ." She scrunched her face. "Not a fan. So boyfriend and girlfriend it is."

"Great." His gaze darted to the house, and his smile widened. "I see a very excited little girl waving at us. Ready to party?"

Freya glanced at the house and laughed. Sure enough,

Daisy was standing on the porch between Matt and Wilson. She was hopping from foot to foot with a giant smile on her face, waving frantically at them.

She patted his shoulder. "Go give the birthday girl a hug, and I'll grab all the presents."

His gaze swung to hers. "You sure?"

She glanced at Daisy again and chuckled. "Uh, yeah."

Freya laughed as she grabbed their gift bags from the back of the SUV, and Xander made his way to the house shouting, "Birthday girl!" Daisy leaped off the porch—fluffy rainbow-sloth dress, sparkly unicorn tiara, and all—and launched herself at Xander with an excited squeal.

"Let me help you with those," Wilson said, heading her way while Xander carried Daisy inside. He grabbed the bags and then held up the three largest, shaking his head. "I swear, the rest of us don't stand a chance of ever getting to be that girl's favorite."

With a smile, she followed Wilson into the house. Xander, still carrying a beaming Daisy, was immediately beside her.

"Hi, Faya!"

"Happy birthday, sweet girl. Are you having a good birthday so far?"

Daisy nodded. "We're gonna have cake and ice cream with sprinkles and popcorn and M&M's! And Xandy's gonna sit right next to me!"

The little girl wiggled in Xander's arms, and he set her down. She flew through the great room and out to the back deck.

"In case you can't tell, Matt already snuck her some ice cream," a woman who was obviously Daisy's mother said with a smile. "I'm Scarlet. I've seen you around, but it's nice to officially meet you in person."

"Same," she said, shaking the other woman's hand.

"If you'll excuse me, I'm going to call the kids in," Scarlet said, resting her hands on her baby bump. "It's cake time. We're doing things out of order since I'm hoping the kids will crash during the movie."

Xander scoffed. "With all the snacks you have planned, not likely, Scar."

The other woman grimaced. "I know. I put out some baby carrots and cucumber slices, but Matt put them next to the gummy worms and Nerds Clusters. Let's just hope they don't all end up puking by the end of the night."

As Scarlet went to wrangle the kids, Xander introduced Freya to the handful of people she didn't know. She was pleasantly surprised to see one of her local clients, Poppy, at the party. The woman owned a popular boutique downtown and was apparently very good friends with Scarlet. Gotta love small towns.

The party was controlled chaos. It helped that there were only a handful of kids, but there were a *lot* of adults, mostly from Hudson Security. The amount of testosterone in the room was high. It was telling how everyone had shown up for their colleague's daughter. Plus, each and every one of those badasses were wearing light-up unicorn headbands.

After dinner and cake and ice cream, they all moved into the great room for presents. Freya stood off to the side, taking it all in, and she marveled at the efficiency. Daisy sat on the couch, flanked by her parents, while Xander and Wilson were in charge of bringing the gifts to her and handling the discarded wrapping and tissue paper. Esme was perched on the arm of the couch, jotting down who gave Daisy what. It was quite a well-oiled machine. But considering this was the Hudson Security crew, Freya wasn't exactly surprised.

She couldn't help but grin at the slew of pink, purple, and unicorn gifts, and at how Daisy was a wonderful mix of delighted and shy as she thanked each person for their gift.

They were coming to the end of the gifts when Xander handed over all four of their gift bags. "Alright, birthday girl, these are from me and Freya."

She snickered as the majority of his friends rolled their eyes, but all their smirks were good-natured. The sweet girl politely thanked them for the pajamas and then squealed with delight at the tent playhouse and furniture.

"Hang on, birthday girl," Xander said, handing Daisy an envelope. "This is also part of your present."

"Oh good God," Tash quietly grumbled from beside her. "Of course he got her another present. Do you know what it is?"

Freya shook her head, curiosity clawing at her.

"It's a mama and baby slothy!" Daisy exclaimed, holding up the photo.

"That's right, birthday girl," Xander said, pointing at the picture. "That's Suzie, the sloth mama, and that's her baby, Coco. We have to wait a couple months for Coco to get a little bit bigger, and then we can go on an adventure and visit them in person. You can even hold and feed Coco."

Daisy's eyes widened, and she gasped. "I can cuddle a real slothy baby?"

He grinned. "You sure can, birthday girl."

Chuckles sounded when Daisy launched herself at him, practically strangling him.

Freya's chest squeezed. This sweet, sweet man . . .

"Ugh." Tash groaned, leaned toward her, and whispered, "I don't even want kids, but *that* whole thing just made my ovaries spring to life."

Freya laughed. "I hear you."

Was it too early to fall in love?

She'd never been one to believe in love at first sight. After all, she was the one who'd had the rule of two dates before you kissed and two *months* of dates before you slept together.

She'd technically kissed Xander before they'd even been introduced. Then she'd *really* kissed him after their first dinner. Then she'd happily jumped into bed with him a few days after that.

Yes, it was fast. And it was most definitely not her norm. But nothing about it felt wrong.

"Xan's a great guy," Tash said, her voice low. "But I'm sure you already know that."

"He is. He's made me throw every dating rule I had out the window."

Tash chuckled. "If it's any consolation, I know for a fact that you've done the exact same for him."

She glanced at the other woman, the woman who was one of Xander's best friends. "Half the time, I wonder how it's possible that he's real."

"What you see is what you get with Xan. And with you? He's letting you see more than any of us. Please be careful with his heart." Tash looked at the man in question, a soft smile lifting the edges of her lips. "You're good for him, Freya. If you give him the chance, he'll be everything you didn't know you needed."

"I think he already is," she whispered. Watching Xander as he laughed with Daisy, warmth filled her soul. "His heart's safe with me. I promise."

CHAPTER TWENTY-EIGHT

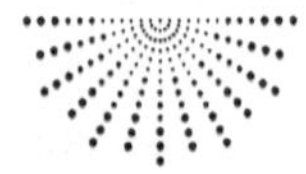

After Daisy's party, Xander had to hit the gym extra hard. Aside from the burgers and cake and ice cream, outside movie night had included a copious amount of junk food. Popcorn, M&M's, Junior Mints, Whoppers . . . Hell, he may have even eaten his body weight in some caramel-chocolate-peanut-butter concoction.

He didn't have a lot of experience with children's birthday parties—Daisy was their group's first kid—but it had been a lot of fun. The way Freya had fit so seamlessly in amongst his friends, Daisy's excitement about visiting the sloth sanctuary . . . It had been great. He grinned as he recalled rubbing his number-one status in his buddies' faces. Immature? Absolutely. Did he care? Nope.

"What are you smiling about?" Freya asked from the passenger seat.

He glanced at her, and his smile grew. Damn, she was beautiful. "Just thinking about Daisy's party. It was fun."

"Uh, yeah. When you'd mentioned an outdoor movie night, I hadn't expected a twinkle-light canopy with heaters.

The twins would love something like that. Just maybe . . . a little less fancy."

"In fairness to Alvarez and Scar, that wasn't their idea. They'd planned on watching a movie in the living room, but Esme got wind of it and . . ." He shrugged. "Her title *is* director of logistics."

"Well, if she ever gets tired of working for Hudson Security, she'd make a killing at party planning." After a moment, Freya's brow furrowed. "Those clouds are pretty ominous looking."

Glancing at the sky, he frowned. The forecasters had predicted another snowstorm, and for once, they may be right.

The days following Daisy's party were more of the same. He drove Freya to work each morning, and since he didn't feel comfortable leaving her alone at his place in the mornings even though he knew it was secure, he'd moved his gym time to his lunch hour.

Work was still busy. They had a number of assignments coming up, and their teams were going to be stretched thin. But on a positive note, he and Gavin had made formal employment offers to the two final candidates they'd interviewed.

Nothing more threatening had happened to Freya. His frustration was building, and he still had that gut feeling that something was off. That whoever was behind the photos wasn't done. He wasn't the only one either. Wilson and Tash were both antsy about it, as well.

It didn't ease his worry, but it reassured him that he wasn't being overly paranoid.

The highlight of each day was Freya. He looked forward to picking her up from work so they could spend their evenings together. Whether it was dinner at home or getting together with her work friends or his, he simply enjoyed every minute with her. But his favorite part was holding her, kissing her, filling her, falling asleep and waking up with her in his arms.

He couldn't pinpoint the exact moment it had happened, but sometime over the last few weeks, he'd fallen hard. The woman was his everything.

Now, as he stared at the dark clouds through his windshield, he winced. They were on hour four of what was supposed to have been a two-hour trip. But a delayed ferry, plus several car accidents on I-5, along with Thanksgiving-morning traffic, had them rolling into Blanchard Bay later than planned. Food was being served at noon, and thankfully, they'd left Hudson Island extra early, so they were still on track. However, they were still about half an hour out, and the last thing they needed was for the sky to start dumping snow on them.

Freya had been fielding numerous texts from her brothers, reassuring them that she'd remembered to bring both the mac and cheese and three Thanksgiving pies.

As they entered Blanchard Bay's city limits, he said, "Run everyone's names by me again."

"Axel's the oldest. He can be kind of an ass, though I've been told he means well. He's a detective with the Blanchard Bay PD. He's a single dad, and his twin daughters—Andie and Josie—are five, in kindergarten, and are freaking adorable. Then there's the twins, Oscar and Jasper. Oscar's super tidy and regimented, while Jasper's basically a slob. But they're both really nice and surprisingly work well together."

"They run the construction company your dad started, right?"

"Correct. They've done well for themselves. Then there's Finn, the youngest." Xander glanced over at Freya just as her nose scrunched. "He's going through his man-whore phase right now, but he's a good guy. Of all my brothers, he's probably the funniest and most laid-back of the bunch. Oh, you'll take a right at the light."

He followed Freya's directions the rest of the way, listening to her commentary—her high school, the elementary school her nieces attended, the pizza joint Finn got banned from. Finally, they pulled into the driveway of a large, two-story craftsman with a wraparound porch. All the spaces in front of the three-car garage were full, so he pulled his SUV in behind a Chevy Tahoe and cut the engine.

"Ready?" he asked.

She let out a breath but kept staring straight ahead, her hands twisting in her lap.

"Baby," he murmured, taking her hands in his. "No need to be nervous. It'll be fun."

She glanced at him, and the worry in her eyes had his chest squeezing. "What if they're jerks to you? I don't want any of them giving you a hard time. They'll try to interrogate you and—"

"Freya, baby, relax." He brought her hands up and kissed her knuckles. "They can ask me whatever they want. Whether I answer will depend on their question. It'll be fine. I promise." His eyes darted to the house, and he grinned. "Now, unless I'm mistaken, there are two little faces pressed against the window waiting for you."

Seeing her nieces, she smiled and squeezed his hands. "If *any* of my brothers give you a hard time or are rude in any way, you let me know. It's Thanksgiving, and if they do anything, I'll pull them aside and kick their asses."

His heart warmed. If he wasn't already in love with her, that ferocity would have done him in. He snaked a hand into her hair and pulled her in for a quick kiss. "You're super hot when you're feisty, you know that?"

She grinned against his lips. "Don't distract me. I need to get my little-sister glare going."

He dropped another quick kiss on her lips. "Sorry, I promise to not get in the way of your sibling glare."

They got out of the car, and he stretched his back. The body wasn't meant to sit for four and a half hours straight. He handed her the gift bags for her nieces, grabbed all their bags of food, and followed her up the porch steps to the front door. It swung open as they approached.

"Auntie Freya!" The girls swarmed her with squeals of excitement.

He hung back as each of her brothers hovered in the entryway, waiting for their turns to hug her.

Xander's eyes widened in surprise. Her brothers weren't what he'd imagined. Freya was a petite little thing, and he imagined her brothers would follow suit. He hadn't expected them all to be nearly as tall as him. They were all fit and had varying shades of dark hair, and they all had the same ice-blue eyes like Freya, leaving no doubt they were related.

After her last brother hugged her, she turned to him. "You guys, this is my boyfriend, Xander." He loved the way the pink in her cheeks deepened. "These two beauties," she said as her nieces attached themselves to her sides, "are Andie and Josie." Then she pointed at each of her brothers and introduced them.

For a moment, they all stared at him with varying degrees of wariness before Jasper cleared his throat and stepped forward, reaching for some of the bags. "Here, let me help you with those."

Xander gave the man one of the pie bags, and the group moved into the large open kitchen. Axel veered off and went out the back sliding door toward a large black smoker.

Placing the remaining bags on the island, he gestured to the deck. "Smoked turkey? Nice."

"Nah," Oscar said, pulling out the pies and placing them on the side counter. "None of us really like turkey—"

"More like none of us can cook one to save our lives," Jasper interrupted.

Oscar shrugged. "Fair. So instead of turkey, we do baby back ribs."

"Sorry." Freya grimaced as she moved to stand beside him. "I think I may have forgotten to mention we don't do a traditional Thanksgiving. I hope that's okay. I mean, we still have all the traditional . . . well, mostly traditional sides."

He wrapped his arm around her waist and dropped a kiss to the top of her hair. "Uh, ribs and pie? You won't hear me complaining, baby."

Finn gagged. "Today's about food and ribs. No PDA. And for the love of God, please don't call her baby or anything like that within earshot." He made another gagging sound before winking at his sister.

"You're an idiot," she grumbled, but Xander heard the humor in her tone.

"If anything, it's payback," Jasper said, slapping Finn on the shoulder. "How many times have we been out to the bars while you suck face with some random chick."

"At least he just kissed her head," Oscar said and then met his gaze. "But please keep it to the top of her head. She's still our baby sister, and that's just . . . gross."

Xander held up his hands in innocence.

"Knock it off, you guys," she murmured, leaning into his side.

The sliding door opened, and Axel peeked in. "Ribs are coming off. Jas, grab me that sheet pan."

As Jasper did his brother's bidding, Oscar checked the dishes warming in the oven. Finn stepped into the hallway and shouted up the stairs, "Girls! Food will be ready soon. Wash up."

"Auntie Freya, we need you!" a muffled voice called out.

"Josie, you're gonna spill the makeup!" another little voice cried out.

"That sounds like my cue." Freya chuckled, making her way to the stairs. She glanced over her shoulder. "Ax is letting them play with makeup?"

Finn snorted. "That'd be a big fat no. And probably one of the reasons the girls no longer have a nanny."

"Yikes," Freya said with a wince before heading up the stairs and calling out, "What trouble are you girls getting into up here?"

"Holy shit," Oscar said, placing trivets and hot pads on the island. "For once, we may get all the food out at once."

"Don't fucking jinx it, dude," Finn mumbled, pulling open the sliding door for his brothers.

The smoky, sweet aroma of the ribs had Xander's mouth watering.

"Ax can't cook a turkey for shit," Jasper said, grabbing the foil and handing it to his brother. "But he's a damn magician with ribs."

"It smells great," Xander said. From the glare Axel was sending his way, he wouldn't be surprised if the guy had poisoned his portion.

Finn grabbed two beers from the fridge and handed one to Xander. "So how long have you been seeing Frey?"

"Thanks." He twisted the cap off his beer. "For a few weeks."

"Funny," Axel said, putting some foil over the ribs to let them rest. "She's never mentioned you."

He shrugged, taking a pull of his beer. "Doesn't negate the fact that she and I are together." Probably wouldn't be the best time to mention she'd been living with him for the last two weeks, but holy shit, did he want to.

Axel shot a glare his way, but he was going to give the guy

some leeway. Freya *was* his little sister, after all. "And what is it you do for a living, Xander?"

"I work in security."

"Like a rent-a-cop? That's nice." The smirk that crossed Axel's face had Xander's fingers twitching. Leeway or not, the guy was a dick.

"Christ, Ax," Oscar muttered as he placed serving utensils beside the trivets. "Give it a fucking rest."

"What? She's our sister. This guy—who we know nothing about—shows up for Thanksgiving, and what? We're just supposed to be all fucking good with that?"

Holy shit, this guy. "Again, it doesn't matter if you're good with it or not. Frey and I *are* together."

"So what was it? You met my sister—a young, impressionable girl—and turned on the charm? You got her to be your little fuck buddy and inserted yourself in her life?"

His hackles rose, and he stepped toward Axel. "Let me be perfectly clear. I don't care who you are. Brother or not, you talk about Freya like that again, I will lay you the fuck out."

"Holy shit, ease up, Ax," Oscar grumbled, forcibly inserting himself between them. "In case you forgot, Frey's nearly thirty. She's not a *girl*. She's an actual adult with a job that pays her bills and shit."

Axel scoffed and crossed his arms over his chest. "Yeah, but you know her. She flits from job to job and—"

"Say one more fucking word about her," Xander growled, moving toward the fucker until both Oscar and Jasper stepped in front of him.

"Shut the fuck up, Ax," Jasper seethed before turning to Xander. "*We* know Freya's got a good job." He shot a glare at his older brother. "*He's* just stupid and can't see her as anything but a broken sixteen-year-old. He's just pissed that she doesn't tell him jack shit."

"And why the hell do you think she doesn't tell you

anything?" Finn asked, sending his own glare to Axel. "Because you're an asshole. You stop being an asshole, then maybe she'll actually talk to you."

"Fuck you," Axel grumbled, but the heat in his words was gone.

As he scrubbed his hands over his face, Xander saw regret cross his face. But fuck him for talking about Freya that way.

"How'd this get so fucked up?" Axel sighed.

"Because you're an asshole," the brothers replied in unison with varying degrees of frustration. They sure as hell weren't wrong, and it was obvious this wasn't their first rodeo with their oldest brother.

There was a pounding noise that sounded like a herd of elephants racing down the stairs. "Ready or not," Freya called out from the top of the steps, "here they come!"

Despite the tension, Xander couldn't help but smile as the little girls stormed into the kitchen—sparkles and glitter and poofy dresses twirling. How such an asshole could have such darling daughters was beyond him.

"Happy Thanksgiving!" they shouted, tossing orange and yellow confetti into the air.

Happy Thanksgiving, indeed. Weren't arguments and fights part of everyone's Thanksgiving family traditions?

CHAPTER TWENTY-NINE

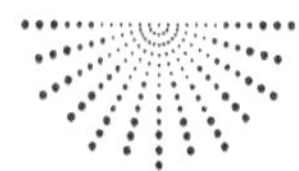

She felt the tension the second she stepped into the kitchen.

"Everything okay?" She glanced at her brothers, but they were ignoring her. Axel was checking the ribs, Oscar was pulling the sides from the oven, and Jasper and Finn were twirling the girls in circles.

Xander was beside her in an instant. "We're good."

She didn't believe him, not for one second. But since the girls were racing through the kitchen, she'd shelve her concerns for now. "Alright, girlies! Grab your plates and let me know what you want." She glanced at Xander. "We do a buffet-style Thanksgiving."

"Yup," Finn said, picking up Josie and setting her on his hip. "Grab what you want, and we all eat in the living room and watch football."

"And because it's Thanksgiving, we don't have to eat any vegetables!" Josie exclaimed, waving her princess wand in the air.

Twenty minutes later, Freya sighed. She was stuffed. Glancing around the room, it appeared as if everyone else was too. What was it about Thanksgiving? It's not like they weren't ever going to get to eat again.

She looked at Xander and let out a nervous breath. Seemingly being able to read her mind, he ran a soothing hand up and down her back. "If you want to tell them, I'll be right next to you," he murmured "If you need help, I'm here."

"Thank you," she whispered before glancing at her brothers once more. Their focus was on the football game, so she waited until a commercial break and then cleared her throat.

"Girls, why don't you two go upstairs and watch a show in the playroom. I need to talk to the guys and then—"

"Did Uncle Finn get in trouble again?" Andie asked as she rose from her little table.

"Hey now!" Finn snagged Andie around the waist and flipped her upside down as she squealed with delight. "Why am *I* the one you say is always in trouble?"

"Dammit, Finn, she just ate," Axel grumbled. "She pukes, you're cleaning that shit up."

"Because you're the naughty uncle!" Josie exclaimed, jumping on Finn. When she was also upside down, she pointed at Axel. "Daddy, you said *two* bad words!"

"That's two quarters!" Andie cackled.

Freya's chest squeezed. God, she missed this. Her brothers drove her crazy, but she missed them.

Xander wrapped his arm over her shoulders. She leaned into him as her nerves built. If it weren't for the man beside her, for his quiet support, she'd probably never have the courage to tell her brothers about what was going on. But as she was coming to learn—first by sharing with Xander and then with his team—the more people who knew what was going on, the more people looking out for her, the better.

"Alright, girls," Freya called out, clapping her hands.

"Upstairs you go. Go watch an episode of *Bluey*, and we'll have dessert after!"

The girls cheered and ran out of the room.

Once she heard their feet stomping upstairs, she turned to her brothers. They all looked at her in concern.

"Everything okay, Frey?" Oscar asked.

Xander took her hand in his and squeezed. She clung to him like a lifeline and exhaled.

"Holy shit," Finn said. "Are you pregnant?"

"What? No!" She glared at her brother, and he held his hands up.

Xander coughed, and when she looked at him with narrowed eyes, he smothered his snicker. Wise man. "Sorry, baby."

She cleared her throat. Loudly. "As I was *going* to say, since we're all together, I wanted to talk to you guys about some stuff . . . some trouble that's come up."

For the next few minutes, she opened up to her brothers. About the photos she'd received on Sarah's birthdays and death anniversaries, about her car getting vandalized, about getting pushed down at the parade, and the photos that had been delivered to her apartment door.

All the while, her brothers sat in stunned silence.

Until Axel surged out of his chair. "Why the fuck didn't you say anything, Freya?"

She bit back a groan. *Typical, Axel. Typical.* She readied her reply, but Xander cleared his throat.

His body had gone tense beside her, but his voice remained calm when he said, "I don't have siblings, so I'm not claiming I'm an expert on family dynamics, but I'm assuming this"—he waved his hand at Axel—"is exactly why she didn't say anything."

"I asked you a question, Freya," Axel said, ignoring Xander.

She was going to kill her brother.

"Uh-uh," Xander said. "You don't get to give Freya shit for not talking to you."

"Stay out of this," Axel spat.

"No way in hell. If she hasn't said anything, it's on *you*, because *you* make her uncomfortable. And after spending time with you—limited as it's been—I can see why."

Axel crossed his arms over his chest, and that smarmy look she'd always wanted to smack off his face bloomed. "Enlighten me."

"You're a condescending prick. As your brothers pointed out earlier, you're also an asshole."

The corners of her lips twitched, and her other brothers snorted. Xander wasn't wrong. But she was pretty sure the only people who ever called Axel out were sitting in this room.

"You look down on her," Xander continued. "A woman who's worked her way up to be at one of the most sought-after resorts in the fucking world. You know nothing about what she does or even who she is, and that pisses you off. But again, that's on *you*."

Xander's defense of her had her falling even harder. This amazing man was something else.

"So what, Frey?" Axel grumbled. "You think this rent-a-cop can help you? You could be in legitimate danger and mall cop here is your savior?"

She narrowed her eyes. "What are you talking about?"

Axel continued as if he hadn't heard her. Hell, considering the rant he was on, he probably hadn't. "Shit happens, and instead of calling me—your brother who's a fucking *detective*—you turn to a security guard?"

Utterly confused, she glanced at Xander, who shrugged. "I may have said I worked in security. Didn't feel the need to clarify."

Shaking her head, she chuckled. "Of course you did." Letting out an exasperated sigh, she turned to her brother. "Xander works for Hudson Security. Pretty sure he's more than qualified to keep me safe."

Axel's eyebrows rose, and for once, he was silent.

Then Finn laughed. A loud guffaw of a laugh. "Holy shit, Ax, even *I've* heard of Hudson Security." He turned to the twins and gestured to Xander. "They protect billionaires and shit."

"Anyway," she said, trying to rein the conversation back in. "I just wanted to let you all know what was going on."

"You should move back here," Axel said. "We can keep an eye on you."

She shook her head. "I love you, but no. Besides, I have a job."

"But between all of us, we can keep an eye on you."

She was shaking her head before he'd finished speaking. "Did you not hear what I just said? Xander works for Hudson Security. I'm fine."

"This person knows where you *live*. That's—"

"Ever since the photos were left at my apartment door, I've been living with Xander."

It was complete silence for three blessed seconds.

"For fuck's sake, Fre—"

"Axel, it's fine. When I'm not with him, he's assigned one of his personal-security officers to be with me at work."

Axel's mouth snapped shut. Finally.

"After the shooting at the resort earlier in the month," Xander began, his voice calm, "Hudson Security was hired to revamp and upgrade the security at Pacific View. Not only do we always have a PSO within a hundred feet of Freya, but we have another security officer on-site as well. Part of the upgrade involved their cybersecurity. Trust me when I say we have nearly every inch of that place under video surveillance."

Axel crossed his arms over his chest and remained silent, but that judgy look remained. God, it took everything she had not to clobber her brother.

"Look," Xander said, releasing her hand. He leaned forward and rested his elbows on his knees. "You and I may not see eye to eye right now. Hell, maybe we never will. But one thing I can promise you is that I'm taking this threat to Freya seriously. Seeing as nothing has happened over the last couple of weeks, I may be going overboard with the round-the-clock security, but I don't care. Overboard or not, I'll do everything I can to protect her."

Axel let out a breath and ran his hand through his hair, nodding. "We can agree on that."

Freya was taking that as a win. "Axel, I'm safe on Hudson. I just wanted to let you all know what was happening. *And* going forward, I'll be better about communicating with everyone." She met each of her brothers' gazes. "I promise."

Oscar nodded. "We will too."

"And we'll get out there and visit you soon," Jasper added.

"Do you get an employee discount at your resort? I mean, shit—" Finn made a face. "Have you seen the daily rates at that place?"

She chuckled, and when Xander's arm wrapped around her waist, she leaned into him. After telling her brothers and being honest with them, she felt like a weight had been lifted from her chest. Yeah, she was sure Axel was still pissed, but at least he knew. Baby steps, right? "I'll see what I can do, Finn. Now, how about dessert?"

The next few minutes were chaos. On top of the three pies she and Xander had brought, there was also ice cream, chocolate chip cookies, and cranberry crumble cheesecake bars compliments of Oscar and Jasper's long-time receptionist.

"Looks like I'm going to need to hit the gym tomorrow," Xander muttered, adding a cheesecake bar to his already full plate of pie. He shot her that lopsided smirk she loved. "Unless you can think of another way we can burn off these calories."

"Holy fucking Christ, dude. I'm standing right here." Finn groaned, disgust all over his face.

"That's the *two*-dollar naughty word, Uncle Finn!" Josie called out as laughter filled the kitchen.

Her eyes tracked Xander as he made his way back to the living room. He settled onto the couch with Andie right beside him. Her heart squeezed as he tucked a napkin into the top of her shirt and spread one out over her lap.

"He's nice," Oscar said from beside her.

She smiled at her brother. "He is."

"He make you happy?"

Her smile widened, and she nodded.

"Good," he said, bopping her on the nose. "I like how he defends you. Continue to stand your ground with Axel though, no matter how big of an ass he can be."

"Thanks, Os." She frowned, her eyes darting around the kitchen and living room. "Where is Ax?"

He nodded to the door that led to the garage. "Probably smoking," he said, lowering his voice.

Her eyes widened in surprise. "He's smoking again?"

"Got a lot on his plate." He shrugged. "Don't tell the girls."

She frowned. "How do they *not* know?"

"He's got a whole fucking setup in the garage before he comes back in," Jasper said, coming up on the other side of her. "A change of jackets, fancy-smelling hand soap, and breath mints."

Adding a slice of pumpkin pie onto her plate next to the

apple, she shook her head. "Ten bucks says he's not fooling the girls."

Oscar snorted. "Not taking that bet."

She grinned as her brothers reclaimed their spots in the living room. She placed her plate on the coffee table and sat on Xander's other side. Leaning close so Andie wouldn't hear, she whispered, "I'm going to talk with Axel. He's outside." She mimed smoking a cigarette.

He nodded, placed his fork onto his plate, and set it beside hers on the coffee table. "I'll walk you out."

"Oh, that's okay," she said, shaking her head.

He tilted his head, and his eyebrow arched.

She grinned. "Right. My favorite bodyguard." She leaned forward and pressed a kiss to his cheek.

Finn groaned. "Stop already, Frey!"

She crossed the living room with Xander, and when she passed Finn, she slapped him on the back of the head. "Don't eat all the pie while I'm gone."

"Want your jacket?" Xander asked as she reached for the doorknob.

She shook her head. "I'm good. I won't be long."

Stepping into the garage with Xander on her heels, she chuckled. Sure enough, just to the right of the door were hooks holding three of Axel's jackets. To the right of that was a utility sink with peppermint soap and a large mason jar full of individually wrapped breath mints.

A gust of wind pushed into the garage's open door. She shivered and rubbed her hands over her arms. Xander draped one of her brother's jackets over her shoulders.

She smiled, glancing at him. "Thanks, I didn't realize it had started snowing."

The ground shimmered with a thin layer of frost. She stepped out of the garage and big fat snowflakes stuck to her lashes. They rounded the corner of the house, and there was

Axel, leaning against the siding, a puff of smoke leaving his lips.

He and Xander lifted their chins at each other in some kind of silent communication.

"I'll be inside," Xander said, pressing a kiss to her forehead before turning and heading back.

"Think it'll stick?" she asked, approaching her brother.

"Looks like. Give it another hour, and the girls will be begging you to build a snowman with them." A soft smile lifted the corners of his lips, but the sadness in his eyes tugged at her heart.

Another gust of wind had snow swirling around them.

"Come on," he said, gesturing to the back of the house.

Tucking her arms into the sleeves of the jacket, she followed behind him. Once they turned the corner, the house acted as a buffer, and the wind died down.

"So you're smoking again?"

He shrugged. "Nasty habit, I know."

"You okay, Ax?" He remained silent for a moment, and the despair on his face turned her stomach.

"I'm sorry I've been such a dick, Frey. I just . . ." He took a long pull of his cigarette and blew it out. He paced a few steps away before turning back to her. "I don't know what I'm doing anymore."

She studied her brother and noted the weariness, the worry lines that were a little deeper since the last time she'd seen him. She vowed then and there to keep in better touch with her family. Yes, this brother in particular drove her extra crazy, but she knew deep down that he meant well. His execution just sucked.

"Sure you do, Ax. You've got a solid job, and the girls are doing great. Sure, they're running through nannies like crazy, but they're Hansens." She shrugged and gave him a teasing smile. "Par for the course, right?"

He chuckled as she'd intended, but then he shook his head. "The girls are great, but that's all them, not me. I fucked up so badly with you—some asshat's been sending you photos for over a fucking *decade*, and you didn't feel safe enough to tell me. Like your guy said, that's on me, and I really am sorry." Shaking his head, he ran his free hand over his jaw. "I'm scared shitless that I'm going to fuck up with the girls too."

Her chest clenched. She stepped toward him and laid a hand on his arm. "You won't. You may be a bit of an asshole, but you're a great dad. The girls adore you. Plus, you have the guys to help you with them. You know they'd do anything for those two. And if you're looking to rein in your asshole tendencies, you know the guys are more than happy to call you out on all your shit."

He snickered. "Don't I know it. That's one thing I don't have to wor—"

Warm liquid splattered her face.

She gasped as Axel's eyes rolled to the back of his head, and he fell toward her. She tried to catch him, but his heavy weight toppled her.

"Ax," she wheezed, but he lay atop her motionless.

He was suddenly yanked off her. Air whooshed back into her lungs but caught in her chest. A man loomed over her. He wore a dark ski mask, and only his hollow eyes peeked through. She opened her mouth to scream, but before she could utter a sound, he swung something at her.

Fire exploded on the side of her head.

Everything went black.

CHAPTER THIRTY

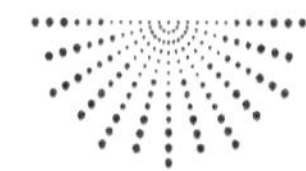

The room erupted in cheers as the Seahawks scored another touchdown. It was a rare treat for them to play on Thanksgiving, and Xander was grateful. Because watching football with Freya's brothers was a whole hell of a lot better than sitting around a formal dining table answering their questions.

"Touchdown tosses!" Finn shouted.

Josie ran toward him with her arms outstretched, and he tossed her into the air as Oscar and Jasper counted aloud to six.

"Me too, me too!" Andie squealed, waving her hands above her head.

Finn repeated the tosses with his other niece and then dramatically collapsed on the carpet. "Soon you rascals will be too big to toss into the air!" He glanced at Xander, and a wicked gleam lit his eyes. "You know what, girls?" He sat up and pulled them both onto his lap. "Xander looks like a big guy. I bet he can get you pretty high. How about he does the next touchdown toss?"

The girls cheered, and Xander chuckled.

Okay, fine. Freya's brothers were good guys. Well . . . He internally cringed. Axel was a bit much. If the man just toned down the asshole bit, he'd be a little more bearable. Maybe.

Speaking of . . .

"Are Frey and your brother still outside?"

Oscar shrugged. "Probably. Maybe Freya's reaming his as—er, butt"—his gaze shot to the girls who were lying on the carpet with Finn—"for being such a douche."

He frowned. They'd been gone a long time. At least fifteen minutes.

He rose from the couch, a knot of worry growing in his belly. "I'm just gonna go and check on them—"

The door to the garage swung open with a bang. Axel stumbled inside, his front covered in snow, blood pouring down the side of his face. For a split second, he swayed, and then his knees buckled.

Xander's insides turned to ice, and he sprinted forward, grunting when he caught the guy. "Finn!" he called out before setting Axel down on the floor. "Look at me, man. Where's Freya?"

He held his breath as Axel shook his head, his eyes unfocused.

"Move over," Finn said, nudging Xander to the side. While he tended to his brother, he called out, "Jasper, get the girls upstairs. Os, call 911."

"Fuck!" Xander bolted out the garage door.

He stepped onto the driveway, he noticed footprints leading to the side of the house and then around back. It took everything he had to not run to the back of the house. He had to think, had to be careful of where he stepped.

Dread and anger pumped through his veins as he reached the back of the house.

Nothing.

No Freya.

The snow was disturbed. There was a large patch flattened where Axel must have fallen. He spotted blood staining the pristine snow, and his stomach twisted. Was it Axel's or Freya's?

His fists clenched. *Focus, Bonetti. Assess first, then act.* Blowing out a breath, he scanned the area.

His eyes narrowed when he saw another set of footprints in the snow, along with dark drops of blood. They led from the back of the house to the street. To an empty space that was void of snow, minus a new dusting that was trying to stick. It was where the car that had taken Freya had sat.

The sound of sirens wailed in the distance.

With trembling hands, he yanked out his phone. He quickly took photos of the footprints and blood splatters. Careful to retrace his earlier steps, he made his way to the sidewalk and took photos of the tire treads in the snow. Within seconds, he'd sent all the photos to his team, then he dialed Frazier.

The phone rang once. "Talk to me, brother."

"Someone's got her, man." A lump formed in his throat, but he swallowed past it. "Someone fucking took her."

CHAPTER THIRTY-ONE

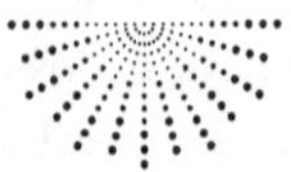

A dull pounding grew louder. Freya winced at the noise, wishing whoever was blaring their stereo would turn down the volume.

She groaned and then gasped as the pounding became more painful.

Ice-cold water splashed over her face, and her eyes flew open. She winced as her head throbbed in time with her racing heart.

"Hello there," the man before her said, his voice eerily chipper.

Though he wasn't wearing a ski mask, she knew he was the man who'd hurt Axel, who'd knocked her out. The dead eyes she'd gotten a glimpse of were the same.

He set the orange bucket down, and bile rose in her throat as he assessed her. "It's been a long time, Freya, but it's good to see you up close and personal again."

It was as if her mind was swimming through mud. He looked vaguely familiar, but considering she saw dozens of new faces each week, she had no clue. Aside from his eyes—a dark brown that was nearly black—he looked like every other guy that visited the resort. A white guy of medium height with a medium build. He was clean-shaven and had a standard businessman's haircut that was shorter on the sides and longer on top.

"I can practically see your mind turning as you try to place me." He stood directly in front of her, unnervingly still. "In due time, Freya. In due time."

His soft, calm voice had dread pooling in her stomach.

For the first time, she noticed she was sitting on something soft, a chair of some sort. Maybe a recliner. She tried to look, but every time she tried to look down, the pounding in her head intensified, became agonizing. She had no choice but to keep her eyes glued to him.

Bile rose in her throat, and she tried to slap her hands over her mouth. Metal clanked, and her arms jerked mere inches from the chair. Her wrists were shackled. She moved her feet, but metal clanked again, holding her still.

Fear had her heart racing, and saliva pooled in her mouth. Unable to stop it, bile surged up her throat, and she threw up. Acid burned her throat as she coughed. The motion and sound sent ripples of pain across her skull.

"You're disgusting," he said, but for once, his voice wasn't eerily calm. Annoyance and anger laced his two words.

Glancing at him, her stomach rolled again. She could make out the darker stains on his light-gray trousers where her vomit had landed on him. She could see discoloration from her puke on the bottom of his white polo shirt.

When he spoke again, his tone was creepily playful. "Do that again, and see what happens. I dare you, Freya."

She may have whimpered, she wasn't sure, but when bile shot up her throat again, she turned to the side. The pain was nearly unbearable, like someone was taking a hot metal rod and shoving it into her skull. Over and over again.

But she heard the splatter of her vomit on the floor. Not

on him. That's what mattered. Because she didn't want to find out what he was going to do, didn't want to have anything to do with his dare, didn't want anything to do with him.

Tears filled her eyes and spilled down her cheeks. Afraid to look at him, she focused on the wall she was facing.

Her eyes narrowed.

She wasn't sure what she was seeing. Her head was pounding, and everything was fuzzy. But when the images on the wall came into focus, she gasped.

Her heart stopped.

Photos of her and Sarah. *Hundreds* of photos of her and Sarah. And in almost all the photos, her face had been violently scratched out.

Tremors shook her hands, and she gasped for air.

Turning away from the wall of photos, she glanced at him again. "Who are you?"

Ignoring her question, he swiveled her chair so she faced a different wall. He pulled over a wooden chair and sat in front of her. The light on this side of the room was brighter and had her wincing.

"She agreed to go out with me that night, you know. Sarah and I talked at the party, and she was looking forward to being my date at the winter formal. But instead, you killed her." He looked over her head, presumably at the photos of Sarah. When he returned his gaze to her, she shivered. Hate. That was the only word to describe how he looked at her.

She averted her gaze, and once again, she wasn't sure what she was seeing. More photos, but only about two dozen. This time, they were of him and . . . Hazel.

Nothing made sense. "How . . . Who . . ."

He glanced at the photos behind him and smiled. "I heard about the shooting at the resort and was worried someone had killed you before I could. Thankfully, they didn't." He pulled a photo of him and Hazel off the wall, a selfie of the two of them on a marina dock. "Then I saw her on television talking about you. Did you know Hazel's eyes are nearly the same shade of green as Sarah's? That's how I knew. When I first saw Hazel, I knew it was divine intervention. Sarah was sending me a message from heaven. It was time."

He glanced at her with a smile that chilled her blood.

"At first, I thought Sarah had sent me Hazel in her place. A reincarnation of souls, a bodily replacement. She even called me Timmy like Sarah did—the only person I've ever allowed to call me that."

A look of pure anguish flashed over his face, and fear twisted Freya's stomach.

"But no. I was wrong. Hazel's been useful, but she's not like Sarah. Not at all. Sarah was pure. Innocent. Perfect. And Hazel—" He sighed and shook his head. "But that's when I realized Sarah sent me Hazel so I could find out more about you. She chose Hazel, with the same eyes and same aura as her, so I'd recognize her. It's quite beautiful, really."

As he spoke, tears ran unchecked down her cheeks. The fog over her mind had eased a tiny bit, and she clung to the hope that Xander would come for her, that he'd find her, rescue her. She desperately wanted the chance to tell him she loved him, desperately wanted the opportunity to build a life with him.

But the longer the man spoke, the more reality set in.

He was unhinged.

She had no recollection of him. Nor could she recall Sarah ever mentioning anyone named Timmy. As each second ticked by, the chances of her getting out of there alive dwindled.

"The best part was that Hazel was so easy to befriend. She loves to talk, and she told me everything I needed to know. The sheer fact that Hazel was your friend—and she even had you wave at me that one night . . ." A far-off smile lifted his lips. "That was it. The final sign from Sarah that it was meant to be."

He rose from the chair, and she flinched. He went to a third wall and scanned the photos tacked up. He pulled three down, grinned, and showed them to her.

She sucked in a breath. The photos were altered pictures of her.

In the first, she was lying in a wrecked car, her limbs broken, and her neck twisted in a horrifying angle, her face filled with pain. In the second, she was crumpled on the ground, tire marks over her body and limbs, and half her face was crushed under a dirt bike's tire. The third was of her, naked and shackled to a dirty beige recliner. All along her body were knife wounds, shallow slashes along her skin. Across her stomach, deeper cuts spelled out *Sarah*. In this one, her face wasn't twisted in pain. No. Her eyes were gouged out with only deep hollows remaining.

"I worked hard on all of these, but I think I like this one the most." He held up the photo of her in the recliner. "I feel like this one avenges my sweet Sarah the most. Because, Freya, what I said to you was true. It should have been you."

With one last spine-chilling smile, he stepped to a cabinet she hadn't noticed. Her eyes widened when she saw what lay on top. She swallowed down more bile. Sweat broke out over her skin, and her breaths became shallow. A long row of knives. Small ones, big ones, hooked ones, jagged ones. So many knives. A shiver tore through her, and she couldn't hold back a sob.

Her heart shattered.

No. She wasn't leaving here alive.

CHAPTER THIRTY-TWO

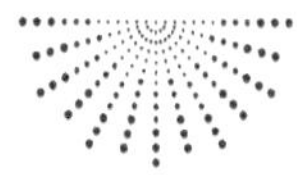

The helicopter flying time from Hudson Island to Blanchard Bay was roughly thirty-six minutes. With the snowstorm wreaking havoc on the Pacific Northwest, the flight time should have been longer, and maybe even impossible for some. Luckily for Xander, their pilot was Hadley Owen, and she made it over with eight members of Hudson Security in twenty-three minutes.

Owen landed in the middle of a street two blocks down from Axel's house, and everyone—minus Frazier—quickly gathered around the kitchen island waiting for next steps. Frazier was busy smoothing out the ruffled feathers of the Blanchard Bay PD. However, seeing as one of their own was injured, and their detective's sister had been abducted, BBPD's police chief was being surprisingly accommodating.

"Bingo," Bean said, her attention focused on her laptop. "I got the plate off that black Hyundai Sonata. Just give me two more seconds."

Xander's heart raced. *Please, Bean. Please find her.*

"How?" Police Chief Horowitz asked as he entered the kitchen with Frazier. She glanced up and pierced him with a look that had him clearing his throat. "Forget I asked. In fact, forget I'm here."

Esme patted him on the shoulder. "Smart man. I also suggest you not hear or see anything that happens while we're here."

He nodded, his eyes wide. "Of course, ma'am. We're here to assist."

"We appreciate that," Frazier said, moving to stand behind Bean.

"Timothy McAllen," Bean said. "Thirty-one. Six feet. One-eighty. Resident of Blanchard Bay." She glanced at the police chief and rattled off a local address.

He immediately shook his head. "No. That's not a viable address. There was a house fire there three or four years ago. The owners never rebuilt."

"That's right. It was a really bad electrical fire," Jasper said. "We were working with the owners on the rebuild design. An elderly couple. They decided to take the insurance money and move to Arizona instead. But they weren't McAllen . . ." His eyes narrowed in thought. "I could have sworn they mentioned a grandson or something?"

"I'll run a search on their family and other residents at that address," Bean murmured, her fingers swift as she typed.

Esme turned to him. "Did you give Freya any kind of tracking device? Jewelry or a tracker for her shoes?"

Xander shook his head, anger at himself building for not having done so. "I should have though."

"Don't start that game, brother," Wilson said from beside him. "You didn't want to push too hard, and there's not a damn thing wrong with that."

"Except she's missing, and we can't fucking find her."

Wilson's hand slapped down on his shoulder. "We will. Hold it the fuck together."

A soft gasp filled the near-silent room, and all eyes

swung to the little girl in her uncle's arms standing in the kitchen entry. "He said the two-dollar naughty word, Uncle Finn."

"That's right, Josie baby," Finn said, running a hand over her dark hair. "I'll make sure he puts his two dollars in the jar."

"Sorry about that, little one," Wilson said, shooting her a wink.

"S'okay. Do you know where my daddy is?"

Xander's gut twisted.

"Remember, sweetie, your daddy got hurt and he had to go to the hospital real quick," Finn said, his voice thick with emotion. "He's sleeping right now, so we have to wait until tomorrow to see him."

Axel was currently in surgery. His skull had been cracked, and according to Oscar, who'd accompanied him to the hospital, the doctors needed to remove a section of his skull to relieve the pressure. The next forty-eight hours were going to be rough.

"If Daddy's hurt, how did he get to the hospital?"

Finn cleared his throat. "He got to ride in the ambulance."

She smiled. "Lucky ducky. That's way more fun than driving."

"Yeah, lucky." Finn sighed, pressed a kiss to his niece's temple, and froze. His gaze swung to Xander. "You said Freya was wearing one of Axel's garage jackets, right?"

The hairs on Xander's arms lifted. "Yeah . . ."

"Were there keys in the pocket?"

His heart rate picked up speed. "I don't know."

"Shit, hang on." He winced as he bolted to the garage with Josie on his hip. "I'll put extra money in the bad-word jar, sweetie." Seconds later, he was back and set Josie on her feet. "I'll give you extra dessert for a week if you can find your dad's phone for me. Go!"

When the girl zoomed out of the kitchen calling her sister's name, Finn turned to them.

"Axel has a Tile tracker on all his keys. Since the girls like to 'help' him in the garage, they always end up losing his keys. So Ax has like five or six key fobs. He keeps a set of keys in his smoking jackets as backup because the girls can't reach those."

"Holy shit," Xander said on an exhale. "If Freya still has that jacket on . . ."

"We'll find her, brother," Wilson repeated. "Hang in there."

Fifty-five minutes.

It took Bean five minutes to pinpoint the Tile tracker on Axel's keys and cross-reference it to a remote cabin at the edge of Blanchard Bay. It took fifteen minutes to get the team geared up and loaded, and because of the cabin's particular location, they had to drive, which took another thirty-five minutes.

Once there, they waited for Bean's thermal drones for more intel. Xander had thought the drive over had been the longest wait of his life. Nope. Not even close.

"Confirming two heat signatures," Bean's steady voice said over their comms. "One moving, one stationary. Stationary is seated. It's a one-room cabin. Door facing south with only two windows facing east and west."

"Alpha Two and Three, you're flash-bangs through the east and west," Alpha One—Frazier—said. "Hold your positions and make sure he doesn't try to slip out. Alpha Four, you're along the north in case there's an exit we don't know about. The rest of us will breach through the south door. Acknowledge."

A chorus of "copy" sounded over the comms.

"Alpha Seven. Not you. You hang back. We'll signal you to retrieve the package when it's clear. Confirm."

Every part of Xander wanted to rebel, to tell Frazier to fuck off. That Freya wasn't a *package*. That he was going to be the first person to enter that damn cabin to get his woman back. But he knew those were his erratic emotions talking. He was currently a loose cannon and that put Freya and his teammates in danger.

Unacceptable.

He let out a deep exhale. "Copy."

"On my mark," Bean said. "Ten, nine, eight . . ."

As she counted off in their ears, everyone moved into position. The whistling wind camouflaged the crunching of their boots in the snow.

At *mark*, all hell broke loose.

The sound was deafening, and Xander could only watch as Alpha One, Five, and Six breached the cabin. He wasn't a praying man, but he sent a prayer up to the universe that Freya was alive. That's all he wanted. He'd help her through the trauma, but he just needed her alive. Because he couldn't imagine his life without her.

"Alpha Seven," Frazier said over the comms. "Come get your girl."

He'd never moved so fast in his life. As he rushed toward the cabin, he paid no mind to the screaming man lying face down in the doorway, easily pinned by Alpha Six, Wilson.

When Xander neared the doorway, there was a loud thud. The man fell silent.

"Shit, I slipped," Wilson said, straightening. He shrugged as he moved to the side to allow Xander to pass. "Don't worry, though, the fucker's still breathing."

Xander rushed past and quickly scanned the small room. His breath left in a painful whoosh when he spotted her. His Freya.

She was seated in a recliner, her wrists and ankles shackled. Her shirt was torn open, split down the center. There were a handful of small cuts along her arms and chest, but only a small amount of blood dotted her skin. Blood streamed down both sides of her face, and her left eye was swelling shut.

He'd never seen a more beautiful sight in his goddamn life.

"You're here," she said, her voice a raspy whisper. "You found me."

He was beside her in an instant. "I'll always find you, baby. No matter what. I'd never stop looking for you. Ever."

He went to press a kiss to her lips, but she quickly turned her head, and his lips met her cheek. "Baby?"

"I threw up all over myself. He was going to cut me up and . . ." A sob tore through her.

His heart ached. No matter what, he'd help her work through this.

Taking care, he wrapped his arms around her as best he could. "It's okay, Frey. I've got you." He glanced down at Alpha Five—Carmichael—who'd just unlocked her ankle shackles. "How much longer?"

His friend glanced up and gave Freya's knee a gentle pat. "We've all got you, darlin'. Just give me a couple more seconds, and I'll get your hands free."

Less than a minute later, the shackles hit the ground. Carmichael straightened and pulled an emergency blanket from one of his pockets. "Here, man."

"Thanks, brother," he said, his attention never leaving Freya.

"Xander?"

Her scratchy voice killed him. "Yeah, baby?"

"My head hurts. I think I have a concussion."

He ran his hand softly over her shoulder, afraid to hurt

her any more than she was. "I think you do too." He opened the foil emergency blanket and draped it over her front. "I'm going to carry you out of here, okay? There's an ambulance waiting."

"No." She groaned. "I don't want to throw up on you."

"Freya, sweetheart, you can puke all over me if you need to. I don't care about that. I love you no matter what."

She let out a tiny gasp, and her eyes flew open. "Really?"

He met her slightly unfocused gaze. "Really. Now close your eyes again, because I'm gonna lift you up. You might get dizzy."

"M'kay, but only if you're sure."

Gently lifting her out of the recliner, he pressed a kiss to her temple. "I'm absolutely sure I love you."

He smiled as she tucked her head against his neck and sighed. "Just so you know, concussion or not, I love you too."

His soul settled, and everything clicked into place. This woman was his everything. And he was never letting her go.

EPILOGUE

New Year's Eve

It was five thirty on New Year's Eve, and she'd finished her last style of the day. It seemed as though every single guest had been through the salon over the last two days, getting their hair done just so for tonight's big New Year's Eve party. The resort usually only allowed guests and staff to the exclusive event, but this year, they'd extended the invite to the Hudson Security group.

She'd been looking forward to going with Xander, but truth be told, she was exhausted. Her feet ached, and right now, soaking in the hot tub sounded better than a party that would be going until past two in the morning. Luckily, she hadn't moved back into her apartment after the incident, so the drive to Xander's place—*their* place—was a quick one.

Oh, the *incident* . . .

After she'd been rescued, she'd had to take a week off for her concussion. Xander had been her rock. He'd not only nursed her back to health, but had held her through her nightmares, held her when she'd cried. He'd also helped her get in touch with a therapist and had held her hand through her first couple of sessions until she felt comfortable going on her own.

He'd not only been there for her, but he'd been there for her family, offering Hudson Security's extensive resources to help Axel with his recovery. Her brother had made it through surgery and had technically made a full recovery. But he was still doing PT and had a long way to go. To say Ax wasn't in a good place was an understatement. Thankfully, the girls were the light of his life, and he'd promised them he'd keep fighting to get better. They—along with her and her brothers, and even Xander—were his biggest cheerleaders.

One step at a time. They'd all get through it together.

"Knock, knock."

The voice pulled her from her thoughts, and she spun around.

Her jaw dropped when she realized who she was looking at. Then she was in motion, wrapping her friend in a hug. "Janie! What are you doing here?"

"My sister and I checked in earlier today," Janie replied, her smile a mile wide. "We're here for the week. And then . . . I'm moving to Hudson Island!"

Joy and excitement had Freya bouncing on her toes, and she pulled Janie in for another hug. "Oh my God, that's so great!"

"Hey, hey, Freya!" Claire said, joining them. "I'd love to stay and chat and catch up, but we're going to be late for our dinner reservations."

Freya gave Claire a hug. "Oh yeah, they're only holding reservations for like five minutes tonight. You better get over there."

"Are you free to get together for dinner tomorrow?" Janie asked.

"Of course! I want you to meet my boyfriend, Xander." She couldn't help the grin that spread over her face.

"Wait," Claire said, her face scrunching. "That name sounds familiar. Was he one of the security guys?"

"One and the same," a deep voice replied. A deep voice that had her insides turning to goo.

Freya grinned as Xander made his way into the salon. "Nice to see you again, ladies," he said, shaking hands with both women.

"Oh my," Janie said, giving her a thumbs-up behind Xander's back. "We'll find you at the party tonight."

Freya chuckled. "Sounds like a plan. Enjoy your dinner!"

Once the women left, Freya stepped to him and wrapped her arms around his waist. "What are you doing here? Not that I'm complaining, mind you."

He looped his arms around her and dipped down for a kiss. "I was in the neighborhood and figured I'd come pick you up. Thought you might be tired since the last couple days have been so busy, and you've been a little sleep-deprived."

Xander was right on both counts.

A crazy number of clients was the cause of her busy days, and her handsome boyfriend who knew how to touch her just right were the cause of her sleepless nights. She chuck-led. "Do you hear me complaining about my lack of sleep?"

"Nope." He flashed her that sexy, lopsided smirk. "I do have a question for you, though."

She ran her hands over his chest, tracing the buttons of his shirt. "Hmm?"

Unlooping his arms from around her, he took a step back and dropped to one knee.

She gasped, and her jaw dropped.

"I was going to do this tonight. I even had a whole plan with candles and champagne, but I can't wait."

Her heart thudded hard in her chest, but when she saw how his hands shook as he pulled a small box from his pocket, everything inside her calmed.

He opened the box's lid. A large ice-blue stone with a ring of glittering diamonds surrounding it twinkled at her. "Freya Hansen, will you—"

"Yes!" She launched herself at him, and of course, he caught her.

He pressed his lips to hers, and she kissed him back with everything she had.

This sweet, wonderful man . . .

When they came up for air, she framed his face in her hands. "Xander Bonetti, I love you. Nothing would make me happier than being your wife."

His eyes filled with emotion. Joy, love, and awe. He blinked back unshed tears and let out a breath. "Freya, I promise to make you happy every day of our lives."

"You already do, Xander." She pressed a kiss to his lips. "You already do."

ENJOY THIS BOOK?

Reviews & ratings encourage other readers to try out a book & I would love your help spreading the word! If you could take a quick moment to rate and/or leave a review on your favorite book site—Amazon, Goodreads, and/or Bookbub—I would be forever grateful! Thank you!

ALSO BY CHRISTINA SOL

Want more of Xander & Freya?

Sign up for Christina Sol's Newsletter for a free bonus scene.

www.christinasol.com

The Spotted Dog Series

Redemption

Reclaiming

Returning

The Hudson Island Series

Shattered Vows

Shattered Illusions

Shattered Dreams

Shattered Secrets

The Hudson Security Series

Out of the Shadows

Into the Storm

ABOUT THE AUTHOR

Christina Sol is an award-winning author who writes what she loves to read—romance books filled with heart, heat, and suspense.

An avid reader from the get-go, Christina was obsessed with The Babysitters Club, Sweet Valley Twins, Sweet Valley High, Christopher Pike, and all things V. C. Andrews. Her love for romance started with the Sunfire books, a YA historical romance series. Caroline by Willo Davis Roberts was her favorite of the series, and a copy of the 1984 novel is one of her most treasured possessions. Then she discovered Danielle Steele and Nora Roberts. And never looked back. She's still a voracious reader and enjoys all genres of romance but leans toward romantic suspense and dark romance.

She lives in the inland Pacific Northwest with her husband and two kids. When she's not writing, reading, or knitting, she's watching football or fueling her planner, sticker, and washi-tape obsession.

To find out more, visit: www.christinasol.com

ACKNOWLEDGMENTS

To my wonderful readers—thank you so much for taking the time to read Xander & Freya's story. I truly appreciate the support you've shown for the Hudson Security crew, and I'm eternally grateful to each and every one of you!

To Heather, Shelli, Jen, and Danielle—I appreciate you all SO much. Your feedback, edits, honesty, and support mean the world to me. I cannot thank you enough!

To Kassidy—thank you, thank you, thank you for sharing your hairstylist knowledge with me & letting me ask you a million questions! I hope I was able to portray Freya in a realistic way & know that any errors in the lingo are *all* on me. :) Thank you, sweet friend!

To Heidi S, L.J. A & Judy Z—thank you for your expertise. I'm SO honored to be able to work with you all.

To my family and friends—a heartfelt thank you for all the support & encouragement you've shown me. Words are inadequate to express just how much you all mean to me.